THE GRADUAL

ALSO BY CHRISTOPHER PRIEST
FROM TITAN BOOKS

The Adjacent
The Islanders

THE GRADUAL

Christopher Priest

TITAN BOOKS

The Gradual
Print edition ISBN: 9781785653032
E-book edition ISBN: 9781785653049

Published by Titan Books
A division of Titan Publishing Group Ltd
144 Southwark Street, London SE1 0UP

First edition: September 2016

1 3 5 7 9 10 8 6 4 2

Did you enjoy this book? We love to hear from our readers.
Please email us at readerfeedback@titanemail.com or write to us at
Reader Feedback at the above address.

To receive advance information, news, competitions, and exclusive offers
online, please sign up for the Titan newsletter on our website:
www.titanbooks.com

To Conrad Williams

1

I grew up in a world of music, in a time of war. The latter interfered with the former. After I became an adult, a composer, many pieces of my music were stolen, copied or rehashed by a plagiarist. I lost my brother, my wife and my parents, I became a criminal and a fugitive, I travelled among islands, I discovered the gradual. Everything affected everything else, but music was the balm, the constant.

When I went in pursuit of my tormentor, I became an inadvertent traveller in time.

Time is a gradual process – like ageing, you do not notice it happening.

2

I was blessed with musical talent, so I never seriously questioned where my future might lie, but the war which dominated my childhood gave a pressing urgency to other things.

Survival was of course a preoccupation, but we, my parents and brother and I, had to eat and drink, had to sleep and learn, had to take shelter more times than we liked, had to become concerned if people we knew were harmed by the war. Both my parents, their careers interrupted when the bombing of civilians began, had found alternative work, but because of the occasional raids what they were able to do had to be intermittent. Neither of them could make enough money to support the whole family. They came and went to their work, and I developed the ability to think for myself, to look out for myself.

There was nothing I could do about the war, but you accept the world you are born into, at least at first. I was born into a musical family, and my talent was prodigious. I took naturally to various instruments as I grew up, uniquely gifted. By the time I was ten years old I could play the guitar and the recorder, but I was accomplished on piano and violin and I had written my first compositions. I am rarely boastful about myself, so I write this in a factual way. Since becoming an adult I have established myself as a well-known composer of modernist classical music. My name is Alesandro Sussken.

Before the air raids started in earnest my father was first violin with the Errest Philharmonia, the principal orchestra in the region where we lived. He had a growing reputation as a virtuoso soloist. The orchestra was disbanded when the bombing worsened and my father had to find what work he could as a teacher. My mother too, who had been a principal singer with a touring opera company, had to take in students. It was not easy for either of them.

Then there was my brother Jacj, four years older than me, who was approaching the age of military draft.

Jacj was also a violinist and a good one, but he remained an amateur and began studying law. His studies were interrupted when the war intensified. I knew that Jacj was fiercely opposed to violence of any kind, and that he intended, if he could manage to avoid the draft, to qualify in international law.

As I grew up and first became aware of the complexity of his problems I realized he was torn several ways: by his music, his devotion to our parents, his concerns about the legality of war, and, of course, the impending draft which would wreck all his plans. Most boys of his age appeared to be fatalistic about military service, postponing their plans for future lives until the days of soldiering were over. Jacj was not like that and in a way neither was I. Music to a musician is a part of life. It has no options or alternatives.

Music and bombing. These were the two main events of

my childhood, running through it from the time of my first awareness until I left school. The enemy, which we all knew was the neighbouring country Faiandland, was firing rockets and sending pilotless bombers against us. Although the raids were never intensive, the bombs hit factories, military installations, houses, schools and hospitals at random. If our side was doing the same in retaliation I never heard about it.

War involves secrecy and a vague but powerful sense of patriotism. The two become mysteriously, inextricably linked. The news and information about the war, which no doubt was controlled and certainly censored by the military junta in Glaund City, was always positive, triumphant, brave. However, I also learned, if not through my teachers, that this country in which I had been born, the Republic of Glaund, had a violent history, a sorry record of disputes with neighbouring countries.

Whatever the reality, and whoever it was who might be thought of as the aggressors, no civilian was safe from attack. At frequent if irregular intervals our lives were disrupted by the sounding of alarms. The town I lived in, Errest, was a provincial industrial city, not the main target for the enemy but because of the huge steelworks on the edge of the city we received more unwanted violent attention than many places. Errest was on the coast but had no port, just a small harbour, but even so that also probably drew in the enemy. The capital city suffered worst, but it was a long way to the west of us and there was a persistent assumption in Errest that any raids were a mistake or a miscalculation. Assumption or not, the bombing continued for the duration of that phase of the war.

In fact, my family and I came through the war relatively unscathed, compared with thousands of other people. Our house suffered damage along with everybody else's, but it was mostly superficial. We lost part of the roof in one raid and several windows were broken at other times. The house was solidly built and it had a deep cellar where we kept our most valued possessions and where we took refuge whenever the alarm sounded. Overall, our neighbourhood was comparatively undamaged by the shells and bombs, while the heaviest bombing occurred closer to the centre of the town. One of the earliest buildings in Errest to be destroyed was the Industrial Palace, the great and beautiful complex of concert halls and auditoria. My father had regularly played in orchestral performances in the Palace before the bombing.

Like all children I lived in two worlds: the outer reality, which was sometimes grim or frightening or depressing, but mostly was simply ordinary, and the inner world of dreams and the imagination. Here, in the privacy of the mind, stimulated and enlivened by the making of music, I dwelt as long as possible each day. Some of the music I heard was of course practical, actual – the long hours of learning and practising, the sounds of my parents and brother playing on their own instruments, the repeated playing of the gramophone records we had – but much of it was a stream of imagined music, welling up somehow from my unconscious mind.

I describe the outer world as ordinary, and so it was for me. I knew nothing else, so I assumed that life in Errest, or even anywhere else in Glaund, was as it should be, as it was known to be. What I then considered to be ordinary was a town which I now realize had originally been a tiny fishing village, but which before I was born had been developed and expanded to become the site of several large engineering factories, and above all the steelworks on the other side of town. This expansion had begun about a hundred years earlier when substantial iron ore deposits were discovered in hilly country not far away. Necessary communications with the rest of the country meant that new roads and railways were built. Errest became a town of dark and dirty factories, a grim environment of poor housing for the workers, a source of the spillage of much disgusting effluent into our only small river, and the instigator of an almost perpetual pall of chemical-laden smoke or fog.

However, state-run heavy industry inevitably brought wealth to the town and by the time I was born Errest was renowned as a centre for the arts. One of the largest art galleries in the Glaund Republic was situated in Errest, with several satellite galleries in other towns in the region. And then there was the Industrial Palace, which incorporated two theatres, three concert halls of different sizes, several well-equipped workshop areas, a huge sports facility, a lending library, a recording studio, two restaurants. Errest was regarded by many of the people in our country as a showpiece town, a monument to industrialization and profit. Naturally, it became an early target for Faiandland's drones and self-guided rockets.

Between the raids – and sometimes weeks and months free of bombs went by in false seasons of hope – I practised on my violin and my parents' piano. I was becoming primarily a violinist, but increasingly I went to the piano when I wanted to write down some of the tunes and harmonies I could hear resounding in my mind.

I joined a local youth orchestra as third or fourth violinist (the actual position depended on who else turned up for each rehearsal or session), and there was a local social club where young musicians were traditionally welcomed on some nights of the week. Jacj and I went along whenever it was possible, discovering folk songs and popular dances, repetitive reels, played with drums and concertinas, fast, loud and long. We enjoyed this relaxed kind of fiddling so much that we both began to let our classical practice fall into inaction – my father soon put a stop to that when he found out what was happening. Afterwards, visits to the club were strictly rationed.

Music was music to me, whatever it was called. But I loved my parents, and was not a natural rebel.

One warm day in summer, early on, when I was about seven years old, I made a simple discovery that indirectly initiated the events that eventually were to change my life.

Because of the confining circumstances of wartime, and because I was still a small child, I had almost no curiosity about the outside world. I was in the house for most of the time. When I went outside it was usually in bad weather – cold, murky, clouded, windy. It was the same all over Glaund, except in the mountains, where it was worse. The roads were often flooded with deep puddles because of damaged drains, or they were made dangerous by the uncleared heaps of rubble. Several times when I was a boy I grazed my knees or shins on pieces of metal or broken masonry jutting out from the ground. People in Errest walked with their heads down, watching where they put their feet, incurious about the world around them.

I was no different. I hurried to and from school, I usually walked after dark to the club where I played. I neither knew nor cared much about what was outside my immediate environment.

On the day in question I was wandering around the top floor of our house when I noticed that the ladder leading to the roof loft had been left down. The loft was often used by my parents, so the existence of the ladder was not a surprise, but they normally slid it up and out of sight. My parents were not around and my brother was downstairs somewhere. I climbed slowly.

It was not forbidden territory – advised-against would be more accurate because my parents rarely forbade anything. They always persuaded Jacj and myself, explained things to us. That was their way. I knew that the roof area was a risky place to be because some of the incoming shells were designed to explode in the air. Many houses had been destroyed from the top down and past damage to our house had been caused by air bursts. But on that day there had been no siren and in fact we were going through one of those periods when there was a lull.

I knew my father kept several boxes of sheet music in the loft and I was curious to find out what was there. The loft space was unlit, but a large window set into one of the sloping roofs let in sunlight. The air under the roof was warm, smelling musty and dry. Dust lay on sheafs of manuscript paper, some of which had written notes, but most of which did not. Old instrument cases and a wooden music stand were leaning in a corner.

I found the printed sheet music in a large box but as soon as I started looking I realized it was not going to be the sort of music I liked. There were vocalists, trumpeters, guitarists, male voice choirs, female crooners – I had been hoping to find something I could learn and play, but none of this appealed to me. I was just a small child. I did not know anything. Thinking back, I can't help wondering what was really there in that box – perhaps some of it might be valuable now. Well, I lost interest and moved away.

I went to the window and because there was an old chest beneath it I was able to clamber up to look at what was outside.

For the first time in my life I had a clear and almost panoramic view of the sea. Not just the grey beaches a short distance from our house, where pallid waves broke listlessly on the polluted shingle. Those I saw every week. That sea had never interested me. It had an oily quality, a sense of tired menace, a worn-out and unwanted threat, like a deep puddle where broken pieces of machinery might lurk dangerously beneath the surface. I was used to its desultory noise, its acidic smell, its old poisoned state. I saw the movement of the tides, and occasionally the sea's different moods when the wind was high, but it was a familiar feature of my everyday life and it had never engaged me. I could rarely see much of it because the air was so dirty.

From the loft window all was different. The air must have been unusually clean that day, with the wind blowing from the south. It did that sometimes, bringing rain or snow in the cold months when it encountered our chill atmosphere, but what I saw that day was a still, shining surface, bright golden where the sun burnished it, mostly blue or grey elsewhere. It dazzled me. I had not realized it was there, that it was like that.

Nor had I known before this moment that there were islands out there. I could see three of them, high irregular shapes made to seem dark because of the surrounding brightness. Fascinated by the sight of them, and completely forgetting why I had climbed up to the loft in the first place, I stared across at those islands. It was impossible to make out details on them because of the distance, but I was certain there would be people living there. Houses and towns must be there but because of the cleanliness of the sea around them their houses and towns would not be like mine, could not be.

I leaned against the grimy glass, gazing and wondering, trying to imagine what it would be like to live in a small place, one surrounded by the sea, one without bomb damage, a steelworks and a mess of factories. I had only the vaguest idea what island life might be like. I had never before thought islands might be real, might be out there, in the sea and visible from the house I lived in.

My father, coming up the stairs from lower in the house, reached the top landing and noticed that the loft ladder was still down. He climbed up to find me.

'If a drone came over you might be hurt,' he said gently, as he stood beside me at the window. 'You have seen how much the roofs are damaged, even if the explosion is not on top of us. We have to survive, all of us. You have to survive the war, Sandro.'

The loft would always be a vulnerable place. Lower down in the house the walls were reinforced as best they could be, the windows sealed with anti-blast laminate. Nothing could protect a house against a direct hit, but these were a precaution against a shell falling a street or two away.

'I was looking at those islands,' I said. 'Can we go across and visit them?'

'Not at present, not while the war goes on.'

'Do people live over there?' I said, pointing with my hand. My father said nothing. 'Who are they? Do they have music too?

'Come on down, Sandro.'

That was the end of the adventure, such as it was. I had glimpsed a distant view I had not known before: a shining sea, the bulking of unnamed islands and the possibilities they enigmatically suggested. I knew nothing of them, but the sight of them was alone enough to charge my imagination. The sounds of waves broke around me, wild ocean winds blustered, tall trees bent on shorelines and high mountains, and there were foreign voices in the towns.

I felt within me unexplained images of beaches, reefs, harbours, lagoons, ships' sirens, violent gales, the cries of seabirds, the suck of a tide moving back over shingle.

I wrote a little piece for the piano, trying to transcribe to real music the delicate and confusing sounds inside my mind. It did not work out as well as I wanted it to, but to this day I think of it as my first full composition. I have not played it for many years.

3

By the time I was fourteen all my plans of becoming a professional musician had to be put aside. The war continued with no apparent conclusion in sight. Militarily it had become a stalemate. An arranged cease-fire brought an end to the bombing of towns, but our lives were still disrupted. The cease-fire was only temporary at first, but it was better than nothing and as the months went by it did seem to hold. Temporariness turned slowly into a feeling of permanence. The political and economic disputes remained – we heard about border infringements, mineral rights disputes, arguments about access to water sources, there was an apparently intractable row about reparations, and of course beneath it all was a clash of political ideology.

The main consequence was that a treaty was drawn up, but not a treaty for peace. The war itself, the actual fighting, was to be continued abroad. The great frozen continent at the southern pole of the world, which was called Sudmaieure, was uninhabited, deemed to be valueless terrain and was appropriated as a pitch for a standing war. Young people were drafted into the military in increasing numbers, shipped south, and made to stand on the pitch and fight for their masters.

No one therefore made the mistake of thinking that because our homes were no longer under attack the war had ended and we were at peace. Everyone realized that it would take years, perhaps decades, to return to that. However, the fabric of civilian lives might at least now be repaired. So many cities had been damaged, houses lost, factories and infrastructure destroyed – rebuilding work began. Ordinary people tried to resume their former lives.

The letter Jacj dreaded most arrived one day. The recruiting of young men and women had redoubled. He threw the letter on our breakfast table for us to read. He was given a date by which he must report for a medical examination. Assuming his health was acceptable he would be drafted immediately. He would be sent south to fight for the honour of our country, and had been pre-selected for something called the 289th Battalion, an active service unit.

Jacj and I often played duets together. Sometimes I accompanied him on the piano, but most often we simply stood side by side with our violins, quietly playing. One day, when we had finished, Jacj said, 'Sandro, we need to talk.'

He led me to his bedroom, which was on the top storey of the house, and closed the door securely behind us. His pet cat,

Djahann, a forest cat, mostly white and long-haired, was asleep on his bed. He sat beside her, pressed his hand lightly on her neck then teased her gently under the chin as she raised her head, large green eyes blinking.

'I've got to join up,' he said. 'There's no way out of it.'

'When will it be?'

'Next week.'

'So soon?'

'You saw the letter that came,' he said. 'That was the third one. I hid the others as soon as they arrived. I destroyed them.'

He told me then some of what he had been doing to try to avoid the draft. The anti-war group he belonged to had various strategies for avoidance, or at best for delay. The group mostly consisted of teenagers like himself, all dreading the call-up. He had tried all their ideas: begging for medical notes, claiming educational commitments, obtaining a letter from his tutor. The response from the army authorities had been implacable. Jacj said that going into hiding was the most desperate method, tried by many young conscripts he knew.

'All were discovered,' he said. 'These people know where to look. It's useless trying to escape them.'

'But Dad said—'

'I know. But in the end I realized that trying to hide only made things worse. It's the coward's way.'

I knew my father had arranged for a close friend from his days at university to take Jacj in. He and his wife had a farm in a remote village high in the Glaundian mountains – Dad said the escouades, the recruit squads sent out by the military authorities to find draft dodgers, were rarely seen in the mountains. Jacj would be safe there.

'It's not being a coward to oppose war,' I said.

'Then how long would I hide from the escouades? A few days? A few months? The rest of my life on a farm in the mountains?'

He said that he had made a decision. He believed that under international law the war was illegal – it was cruel, it had killed many thousands of innocent civilians, it had no social worth, it had no moral justification. Hostilities would have to be brought to an end soon, and in the meantime he would yield to the draft.

There was little any young recruit could do alone, but at the least he would learn the system from the inside, gain and collect evidence, and one day after he returned to civilian life, and had completed his law studies, he would be able to act.

We were two boys: I was fourteen, Jacj barely eighteen. The draft was more than just a vague threat to me: I knew that in four more years my turn would come. To me, Jacj's plan seemed, for a short time at least, to be brave and workable.

Jacj lifted Djahann from the bed, her legs drooping. She was still half asleep. He let her spread out on his lap, purring. He stroked her back, played with her paws, tickling the pads behind her claws in a way she loved.

'She's my priority, Sandro,' he said. 'Will you look after Djahann for me, until I'm back?'

We both fell silent, staring at the cat. She rolled on her back, raising her paws towards him.

A week later I walked down to the centre of Errest with Jacj, where he was to report to the recruitment building. Our parents, tearful but supportive, stayed at home. Following instructions, Jacj carried no luggage, but he was allowed one luxury. The letter had suggested a book, a photograph, a diary. Jacj had decided to take his violin, and it was strapped across his back.

We came to a line of white plastic tape, forming a barrier in front of the building. Here we said goodbye: too young to show the emotion we felt, too old not to feel it. We mocked a couple of brotherly punches, then he turned away and headed for the building. Halfway across the concourse a uniformed soldier directed him instead towards a grey-painted bus that was parked to one side. It had windows, but they were silvered against the chance of people being able to see inside. I waited for a while, watching other young recruits shepherded on to the same vehicle, but I was finding the scene depressing. I headed for home.

A few minutes later the bus was driven along the street past me. It left behind a cloud of oily black smoke.

A few days later my parents received an official letter from the Staff Strategy Office in Glaund City – this was known to everyone as the headquarters of the military junta. The letter was signed by Jacj himself, as if he had written it, but the countersignatures of two junta officers revealed the true source of the letter. The letter confirmed that his battalion was being sent to join a large operational division. Because of the conditions of war he would be unable to contact us until he returned to this country.

At the end of the letter there was an extract from something called an Article of War, which imposed secrecy and confidentiality on all the next of kin of serving troops, but it added that his family would be notified immediately the 289th Battalion was released from active duty.

Jacj's drafting into the army was a terrible matter for my parents to bear, because it was known that conditions on the southern continent were harsh and dangerous. There were already many stories of young people who had not returned. The only consolation my parents had was that the battalions were normally demobilized in numerical order, so that they would eventually be able to work out when Jacj would come home. Around this time the 236th Battalion was said to be returning from duty, so we knew there was going to be a long wait.

4

We three remained at home. My parents were still both having to work as freelance music teachers, but as the conditions of the half-peace took hold they were hopeful of finding more permanent employment. There was talk of the possibility that the Industrial Palace would be rebuilt, although this would of course take several years to complete. My father said there were already moves to re-form the Philharmonia Orchestra.

I was wrapped up in my own worries, aware that it would be only a matter of time before I too was drafted, even though there were still four years before the problem became actual. I was desperate not to have to follow Jacj into the army. A full-time course at the conservatoire in Glaund City would defer the draft for two years, but even that postponement was not a possibility for me – the main building had been damaged in a raid and student places were few.

When I left school at the age of sixteen I had to look around for a job, and by a stroke of good fortune managed to obtain a lowly position as a trainee cost clerk with an electronics company in Errest. They had a contract to supply missile guidance systems, so although I was an insignificant member of the staff, without technical skill, their role as an arms supplier meant they were a safe haven for me.

The work I did was administrative and dull, but it gave me an adequate income while allowing me to develop as a composer in my spare time. So long as they went on selling their weapons systems to the junta I would be spared the army.

With a regular income I was eventually able to leave home. I rented an apartment with three good-sized rooms in a tall house not far from the sea. The area had been badly bombed, so rents were low. Music became my obsession and commitment once more – I spent most of what was left from my wages on gramophone records and printed scores. It was the period when long-playing vinyl records were available at affordable prices. I slowly built up a collection of the works I most loved. I borrowed books on composition from the local library, and read biographies of the great composers. I listened, I played, I wrote. Music rang through my head.

The cease-fire continued to hold. Many people were nervous that without a formal armistice the violence could break out again, but even so life was returning to what it had been before the raids. I managed my job so that I had as much spare time as possible, attending almost every concert I could find, sometimes having to travel a long way.

One summer I took a week's holiday and stayed alone in a small hotel in Glaund City, which was about an hour's train journey along the coast from Errest. By this time the worst damage to the centre of the capital had been repaired, so that public concerts were once again taking place. Live music was at last emerging from behind the alarms and from inside the shelters where we had all been forced to hide. It was a thrilling time. I used up most of my savings during this one week, but afterwards regarded it as an important period. It confirmed to me what I had been reading in music magazines, and had heard from a few other musicians, that although the traditional repertoire was as popular as ever modernist music was once again being composed and performed.

The music I was writing soon started to make a mark, albeit a small one. Through my father, and other contacts, I arranged local performances of some of my pieces. One was a song cycle based on the verse of the Glaundian poet Goerg Skynn, another was a suite for piano and flute, my most complex work at this time was a piano sonata and when I was twenty-seven I mounted an impressionistic piece for piano and violin at a recital in Errest Town Hall. It celebrated Memorial Day and it was called *Breath*.

Breath was a composition inspired by and depicting moorland scenes on the hills I could see in the distance from the windows of my apartment. I made several solitary trips to the moors, soaking in the feelings and sounds. I went the first time because I wanted to breathe unpolluted air, and I guessed that the altitude of the moors would be above the layer of airborne muck that we normally had to take in, but once I was there I began to appreciate the greater subtleties of the area. Much of the landscape evoked silence: the spaces in the music represented the absence of sound when a bird or an animal sprang away from me as I trudged over the tussocks and along the paths. Wind flowing through the coarse grasses was suggested in the background. Windless days created a quietness I had never known before. The sounds of steeply flowing streams wound their way through my melodies.

For this recital I played the piano myself, with a young woman called Alynna Rosson taking the violin part. I had met Alynna at one of the concerts I went to in Glaund City, and we had become friends.

Neither of us had played in front of an audience, even one so small as ours that night, and it was an emotional experience for both of us. Afterwards, in the bare room behind the platform, where Alynna had left her violin case, we were both crying. For me it was partly the relief of having completed the performance without obvious mistakes, but also I had been living again the emotions I felt while conceiving and writing the piece. Imagining she must be undergoing the same feelings of release I tried to comfort Alynna by putting my hands on her shoulders, but she shrugged me away.

'I felt I was alone up there,' she said, and her voice was low, but not because she was crying. I realized only then that she was angry with me. 'I could not hear you playing,' she said, and her voice broke up.

'The score has many silences. I was with you, but it was the same for me.'

'When we rehearsed—'

'A rehearsal is never the same,' I said. 'You played perfectly tonight. I found it very moving to hear you playing like that.'

'I was only following the score.'

'That is how it should have been. The score is the shape of the music. You are still shaking.' Once more I tried to console her with a hand on her arm, but again she pulled away from me. People were passing and the door opened and closed a couple of times. The lights in the corridor outside went out. The staff wanted to close the building. 'You are upset,' I said stupidly, wishing I knew how to make things better for both of us.

'It was those silences,' she said. 'I could not hear them properly and I was trying to count the bars. I was terrified of missing them.'

'The notes were written to go around the pauses. They describe and define the spaces. It is only in silence that music is pure.'

She was staring at me, frowning, not comprehending. I wished neither of us had said anything.

'I saw the silences on the score. I didn't know you were going to mark them with red ink.'

'The score has to show the pauses as well as the notes. I am giving another recital next month,' I said. 'Would you like to be there with me?'

'After what just happened?'

'Please, Alynna.'

For me, what had just happened had been a transcending experience, with a purity of note and expression from her violin that made me shake inside. Her sensitive playing made me want to wave my arms with excitement. Her negative response was really confusing to me.

'I don't think so,' she said, putting away her violin.

Soon after this Alynna left without saying goodbye. I was in turmoil. My constant need to be writing and playing meant that I had never formed proper relationships with anyone of the opposite sex. The events of that evening reminded me painfully of my inexperience. Alynna made me think I had failed her, frightened her, and because I was blundering I had actually damaged whatever it was that had seemed sensual and intimate when we were playing together. In those few minutes of playing *Breath* she had come to seem beautiful to me. I had a lot to learn.

Outside, as I left the hall, a few members of the audience were waiting in the cold darkness to greet me, to congratulate me. Nothing of the sort had ever happened to me before, and I was unprepared. I tried to respond graciously to the polite compliments but as soon as I could I retreated to the yard at the back of the town hall, found my bicycle where I had left it and pedalled home through the chill fog.

My route led me for part of the way along the shore, a narrow road close to the edge of a cliff. As always I glanced to the south, across the sea, towards those islands that had so briefly enchanted me in childhood. I could see nothing of them in the murky darkness, no hint of lights, not even a sense of their bulking shapes. I had stared at them so often, though, that I knew their dark outlines, their silent mysteries. I hummed a fragment of music, imagining myself walking on the hills of one of the islands.

5

When I was thirty years old I made the breakthrough I had been hoping for. An independent record label based in a small town a long way from Errest, on the far side of Glaund City, approached me. They specialized in commissioning recordings by new or emerging musicians and featured small orchestras. They packaged their records well, priced them reasonably and for a small label managed to have most of their catalogue distributed through the shops. They had decided to release a long-playing record to showcase contemporary Glaundian music.

As soon as I heard about it I submitted several recent pieces. The first scores I sent in were returned to me, often without comment, but at least two of them were described as unsuitable. They gave no reasons. I kept trying, and finally they accepted a short piece I had written the year before. It was called *Dianme*.

Dianme is a single-movement quartet for piano, flute, violin and viola. It was inspired by the island of the same name, which was one of the islands in the bay offshore from Errest.

Using the name *Dianme* was my way of revealing a personal discovery of the island, but a few people remarked, sometimes in print, that it was a political act too. I was politically naïve, so when I went on a quest to find out what the island was called I accidentally discovered the Glaundian government's deliberate attempt to control what information could be allowed to the public.

I established the island's name only after much searching around, using old directories, atlases, charts and so on. I had assumed that such a search would be routine. In reality I discovered there was a cloud of obfuscation about all the islands in the region. A librarian told me in confidence that a directive had been issued by the military junta several years before to the effect that all reference books and maps about the islands must be surrendered to the government. Quite apart from covering up what the islands' names were, the secrecy extended to photographs and drawings, descriptions, even encyclopaedia entries about population statistics, agriculture, trade, and everything else. It was as if the islands had been declared not to exist at all.

Most contemporary maps naturally had to include our shoreline, but nothing was depicted in detail of the sea itself. Some of the maps marked the ocean as the 'Midway Sea', and in much smaller type the words 'Dream Archipelago' appeared, sometimes in parentheses. I had heard the name somewhere – perhaps it was mentioned at school? – but I knew nothing at all about where or what the Archipelago might be. No islands were ever depicted on maps.

One day in a second-hand shop I came across a dusty old book about the Glaundian shoreline. A footnote about a tidal surge mentioned the three islands in a factual way, and named them. The smallest of the three was called Dianme, named after a benign goddess of mythology, alleged to have stirred up a warm wind from the south-east. This usually brought the spring early to our coast.

Charmed by the discovery, I wrote my quartet. I was happy to have the name at last.

The other two islands, larger and further away from the shore, were called Chlam and Herrin, again named after mythological events. I mentally stored them for future use.

Physical details of the islands were still difficult to make out, even when magnified by the bird-watching field glasses that used to belong to my father. The glasses were not strong enough to clarify much, but the images I saw through the instrument gave me a sense of compressed space, a feeling that time was being shortened by this view.

The normal hometown sounds I heard as I stood on the coastal road, staring out to sea through the binoculars, became in my mind a rhythmic counterpoint to the calm, static islands, apparently locked out there in distance and time. The flute and violin reproduce the homely sounds of birdsong, children's chatter, while the viola and piano suggest the distance, the boom of waves, the gasp of the warm wind from the south-east. Dianme, the closest of the three as well as being the smallest, particularly charged my gentle, harmless fantasies.

Facts about the Dream Archipelago were hard to come by and fragmentary, but I was slowly piecing together what I could. I knew, for instance, that as a citizen of the Glaund Republic I would be forever forbidden from crossing to any of those islands. Indeed, the entire Archipelago, which I learned circled the world, was a closed and prohibited zone. Officially, it did not exist. However, the islands were in fact there, were neutral territory in the terms of the war Glaund was involved in, and their neutrality was fiercely protected by their local laws and customs. For them, Glaund was still a belligerent country, as was, I assumed, Faiandland. A real or lasting armistice with

Faiandland and its satellite states was as far away as ever, and only a complex network of diplomatic compromises kept the fighting away from our homes. This clearly did not mean peace. The Dream Archipelago was the largest geographical feature in the world, comprising literally millions of islands, but it was closed to warmongers.

The discovery of these islands was like hearing a great symphony for the first time. The realization that I should never be allowed to explore them was like having a door slammed in my face as an orchestra started to tune up.

My *Dianme* quartet reflected and expressed both the quietude of the seascape as I perceived it from the shore, and the feelings of defeat induced in me by the denied existence of the islands. The normality of the local sounds, picked out and expressed by the pizzicato violin, was discordant and intrusive. The main theme that suggested Dianme herself, declared in the first few phrases and reprised towards the end, was a restful melody, intended to signify the beauty of beneficent nature.

I was of course pleasantly surprised when I heard that the recording manager had accepted my composition. Because I hoped to be involved with the making of the record I took two days off work and travelled to Glaund City for the session. When I arrived at the studio it turned out I was allowed only to sit in the recording booth while the piece was being played. Even so, I found it a profound and moving experience.

When the record was released a few weeks later I managed to persuade my local record shop to stock three copies, although in the end I had to purchase them myself from the shopkeeper. For two months the record was received in silence by the music critics, but finally a short review appeared in a weekly magazine of political satire and news. The reviewer was dismissive of all the pieces on the record, but did mention *Dianme* in passing, stating that it was 'melodically pleasant'. The magazine misspelled my name 'Alesander Suskind'. I was just pleased to have the record.

6

Not long after the release of *Dianme* I met a fellow composer from one of the islands in the south, whose name was Denn Mytrie. Mytrie was to become a friend, although our first encounter was fraught with misunderstandings.

Our meeting came about after I had completed the piece of music that followed *Dianme*. It was called *Tidal Symbols*, an interpretation of what I saw as the episodes of calm and bluster along our shores. I sent the score to the same company that had recorded *Dianme*, and felt happy when they responded within a week, writing enthusiastically of its modernist approach, its harmonic innovations and its unusual treatment of melodic surprise. I was delighted by their reaction. Although what they said of my music was not exactly how I would have described it myself, I answered their letter with alacrity and a contract for the new work was drawn up immediately. I signed it and sent it back the same day.

A long wait ensued – I later found out that the reason was because of the length of *Tidal Symbols*. It was only long enough for one side of a 10" long-playing record, and they were waiting for a suitable piece of the same sort of length to go on the other side. One day they told me that they had accepted a work by a composer named Mytrie. I had never heard of him, or perhaps her, as had no one else I knew.

When I asked the record company for more information, they told me that Denn Mytrie, a man, was from Muriseay in the Dream Archipelago, newly arrived in Glaund on a cultural exchange programme. I said nothing about what I had learned of the denied existence of the islands.

The day of the recording finally came around. This time I caught the first available train to Glaund City, so I was early and in the studio before most of the other people. I was startled to see more than thirty musicians arriving to perform on the record. I recognized a few of them by sight, but most of them were strangers. However, I did instantly recognize Alynna Rosson taking up a position with the violins. I had not seen her to speak to since the evening we performed *Breath* together.

To my surprise, when she noticed me she raised a hand in welcome and walked quickly towards me.

'Sandro! I was hoping you would be here today.'

'I'm glad to see you again,' I said, while knowing that in reality I had abandoned all hope of keeping her as a friend. A year had passed since that evening.

'What have you been working on?' she said. 'I heard you had a record out.'

'The new one is called *Tidal Symbols*,' I said. 'One of the pieces I imagine you are here to record.'

'No – I'm only on the first. The one written by Denn.'

'Denn?'

We were standing in the centre of the sound stage. Pointing to the side she indicated the tall young man who had been at the studio when I arrived. He was standing confidently with one of the recording engineers, discussing the score, marking up one of the pages before the session began. I had seen him when I arrived, but I had been too shy to approach him, thinking he was something to do with the studio. Anyway, he exuded a kind of free confidence I notably lacked, the sort I always felt intimidated by. He had an athletic body and a shock of long blond hair. His easy manner radiated his pleasure that he was working in this studio.

'That's Denn Mytrie,' Alynna said. 'He's a wonderful musician. You probably know his work?'

'Is he the composer from Muriseay?'

'Yes.'

'And you say you know him already?'

'He's a friend, someone I happened to meet a couple of weeks ago. He recommended me for this job today.'

'I had no idea people could come to the mainland to work. Muriseay is one of the islands, isn't it? I thought the borders were closed.'

'The regulations have been eased. And apparently Muriseay is situated more or less due south of Glaund, which makes a difference to people travelling here, or going back. He's on a cultural exchange of some kind. There's even talk of orchestra tours, here and in the islands. Have you heard anything about those?'

'No, I haven't,' I said, beginning to realize how my endless preoccupation with work was isolating me from other people, even those in my own profession, and the subjects they would be talking about. 'What difference would travelling north or south mean?'

'He said it makes getting a visa less of a problem.'

I shook my head, not understanding. 'What about you?' I said to Alynna. 'Are you living here in Glaund City now?'

'No. I'm still in Errest. You too?'

'Yes, the same. I'm really pleased to see you again, Alynna.'

'Why did you think I had moved away?'

I was feeling again my lack of experience with women, in particular with Alynna, who to my astonishment appeared genuinely happy to see me. I was struggling with a feeling of possessiveness, brought on when I found out she was already on first-name terms with this other composer. What had been going on between them?

When Alynna went back to take her place in the orchestra I noticed that Mytrie went across to speak to her, making her laugh. Mytrie had a generous smile and briefly touched her hand with his while they were speaking.

Alynna's presence in the studio took my mind off other concerns as I watched her first rehearsing with Mytrie and the other musicians, then playing his piece. It was called *Woodland Love*. One of the recording engineers told me that it summoned up life on Muriseay, using variations on certain folk tunes. Ordinarily that sort of thing would have interested and involved me, but I had trouble concentrating. It sounded smooth and conventional to me. All my interest was absorbed by the small, dark-haired woman sitting in the second row of violins. I watched the intentness on her face as she played, the responsive movements of her head. She sat, poised and elegant, her shoulders and neck straight, her control of the instrument fluid and expressive.

The recording was completed after four takes, but the Muriseayan rhapsody had barely impressed itself on me. It sounded sweet and familiar, music that gave comfort, not stimulation. I felt that my work was at a different intellectual level, and that it was wrong that this Mytrie and myself were being packaged together. The fact that his work and mine were to occupy different sides of the same disc suggested a link of some kind, a similarity of purpose where none existed.

I was hoping to speak to Alynna again, but as soon as the recording manager announced that the session was complete she left her seat to mix with the other musicians. When she had put away her instrument she left with the others. The remaining musicians took their places for *Tidal Symbols*. The other composer walked across to me.

'Sir, I believe you are Alesander Suskind. Would that be right?'

'Yes,' I said, too startled to correct what I knew was becoming a common mistake about my name.

'I am Denn Mytrie, and I am visiting from Muriseay. I'm proud to meet you, sir.' I shook hands with the young man. I immediately liked his firm grip, the open way he looked at me, the sincerity he radiated. His words were unaccented, but there was a lilt to his voice, a kind of musical inflexion that you would never hear anywhere in Glaund. Previously I had no idea how islanders might sound, and briefly wondered if this might be it. 'This is a great honour, Msr Suskind,' he continued. 'When they told me we would be recording together I could hardly believe my good fortune.'

'Well, thank you,' I said, embarrassed, pleased, feeling my prejudices against this young man dissolving away.

'May we get together briefly for a drink after this? There is so much I'd like to discuss with you.'

'Well, I will have to catch a train home—'

'Let's see if we can make the time,' he said. 'I would love to discuss your quartet *Dianme*. I listened to the record properly for the first time just before I had to come away.'

'I didn't know it had been distributed—'

'My publisher sent me a copy, but it is already popular on many of the islands. You hear it on the music radio channels.'

'In the Archipelago?'

'Of course! You are becoming well known, at least on Muriseay, but many of the other islands too. My publisher said I must talk to you, because of the new ground you seem to be breaking. I should like to know where the inspiration comes from. I could feel your excitement in every phrase.'

We were standing together by the rear wall of the studio, partly concealed from the main area by two diffusers, but I could see the engineers already taking sound levels as the musicians tuned up. His enthusiasm radiated at me, seeming entirely genuine.

'It was the name of the island,' I said, thinking of the search for a map or chart. 'When I found out why the island was called Dianme I heard the music taking shape. It just – flowed. I was imagining what the winds might be like on that island. Dianme's winds.'

'That explains so much. But when I heard the music I wondered if you had meant one of the other islands. Chlam, perhaps?'

'No – Dianme.'

'It is a superb piece of music. I have so much to learn from you.' He seized my hand again and shook it vigorously. 'They're about to start. Let's speak together again later?'

'It has been a pleasure to meet you,' I said, meaning it.

He smiled affably at me, turned away and was gone. I went to take my place at the rear of the control room.

There turned out to be problems with the performance of *Tidal Symbols*, and the orchestra had to make several attempts before they could get it right. The leader of the orchestra complained that they had not been given enough time to rehearse, and there was a surprisingly angry exchange of words between him and the recording manager. Embarrassed, I stayed out of it, dreading that I might have scored the orchestration inexpertly. I had been revising the score until two or three days earlier, and I had sent in at least four separate revisions, one of them restoring deletions from an earlier draft, then a few days later I changed them back again. In the end, the studio managed to get a good take, by which time it was late in the afternoon. Everyone, including me, looked and felt exhausted. There was no sign of Denn Mytrie.

Three days later, when I was back in Errest and the rather mixed memories of the recording were starting to fade, I was still thinking about Alynna. I braced myself against the dread of being rejected by her and made contact. She came to the telephone, said she was pleased to hear from me again and reassured me when I described some of what had seemed to go wrong during the recording. We spoke on the phone for nearly an hour, then arranged to meet the next day. I was happy and full of confidence. We walked along the deserted seafront, becoming closer by the minute. We met again the next day, and also on the next. Within four months we were married. Our friend Denn Mytrie was an invited guest to the wedding, but he sent a note saying that because of travel difficulties he would be unable to attend.

Alynna and I made a home together in a large rented apartment in a small town further along the coast from Errest. It was convenient for my dull but necessary job, and it had a railway connection direct to Glaund City. The apartment had views of the sea. I set up my studio in a room with a high window, looking down across a strand of tussock grasses and low dunes. The island of Dianme was slightly to the left of the view – her companions Chlam and Herrin lay further out to sea, darker than she, more closed with their secrets, intriguing as ever. I mused when I stared towards them. I could not free myself of their insistent harmonies, as they seemed to drift across to me above the constant waves.

7

Tidal Symbols was reviewed well and the record company, after a few weeks of silence, suddenly announced that the record was also selling well. I was later able to measure this, when royalties from sales started to reach me. I was pleased and astonished but even more surprised to discover that a high proportion of the copies sold were within the islands of the Dream Archipelago.

Denn Mytrie, who had returned to Muriseay after completing his exchange visit, wrote me several letters, sometimes enclosing reviews which had been published on one or other of the islands. We both exulted at our success, each generously saying how fortunate we had been to have appeared on the same record. In truth, I secretly believed that Denn Mytrie's populist melodies were the magic ingredient in our sales mix, and that my more austere composition would never have appealed to so many people, but he would have none of that. We were both satisfied.

I was going through a period of general contentment. I enjoyed being married to Alynna, and the first excitements we had for each other went on undimmed. I liked the feeling of being settled, of having a secure emotional base for my life. Alynna's musical prowess was improving steadily and she was regularly invited to play: her session work brought money in reliably, and her occasional invitations to sit in with an orchestra or a smaller ensemble produced welcome cash bonuses.

While Alynna played, I composed. I was working steadily, trying out new approaches all the time. The income from *Tidal Symbols* enabled me finally to leave my day job in the cost accounting department – I was now old enough to be low in priority for the draft, and so no longer needed the extra protection the job afforded me.

I was never entirely free of dread thoughts about the draft though, because I could not forget the likely fate of my brother Jacj.

A letter had arrived from Jacj not long after I married. It was sent to my parents, although I was named too at the top. It was on notepaper with the Battalion insignia printed as a heading, and although it was written by hand, for some reason Jacj had printed every word in capital letters. It was a short note in a mechanical style, as if he had been made to copy it from a pro forma, or someone had dictated it to him. It simply said that he was embarking on the great military campaign that would bring an end to the war, that he was travelling in the company of fellow soldiers he liked and admired, and that he wanted us to buy the war bonds sold by the government to protect him by helping to finance this great adventure.

I imagine every family of every young recruit received a letter like this, and because we understood the way it was written and why it was sent, it was not in itself upsetting. However, from the date of the postmark it seemed to have been written not long after Jacj had sailed away, yet it had taken more than ten years for it to reach us. My parents, who were by this time moving towards old age, were upset by the thought that this letter had been lost or delayed en route.

It had been sent from one of the islands: with a magnifying

glass it was possible to read the faded red-ink franking on the front: *Island Protectorate of Winho*. Where was Winho? We had no maps, we knew no one who could tell us. Was it an island close to our shores, or was it far away on the other side of the world? This extra enigma only deepened the feelings we all had of worry, upset and apprehension about where Jacj was and what might be happening to him.

I wrote to Denn Mytrie and asked him if he knew where the island of Winho might be. When his answer came, several weeks later, it was to say that he did not, but that people he knew on Muriseay believed it to be somewhere in the southern hemisphere. He told us that although maps were not forbidden in the Archipelago, it was always difficult finding any that depicted islands not in your own group or immediate area. He said that this was a problem throughout the Archipelago, and something to do with the gravitational anomalies. (He did not explain, and from the vague way he wrote I had the feeling he couldn't.)

Whenever I contacted Denn Mytrie, I felt I was groping across unknown seas, to an island I could not imagine, through delays and wasted time.

8

I made several more trips to Glaund City, partly to promote my music to the record managers, but also because I was sometimes offered session work in the studios. The money was helpful. Two more contracts were eventually signed and for one of the recordings I was allowed to rehearse the musicians and manage the actual performance. My reputation was slowly growing, and so too was my confidence. Alynna sometimes worked with me – these were occasions that were especially enjoyable for us.

The music I produced that I was most proud of at this time was my *Seasonal Gods* oratorio. I had loved writing *Dianme* and I treasured the recording that had been made, but I knew that my lack of confidence at the time had prevented me from developing the work as much as I should. Working on

Seasonal Gods encouraged me to try.

It was a commissioned work: the Metropolitan of the See of Glaund City had heard *Tidal Symbols*, and through an intermediary enquired if I would consider a liturgical piece for his church. I am not religious, but the money was good and the brief was in musical terms open. I used as my text five of the psalms suggested to me by the Metropolitan's staff. The format was complex, involving soloists and a choir, an organ part, and a small orchestra. I structured the music around the five psalms, which were followed by sung recitative and responsorial gradual. Passage of time was depicted by the antiphonal gradual.

Seasonal Gods occupied me for the best part of a year. When it was complete, and the first performance had been achieved, I was free of financial worries for a while and felt inspired to return to *Dianme* and make it part of a larger work.

It was a natural progression to conceive of making a trio of pieces, based on the three islands I thought of as my own: Dianme, Chlam and Herrin. The title of the overall work was suggested by the myths that were associated with each of the islands: *Detriment in Calm Seas*. With the thought came the imagining and the conception, and I was soon concentrating hard on the final two pieces of the suite.

Chlam was disruptive, singular music. I wrote for instruments I had barely used before: a silver trombone, snare drums and two electrically amplified string instruments. I had learned that Chlam, the mythological being, had brought ruin to the island by making a pact with a diabolical creature.

My piece called *Herrin* was different again. The myth on this island was one of calculated deception. Herrin had seemed to bring peace and wealth to the island, making the inhabitants trust him, but there was a price to pay. Time hung heavy. I orchestrated long romantic passages for the chamber orchestra, but these themes were gradually undermined by a creeping disharmony, until in the climax of both the piece and the suite every instrument was scored against every other in a cacophony of clashing notes.

My career progressed. As well as my recordings I was honoured by two live performances of my music in Glaund City.

I went to an inland town, high in the mountains, where I gave a performance on piano of my *Travelling Circus* suite – this was later chosen as the opening work of a concert by the eight-strong Academy Players at the Trade Hall in the industrial city of Leeth. I began writing a column of personal observations of the musical scene for one of the monthly magazines aimed at the serious listener. I reviewed records by other artists. I gave lectures and talks to students, and for one three-week period I was running a composition workshop for the best students in the conservatoire.

Gradually, things were improving for me. The liveable income I was making from my music started to seem steady, reliable.

Then, things started to go wrong.

9

The letter that arrived seemed innocuous at first. It was from someone who bought my records, and who had been to some of my concert performances. Towards the end of his long and mostly admiring letter, he wrote:

> I will not embarrass you, Monseignior Sussken, by noting my reactions to every single piece of music you have written, but I have enjoyed all your work. When a record is available I have always bought one, and several times I have bought extra copies to give to friends. I have particular admiration for *Tidal Symbols*, for *Breath*, and for your early masterpiece *Dianme*.

So far so good. I had not received many letters like this, and I was glad to have this one. However, the writer went on:

> A few weeks ago my son, who had been on a school exchange trip to one of the islands to the south of us, came home with a record he had bought. It had the unusual title *The Lost Aviator*, or in its original language (the island demotic) *Pilota Marret*. It was rock music, which I do not like, but when I heard my son playing it my attention was immediately caught by some of

the tracks. Much of the music sounded uncannily like yours, if you can imagine your work played in a raucous manner by a band of young men on electric guitars and drums. I'm sure I am not mistaken – at least half the tracks are either based on your work, or are crude transpositions of it. I have noticed distinct traces of *Dianme* and the rest of the *Detriment* suite, *Tidal Symbols*, at least three of your magnificent flute sonatas, your first piano concerto, and here and there many phrases and passages which are uniquely in your style.

And so he went on, listing several more of my compositions, transcribed into music for amplified guitars.

In fact, I did not mind the idea of this transposition as much as my correspondent said he did, because for me all music has a common purpose. I was too old to involve myself in rock music. I knew it was not for me but I had nothing against it. I did not, though, like the idea of someone stealing what I had written.

The name of this rock musician is And Ante, which is also the name of his group. My son tells me that 'And' is a common first name for men in the Dream Archipelago – 'Ante' might be an adopted name as a performer, or might be his real name. I was wondering if you have been in touch with Monseignior Ante directly, and whether you have heard his record?

He then added the name and address, in Glaund City, of a specialist importer of records, who was carrying a stock of Msr Ante's *Lost Aviator*, in case I wanted to get hold of a copy.

I wrote back to thank my correspondent, and in the same mail I sent off an order for a copy of the record.

During the week that followed I was overseeing a composition workshop for a second season, guiding half a dozen young musicians at the start of their careers. I barely had time to think about what the letter said, and mentally postponed any reaction until I received my own copy of the record. The postponement was longer than I expected – the importers responded to my order with a note saying that they were waiting for more copies to arrive at their office. They enclosed a page from their recent catalogue.

This described *Pilota Marret*. The company who had issued the record was based on an island in the Dream Archipelago called Temmil – another place I had never heard of. The record consisted of ten tracks, with And Ante listed as the writer of all the songs. There were four musicians in the band, including Ante himself, who played lead guitar. The other three played bass guitar, trumpet and drums – the bass guitarist was credited with most of the singing. The longest track on the record, with a running time of nearly fifteen minutes, was an instrumental called 'Pilota Marret', giving the album its overall name.

I took what I believed was a sensible approach. Plagiarism aside, there was an element of flattery, a compliment almost, in the fact that someone thought my work was worth pilfering. I could never condone it, and if I should ever run into Msr Ante in person I would tell him what I thought of what he had done, but that was unlikely and I had other things to worry about.

Then the record itself arrived. Alynna had to travel to Glaund City that day for another recording session, so I waited until she was out of the house before putting the disc on the turntable.

The reality of what this man Ante had done was greater than I had thought, or even feared. Every single track on his record contained, at the minimum, a reference to something of mine: a particular harmonic progression, a brief snatch of melody, a way of introducing a key change. But more than that, one track was virtually a note-for-note transcription of one of my *Wind Songs*. Another took the tiny cadenza of my flute concerto, a delicate, flowing piece, a mere eight bars in length, and made it into a six-minute sonic assault of screeching guitar and a maddening, thudding drum beat. I could even detect the silences of *Breath* in one of the songs.

The main track, the title track, *Pilota Marret*, was not translated on the album sleeve. The man who had written to me had translated it as *The Lost Aviator*, which for a time I accepted. I was soon obsessed with trying to work out what this Ante person had been thinking, what clue that title might contain or perhaps reveal. I went to the Central Library in Glaund and found a tourist guide to the island demotic. The demotic did have a written form, and it obeyed rules of grammar, declension, syntax and so on, but because of the immense size of the Dream Archipelago, and the literally innumerable island patois, there were dozens, hundreds, of dialects. Island demotic was, in effect, best understood as an oral form, but with no one around me who spoke it, all I had to go on were the rules set out in the book.

It turned out that 'The Lost Aviator' could be regarded as an adequate translation of the demotic spoken in a group of islands called the Torquil Group, which happened to be the islands closest to the Glaund coastline. Presumably the man who had written me the letter thought the Torquil version of the demotic would be accurate enough. In fact, Ante's home island, Temmil, was on the other side of the world from the Torquils. I had no idea where. It was located in a sub-tropical island system known in demotic as the Ruller Islands – in the local patois 'temmil' meant 'choker of air', and 'ruller' meant 'drifting flower scent'.

I was getting lost in all this and feeling increasingly obsessive about what had been done to my music, but I was eventually able to rough out a translation of the album title as *Sea Images*. I believed this was as close to *Tidal Symbols* as made no difference, and with this detective work completed I suddenly felt deflated and worn out, the excitement of pursuit leaving me. I also felt as someone might whose home had been burgled, the contents ransacked, all the best possessions stolen and removed.

There was nothing I could do, at least that I could think of doing. Of course I thought of trying to start a legal action for copyright infringement, but the difficulties of that – my ignorance of the law in the islands, the time it would take, and so on – not to mention the expense of hiring lawyers, made it impractical. I knew I had been wasting too much time. I grew tired of staring at the photographs of the band members on the front cover of the sleeve: four dishevelled young men posing with dissolute, even rebellious expressions, too thin in their bodies, dressed untidily. Their facial images had been mangled by the sleeve designer, who for some reason had rendered their photographs in median threshold: stark monochromatic faces, deep shadows and bleached highlights, making them skull-like, lacking in all detail. The photographs could literally be of anyone.

They were young men half a world away, so removed from me musically and artistically that there could not be anything interesting to say to each other, certainly not about music. Their music, their record, seemed a crude thing to me. In spite of its apparent success, I assumed it would soon fade into obscurity.

I felt tainted by the disdain for young musicians in the letter that had been sent to me, and could not entirely throw off the feeling, but I knew that the only way to deal with the problem was to try to ignore what had happened, move on. I had not created the situation. I did not want and could not afford a dispute with Msr Ante and his friends, but I wished he had not stolen my ideas.

Other than this distraction I was busy and productive. Two more long-playing records were released, one of them to coincide with and celebrate my fortieth birthday. This brought my first symphonic work to the public. It was formally called Opus 37, Symphony No. 1 in E Flat Minor, but it was also known less formally as the 'Marine' Symphony. I had scribbled this word in pencil on the first page of the score and someone at the recording studio noticed it and picked up on it.

The Marine Symphony was about imaginings, about dreams, wishes. It celebrated islands I was not supposed to know existed, it depicted the seas around them, the life that was in, of and on the sea, the ships and boats and the people who worked on them, the creatures who swam beneath the waves, but most of all it was about my imaginings of the beaches, houses, harbours, reefs, mountains, endless glowing vistas of the islands that crowded the shallow sea.

Settled, feeling creatively fertile, I began to forget about Ante. It was a false dawn, though, because an experience much worse than plagiarism was soon to happen to me. This was a real crisis, a disaster, my life thrown into chaos – but there was no hint of what was to come or how it would develop. It started so well.

10

I was negotiating with the management of the Federal Hall in Glaund City for the first live performance of the Marine

Symphony, when a large sealed envelope was handed to me. It contained a letter of invitation. There was to be an overseas orchestral tour – I was requested to join it.

The plan was for a series of concerts on a few prime islands in the Dream Archipelago. 'Requested' would be an inadequate way of describing the words they used. I was implored to grace the adventure with my presence, my lustrous genius, etc.

I read the letter many times, savouring not the flattery and the blatant appeals to my vanity, but the thought of travelling at last in those islands so sacred to my inner world. There was a condition to the invitation, though, one I was not happy with. It created a conflict for me.

As soon as I was home again I showed the invitation to Alynna, handing her the envelope, urging her to look inside. I tried not to reveal my feelings as she scanned the extravagantly polite letter.

'Are you pleased?' she said, still holding the letter.

'Of course! Of course!' I said, knowing I was shouting the words at her, but I had for the moment lost control, such were the feelings pouring through me. I had been holding back the excitement all day, waiting for this chance to share the news with my wife.

'I thought you would be,' she said, and we embraced and kissed.

'Then you knew this was coming.'

'Sandro, I have been trying for many weeks to find a way to have you included in this tour. They wanted you from the outset, but they were afraid to ask, did not know what to offer you, were concerned that you would reject them.'

'Why didn't you tell me?'

She hugged me again. 'You can be difficult to please sometimes.'

I stepped away from her, taking up the letter again. I took what she said as a cue, because she knew me so well.

'You know I would love to be on the tour,' I said. 'But they don't want me to play. How could they do that to me? I have two concerti, several sonatas, the new symphony. Those suites about the islands! They are begging to be played by me. I am the best person, the only person, to perform them. I could conduct if they don't want me to perform—'

Alynna stood quietly beside me, waiting for me to subside. We knew each other well – I could feel her patient regard, but I also knew that first I had to relieve the pressure of disappointment.

Finally, she said, 'Sandro, they want more of you than you think. You are not a player any more – you have grown beyond that now.'

'They want me to stand by, wait around in the auditorium while other people struggle to play my music?'

'You haven't read the prospectus yet, have you?'

'I don't need to,' I said. The three or four extra sheets of paper had been tucked into the envelope, a firmer fit than the small, elegantly hand-written letter of invitation. 'I'm being marginalized again.'

'Sandro – read the prospectus.'

She sat down on the small hard chair that was on the opposite side of my writing desk. It was unusual for her to be in my studio with me. She knew all along what the letter contained. Was she complicit in the plans? Had she realized the conflict of feelings they would arouse? I extracted the extra sheets and glanced at them dismissively, skimming.

The whole thing felt irrationally to me as if it had been spoiled. Part of me accepted how temperamental I could be. Alynna had known for some years what I was like to live with, my preoccupations, my sudden changes of mood, my long silences. I was driven by my art, the giving, the expressing, but I was also ambitious, conceited, quick to jealousy. I was a cocktail of artistic urges and motives, all ultimately caused by the music that surged through my mind. I tried hard to temper my passions, make myself seem normal, modify the impulses that otherwise I would yield to. I loved Alynna, she was everything to me, but I had the devil of music in me, the unavoidable obedience to its demands. This, I knew, was one of those difficult times, but I was annoyed as well as disappointed.

I did not recognize the name that was signed at the bottom of the letter. But as I read hastily through the prospectus I did glimpse several names I knew: principals from orchestras I had worked with, musicians I knew, solo singers, two conductors based in Glaund City, three more guest conductors whose names I did not immediately recognize.

Then the list of works that would be performed on the tour: it was the familiar repertoire: symphonies and concerti, operatic arias, several popular light classics, a handful of short modernist works. (Two of mine were included.) All well chosen, varied, acceptable, enjoyable to perform and be listened to.

On the final page my name appeared. Written large. *Composer emeritus – Alesandro Sussken.*

I was to mentor young musicians, conduct masterclasses, tutor singly, run seminars, give private demonstration recitals.

'It's the kind of work you're best at, Sandro,' Alynna said, leaning towards me intently. 'Please don't be too proud to accept this. The tour could change everything for you: work, career, even your life.'

Hindsight recalls that moment of inadvertency. Prospects are always ambivalent: Alynna meant changes for the better, and I understood them to mean what she said in the same way. Neither of us then knew any different – but hindsight is the opposite of foresight.

If the future by some miracle became knowable to us, how would we really behave? Alynna spoke the words at the moment I was feeling my disappointment and annoyance fading away. The tour glittered before me, a prospect of sea and islands and the music I loved. I saw what was intended for me, I realized the great potential.

'Tell me what you knew about this, Alynna,' I said.

'I had little to do with it.'

'But you knew the letter was coming.'

'The man who wrote the letter, the one who is promoting the tour, is called Ders Axxon. He's an islander and this is his first major tour. It's incredibly important to him. He comes from a small island, one called Memmchek, but he works from Muriseay. You remember Denn Mytrie?'

'Of course.'

'Msr Axxon made contact with you because of Denn. He is here in Glaund to set up the tour and book the artists. He didn't know the correct way to approach you.'

'Couldn't he have called me?'

'Sandro, he's terrified of you.'

'Terrified of me?'

'You frighten some people. You have ... a reputation for irascibility.'

'Me? Irascible?' I said.

'You are often short with people,' Alynna said. 'Some of the people you most need are frightened of you.'

'But I mean no harm,' I insisted, feeling defensive.

She moved around my desk, leaning over beside me as at last I read the prospectus carefully. She rested her hand gently on the back of my neck – these days there was not much physical intimacy between us but I still enjoyed having her close to me.

We had grown over the years into a working partnership, confiding, supporting each other, working separately but in harmony, planning our lives, but the excitement of the early days had passed. It seemed to suit us both, but at that moment I liked the warm companionship conveyed by the feeling of her fingers against my skin.

'What about you, Alynna,' I said finally. 'If I decide to go on this tour, will you come too?'

'This is for you. They have already asked me if I would like to join the tour, but I said no.'

'Wouldn't you like to be there with me? To see the islands?'

'Obviously I've thought about it. But for you the islands are unique. You must go, make the most of the opportunity. You've always wanted this. I've all the usual things to do here.'

I turned back through the pages. 'But I'll be gone for – what is it? Eight weeks?'

'Nearly nine.' She reached back to her music case, which she had brought in with her and laid on the floor behind her. She pulled out her diary, showed me the entries she had already made, blocking out the period when I would be away. 'Look – I've been preparing. I'm taking on two extra students. I'll be busy all the time you are away.'

Later, while I was browsing through the itinerary, a list of towns and islands and island clusters I had never heard of before, I noticed that one of the places we would visit was the island of

Temmil. The home of the man who plagiarized me. The choker of air, amid the floating of flower scent.

So it began.

11

So, immediately, it went on. Time was short, and in the whirl of necessary preparations I found it more or less impossible to work. The duties I would have to perform during the tour were obviously designed to be light. There would be an opportunity for workshop meetings in every city and on every island. Spare days were set aside for me to fill with whatever I wished. I could take on extra tutorials or masterclasses as suited me, but there would also be abundant time for me to explore some of the places we visited, or even to find some solitary time for a little composing. It was, in short, designed as a working holiday, a reward perhaps, something I would find attractive.

But I still had to prepare and three trips to Glaund City were necessary. I had to meet the organizing staff, fill out innumerable official forms from various island states, make sure I had a passport and various visas, succumb to inoculation against a range of tropical diseases and possible insect stings, create a list of which musical instruments I intended to carry with me (I opted for my violin), and in general discuss any other requirements. The staff who helped me with my preparations were all native Glaundians like me, so they had only the vaguest idea of what we would discover during the trip.

They told us there would be a full briefing by the tour promoter before we departed.

My commitments during this period were lighter than those of the orchestra members and soloists, so in spite of travelling to and fro, fretting about what clothes I should take with me, and so on, I did have time to reflect.

I had spent so much of my time dreaming and fantasizing about the islands that I had created a plausible but totally imaginary Dream Archipelago in my mind. I had drawn music productively from these fantasies, but would the reality live up to the dream? What in fact was I going to find, and how was I going to react to it?

Three days before the actual departure I travelled to Glaund City for the final briefing. Once I arrived I realized for the first time how many people were going to be involved: the full personnel of a symphony orchestra, other musicians who would take part in smaller recitals and chamber pieces, many soloists and singers, sound and stage crews, admin staff.

I was in good spirits – so too was everyone else I spoke to. If nothing else we were leaving Glaund as the cold weather was about to set in – the damp darkness of a typical winter was imminent, where inversion layers intensified the fog and fumes of the industrial pollution, the ground was permanently frozen, the winds bore down from the northern mountains. We would miss the first weeks of that, always the worst because there was no hope of a change for the better for several long months ahead.

Eventually, everyone was asked to take a seat and the unfamiliar figure of Ders Axxon, our promoter, addressed us. I loved the sound of his voice from his first words: he had the same musical lilt, the sound of the islands, that I had discovered in my friend Denn Mytrie.

He spoke briefly and amusingly about the prospects for the orchestra and the players, how enjoyable the entire excursion was likely to be, and how important it was for us to take our modern musical culture out to the islands. He explained that many islanders considered themselves to be isolated, and gave a mock warning that our concerts would be greeted with an enthusiastic appreciation that would be more effusive than anything we had experienced from northern audiences.

He concluded his presentation by introducing the many notables who would be participating in the tour: the conductors, soloists, singers. I was among those asked to stand up, and everyone there applauded encouragingly.

After this, members of Axxon's staff gave some extra information about practical arrangements: the travel plans, how to deal with small emergencies, who to contact for particular requirements, and more. A Q&A followed, where several small concerns were raised and dealt with.

Finally, Msr Axxon returned to the podium.

'I have to conclude on a serious note,' he said, after we had quieted down. 'Music is an international language. It crosses and eliminates borders. But I am afraid there are other borders you must never forget. While you are travelling in the Dream Archipelago, remember that the country you are representing, this one, is still engaged in war. By law, by custom, by habit, by agreement, every island you are going to visit is neutral territory. Islanders are accustomed to peace and it is a peace that has lasted hundreds of years. They will come to your concerts for the music, for the fact that you are artists, they will know that you yourselves are not belligerents. They also know that the war this country is engaged in happens to be, thankfully, in a sort of abeyance for the time being, but even so you will be expected to respect their neutrality in every conceivable way.'

He reached behind him and produced a compact holdall, sturdily made. He held it up.

'This is something you must have with you at all times,' he went on. 'There will be no official interference with you while you are on tour – you can be certain of that. There is no overall government authority in the Archipelago but there is a diplomatic body known as the Seignioral Council. The Council have authorized this tour, but they have to be certain that every one of you is fully prepared for your short visit to the islands. It is therefore a condition that each of you must carry one of these packs.'

He opened the top flap, gave us a glimpse of what was inside.

'Now – I know you'll be pleased to learn that not everything in this pack is the product of bureaucracy. You'll find an informal jacket which will identify you as a member of the orchestra. Also, a cap, just for fun, but the sun can be bright in the islands. All your travel and identity documents have been placed inside, entry and exit visas, and so on. Before you go home tonight you must be sure to collect your own pack and sign for it. You'll also discover that your hosts have been generous to you. In each of these holdalls you will find a selection of vouchers, which can be used while travelling.

They include restaurants, shops, museums, even some of the bars in the towns you will be visiting. There is money inside your holdalls. The currency in the islands is called the simoleon and the Council have given everyone on the tour one hundred simoleons for day-to-day spending. This money is not part of your agreed fee for the tour, which will be paid separately.'

As he delivered his agreeable speech, Msr Axxon was unpacking the holdall he had in his hand, showing the various items to us, then placing them back inside. I was smiling as cheerfully as everyone else, truly looking forward to the adventure that lay ahead.

Alone on the train returning home, I opened the holdall I had signed for and checked through the contents. I was relieved to be reunited with my passport, which I had obtained only two weeks before. I looked at all the various visas that had been carefully impressed on the inner pages. I found the Archipelagian currency and transferred it to my wallet, wondering how much it would be worth.

At the bottom of the holdall was a hard object. I pulled it out to have a look. Msr Axxon had shown us one while he was at the podium, waving it aloft like a small sword and saying it was called a stave. The familiar musical word had raised a brief laugh of recognition from the crowd. Axxon had not said much about it, except that it should be kept safely inside the holdall and carried throughout the journey.

The stave was a short wooden stick or staff: the wood was bare, unvarnished, but sanded to a fine finish and so smooth that it was almost soft to the touch. The end of the stave had been shaped and rounded. At the other end it had a handle made of metal and another kind of wood, bonded to the main shaft. Engraved into the metal part of the handle were some words which I could not understand but which I assumed were in island demotic: *Istifade mehdudiyyet bir sexs – doxsan gün.*

I gripped the stave, held it up, looked closely at it under the lights of the railway carriage. I wanted to wave it about, in the way Msr Axxon had done, but there were other people on the train with me. I slipped it back into the holdall.

12

The next day I went with Alynna to visit my parents. They were still in our old family house, which always appeared to me far smaller and more cramped than it had been when I was living there as a child. Because I had been so busy in recent months, and because I maintained regular contact with my mother over the phone, we had not visited them in over a year. But as soon as we arrived I realized their lives had deteriorated noticeably since my last visit.

The place was looking shabby and cluttered: cardboard boxes were stacked in the hallway and up the staircase. The main room at the front of the house was crammed with furniture and more boxes. My parents appeared to spend their days in the cosy music room at the back – the piano was still there, but also mounds of sheet music, as well as hundreds of old newspapers stacked in and around the fireplace. Unwashed food plates and odd pieces of cutlery lay on the floor. The curtains were closed but hanging irregularly from the runners, one of which was coming away from the wall. Sunlight glanced in at an angle. There was an unpleasant background smell.

Alynna and I had brought our violins with us, thinking of our last visit when we had played together with both parents late into the evening, but this time, as soon as we realized what was happening, we placed our instrument cases out of sight in the hall.

Throughout most of the time we were there my father remained seated wordlessly in an armchair behind the grand piano, almost hidden from the rest of us by the framed photographs on the lid. He raised a hand in greeting when we arrived. Alynna went around and tried to speak to him.

Grief had taken my parents, denying them any pleasures of life or hopes for the future. I knew as soon as we walked in what was causing it. It was because of Jacj, still missing, still at war somewhere, years and years later. There were photographs of him on the piano – he looked like a boy, he was still a boy in those pictures. The letter he had sent before he was shipped away to the south was in a frame, standing at the front of the photographs. The only hope we had of ever seeing Jacj again lay in that letter, those fading photographs. So many years had passed without him.

Jacj's absence was eternally in the background of everything I did. Whatever had happened to him gave me feelings of dread, misery, guilt, horror, helplessness, but you cannot work up these emotions every day, every hour. I feared for him, was terrified of the news that I felt would come inevitably: he was dead, he had gone missing in action, he was horrifically wounded, he had deserted and been shot by officers. All these I pondered.

Yet the time went by, I had my own life, no bad news came, but neither did Jacj return. I never forgot him, was always aware of how he had been taken, but also, as the years went by, I found it increasingly difficult to remember him. Dread, misery and helplessness were bad enough, but guilt was the hardest to deal with.

'They will bring Jacj home soon,' my mother said that day. She mentioned units of other young men who had been drafted a few months before Jacj. 'The 275th Battalion returned safely. They release them in order, don't they? It can't be much longer before Jacj is home.'

She was waiting for the return of the 289th. She spoke optimistically but vaguely of the regular bulletins broadcast by the military junta. News came through every week – I had listened to some of those broadcasts until I realized what they really were.

My mother took comfort from the junta's imprecise announcements of a successful skirmish here, a routing of enemy troops there, a victory, a tactical retreat, a new stronghold established, a long march across icy terrain to reinforce other sections, a minimum of casualties. She pointed to the heaps of old newspapers. The facts were always encouraging. Few young Glaundian soldiers ever seemed to be injured, while the other side, those fighting for the Faiandland Alliance, were said to suffer horrific losses. The war was not likely to come to an end soon, but our cause was prevailing. Victory was inevitable. One day.

We stayed with them as late as we could but it was depressing to see my parents in such a state. Alynna had cooked a light meal while we were there, and my father sat next to me while we ate.

'I have played your records, Sandro,' he said.

'Do you like them?' I was pleased.

'I do like them.' A little later he said, 'I have played your records, Sandro.'

'Thanks, Dad.'

I tried to explain about the tour, about to begin in less than forty-eight hours, but I don't think either of them understood.

As we returned home, Alynna said, 'Do you realize you have almost never talked to me about Jacj? What you remember about him, what he's like, what your feelings are.'

'I don't know what to think,' I said. 'Therefore I never know what to say. I lost my brother before I knew I was going to lose him. I don't know if I'll ever see him again.'

'How old is he now?'

'He's just over four years older than me.'

'So he would be … middle aged now?'

'Early middle age,' I said.

'Isn't that too old to be a serving soldier?'

'I always thought he was too young to be a soldier. The longer this goes on the more I think that. Seeing those old photographs today—'

She said, 'We ought to visit your parents more often.'

'Yes,' I said, but I was thinking of the tour, unavoidably close. 'We'll go to see them again as soon as I'm back.'

'Would you like me to visit them while you're away?'

'It's only a few weeks. Let's wait until I'm home again.'

I remember those words. Now.

13

I was demoralized by seeing my parents. I should have cancelled the tour but I did not. The heart of my work would have died. I knew that my images of the ocean and its clustered islands were the product of dreams, of fancy, of guesswork, of uninformed wondering. To complete my work, to take on the great and serious works that I then believed lay ahead, it was essential to experience the Dream Archipelago directly.

The tour began with a gala concert in the main auditorium of the Federal Hall in Glaund City. Alynna was there with me – I had no formal part in the concert, so we sat together in reserved seats close to the front, soaking up the sumptuous, subtle sounds of a first-class orchestra playing three works from the repertoire of great classics. At the end, flowers were presented, speeches were made, tears were shed. The applause was thunderous, the orchestra played a brief light-hearted orchestral encore, then left the stage while the audience stood and cheered. Alynna and I spent our last night together in a hotel, and in the morning we said goodbye.

14

The port adjacent to Glaund City is called Questiur, and our first ship to the islands was moored there, waiting for us to board. In common with everyone else I had never been into Questiur. For years it was used exclusively as a naval base, and all civilians were barred from it. Because the war was in a kind of limbo, at least as far as the home countries were concerned, an area of the main harbour was open for non-military shipping.

We were driven in a convoy of buses from the hotel straight to the quay. There was a delay boarding the ship because we had to be sure all the instruments were with us and accounted for. I saw my violin case being unloaded in the first batch, so while I waited for the others I walked briefly along the huge quay, past where our ship was moored.

Now that I was breaking free of a world based almost entirely on the inner mind, I was curious to see one of the places which for so long had been a state secret. The day was dark under a sky of grey, scudding clouds. The wind bore stinging pellets of ice. The harbour was a bleak and disquieting place, with many of the dockside buildings derelict. I was glad to hurry back down the quay and stride up the gangplank into the warmth of the ship.

I was late into my bunk that night, because for all of us on the tour this journey was a step into newness, an escape into a different life. Everyone I spoke to seemed uplifted, excited, speaking more loudly and emphatically than usual. The mood was infectious. The saloons and dining areas of the ship were luxurious and well stocked. The ship must have moved away from its mooring while we were eating, because a background vibration from the engines, which I had been aware of since I boarded, became louder and more insistent. The ship was soon under way as we went out into the open sea.

After our first onboard meal many of us moved to the nearest bar and our celebrations continued. Standing there with the other musicians, listening to what people were saying, joining in, laughing with the rest of them, I was relaxing in a way that was almost unique in my life. Glaund was away, Glaund was behind us. We were sailing to peace and neutrality, the calm vigour of island air, island seas. I wanted to be there now – I was already there now, I realized, enjoying the unfocusing effect of the alcohol.

In a period of relative quietness I stood alone by the bar with a large glass of whisky in my hand, feeling the ship moving beneath me, to and fro, up and down, a twisting motion side to side – gentle, unthreatening, a sense of movement forward, a purpose, a destination. Some of my colleagues had said the ship's movements made them feel queasy, and they had left the saloon, presumably to return to their cabins, but I felt no such malaise. I wanted the ship to thrust forward into the swell of the sea, speed up, take us more quickly to our first landing on an island.

By the time I returned to my cabin, finding my way there somehow through the muddle of all that drink, I was mellow and sleepy. I rolled into my bunk with a feeling of pleasurable surrender to the comforts of onboard life.

In the morning I was aware of the ship's noises and movement before I was fully awake. I turned over, then back again, stretching and snoozing, feeling the vibration of the engines deep beneath me. I pressed my fingers lightly against the metal wall: the gentlest tremor teased me, like the touch of violin strings.

Bright sunlight was shafting in through the porthole but I kept my eyes closed against the glare for some time, wanting to prolong the feeling of luxury. Also, my head was hurting – I knew I had drunk too much the evening before. Finally I climbed carefully out of the bunk and leaned towards the porthole. I rested my hands on the circular metal rim and I peered blinking into the daylight.

I was assaulted by a blaze of brilliant colours. For a moment I was so surprised that I found it difficult to register what I was seeing. Then I focused. The ship had been steered towards a shore and was sailing slowly. We were so close to land that it felt as if we were passing beneath a steep rocky wall, or cliff, thick with multi-coloured foliage. At first it was so close that I was sure that if I could somehow wrench the porthole open I would be able to reach out and take hold of some of the flowers, or let my fingers drag against the jagged rocky wall. But of course the ship could not be so close in as that, and as I peered up and to each side the perspective made sense. The ship was probably at least fifty metres from the rock face, but the escarpment was so huge and steep that it loomed above and against the ship.

I had never seen anything like it. I was dazzled by the colours.

I had grown up in a drab country. The environment of Glaund was a nation of cinder-grey stone and pale concrete buildings, black roads, pebbled beaches, dark trees that never lost their evergreen needles, steep mountains that when they did not present their bare rock faces were clad in snow. The plazas in the towns were paved with slate flagstones, the old buildings had mullioned windows that reflected in small fragments the cloudy skies.

Outside the towns there was of course the countryside, but most of the land was given over to monoculture crops, or where it was not cultivated it revealed vast areas of stone and sand scrubland. There were few open spaces in Glaund's cities – no parks or playgrounds, no tree-lined avenues. The heritage of heavy industry was evidenced everywhere. Because of the effects of the war, because of the deadening social levelling of the war, there were few bright lights, only modest advertising placards, understated signs outside offices and shops, curtains drawn behind every window, doors that were closed all year round. Even our national flag was almost monochrome: the main ground was dark grey, and the emblem of St Sleeth, his Cross, was a deep red, surmounted by two narrow crossing lines.

When I had been at home, staring longingly across the pallid coastal waters towards beautiful Dianme, troublesome Chlam, unreliable Herrin, even then I could only view those in virtual silhouette, dark mounds bulking against the south-lit sea, hidden in the day by the dazzle of sunlight, hidden at night by the darkness. Mostly there was a haze, a dirty miasma, which drifted away from our coastline and spread sluggishly across the surface of the sea, blurring and concealing. From those islands I had gained no idea of what the Archipelago might really be like. Now I was seeing!

This island against whose flower-clad wall we were sailing – was this one that might also be seen from the mainland? How far had we sailed from grim Questiur while I drank myself to sleep, then slept? And how long had I been sleeping?

Although I fell happily into a whisky-fuelled sleep I had stirred several times in the night, once to visit the toilet, and after that I drifted between states of semi-slumber and semi-excitement until the daylight started lightening the sky beyond the porthole. I found my wristwatch – it showed the familiar time that at home I would normally get out of bed and wander down to find myself a breakfast. That was good, because I had not wanted to sleep through the day.

I washed and dressed as quickly as I could, and while I was doing so I noticed that there were two clocks, or chronometers, already mounted in the cabin. They were built into the wall next to the door. One showed the same time as my watch, but the other was more than four hours ahead of that. I imagined that this must mean we had crossed one or more time zones during the night.

Both clock faces had words inscribed on them that I could not understand. I guessed they were in island demotic. The one on the left was labelled *Mutlaq Vaqt*; the other was labelled *Kema Vaqt*.

As soon as I was dressed I left the cabin and hurried along the companionway to try to find a way out to the upper decks. I passed several other members of the orchestra as I hurried along – I did not stop to speak to them. I found a door and broke out of the interior of the ship into hot, blinding sunlight. The white-painted superstructure of the ship reflected the glare, and I protected my eyes with an arm thrown across my forehead, but already I could see what I had come outside to find.

We were passing through a waterway that was so straight, so neatly laid between the two sheer cliffs, that it could only have been artificial. The canal was just about wide enough for our ship, but there was not much spare. On the high cliffs of the canal there were a few bare areas where the blasting of the rock had left steep patches of baldness, but otherwise bushes, vines, flowers, grew in profusion. The scents from them were almost overwhelming.

Ahead I could see that the narrow cleft was coming to an end. A stretch of open sea lay beyond. Soon enough the ship came to the end of the passage and as we moved out into the open it was possible to see when I looked back that a line of mountains ran across the island we had traversed, and that the canal was a deeper extension of what had once been a valley. The mountains stretched away as far as I could see in either direction.

Other ships were hove to in the bay we were starting out across. As soon as we were clear of the entrance to the canal, the one waiting closest began turning, then headed towards it. It was a transport ship, an elongated tramp steamer of some kind, lying low in the water. Two large cranes stood on its deck. Its aft-mounted superstructure was dark and stained, and the hull was pock-marked with spreading patches of rust pushing up through the paintwork. There was an exchange of sirens between our ship and this one. A smell of coal dust drifted across to us.

I saw another man standing at the rail. I recognized him as Ganner, a cellist who had sometimes played alongside me as a session musician. I walked across to him, glad to see a familiar face.

'We seem to have travelled a long way already,' I said. 'Do you happen to know where we are?'

'You've slept late,' Ganner said unexpectedly.

'Why do you say that?'

'You missed a briefing session this morning, after breakfast. One of the ship's officers described the route we were taking.'

'Breakfast?' I said. 'What time is it now?'

He held out his arm for me to see his wristwatch. It was long past midday – my own watch was four hours slower than that. I made what I hoped was a self-effacing comment about having had too much to drink the night before, and slipped off my watch. I adjusted it so that it was showing the same time as Ganner's.

'There are chronometers in every cabin,' he said. 'The crew recommends we use those, and not bother with our own watches.'

'I saw them,' I said. 'Two dials showing different times. Any idea why?'

Ganner shook his head. 'Things are different here. Several others missed the briefing. I don't suppose it matters much. None of the place names meant much to me, or anyone else.'

I was frustrated to hear this – I should have loved to have heard island names.

'Can you give me some idea of what was said? Did they say what that island was called, the one we just left?'

'He said the name of the island, but I didn't really pay much attention. Sick? Seek?'

'Was it the island of Serque?' I said. I had noticed that name as a transit point on one of the documents. Two names in fact: Grande Serque and Petty Serque, intriguingly.

'It might have been,' said Ganner. 'Why do you ask?'

'Just interested.'

I didn't want to say any more – I could feel the annoyance in me cohering around a sudden idea, a sound of words, a line of music, brilliant in my mind.

Serque, Serque – I read you!

That was mine, that was not for conversation.

Ganner glanced up at the sun and wiped a hand across his shining face. 'I'm not dressed for this climate,' he said. 'I'm going down to my cabin to change.'

He went away, leaving me to marvel alone at the scenery. The sea was silver and calm, the ship punching white churning foam away from us. The azure sky was unbroken by cloud and the sunlight was intense. I walked to a side rail, staring back at the bulky mountains of the island we had just traversed. It was already no longer possible to see the narrow entrance to the canal, although the place where it lay was indicated by the fold in the mountain range.

I thrilled to the constant sound of the engines, the rush of the wind, the accompanying seabirds who glided and swooped behind us, the constant but unidentifiable noises of a ship thrusting powerfully through the waves. My senses were alive: I could not resist hearing a rhythm in the deep beat of the engines, far below. The hot wind blustered my ears and the sun glossed the sea. Everything around me was trembling with sound, and the impressions flooded in.

15

Mutlaq Vaqt was a phonetic rendering of a demotic phrase meaning 'absolute time'. *Kema Vaqt* was demotic for 'ship time'. (They appeared never to be the same.) The island we had passed through was called Serque, as I had guessed, and it was divided by the canal into two artificially created regions: Grand Serque and Petty Serque. Serque was a long island that sprawled inconveniently in the path of many preferred shipping routes, had difficult areas of shallows at its extremities, and so the canal had been constructed about a century before. Serque itself was the main island in a huge group called the Greater Serques. Apparently there was a second island group, half the world away, even more huge in extent, and paradoxically called the Lesser Serques. That group too had an eponymous island called Serque. Serque and Serque were emphatically not the same island, although they were sometimes confused for each other. They were rivals in a passive sort of way. Both had a thriving tourist trade, both were seats of learning, both had important historical figures, both were going through a programme of industrialization, both were heavily forested, both had huge mountain ranges, and both spoke a local language called Serquois, although the two languages were completely unalike, even to the use of different alphabets. People from one Serque rarely visited the other Serque. There was not thought to be any reason for this other than the immense distances involved.

I garnered this confusing information from a young woman called Jih, who worked as a publicity assistant to Ders Axxon, and who had been one of those at our pre-tour briefing who had offered to help and advise us during our travels. I found her on the second evening before dinner, and asked her to sit at my table so that I, and the three other musicians who were with me, could be given a little information. When we were seated I asked her if she knew through which part of the Archipelago the ship was presently sailing.

'We are still in the Greater Serques,' she said, and it was then that she attempted to explain about the confusion of the two identically named islands and their groups. When we had cleared this up, she added, 'At the moment we are heading for an island called Wesler, and we expect to be docking there early tomorrow morning. Wesler is the place of your first scheduled concert booking.'

I remembered then, as I suppose so too did the others, that I had seen the name Wesler in our itinerary.

'Do you recognize any of the islands we have passed?' I said.

She looked concerned, as if my questions were challenging her role as a provider of assistance. I wasn't trying to do that – I merely wanted to know where we were. There were no charts or maps anywhere on the ship and none of my colleagues knew anything more than I did. Most of them appeared to have missed the early-morning briefing that Ganner had told me about.

In a moment Jih said, 'I wasn't born in this part of the world. I come from Goorn, which is not at all like this area of the Archipelago.'

'How is it different?'

'Goorn is in the north, close to the arctic circle. In the Hetta group of islands?' Her rising inflection seemed to suggest that we might know where she meant, but I shook my head. It was another fragment of information about the Archipelago, another name to add to the others, which I seized on. Goorn – it sounded uninviting. The word did not resonate. 'Goorn has a long winter,' Jih went on. 'Only a few weeks of summer. The sea is frozen for nearly half the year. The island is mountainous and the northern coast has many fjords. It's not like the islands here. I love this heat, don't you?'

'Yes – but I had no idea there were parts of the Archipelago where the sea froze. I thought the islands were tropical, or sub-tropical.'

'Not all of them.'

'What can you tell me about Wesler?'

'I have some photos in my cabin of the main town, where you'll be staying. It's called Wesler Haven. I'll bring the photos tomorrow but by then we will probably be about to disembark. I have the hotel bookings confirmed for everyone, so there should be no problem with those. The venue where you will be playing is called the Palacio Hall. Wesler lies to the south, so it's likely to be warmer than here.'

'Is it tropical?' one of the others asked.

'Not exactly – I mean, I'm not sure. It's my first time too.'

She went on to tell us that after we had finished in Wesler we would be on another ship heading towards the west, no longer moving so directly into the south. Many of the islands in the equatorial regions were uninhabited, or undeveloped, she told us. Msr Axxon and his team knew the effect a humid climate could have on some musical instruments so we would be avoiding the hottest places.

That night, alone in my cabin and waiting for sleep, I replayed memories of the day: the scenery I had viewed from the ship's deck, and also the general experience, novel to me, of being on a ship, living a marine life, responding to the subtle movements as we navigated our course. I had already grown to love the slow, repeated rhythms of a big ship sailing on a calm sea, the gentle rocking, the sense that the boat was, in some way I could not define, alive. And of course the islands themselves, visible on all sides, an interminable variety of shapes and sizes, the endless passing show whose sights seduced me and whose scents drifted somehow across the quiet waves towards me.

Sleep was failing me. I had not wanted another extended drinking session in the saloon so I had come sober to my bunk, because that was how I slept most of the time when I was living at home, but everything was different on a ship. I was in a ferment of excitement, even when I tried to relax, to still the thrill. As the long night went on I began to realize something about the experience that was perhaps a warning.

Until I started out on this voyage the Midway Sea and the Dream Archipelago had been hidden, their existence more psychic than physical. Before, they had spoken to me in imagined sounds and tones. I felt they were a part of a system of secrecy – why were there no books or maps, or none that might easily be found? Why should the government of my country try to deny their existence?

The islands formed a pattern, a format, a structure in the way I understood structure: movements or parts that while being single and separate made up a whole. Islands, I had thought, would be like a sonata: my beloved Dianme becoming in effect an allegro introduction to the Archipelago, Chlam an andante variation on the theme, Herrin a rondo finale.

But this was academic music. Real music was about heart, passion. I had presumed to think of the islands as individual notes, groups of islands as bars or chords, a transit of the islands a kind of harmonic progression, the entirety of the Archipelago an immense and unwritten symphony waiting to be made coherent. Perhaps it was, but that I would never know. Even if I were to spend my life discovering islands by shape alone, by their practical existence, it would be like trying to understand a five-movement choral symphony from three or four semi-quavers spotted at random.

Music emerges from within – it is not composed by the fingers pressing the keys of a piano, or bowing the strings of a violin, or the lips pursing against the mouthpiece of a flute, or even by the scratching of a pen across the staves of manuscript paper. That sort of music was suddenly irrelevant to me. I knew that my task was to understand the island music, how to detect it, sense it, feel it.

So it became a night of having to re-evaluate. Perhaps I slept for short periods – there were moments when I was more alert than at others. I felt restless the whole time. At one point I was pulled into full consciousness by a soft, mechanical sound coming from somewhere within the cabin. I sat up, switched on the little lamp mounted on the shelf beside my pillow, and in the cone of light that flooded out I looked around to try to see the source.

The hands of one of the two chronometers were slowly turning back. I sat up: it was *Kema Vaqt*, the keeper of ship time. The hands described a reverse arc of more than a full hour, then halted. A moment later, *Mutlaq Vaqt*, absolute time, moved more quickly in a forward direction. When both clock faces showed the same time, no further adjustments were made, from whichever central point in the ship they came.

I turned off the light and resumed my efforts to sleep.

Because of my restlessness I was fully awake soon after sunrise. I did not want to run the risk of missing any more briefings from the crew, so I showered and dressed, then went up on deck. I was still curious to find out what I could about our route, our various destinations. I glanced at my watch as I left the cabin, hoping I would not be late for breakfast again. My watch was consistent with *Kema Vaqt*. It was several hours behind *Mutlaq Vaqt*.

Even as I walked along the companionway towards the dining saloon I could see that the ship was moving slowly. Through saloon windows I glimpsed cranes and winches, tall warehouses and the superstructure of other ships. The ship's engine made a deeper grinding noise and I saw that we were sidling towards a concrete berth.

By the time I had finished breakfast the ship had completed docking and everyone was preparing to disembark. It seemed that yet again I was later than all the others. As I quickly packed my bag in my cabin I checked my watch against the chronometers. They were out of agreement again, one behind the other, or maybe the opposite. My wristwatch showed yet another time, running slow compared with them both. I wound it fully, reset it to *Mutlaq Vaqt*, then finished my packing and joined the throng by the gangway.

16

We moved down from the ship, crossed the broad concourse next to where we had berthed, and were herded towards a long, low building set back in its own compound. We all had to carry our baggage, suffering under the relentless sun. As we reached the gate into the compound we were held up because we were admitted only one by one.

The building had a fairly imposing doorway, with two brick pillars on either side. Above, there was a large metal sign, written in demotic, but underneath it said:

WESLER SHELTERATE SERVICE
HAVENIC BUREAU

A flag was flying above this: a white ground, rimmed with dark blue, and with the symbols of a large graphical star and a tree set in the middle.

We shuffled forward slowly, sweltering in the heat. Few of us said anything, but one or two people were complaining about the delay. I saw Jih moving quickly around the edges of our small crowd, a clipboard pressed to her chest. She was wearing a large, shading hat, but even so looked uncomfortably hot. I was finding the humid air difficult to breathe, and I realized that the ship with its air-conditioned saloons and cabins, and its breezy open decks, had not prepared us for what the conditions might be on land.

Eventually, I reached the gate. Beyond it there was a small area, largely grassed, and with a bed of huge, exotic leafy plants standing at the centre. Along one side, set back from the path, there was a canopied shelter, with a long bench and a few extra seats set in the shade. Here sat or sprawled a group of seven young people of both sexes. They took no apparent interest in our crowd as we moved slowly through the garden, although most of them were looking vaguely in our direction. They were all dressed casually, and in two or three cases minimally. They all wore broad-brimmed hats, light shirts, sunglasses, sandals.

I stared at them, wondering who they were and why they were waiting there. One of the young men noticed my stare and immediately looked back, but I suppose he then intuited that I was only mildly curious so he glanced away again. Before I reached the doorway into the building, one of the young women also looked directly at me, as if in surprise. I made a non-committal, neutrally intended smile of greeting, but she did not respond and looked away again. I noticed she had a long-bladed knife dangling from her wrist by a silver chain. She swept it behind her so that I could no longer see it.

Then I was inside the building where it was cooler, if not cool. Here our passports and entry visas were examined slowly, and we were all questioned individually about the purpose of our visit. By this time, Jih had also entered the building and was standing next to the counter, watching and listening. I wondered why everyone was being put through the same aimless grilling, and also why Msr Axxon or Jih herself had not managed to spare us this. However, we were in no position to argue, and anyway it was soon over.

Outside the building two large buses were waiting to transport us to the hotel. The refrigerated air inside the vehicle was a calming pleasure.

17

So began our few weeks' tour of the islands, performing, working and travelling. Most of the concert selections for the tour were from the classic repertoire, but a few modern pieces were also included, to showcase some of what was being written in Glaund at the present time. Two of my better short works were among them. The musical director had chosen my Concerto for Piano and Orchestra in E flat major from a few years back, and a more recent piece, an orchestral fantasia called *March of the Soulful Women*.

The concerto was scheduled to be performed only once, at our final appearance, with a brilliant young pianist called Cea Weller. She was not on the tour with us at present because she was an islander who lived on Temmil, where our last concert would take place. None of us had performed with her but her records were available in Glaund. A period of rehearsal would be required before her performance but her reputation as a virtuoso was formidable.

The *March*, my fantasia, had a twenty-four bar cadenza for solo violin, which I had been invited to perform myself in one of the concerts. The piece was inspired by a demonstration against the war in Glaund City, by the women of Glaund. Unsurprisingly, in view of its political nature, the choice of this music had been controversial because of the Neutrality Covenant which governed the islands. Msr Axxon himself had declared it was unsuitable for an island audience, but I had vigorously defended it. It was of course profoundly anti-war. It was against all war, not just the war in which we were involved. In any event the music really mattered to me because Alynna had been one of the peaceful protesters. Finally, after a delay of about a week, everyone had agreed the *March* should be included. It was to be performed several times as a short introductory piece, with myself as soloist scheduled for one concert late in the tour, on an island called Eger.

Otherwise, my actual musical contribution was more or less as it had been planned at the outset. Most of my work was carried out away from the public view. On all the islands, starting with Wesler, I went to schools, colleges and music studios, met and worked with many young or developing musicians, listened to what they were playing or writing, commented, encouraged, praised. I was always positive and expansive in my remarks.

It was not false. I was genuinely impressed by the quality of the young players and composers. Much of their music was more traditional, lyrical and romantic than the music we wrote and played in Glaund, which was heavily influenced by the militaristic mood that had prevailed for most of my life. For me it was an enjoyable novelty to hear sea sagas, celebrations of sporting victories, love songs, epic tales of bravery, fantasias, folk dances.

We carried on through the Archipelago. I had brashly assumed it would look and feel much the same everywhere, but there was an endless variety of islands and a huge range of cultural differences.

I tried to keep notes, I took many photographs, but in the end the sheer pressure and complication of constantly relocating from one island to the next overcame me. I was soon content to find a seat somewhere on the shaded deck of whichever boat I happened to be on, and idly observe the lovely islands as we sailed slowly past.

As for the ships: the air-conditioned luxury of that first ship from Questiur was rarely to be enjoyed again. Many of the later ferries we boarded were, to say the least, uncomfortable. One was practically unseaworthy and I dreaded a storm might blow up. I was convinced the vessel was a death-trap. Most of the boats were old, noisy or unclean. Some had no food or drink available. On one ship I had to share a cabin with three other men – on another ferry there were no cabins at all and we passed a long night on the open deck. One or two of the ships, though, were reasonably modern and comfortable.

I was also surprised by the degree of bureaucracy in the Archipelago. The people of the islands were easy-going, generous, uncritical, amiable, languid. However, the keepers of their gates were a different matter. I had noticed a certain official thoroughness as we entered Wesler, but as we left that first island we experienced what turned out to be a regular aggravation, almost a routine of intrusive questions, examination of papers and occasional body searches.

18

It was fortunate that Msr Axxon had warned us before we departed. Everyone was carrying, or had brought, the little pack we were given at the last briefing meeting. It turned out to be necessary.

By the time we were about to depart from Wesler the orchestra members had largely freed themselves, ourselves, of the collective tour mentality. We headed singly or in small groups to the port on our last morning in Wesler Haven. I myself wandered alone through the narrow streets to the harbour. There was a small queue ahead of me – I recognized everyone there.

Once again I saw the group of informally dressed young people waiting around outside the Shelterate building, but they were not in the same place as before. They were now on the town side of the building, where we had to line up for our exit visas to be checked. They were watching us again but it was casual and not intrusive or intimidating. They seemed to be waiting for us to approach them but I could not imagine what it would be for. They were not apparently selling anything, for instance.

Inside the building I approached a vacant part of the segmented counter, placed my baggage in sight. I took from the holdall the documents I carried – the same ones, of course, that had been examined a few days earlier on arrival. The official, a woman, took these documents and spread them on the table in front of her. Leaning forward on her hands she read them slowly, touching each sheet with the fingers of one hand, turning it over to examine the other side – usually blank – then turning it back and reading it again. I waited silently. Along the counter some of my colleagues were standing as I was, not at all understanding what was behind this.

Finally, she said, 'What is your name?'

I told her, even though it appeared prominently on every single sheet of paper before her.

'What was the purpose of your visit to Wesler, Msr Sussken?'

I was certain that everyone who had passed through before me must have been asked the question. I said, calmly, 'I am a member of an orchestra on a cultural tour. The same as everyone else.'

'I am not asking everyone else, Msr Sussken. What sort of cultural tour would you describe it as?'

'We gave a series of classical concerts at the Palacio Hall here in Wesler Haven.'

'What music did you perform?'

'Do you require the type, or the names of the pieces?'

'What music did you perform?'

And so went the questions for several minutes. Her tone was mechanical, uninflected, persistent. I felt threatened by her questions, and as the minutes went by I started to feel irritated, but at the same time, rather oddly, I felt sorry for her. She had to work in this unventilated shed all day, a noisy and comfortless place, questioning strangers about their reasons for travel. I kept my replies factual and brief. At no point in the interrogation did the woman look directly at me but kept her head bent down, as she appeared to keep comparing my answers to the documents.

Finally the questions came to an end, with some enquiries about our next planned destination – fortunately, we had been reminded the evening before that the island of Manlayl was to be our next stop. I was always strong on impressions, weak on practical details, so I was glad I had been told.

'Manlayl,' I said, not even being sure how to pronounce the name. It seemed not to matter. She slowly picked up my papers. These included the itinerary, where the names of all the islands we were going to visit were printed prominently. She slid them one by one under the plate of a franking machine before handing everything back to me.

She did then look up at me, and I saw her face clearly for the first time.

'Your stave, Msr Sussken.'

'My what?'

'You are required to carry a stave when travelling between islands. I wish to register it.'

I remembered it then, lying half-forgotten under everything else. I pulled it out and handed it over, realizing as I did so that there was nothing on it that identified it as mine. Should I have written my name on it? Had anyone else done that?

She held the rod in both hands, looked closely at it, rotated it lightly in her fingers. Then she turned away from me and stepped across to a machine painted a dull ochrous colour, mounted on a shelf behind her. It looked as if it had been in use for many years. She pushed the end of the stave against an aperture and the whole wooden rod slid down inside. There was a short wait, the stick was sucked down a little more by something mechanical inside, an indicator light came on and went off, and then the stave popped up and free of the socket. She handed it back to me.

'Thank you for visiting Wesler, Msr Sussken. I hope you have a pleasant onward voyage.' She glanced at the people waiting behind me, and raised her voice. 'Next!'

I picked up my luggage and was glad to move away towards the berth where the ship was waiting. I looked at the stave to see what her machine had done to it, but I could see nothing. No marks on it, no impressed stamp, no sign of anything. Perhaps there was a concealed strip buried inside the wood? Magnetized metal? I was glad to be through the process. I pushed the stave back into the holdall.

When I reached the ship I discovered that the gangplanks had not yet been lifted into place. I put down my bags and joined the others, already waiting on the apron. It was still fairly early in the day so the midday heat was not yet on us. After a few minutes I went across to the edge of the quay, close against the vertical wall of the black-painted hull of the ship. I looked down at the narrow strip of water that lay there, a deep greenish colour in the shadow. Staring at it I thought about this fragment of the sea, this ocean, spreading across the whole world. Why should they have attempted to keep it a secret? All these islands, unimaginably numerous, shaped but unstructured, washed by the seas, these fragments. I ached to understand the islands, but the reality confused the image.

That evening, as we sailed slowly westwards, it became apparent that the intrusive questioning of the Shelterate officials had bothered many of us. It seemed so out of step with the mellow, uninquisitive lifestyle of the islanders we had met on Wesler.

Jih was sitting with us in the saloon.

'There's an alert on, for army deserters,' she said. 'It's a problem for the islands. When the conscripts manage to escape from their units in Sudmaieure the only direction they can take is to the north, which brings them to the islands. Most of them try to settle on the first place they come to, in the southern hemisphere, but most of the southern islands are unfriendly to deserters, or have been designated as military bases. Because of that many of the deserters have to keep moving on. A few of them find their way up to these latitudes. Different islands have different policies. Some offer automatic shelter and protection to deserters, some refuse it, some haven't made up their minds.

Shelterate arrangements are an issue all over the Archipelago. Every island has the same problem: the armies come down hard on deserters and any island which becomes a haven for them, even inadvertently, is likely to see squads of armed troops roaming the streets.'

'Is that legal?' one of the others asked.

'Strictly speaking, no. We're neutrals. But they come anyway. You will probably never be troubled by them, but because of the deserters entry procedures at most of the islands have become tightly controlled.'

The questions from my colleagues continued, but I was suddenly deep in thought about my brother Jacj. Did this explain what had happened to him? Had he become a deserter, fleeing from the army he detested? He could be anywhere, and hiding. How would I ever be able to find him?

And how would I know where to start searching? I had only short periods of time to myself, which was not what I had been expecting. Already, during our sojourn on Wesler, I had discovered that every day was filled. The daily round of hotel life, meal breaks, then all the travel to and from the venues, was time enough taken.

But other delays had emerged as matters to be dealt with.

Rehearsals, for example, had exposed a problem with uneven tempi – none of us had ever had to deal with this before. The percussionists claimed that the orchestra was constantly slipping behind them, the conductors said that the percussionists had not rehearsed adequately. There had been at least two unpleasant rows about this, and extra rehearsals followed as a result. Then we had all discovered that our performances would not run to time. They over-ran even when we began punctually, and even when we consciously tried to keep to the schedule.

And other problems: in my own case the workshops and masterclasses usually took place in areas away from the town centre, so I had to spend time travelling to and from them. More generally, a host of minor administrative crises had to be solved, dignitaries turned up unexpectedly and had to be greeted and dealt with courteously, things were always going wrong, expected events were not happening when they should, people were often getting lost, lateness was endemic, there were disputes between some of the brass section and the woodwinds, and constant tiredness, tiredness ...

19

The ships, ancient or modern, mostly the former, gave a temporary relief from the stresses of the tour venues. The island we visited after Wesler was, as planned, Manlayl – after that came Derril. After Derril – well I can only say that although each island, each concert performance, was different, after the first three or four they tended to blur in memory. I recently found a copy of the itinerary I had been supplied with, and now I see a sort of cadent continuo, a steady beat, of mysterious names: Wesler, Manlayl, Derril, the Reever Fast Shoals, Eger, Tenkker, Ganntens. Most details of these islands fade away into the collective experience, but images remain, unlocated to particular names. They are vivid memories, unique and arousing.

We zigzagged our way across the Archipelago, veering sometimes slightly to the south, sometimes to the north, but ever westwards, disembarking, re-embarking, carrying our instruments or worrying about other people transporting them, eating, sitting, meeting and greeting more dignitaries, trying to sleep, rehearsing, performing, taking the airs of the Archipelago.

The end of the tour was approaching. Glaund and its industrial blight and its military junta seemed a world away. It was in every sense a real world away, halfway around the globe, and past concerns seemed for the time being minor and irrelevant. The music I lived for was finding fruition. I wanted to stay in these islands forever.

The weather remained hot and calm, the sea was almost invariably smooth. It rained torrentially one night while I was sleeping in my cabin deep in the accommodation deck, but I only heard about it the next morning. The prospect of islands continued and some of those delightful places turned out to be our destination of the day. I never lost the sense of excitement, the sensation of escape, as we stepped down from the ferry, went through the now predictable Shelterate and Havenic interrogations, breathed the scented air of whichever new island it was, prepared for the shock of the unexpected, took in the verdant greens of the forests, the brightness of the sandy beaches and the white-painted villas, the daunting height of the mountains, the glowing blue-white of the lagoons, and ventured into a new country.

Every port had its starkly built Shelterate office – we were learning to get through the interrogations more quickly, so everyone on the tour saw the delays as no more than a temporary irritant. Rather more interesting to me was the invariable presence of the group of young people I had noticed on arrival in Wesler.

Some of them were always there, gathered outside the Shelterate offices, casually dressed, lounging about in the sun or hanging back under their canopy. They seemed to be waiting for us: there on arrival, there as we left. For some reason I felt awkward in their presence.

I had a worrying but imprecise feeling that at first I had interpreted as threat. Why were they there? What did they want? Why did some of them carry knives? But they never approached any of us, they never said anything to us, and in fact when you looked directly towards them they barely seemed to notice us at all, letting their gaze fall. I slipped into the habit of looking quickly towards them but immediately looking away again, averting my gaze, so that I registered them without properly observing them.

After we had landed at a few islands I realized that some of them were the same individuals we saw on every island – somehow they managed to arrive at our destination before us, somehow they knew when and where we would arrive. There was a core of about five of these people who were always there to greet us.

But there were others who appeared less regularly – they all were roughly the same age, wore the same kind of scruffy clothes, lounged around in the same mannered body language of indolence or disdain. These extra people came and went, different faces, similar appearance. On the island of Quy the group had swelled to about fifteen, but other islands attracted smaller groups. The core of them remained. They did not like us, I decided, not knowing who or what they were.

Oddly, I seemed to be the only member of the tour who took any notice of them. No one else seemed to notice them, or react to them if they did.

The tour ended on Temmil, island home of the man who had plagiarized me. This fact added a piquancy of interest to my visiting the place, but by the time we arrived I was barely thinking about him at all. Everything still felt as if the tour was going to work out well, that there was nothing that could go wrong.

Nothing did, on Temmil, Choker of Air.

20

The main town on the island, and the only large port, was called Temmil Waterside. There was a newly opened concert hall in Waterside, a matter of great local civic pride. We were shown around it soon after we landed. It had a large and comfortable auditorium, and the best acoustics and backstage facilities I had ever encountered.

We were concluding our island tour with a gala concert – five main works would be performed, with two intervals and a period at the end set aside in case there were calls for encores. My piano concerto was to be played after the first interval – the soloist Cea Weller lived in Waterside and during our first day in the town she came to be introduced to the orchestra.

I was keen to meet her, to discuss her interpretation of my work, but our guest conductor for the night, the world-renowned Monseignior Bayan Cron, did not like the idea. I had expected that might happen, so I did not insist. However, Msr Cron did suggest I could have a brief meeting with her. He would be present.

I was with Cea Weller for only a few minutes. I found her personal manner soothing and encouraging, her approach to music brisk and professional. Her questions and observations were germane, polite and accurate, but we had barely begun to speak when Msr Cron steered her away from me.

The rehearsals went on without me, because from the second day I was running a compositional workshop elsewhere in the town. I was able to see something of the surrounding countryside. The town and harbour of Temmil Waterside were picturesque, but most of the interior was on a different scale of grandeur. It was a mountainous terrain, dominated by an active but presently quiescent volcano called the Gronner, situated in the western range. My workshop was taking place in the local secondary school. The windows of the main hall looked out across the hills, with the peak of the volcano clearly visible in the medium distance. Wisps of gases or steam were drifting about, high around the summit.

During the afternoon of the second day I was walking alone from the school building back to the hotel, when I suddenly remembered And Ante, the young man who had plagiarized my music.

I had been so absorbed by the experiences of the tour that I had all but forgotten him. Of course I had taken a mature decision, as I saw it at the time, to let the matter pass me by, but here I was, on the island where he lived. No longer was Temmil a remote place, a distant island at the opposite end of the world – it was here, this was the place, with these mountains, this town, that sea. It was even possible, probable perhaps, that Msr Ante lived here in Waterside. The recording studio where he had played was somewhere in these streets. I might even have seen him about the place without realizing it.

The days and evenings were packed. I was happy, engaged, involved in a thrilling musical adventure. I had no time for the electric guitar music of And Ante, whoever he might be.

In the day and a half before the night of the gala concert I was trying to make contact with Alynna. Before I set out, because we both knew that communications between islands and the mainland were almost non-existent, we had agreed that if we heard nothing from each other while I was away we should not be too concerned. After the final briefing before we left, I had been able to pass on to Alynna two poste restante addresses, one bureau on the island of Quy, the other here on Temmil, but when I checked with the collection bureaux nothing had arrived from her.

Even so, from every island where we had called, even for the briefest of stops, I mailed her either a short letter or a picture postcard. At least some of those, I reasoned, would work their way through the impermeable barriers that seemed to lie between us.

The hotel where we were staying told me that phone calls to Glaund had become possible recently, so I went immediately to my room and booked one. I was made to wait for more than an hour while connections were attempted. I don't know what happened, what went wrong, but getting through turned out to be impossible. I was told, variously, that the number at my home was not obtainable, or that all lines to the mainland were busy, or after one protracted attempt with strange and disjunctive noises rattling in my ear, even that my phone at home appeared to have been disconnected.

Later that day I wrote Alynna another letter telling her about this and saying that in a few days' time we would be heading home. Whether it would reach her before I did I had no idea. I mailed it anyway.

In the morning of the day of the concert I went with several of the other musicians on a short tour of the island, driven around the hinterland of Waterside in a modern, air-conditioned bus. The climax of the trip was an ascent of the roads and tracks that led to the summit of the Gronner.

As we climbed, circuiting the precipitous sides and terrifying slopes beneath us, the driver guide gave us an account of the importance of this volcano to the island. She described it as one of the few active volcanoes anywhere in the Archipelago. It was the icon of Temmil, she said: the profile image of the Gronner was on the island flag, it appeared on the reverse of Temmil-issued simoleons, it was used as a brand by many businesses and shops. The rich soil of the lower slopes produced fine wines, appreciated in countries around the world. The mountain had not suffered a major eruption for more than a century, but a haze of hot smoke and gases swirled constantly around the main crater and issued from numerous fumeroles on the broken sides below.

When we were as close to the summit as possible the guide parked the bus. She invited us to ascend the remaining distance to the lip of the caldera on foot. I began to follow the others but as soon as we clambered down from the vehicle I changed my mind. It was freezing cold at this altitude and the air was smoky, smelling of ash and sulphur dioxide. It made me cough more than I liked. I waited inside the bus with a few other unadventurous souls, while the rest stepped away and up, soon moving out of sight as the smoke and steam concealed them.

I was content to remain inside, looking down from my window through the wisps of passing vapour at what I could see of the fantastic view far below: the aquamarine sea, the dense forest on the plain to the north of the mountain, the white fringes of the coastline where the surf broke on the shores. Music sprang spontaneously to mind – I hummed happily to myself. Above everything else I relished the stunning, directionless daylight of the high-clouded sky, the sun brilliant but lost to sight above the nacreous layer.

Sitting there peacefully, breathing warmed and filtered air, I wondered if it would ever be possible to return to this place, to become a deserter, so to speak, from the grim belligerence of Glaundian life. I wanted to live out my days in this paradise. That is how Temmil seemed to me then: an island of physical perfection, where music constantly vibrated through my soul.

I was aching to return to my studio at home, fulfil the dreams of melodies and harmonies that flooded through me, but I did not ever want to leave this place.

That night, the final concert. That night, Cea Weller.

21

I was in my reserved seat in the front row. My piano concerto was the third item in the programme, immediately following the first interval. I listened intently to the orchestra, conducted by our guest Bayan Cron, as they opened with the familiar and well-loved humoresque *Musical Explorers*, by Micckelson. This was always popular with audiences, because of the way different instruments took turns to deliver one of a series of semi-comic solos. It required a light touch, and Msr Cron, who in person I had found imperious and self-centred, handled it well. He appeared to be enjoying the comic pieces, and from time to time would turn to the audience and let loose an anguished or roguish smile whenever one of the famous dud notes was blown or struck. After this came a selection of theme tunes from classic films. The audience was loving all this.

After the interval, the music became more serious, beginning with my piano concerto. A concert grand was wheeled in for the performance. The interval felt to me as if it was lasting forever, but in the end the orchestra re-assembled, Msr Cron returned to the podium, and Cea Weller made her entrance. Clearly a well-known figure on Temmil she was greeted with enthusiastic applause from the audience. I joined in, of course, but by this time I was in a state of nervous tension, as I was whenever something of mine was played in public.

Cea Weller played the first movement well, but I was still anxious about how she would handle the second, slow movement. This includes a long cadenza requiring several intricate passages, the right hand slightly out of time with the left. She performed it brilliantly, and she and the orchestra swept, without a break, into the final movement, the rondo allegro. I could hardly bear to stay still, and at the climax I leapt to my feet, my arms waving excitedly. Fortunately, many members of the audience also rose to their feet, so I was not alone.

As the applause continued, and the conductor, the soloist and the various sections of the orchestra took their bows, I was invited up to the stage by the maestro, and stood beside Cea Weller as she repeatedly bowed and waved to the audience. She was cradling a huge bouquet in one arm.

Then Bayan Cron led Cea Weller and myself backstage, as the applause at last died away.

I was too excited to return to my seat in the auditorium so I sat through the remainder of the concert in the hospitality room behind the stage. Two large video screens showed the concert continuing, with the music relayed through speakers. I was on my own, with just staff from the concert hall readying themselves for the celebratory reception that would come at the end of the concert. Cea Weller had been taken away by Msr Cron to another part of the building, presumably to her dressing room, so I did not see her again.

Finally it was over. The second encore was played, the ovation rang out, and at last the conductor and the musicians came down from the stage and filled the room. In no time at all everyone was drinking fast and talking noisily. It was the end of the tour, and it had come to a tremendous and successful conclusion. Short congratulatory speeches were made, there were jokes and a little teasing – the chief timpanist was presented with a metronome, to acknowledge the fact that he had made so many insistent claims that the orchestra was stepping out of time from him. Our guest conductor, Msr Cron, was handed a stave, one of the odd little devices we had been told to carry with us everywhere. He seemed pleased but nonplussed. It was all in good part.

'Msr Sussken?'

A quiet voice at my side made me turn away from the others. It was Cea Weller. For a moment I had trouble recognizing her. She had changed out of the formal gown in which she had performed, and was wearing a blouse and skirt. Her hair, which had been pulled back into a stiff bun while she played, was now loose and at shoulder length. She was holding two glasses of sparkling wine and she handed me one of them.

'Congratulations on your performance,' I said politely. 'It was magnificent.'

'I wanted to say how much I love all the work of yours I've been able to listen to,' she said. 'It's sometimes difficult to find recordings from the northern countries, but I have bought everything of yours that I've found.'

'Thank you.'

She said, 'I have some friends here who would love to say hello to you.'

I realized that behind her and around her was a small group of people, who were standing attentively while she and I spoke.

She introduced them to me one by one: they were all involved in music in one way or another. Four of them were professional musicians, while two others were journalists: one was a writer for a magazines, while the other was a critic and musicologist. I only barely caught their names. We chatted politely and conventionally for a while but the party was getting under way and the noise level was rising. The concert had been a triumph and everyone was high on adrenalin. I exchanged a few opinions with Cea and her friends, received and gave several compliments and as the staff went past with the trays of glasses, we drank more and more wine. Gradually, the others moved away. After a while, because of the noise in the room, Cea and I backed out of the crowd and stood by ourselves in a narrow corridor outside.

We were talking much more informally – about some of the pieces I had written in the past, some of the conductors and orchestras she had played with, islands we had both visited. I told her my worries about Jacj, and she gave me a little information about charities in the islands which attempted to trace soldiers who were on the run from their units. People came down the corridor and as we moved briefly aside to let them pass, she and I returned to our place, standing a little closer to each other every time. I told her I was married – she said she was too, but she and her husband had separated the year before. She said her father and mother were both musicians – her father was still playing regularly, but her mother had retired. Her father was apparently one of those people she had introduced to me earlier, but I hadn't heard all the names and I wasn't sure which one of them she meant. She told me she was working hard at the moment: the concert tonight had been a highlight, but she had a full diary for the next few months, and the next day had to travel to an island called Demmer. She was to perform a series of recitals.

At one point she asked me about my part in the tour, and I talked about that for a while, but it led naturally into me telling her about the rock musician who had been copying some of my music. When I said he lived on this island she said there were a lot of young musicians here. Temmil Waterside was renowned for its music scene and there were many bars, clubs and other venues where music was played. I told her the name, And Ante, but she said it could be anyone – many men on Temmil had names like Cornand, Anders, Stephand, Ormand – some of them abbreviated it to And. We laughed about the musical pun.

The party continued but Cea and I left together, walking down the hill from the concert hall complex. She had her hand on my arm – I later put my arm around her and she leaned her head on my shoulder. We saw the night sea, the lights in the harbour, the bustle in the town centre, the doors open to the hot night with music and voices spilling out from within. Hundreds of people were walking about. It's called the *promenadá*, she told me. When we reached my hotel she went inside with me and we spent a happy night together.

Then came, inevitably, the awakening to a new morning, a bedroom in a hotel, a virtual stranger beside me. The memories of the excited post-concert party no longer seemed to provide the context, the excuse. That was already over – normality had returned. While Cea dozed in the bed next to me, slowly rousing, I began to think guiltily about the implications of what I had done. I was about to return home to Alynna, to whom I had always been faithful. I blamed myself – Cea had done nothing.

Then she was awake, and after a brief affectionate hug we went about the slow business of the morning after. We had both drunk too much at the party so there were those after-effects to cope with, plus the unfamiliarity we had with each other. I knew so little about her, what I had seen of her, how she had played. She must have been feeling much the same about me. What was there in her life that she must return to?

When we were both dressed I walked out of the hotel with her and we stood together for a few minutes in the ornamental garden at the side of the building.

'What next, Sandro?' she said. 'The tour is about to move on, isn't it?'

'We're crossing to Hakerline Promise this afternoon – they've laid on a special boat. There are no more concerts. This will be a break before we return home.'

'I'm leaving for Demmer today,' she said. 'Two weeks of recitals.'

'So we're unlikely to meet again?'

'Unlikely – but not impossible. Maybe we shouldn't try.'

'I think so too. You all right with that, Cea?'

'Of course. We're both adults. It was a great party – let's leave it at that. It was good while it lasted.'

There was a taxi rank at the hotel. When her car had driven away, I returned to my room to pack. I realized then that I had said nothing to her of my hopes and plans of one day moving to Temmil permanently. That was probably as well.

22

We tour members settled into a large, modern hotel a short distance outside the town centre of Hakerline Promise: it had its own beach, boats for hire, fishing areas, restaurants, bars. The remaining admin staff from Ders Axxon's organization left us there.

On the second day in Hakerline Promise I walked down to the beach below the hotel and stared across the strait at nearby Temmil. The dark shape of the Gronner stood against the sky, a thin stream of its outflow drifting with the wind away from the island. That small island represented my future – of that I was certain. It was difficult, painful, all but impossible, to contemplate returning to the dour northern landscape of Glaund and trying to write there. Restlessness filled me. Guilt about the night with Cea – other uncertainties too. What would happen when I returned home? Would Alynna want to come with me to Temmil?

I had felt my ideas about music changing as I travelled. My ascetic, theoretical modernism, with its experimental clashes and pauses, a delight to the intellect, was being drastically challenged. I now longed for the surge of romanticism, the delirium of colour and rhythm, the exhilaration of wide-open lyricism. I wanted to write sea shanties and children's musicals and I wanted to celebrate the love affairs of famous people.

It made me smile to think such things.

I could not help remembering Denn Mytrie, the young Muriseayan composer I had shared a record with, years before. I had privately scorned his romantic composition, then grown to like both him and it. I had seen some of the reviews in Glaund City newspapers of our shared disc: at least two of the critics openly sneered at what they saw as his naïve musical values. (I had never sent him copies of those reviews and I hope he never came across them.) At last I was understanding how his music came into being, the texture of his open society of islanders, the enjoyment of simple things. I now wanted to write music that would make those same musical prigs disdain me too. But first I needed to return home, spend a great deal of time with Alynna, and in due course let the new music of these islands take me wherever it willed.

23

The return journey to Questiur took more than eight days. Every day my watch appeared to lose or gain time – one day it gained four hours, or lost eight. I was not sure which.

We had to change ships several times, a nuisance, a delay and a vexation. Our baggage and musical instruments were often examined by officials. With the concerts behind us all we wanted was to go home. For part of the journey I stayed below-decks, annoyed and sulky because of the maddeningly slow progress.

One day, one ship, it was intolerable – the ship had been wired up with loudspeakers on every deck and in every companionway. From the moment we boarded they were playing popular music from which there was no hope of escape. At first, for a few minutes, I was intrigued. I wanted to learn something of the Archipelagian musical popular culture, which was for me a novelty, but it soon became tiresome, unavoidable. Then they played a track I instantly recognized – it was from *Pilota Marret*. And Ante's screeching electric guitar shattered any remaining peace of mind. As that long day passed with agonizing slowness, one track after another from his wretched record was played.

Played at me, or so it felt. I spent most of that day on the aft boat deck, as far away from the sound as possible, letting the sea wind bluster about me.

At other times, on other ships, I stood or sat on the open decks. I knew this might be my last chance to take in the unique ambience of the Archipelago. I was watching, watching, thinking about colours and winds and seabirds and mountains and light and waves, and the secret codes of music they all somehow imparted to me.

The weather gradually cooled.

Every change of ship meant that we had to disembark and briefly enter the island as transit passengers. The grudging, pedantic methods of the officials were no better than they had been anywhere else, but to us the process was simply pointless. We produced our documents, our visas, our travel passes, our staves – all were routinely examined, and the staves were dipped into the mysterious scanning machines.

We noticed the attendant group of young people at every stop, but by this time I was no longer intrigued by them and barely registered their presence.

My stave never elicited any response from either officials or scanning machines. None of the officials remarked on that, or anything else. Always the cool, unexplained transaction: the stave handed over, the few seconds of silent examination, the insertion into the machine, the stave returned. It remained unmarked, apparently not changed in any way or officially approved. Mine was no different from anyone else's. We all submitted to the perplexing procedure. My stave was beginning to look slightly travel-worn, but the smooth surface of the main wooden shaft remained unblemished.

On the eighth day I was standing at the rail of the ship we had boarded that morning. I was cold and miserable. Most of the clothes I had brought with me were lightweight, what I had thought would be suitable for the warmer south, so all I could do to ward off the cold was put on an extra outer layer, another shirt, a jacket. I felt bulky and unhappy. A bitter wind was blowing. All the islands I could see from where I was standing looked windswept and barren. Never more had I wanted this long journey to be over.

One of the orchestra's second violinists walked across and joined me at the rail.

'Have you noticed that?' he said, pointing directly ahead of the ship.

I saw what I thought at first was another large island. It was low on the horizon, spreading across it indistinctly. I could see rocky peaks, but not much more.

'I think we're almost there.'

'Glaund?'

I was surprised. I had not expected we would arrive before late in the afternoon. I looked at my watch, a habit, but it was a long time since it had worked properly. Every day it gained or lost time.

I continued to stare ahead as the ship bore us gradually nearer. The land became a more distinct sight. The iron-grey mountains were what drew the eye, and I could see that most of the higher peaks were covered in snow. Lower slopes were dark and unclear to see.

Soon the coastal plain was visible, or to be more accurate it was possible to see where the coastal plain lay. A miasma of fog or mist or pollution ran from the sea, where it merged indistinguishably, back as far as the foothills of the mountain range. Nothing beneath the fog could be discerned.

It induced a strange mix of feelings in me. This was home: my country, my parents, Alynna, friends and colleagues, most of my memories. My work and reputation were based in Glaund, but I had been away in the islands. I yearned to be home but in truth I wanted little of it.

We were sailing ever closer to my dark and damaged country and I wanted the ship to slow down, veer away, turn back.

One by one, other tour members were coming up from below, standing around me at the rail, watching as the boat drew us near, manoeuvring to line up on a dark smudge of town. We knew it must be Glaund City, or at least its port, Questiur. A few people commented, but there was not much to say.

Soon there was no mistaking where we were headed as the mountains behind the town took on a familiar aspect and we could make out, through the smothering murk, large buildings we recognized in Glaund City. The voice of one of the crew crackled out through the public address system: we would be berthing in fifteen minutes, all passengers should collect their belongings and move to the gate number they had been assigned when boarding the ship ...

So for the last time we prepared to disembark. For me at least it entirely lacked the feelings of surprise, anticipation, excited pleasure that had been the feature of so many arrivals while we were in the islands. We all clambered about below-decks, pushing in and out of our cabins, collecting our baggage, what souvenirs we had bought, what instruments we could carry, trying to locate the gates of disembarkation.

One of the sailors opened the metal gate to which I had been assigned, so I was able to watch the concrete quays sliding slowly past, feel again the chill from the mountains, breathe once more the smell of industry, engines, chimney discharge, the odours of millions of people, the output of their workaday lives.

I was wearing on my back the holdall that Msr Axxon had handed out so long ago.

'We won't be needing that any more,' someone said, behind me. He said he had left his behind somewhere. I had already decided to keep my own holdall – it would be a reminder of being away.

I could see the open quay, with no sign of a Shelterate building, no small group of casually dressed young people. Once again I was in the world of bare functionality, the unattractive place where I had been born.

The ship came to a gradual halt, sidling in to the quayside. Sirens blew, men on the quay shouted up to the crew on the bridge of the ship. Ropes were secured. The vessel lurched in a familiar way as it ground against the cushioned bulk of the quay. I was standing in a small group by the hatch and we jostled against each other.

A gangplank was being swung across from the shore to the hatch where we stood. With the other musicians I picked up my heavy luggage. But no one moved. The gangplank remained aloft, hanging on its chains. I could see along the wharf that a second gangplank was aloft, also waiting to be lowered.

A detachment of troops had marched on to the quay and they were dispersing to take up positions against the places where the gangplanks would be. They stood in a disorderly way, carrying their weapons. They looked young and nervous, probably recently drafted. An elite squad had clearly not been sent to meet us. Several of the soldiers were staring up at the ship as if they had not been so close to one as large as this before.

A couple of non-commissioned officers appeared – one of them shouted at the troops, while the other strode along the quay blowing on a whistle. The gangplanks moved again, lowered slowly towards the side of the ship. I did not want to be the first ashore, the first to be halted or questioned by the army, so I hung back, but soon I was on the gangplank, feeling it wobble and lurch beneath me.

It was a homecoming but not one I wanted. I was still full of my dreams, the plans, the hopes, but for now they were to be buried beneath the suspicions of the ruling junta which had sent these troops to find out where we had been, what we had been doing, what we had seen, who we might have met, and perhaps also what we now wanted.

I stood on the quay, my baggage on the ground beside me. While I waited to be singled out for the next questioning, I checked my watch against a huge clock on the wall of the wharf. Since I woke up on the ship that morning it appeared to have lost another seven and a quarter hours. Or maybe it had gained four and three-quarters.

The air smelled of soot, of something acidic, of something I did not wish to breathe. I did not want to be there at all.

24

It was strange to be walking on solid ground again after more than a week at sea. Now that I was in the town of Questiur, buildings on every side and away from the coast, the air was not as icy cold as it had felt while I waited on the quay. I was laden with my luggage: the holdall and my violin case were strapped to my back, I had one large bag in each hand. I had no idea of the date and only an approximate idea of the time. Late afternoon? It was gloomy in the city but that was often the case under Glaund's familiarly leaden sky.

The weather was concerning me. We had sailed away to the islands as winter was about to break and we were absent on the tour for about two months. At the back of my mind, as I revelled in the hot and gentle airs of the islands, I had sometimes had the thought that we could not avoid returning to Glaund during its worst weather profile. Once winter set in we normally suffered several freezing months, usually with dirty old snow on the ground and new snow falling regularly. This weather – a dank, pollution-rich mist, stiff with the residue of smoke and waste materials, but still above freezing temperature – was more like what we had to suffer before and after the worst of winter.

I came to a subway station and was glad to catch a train to the main rail terminus. I had to squeeze into the compartment, pushing myself and my bulky luggage against the people already crushed inside. I looked around at the faces. There was no mistaking which town I was in. Those fixed, tolerant, patient faces, putting up with life, carrying on. No eye contact, no signs of happiness. Everyone ignored me, even those whose bodies were pressed against mine, whose faces shadowed my own.

Warnings about trains delayed by the fog greeted me at the main station, a familiar problem in Glaund City, but while I was in Questiur the fog had not seemed too thick. I could see it lowering heavily under the arched roof, though, and felt a familiar sense of resignation about being delayed yet again. However, I was fortunate. An earlier train, delayed by the weather, was still held back in the station. Darkness was falling now. I bought a single ticket, hurried across the vast central concourse to the platform. Grey-blue smoke from the noisily idling engines of the waiting trains billowed up into the murk. I lurched along the platform with my heavy load of luggage and found a row of empty seats in a central carriage. In spite of the chill weather I was perspiring with the effort and my anxiety to catch this train. I made myself comfortable, my bags and violin case stowed overhead, and after a few moments, amid the noise of the station and the train doors intermittently slamming as other people boarded, I began to doze.

I was dimly aware of the train shuddering and swaying but it was only a while later that I woke up completely. It was dark outside, with few lights showing. The train halted soon after this and I recognized the station name. I was already more than half the distance home. I tidied my clothes after the earlier rush to get the train, made sure my baggage was secure, and when we finally halted in my own station I was ready for the final stretch. I wished I had had time to phone ahead to Alynna, but it was too late for that. I found a rank of taxis in the station yard so I took the first one and gave the driver the address. Five minutes later I was outside my home.

All the windows were shuttered.

No light showed. I felt a chill in my heart. I went through into the shared entrance hallway.

Stupidly, I pressed the bell-push, and heard the familiar chime inside. There was no noise or movement from within. I scanned the window by the door for any sign of life, then I used my key and it turned at the first attempt. The door would not open. I used the second key on the deadlock, the one we never had need for when we were at home, and after this the door swung open. It brushed against a pile of unopened mail that had accumulated.

I stepped into the darkened hall, dragging my luggage after me, and slammed the door. Alynna was not there and as I hurried around the unlighted rooms it seemed she had not been in the apartment for many weeks. I looked for her in the dark, frightened, feeling desperate. I called her name, fearing everything: an accident or illness, a break-in, perhaps worst of all a departure of some kind, an angry exit. None of the lights worked, but then I went to the fuse box and threw the master switch.

I renewed my search, in less of a panic but fearing more. The furniture was all in place, the windows were closed and locked, the whole flat felt airless but clean. My studio was intact and my piano was locked with the stool parked neatly against the pedals. Papers I did not remember lay on my desk, many of them still in unopened envelopes.

The place was chilling me. There was no food in the kitchen but the cutlery and crockery had been washed and put away. The refrigerator door hung open, revealing more unlighted emptiness.

I switched on the heating and was reassured by the sound of the boiler coming to life. With the apartment gradually becoming liveable again I made a third search, meticulously, trying to discover what had happened.

There was no trace of Alynna at all. Her clothes had disappeared from the closet, her various ornaments and books had been removed, the room she used as a studio was empty. Even the carpet had gone. I looked for something she might have left, to explain to me why she had moved out. A forwarding address, perhaps, or a note. But nothing.

I was shocked. Before I left there had been no suggestion that anything like this was going to happen. We had been contentedly married for years. True, it was based more on mature companionship, understanding and loyalty than on romantic passion or physical love, but we had been happy. Or so I thought. We each had our own lives but still felt closely connected, which I had assumed after years of living together was something we were both used to and accepted. There had been no hint that a break-up was about to happen. My feelings of guilt about Cea briefly gripped me – could Alynna have somehow found out? I could not see how.

I had not eaten since that morning while on the boat, but there was nothing at all in the apartment. I went out and bought some food from a shop that was still open, then took it home and tried to eat. I had little appetite.

I spent the night alone in my bed – the mattress was bare but I found dry sheets and a blanket. I barely slept. Every time I roused in the night I was aware of absences, like the silent pauses in the compositions I once had thought so daring and essential.

One of my first tasks in the morning was to look through the mail that had accumulated, some of the correspondence Alynna had placed on my desk before she left, as well as the unopened envelopes.

The first thing I noticed when I started looking through them was that not one of the letters or postcards I had sent to Alynna from the islands was there. Did this mean she had received them and taken them with her? Or had they simply not arrived?

Among the first envelopes I opened was one with the words URGENT – LAST WARNING printed in red ink on the front. Inside was a disturbing letter from the property company from whom I rented the apartment. The letter warned me that because the rent had gone unpaid for more than six months they were taking immediate action to evict me, confiscate all my property and sue me for the arrears. My first reaction was that it was an error. I had settled all my bills before I left for the tour and Alynna knew exactly what had to be dealt with while I was away. I had made sure she had enough money in her account. Why had she stopped paying the rent?

I ransacked the pile and found earlier letters from the same company. One by one the letters detailed a growing backlog of unpaid rent: reminders, demands, warnings, threats. Their patience was exhausted.

Although I was stricken with a sense of unfairness as well as shock, the sheer mystery still bothered me. How had this happened?

I looked through the other letters, many of which were from statutory suppliers: payments for town gas, electricity, fresh water, waste disposal, property taxes, telephone – all these were in arrears. The tour had made me cash rich, temporarily at least, so as I mentally totted up the outstanding amounts I knew I could settle the most urgent ones at once, while the rest could certainly be paid within a day or two.

When I looked at the accounts from my bank – their statements too were buried in the pile – I discovered that financially I was better off than I thought. My agent had been sending regular payments for royalties on my recordings and these had mounted up. I was not wealthy, but at least the crisis of unpaid debts could be resolved.

Then at last I noticed the dates on these letters.

25

There was worse to come. Before the end of that first morning I learned that both my parents were dead.

My father had died first – he was seventy-eight, in poor health and his death occurred only six weeks after I left on the first ship south. From a sad, erratic note written by my mother I learned a little about what had happened. She must have written the note not long afterwards. Her tone was mock-understanding, but the true feelings were there: 'I know you are away and that your journey is important to you, but—' She finished few of her sentences and her handwriting was uneven. She had always prided herself on her steady, beautiful hand. She seemed to be muddling up my father's death – it sounded as if he had suffered a stroke – confusing it not only with the still unexplained absence of Jacj but also with me. She had lost all three of us. One sentence asked me when I was going to leave the army. Another said she was missing me endlessly. I could barely make myself read these words. There was a mention of a funeral, but she did not say where it had been. She said nothing about her own health, what she might be going through beyond the great loss of husband and sons. She said she had tried to visit me at the apartment (even though she knew I was away?), but had found neither me nor Alynna at home.

When was this? Her note was not dated. Had she written the note during that visit, sitting in the communal entrance hall outside our door? Or did she come back later and deliver it then? How much time had passed since?

The saddening note had been pushed through the door so that it landed in the heap of everything else. There was no envelope, no stamp, and therefore no postmark or any other clue to when it had been written.

Elsewhere in the pile of mail I found a letter from Sella, my mother's younger sister, a distant and disapproving figure for most of my life. This letter was dated, so I could tell it had been written about six months after my mother's note. Sella made no secret of what she saw as my culpability for being away so long ('you have chosen to allow *month after month* to elapse with no news of your whereabouts, or how we may contact you, or an explanation of when you will decide to return – Malle said she would forgive you but I am not sure anyone else but your mother ever would'). At least she gave me the date of the funeral, where it had taken place and where both my parents were interred. She enclosed a bill from the undertakers.

These dates! Even as I discovered them they made no sense. Everything was wrong. According to Sella my mother's funeral had been about eight months after I left, but I had been away less than nine weeks!

I read more letters, opened more demands for payment, and I began to piece together some idea of when things had happened, but I still could not see how. Months had passed, a year, maybe more? It was impossible. Either every letter and bill I opened carried a deceptive date, or I had lost several months of my life.

Perhaps I had gained those months. I couldn't grasp the meaning. Had I suffered a period of lost memory? If so, how and when, and where was I at the time? Nothing traumatic had happened to me, I had suffered no blows to the head, or concussion. I remembered the whole trip vividly, the islands, the ships, the concerts, all the events and thoughts and experiences.

I was sitting on the floor of my hallway, leaning back against the wall, envelopes and letters and bills spread around me, and my life, or my memory of life, was betraying me. I had lost Alynna, lost my parents, bills were mounting up, the flat had been empty and cold and sealed up. My entire past had disappeared.

Later, when a horrid, frigid calm had come over me, I tried to estimate how much time I had lost, or gained. From the dates, known events, the escalating and dated demands from the landlord, it seemed the time period was about one year and eleven months. At the end of that grim morning I confirmed this when I walked out of the apartment and bought a copy of the daily newspaper.

Objective evidence! I had been touring in the islands for just under nine weeks. That should have put my return in midwinter, but I now knew that I had missed that winter, the summer following, the winter that followed that, another summer, and here I was in the late autumn, first weeks of winter, nearly two years after my date of departure, season of fogs and gritty Glaundian air.

I began to calculate back. Alynna appeared to have stopped paying the rent for the last six months, so that must mean she had abandoned the apartment between about five and seven months ago. My father had died during the first winter I was away, my mother, heartbroken and feeling abandoned by her sons, had followed him to the grave nine weeks later. So Alynna stayed on in the apartment for about another year after that, before leaving? Until the spring of this year? But she was apparently not here when my mother visited and left the note. That was much earlier. Had Alynna already moved out at that time? Perhaps a simple explanation was that she had been away from home that day.

I tried to imagine how their deaths affected Alynna, in my absence. She had always been affectionate with them both, but it was a dutiful and cool affection, warmed only by respect.

Feeling stunned and disorientated I spent the afternoon in town, calling on my creditors, making payments, apologizing for the lateness, promising it would never happen again, settling the interest surcharges, the penalty fees, the collection demands, the outrageous costs of lawyers' letters.

The music of the islands fled.

The contaminated air made my lungs hurt, my eyes water and my throat sore. My mind was empty. I could not see the ocean – I could barely see the sky. I was dealing with the sordid reality of a broken marriage, an abandoned home, bereavement, isolation, loss. And inner silence.

26

What was I to do about Alynna? Firstly, how would I find her? She had left no messages, no forwarding address. Not even any clues I might try to follow. Then, even supposing I might see her, what would I say? What would she say to me?

The world of classical music in Glaund is relatively small, so

I asked my colleagues what they knew. People helped. Within a week of returning I had been able to find out where she was living. She had moved back to Errest, and she was living with someone. No one said who it might be, whether it was someone known to me or not, male or female. I was not able to find an address for her, or a contact number. I was told she was still giving lessons, and she played violin occasionally with one of the smaller orchestral ensembles in Glaund City. I knew it was possible, even likely, that I would run into her sooner or later.

Then she contacted me by telephone.

'I hear you're back at last,' were her first words.

'Alynna?'

'Were you expecting someone else? Of course it's me. What happened to you?'

'What happened to you?' I said, before I thought.

'I'll come round to see you now.'

She put down the phone. I had been cooking some food when the phone rang, so I turned it off, suddenly not at all hungry. I took two bottles of beer from the refrigerator and opened one of them – Alynna preferred wine but I had none.

I climbed up the stairs to my studio and went to the window while I waited. I sat in the dark and drank beer from the bottle. Across the coast road that ran past the building, across the narrow strip of clifftop scrubland, I could see the sea and in the distance the dark, indistinct shapes of the islands. Everything had begun with Dianme, Chlam and Herrin. I was in a turmoil of conflicting feelings: guilt, incomprehension, unhappiness, defiance, anger, expectation ... but in truth the guilt was foremost.

I heard Alynna at the outside door, letting herself into the apartment with her own key – when I first came home I had deliberately not changed the lock in a sort of blind hope that she would return. Since then I had lost all impetus to change things. She came up the stairs, opened the door to my studio, switched on the light.

We stared at each other across the room, two people in need of explanation but not knowing how to start. She looked larger than I remembered her: stronger, taller, her hair was cut differently. I stood up and felt her regard. She was dry-eyed. I was angry, but also scared and nervous. I realized I liked seeing her, but dreaded what we would say. Sorrow appeared to have abandoned us both just then. How would we start explaining to each other?

'Why didn't you wait for me to return?' I said.

Why didn't you return when you said you would? she said. You've been gone so long. How could you expect me to wait?

'Why didn't you pay the bills?'

You didn't even write to me. Why not?

'Have you moved in with someone else now?'

I think you met someone else while you were away. That's why you didn't come home. Why won't you admit that?

'I had no one to meet, no one I wanted to meet. That wasn't what happened. There was never any chance of that. Are you happier now? I wish I knew what I could say.'

You're lying. There must have been someone else. Another woman.

'I had a brief fling. It was not planned, not serious, we had been drinking and we didn't think what we were doing. She is a professional woman with a life of her own. She is also married, and separated. She isn't important – not the reason I was away from you. We spent one night together. It won't happen again. It can't happen again.'

I knew that was what it was. You don't have to lie about it.

'I'm not lying. She isn't what happened. There's some kind of problem. I lost time. I can't tell you what it means.'

You're looking younger. You've lost some of that weight. It makes you look fit again. The trip must have done you good. Why won't you tell me what happened, why you stayed away so long? Why didn't you come home when you said you would?

'There's a problem with time and I don't know how to explain it to you.'

I waited month after month for you. I was desperate. There was no news, no information.

'What happened to my parents? Were you able to help them?'

You never wrote to me, you never phoned. I asked everyone who might know, but they had no news. The orchestra management didn't know how to contact you.

'I was travelling. Much of the time I was on ships and small ferries. We went to nine different islands. I tried to phone you whenever I could, but they said the lines weren't working. I wrote letters and cards and sent them from every island, sometimes more than once. I worked, I travelled, I sailed on ships. You know how you and I have always been. I am no different without you. I came home as soon as I could. There's a problem with time and I don't know how to explain it to you.'

You've got a look about you. Something changed while you were away. You're concealing it from me, whatever you might say now. I heard nothing from you. No one knew where you were.

'I never forgot you, but I had to devote myself to the orchestra and the other musicians I met on the way. That was what I was there to do. You knew all that. You encouraged me to go on the tour. There's a problem with time and I don't know how to explain it to you.'

I had no money. Just the cash you left when you went away, and what I could earn. The cash started to run out. It would have been enough if you had come home when you said you would, but you never came back. At first your parents said they would help but your father died soon after that and then your mother was ill. There was another war scare and the economy nose-dived. Some of the banks seized people's accounts. Your account was locked for a few days, but then it opened again. It made no difference – I couldn't get at the money that was there. Almost all my students stopped coming here for tuition and because of the emergency I could find no new ones. All abandoned me except Pyotr, who came every week and then every day.

'Pyotr? Is that his name?'

For a while Pyotr had nowhere to live so he came in here with me, for company, to save money, nothing more than that. I was so frightened, so lonely! We shared expenses, but after a few months we couldn't afford the rent on this place, even together. Pyotr was offered a small flat in Errest. The rent was much lower. He moved to it and at first I stayed on here. I was still waiting for you, but more than a year had passed and I didn't know what to do. Pyotr said he wanted to live with me again, so I went back to Errest. We are together now and we want to stay together. I'm in love with him. I'm not coming back to you, Sandro. You abandoned me. It's too late to put things back where they were. Why aren't you saying anything?

'There's a problem with time and I don't know how to explain it to you.'

I don't see what that has to do with anything.

'That's what I can't explain,' I said. 'It's a problem and I don't understand it myself.'

After she had left, a quiet departure when it was clear there was nothing more we could say, I opened the second bottle of beer. I stood at the window and watched her walking away along the road, under the street lamps. At the turn of the street I noticed the indistinct figure of a man waiting for her. They met, then went out of sight together. The moon glinted on the sea beyond where she had walked. I stared out towards the islands. I drank the full bottle of beer in one draught. I was not thirsty and I did not want to get drunk, but in the silence she had left behind her there was nothing else I could think of doing.

The next morning the first of my postcards was delivered in the mail.

Dear Alynna, I am on an island called Wesler, but I'm not exactly sure where it is, or how far we have travelled. This evening we are putting on the first of our concerts, and tomorrow I am going to be running a masterclass at one of the colleges here. I love you and I am missing you, and I promise I shall be home very soon, much sooner than you think. With love, Sandro.

(By the way, the watch you gave me years ago seems to have gone wrong.)

That was what I wrote to her. Back then, when the mysteries of time could still be explained. Or if not understood then guessed at.

27

As I began slowly to dig myself out of the trough of misery I knew I should have to work again. As far as composing was concerned I felt silent inside, but I could still play and session work was available. I began regular trips to Glaund City and naturally I saw again some of my colleagues from the tour.

I immediately discovered something I should have realized. I was not the only one suffering from lost, or possibly gained, time. Everyone had experienced the same as me, and their lives were as blighted as mine.

We had a lot in common, I found. We shared our stories, did what we could to reassure each other. It was a way of explaining, of asking, of venting some of the feelings of anger or frustration or loss. Some of the stories I heard were horrifying. One of the principal violinists on the tour, a young woman of immense artistic promise whom I had known well, had committed suicide. She split up with her fiancé when she returned, or she found the fiancé had not waited for her – no one was sure what had actually happened. A week later she was dead of an overdose of painkillers. My own loss was not unlike hers, but still the news shocked me. Others were said to be drinking hard, or had given up playing music professionally – one of the four cellists on the tour had been sent to prison, although it wasn't certain what he was said to have done.

There were many other stories of broken relationships, lost homes, alienated children, violent disputes, claims for money, betrayals, desertions.

I listened, tried to make sense of it, as we all did. Many of us had devised theories to explain the phenomenon, but they did not help. Nothing helped. On the evenings when these meetings took place I would usually stay overnight in a hotel in Glaund City, because it was better sitting around in a bar with fellow sufferers late into the evening than returning to another lonely night in my apartment. The hotel was as lonely, but it was at least free of unwelcome reminders.

The first few of these meetings were casual – some of us would get together after a recording session – but gradually other people who had been on the tour heard about us and they turned up too. It was not an answer, but there was a feeling of safety in numbers, a common cause of grief. One evening, nearly two-thirds of all the people who had been on the tour turned up, and after that we decided to make the meetings semi-formal. We knew of a restaurant with an upstairs function room, so we met there one night of every week.

After several of these occasional gatherings I was beginning to come to terms with what had happened when I read in one of the specialist musical magazines that my distant nemesis And Ante had released another record. As before it was available only through a specialist importer. I tried to ignore it.

Things had changed, though, since Ante's first theft of my property. My work was better known, many more people had listened to it, and several of my compositions had been discussed in the most serious critical terms. While I tried to ignore Msr Ante, other people were listening to his record, and it was not long before new similarities to my music were being identified. At one of our informal self-help meetings, one of my colleagues showed me a page of reviews in a recent magazine. He held it across towards me, and asked me if I knew about it.

'It mentions you,' he said.

I took it from him, looked more closely. Who could blame me for doing so? Every instinct warned me to ignore Ante, told me not to interest myself in what he might be doing, but curiosity did get the better of me.

My colleague said, 'Do you know this guy? Did you meet him while we were out there?'

It was actually the picture that first gained my interest: next to the printed review was a colour reproduction of the sleeve of Ante's new album. The photograph depicted a scene achingly familiar to me: it was the view from Hakerline Promise across the shallow strait towards the island of Temmil. The great conical mound of the Gronner was silhouetted black against a red and gold sunset sky. A plume of grey smoke or steam, illuminated in many shades of yellow, orange and pink by the lowering sun behind it, drifted serenely away from the high crater, gradually dispersing in the calm evening air. White-painted boats rode the sea. The tiny town of Temmil Waterside could be made out, a cluster of colourful buildings set between the sea and the foot of the coastal hills.

Ante's name was blazoned across the top, blocked white letters with red outlines.

The magazine had printed another photograph of Ante lower down the page: it had been reproduced in black and white and he was standing with his face lowered and half turned away.

I glimpsed words, lines, phrases in the review. I saw my name several times, Ante's name, a reference to one of my piano sonatas, my orchestral suite *Breaking Waves*. I turned away from the magazine and handed it back.

'Thanks,' I said. 'I do know about that.'

Whatever obscure threat Ante's activities might once have seemed to be, I felt myself no longer vulnerable.

'They say here that he's stealing your music.'

'Let them. Let him.'

'Doesn't it bother you?'

'Not now. It did once, but he's young and foolish. He'll grow up and regret it one day.'

Part of this was bravado, part of it was denial. But in truth I felt that after what had happened to my life at the end of the tour I had more to worry about than a young rock guitarist copying my work.

A few more weeks went by. Our self-help group continued, but after the first flurry of activity our numbers gradually reduced, as we should have known they would, to a core of regulars. There were soon only at most fifteen of us who went along for a meal in the restaurant and then some drinks afterwards in the private bar upstairs. The others drifted away. I was aware the meetings were futile, but they were all we had.

I had never been particularly friendly with the cellist Ganner, who in a different era of my life, as it felt, had first made me notice the time slippage when we were aboard ships, but one evening he and I were sitting at a table together in the upstairs bar. On that occasion I had brought with me my stave. For some reason I had kept it. After I returned to the chaos of my wrecked life I had put it away in a closet with most of the other stuff I acquired during the trip. There it had remained while I tried to make sense of what had happened. That day, knowing we would be having our regular meeting in the evening, I had come across it and taken it with me.

I was not entirely sure why – perhaps it was an unconscious indication that I was coming at last to the end of the first stage of recovery, a closure, a step towards whatever came next.

I took the stave out of my music case, and laid it on the table between us.

'You've kept yours, then?' Ganner said immediately.

'Have you?'

'I wasn't sure what to do with it.'

'But you didn't throw it away.'

'I like the way it looks. The way it feels in your hand.'

'Did you ever find out what it was for?' I said.

'No.'

I picked it up and held it in the fashion I had seen it handled by all those border guards, Shelterate officials, whatever they were properly called. I held the metal handle in one hand, and rotated it while the fingers of my other hand lightly touched the smooth surface. The sensation was close to how you might expect a rod of finely sanded softwood would feel if you rotated it lightly in your fingers – but there was something else. Not quite a sensation of static electricity, not a vibration, nor any physical response at all, but a feeling of *contact*, of a new *awareness*. I had felt this every time I had done it. At first I assumed it was the finely grained surface rubbing against my fingers but later I noticed that the same feeling was detectable if my fingers never actually touched the rotating surface but were a millimetre or two away. Any further away than that and the sensation disappeared. It made me wonder if the thing was emitting or radiating something other than friction.

I performed this familiar action while Ganner watched. Then I described the feeling.

He shook his head. 'I have never felt that.'

He took the stave from me, held it the way I had done, and turned the rod against his fingertips.

Then he put it back down on the table.

'Nothing?' I said.

'No. It's just a piece of wood that's been smoothed,' Ganner said. 'But that's probably what I like about it. You know how long instrument makers have to polish the bodies of cellos, and the other string instruments. How they achieve that superb finish. Not the varnish but the fine texture of the belly's inner surface. Whoever made the staves was an instrument maker, and he or she did the same with them.'

'So maybe it's a musical instrument?' That in fact had not occurred to me before.

'I don't think so,' Ganner said.

'Then there's this.' I picked up the stave again, and held the handle so that Ganner could see it. I rested my thumbnail beneath the words deeply and perfectly engraved into the metal. I couldn't pronounce them, but they were *Istifade mehdudiyyet bir sexs – doxsan gün*. 'Have you any idea what that means?'

'Have you?'

'I've deciphered what the words say, but I'm still at a bit of a loss.'

While I had been in Temmil Waterside I noticed a shop selling tourist maps and books, and I had seen a basic introduction to the written form of the patois used throughout the Ruller Islands. During my travels I learned that nearly all the patois forms spoken in various parts of the Archipelago were vernacular, purely oral, but that some of the island seigniories, particularly in the island groups most visited by tourists, made attempts to produce a written form, even if only as a primer, a rudimentary lexicon. The Rullers were one such island group.

During an idle hour on the voyage home, I had used this book to try to interpret the words on the stave. It was only a rough translation, and probably unreliable, but as far as I could tell the inscription said: *Unlimited use of one person – ninety days*.

I told Ganner this.

'So what do you say that means?' he said.

'I think it means what it says. The stave is usable by one person only, on an unlimited basis, but only for ninety days. It's like an expiry date.' Ganner was looking uninterested, so I said, 'The point is they wouldn't put information like that on the stave if the stave didn't have a function.'

'But you don't know what.'

'I don't think any of us did.'

I remembered the often repeated ritual in the Shelterate buildings, with the officials running their fingers over the staves, then mysteriously inserting them into the scanner and handing them back without comment. Clearly they knew what the use was – it would tell them something their job required them to know, and at the end of the process the thing was handed back to the one person who had unlimited use of it for ninety days.

28

It was a few days after the conversation with Ganner that I heard a second orchestral tour of the Archipelago was being planned. A new promoter was involved – there was no word of Msr Axxon, from before. As soon as I heard about the new tour I made it clear, presumptuously perhaps, that I did not wish to take part in any way. I certainly did not wish to be taken around the islands once more.

When I later discovered the planned route – it was to be a longer tour with more island visits, Temmil to be included again – I felt an unmistakable yearning to go back. I stayed on the sidelines, alert for news, but I felt then that there was nothing in reality that would draw me back. I later discovered that not a single person who had been on the first tour either agreed to go on the second tour, or volunteered for it.

A few weeks later the tour party set off to the Dream Archipelago: a major concert programme was planned for each of twelve islands, with a number of extra recitals and performances at smaller venues. There would be a stay of between seven and ten days in every place. The repertoire was more extensive than our earlier one and more varied, and I heard about complicated arrangements involving guest conductors and soloists who lived on islands in the Archipelago, not all of them on the itinerary islands. For part of the tour my friend Denn Mytrie would accompany the players, conduct workshops in partnership with them, introduce his own concert of island themes. Once again, briefly, I wished I could be a part of that. I had not seen Denn for a long time.

My only direct involvement with the tour was to deliver a celebratory farewell lecture to the tour party. In the days before I gave the lecture I wondered for a long time how much I should say about what they were likely to discover when they returned. I was still not sure what exactly had happened to me, and even if I found out I would have no idea how I could explain it.

On the night of the lecture I took what I saw as a safe approach and spoke to them about music only, told them anecdotes about the conductors they would be meeting and working with, mentioned technical or acoustic details about some of the concert halls they would be going to that I had already experienced, and so on.

At the conclusion of the speech, I suddenly felt compelled to allude at least to the time distortion effect. Departing from my prepared text I reached down to my side and produced my stave.

'You have all been given one of these?' I declared, brandishing it in the way I had once seen Msr Axxon brandishing his. I saw recognition in many of the faces close to the stage. 'Be sure to use it in the way you have been instructed! Never forget this. It is most important. Good luck to you all!'

The response was an outburst of clapping, which became prolonged when they realized that it was also the conclusion of my speech. I stood beside the lectern, acknowledging the applause, smiling around, modestly accepting the compliments of the chairman of the event, but thinking to myself, What advice have I just given? On what experience of my own was it based? It was advice I had not followed myself because I did not know how. It was advice I knew nothing about because I had had no instruction.

While the applause continued I raised the stave so that the wooden rod rested lightly against the fingers of my other hand, and I felt again the sensation of contact being made, of an awareness that was beyond the moment.

The next morning I was on the quayside at Questiur to

watch their ship depart, to wave them away, to wish them well. I stood there on the cold concrete wharf long after the ship had disengaged from the quay and headed out into the bay. I remained there long after most of the relatives and friends had dispersed. I watched the ship while it steamed across the bay until all sight of it had been consumed by the chill sea-mist that obscured the Glaundian coastline in the morning hours.

Most of my thoughts were guilty ones, wishing that I had had the strength to try to warn them while I had the chance the evening before, but there was still a part of me, a substantial part, that deeply envied them. I did want to be on the ship with them.

How profoundly I wished to return to the sea! To the islands, to the dreams they contained, perhaps to vanish forever into the vague tides of distorted time, days and weeks gained, or days and weeks forever lost.

The fourteen-week orchestral tour of the Dream Archipelago returned to Glaund City exactly fourteen weeks and one day later. I had not been expecting them. I was not there to greet them when their ship docked.

29

Five years passed – I had reached the age of, what? Did I count the two years I had lost? Were they to be added to or subtracted from my calendar? All that was certain was that I was somewhere around fifty.

I felt myself to be in my prime, if not physically then certainly creatively. After I discovered that the people who took part in the second Archipelagian concert tour had returned exactly when expected, with no apparent trauma of lost time, I was drained emotionally by the news.

I was confused: was their experience the same, subjectively, as mine had been, subjectively? Or had they somehow avoided the time paradox? Or, worst of all, had I imagined the whole thing? These thoughts confounded and scared me for a long time.

But the deep store of music I had imagined while I sailed

between the islands became something I could explore at last.

I calmed myself, I turned my mind away from my troubles, I thought about my experiences in the islands. Memories poured in, vague and precise and allusive. Finally, I settled down to work. Those two years following the return of the second tour became one of my most fecund periods. I composed two short symphonies, a suite of piano sonatas, two dozen songs, five concerti, a volume of trio and chamber pieces – one followed the other.

The critical reception was positive but the popular audience left me with mixed feelings. I believed my work was under-appreciated by audiences. At worst I assumed I was misunderstood, or at best that my music was taken for granted.

How should one read the response of a live audience at the end of a concert? I sampled many such evening events, where my work was performed. Applause followed invariably, often there were cheers, sometimes flowers were thrown appreciatively on to the platform, but I always left the concert hall with an inexplicable feeling of anticlimax.

My record sales increased steadily, though. My new work received good reviews, it sold well in the shops and my back catalogue was often re-released. I found these apparent contradictions confusing.

And Ante returned unexpectedly into my life. One morning I received an email from a record dealer in Glaund City, saying he understood that in the past I had shown an interest in the work of the 'progressive jazz/rock fusion musician And Ante' – was I aware that Ante had recently released a new record? The dealer said he had imported a small stock, and would be pleased to receive an order from me.

The disc arrived in the mail a week later. I did not open it straight away, feeling unexpectedly fearful of it. What had Ante done with my music this time? How would I react? From the size and shape of the outer packaging I could tell that what was inside was a digital record – at this time digital records were still something of a novelty and I had not expected the technology to be available in a remote place like Temmil. However, I had already bought a player for myself, so I had no excuse not to play it.

I was astonished by what I heard. Ante had taken nothing away from me: none of my melodies or themes, none of my harmonic progressions, no signature tempo changes, nothing. I would never like the kind of vaguely jazzy music Ante was writing and playing now, but at least he appeared to be working with original ideas. I played his record three times, listening closely to each track, but finally I was satisfied, pleased even, that I had nothing to worry about.

Only the following day did I think to look more closely at the printed sleeve notes. The plastic case included the usual inlay card, but I had skipped it at first because of the small print. I put on my recently acquired reading glasses and read what was there. Although the notes were written by someone who was an admirer of Ante's work, and therefore totally uncritical, it was possible to see beyond the praise to understand some of the traditions Ante was drawing on, who his influences were, what he aspired to. He was quoted directly a few times. Answering a question he listed the musicians and composers who had most influenced his work, singling out two or three of them for special praise. I knew all the composers he mentioned, of course, but also could not help noticing that my own name was not among them.

Not long after this, And Ante released two more records in short order. Astonished that he was so prolific, I ordered copies from the same dealer. Once again I was pleased to discover that Ante's career as a plagiarist had apparently come to an end, perhaps for good. He had moved on in another way – his interest in jazz/rock fusion had evidently soon passed and he was now experimenting with more ambitious music. One album was a film soundtrack, with a full orchestra, Ante conducting. The other was a suite of jazz-influenced tracks, with a five-piece band. I noted with surprise that my friend, Denn Mytrie, was listed as playing the piano on every track.

30

One day while I was listening to the news on the radio I heard a short item that electrified me. The Ministry of National Defence – a government department which served as a source of instructions, warnings and propaganda on behalf of the ruling military junta – announced that the 286th Battalion had completed its war duties and that the troops would be returning to a heroes' welcome in Glaund City. They were already aboard their troop carrier and heading for home. The item was over within seconds and spoken by the presenter in a monotone, immediately followed by a story about a dispute between two business corporations which would be going to court for an adjudicated hearing.

But I had caught what was said. I noted down the day that had been announced when the troops were expected to arrive home, and as soon as I could afterwards I made enquiries about them.

Throughout my life, as the years passed, the unexplained absence of my brother Jacj had been like a background droning sound of depression, worry and sadness. I had never given up hope about him but it had become more an act of faith than a genuine expectation. It was decades since I had seen him. Jacj's battalion was the 289th – three away in the numbered sequence. Two or three battalions were recruited and sent south to the ice-bound battlefields every year. The numbering sequence was closely followed – the troops were demobilized in the same order as the one in which they had been drafted.

A nation at war is a secretive place. The war that was being fought against our enemy, the Faiandland Alliance, was managed and contained within a structure of secrecy. Once the fighting was moved to Sudmaieure, the unpopulated southern continent, the deception that normal life could continue was enabled. That was what they intended and after a few months that was how we learned to act.

It was sometimes easy to overlook the fact that we were at war. So much was held back from the ordinary people – national security was invoked in many different guises. All my adult life I had been encouraged to believe, along with everybody else, that the war did not endanger me, nor even inconvenience me.

Of course there was a price for this and I discovered it as soon as I began to enquire about the return of the battalions, and in particular when I tried to find out about the 289th.

Letters, emails and personal approaches to the Ministry, to my elected parliamentary deputy, and to various other authorities, were all nullified either by a lack of response, or by bland stonewalling. The fact that I had become by default Jacj's only living relative made no difference at all.

Meanwhile, the day of the arrival of the 286th Battalion came closer.

I reasoned that if the return of one of the battalions could be reported on the radio, then similar information must be discoverable in newspaper archives. One day I went to the Central Library, asked to see the archive of the *Glaundian Times*, and was taken to a computer terminal by a helpful librarian. She showed me how to access the software and how to search the archive, and also how to narrow my search to find and focus on the material I wanted to read.

If these notices had been published in the newspaper on the days I was reading it, I would have missed them. They were certainly there, made publicly available, but the release was a technical one. They were not printed or displayed prominently. Whenever the software located one of the announcements by a data search it was invariably written in a short paragraph, usually without a headline, and almost always placed on a page of classified advertisements and government directives, buried among planning applications, declarations of bankruptcy, statutory information, and so on.

However, I had soon identified and downloaded all the announcements of battalion returns from the last two or three years.

The information was not clear and it was often ambiguous. It appeared true that a battalion arrived back in Glaund City, or more accurately in the Questiur docks, about once every three or four months. The troops arrived in roughly the same order as the numbering sequence of the battalions themselves. Much else was left unsaid.

In the period I was searching, the 276th, 280th, 279th, 282nd and even the 288th had all reached home, but they had arrived in that order, not according to the battalion numbers. Two of them had docked more or less simultaneously. One, the 277th, appeared to be entirely missing – I found a vague note about 'redeployment', which revealed nothing. As I already knew, the 286th Battalion was expected next, but I could find no information about any of the others. My brother Jacj's battalion, the 289th, was mentioned nowhere.

A second visit to the library, using slightly different search terms, established that battalions were occasionally merged on the battlefield into fighting divisions under a different numbering sequence, and in other cases were broken up and divided into smaller operating companies, again with another numbering sequence.

I also came across a government notice announcing the creation of an email helpline, so that if troops had changed battalion identification it should be possible for relatives to trace them.

I therefore immediately emailed the helpline, asking for information about Jacj. No reply came. I followed it up with a letter sent by mail and I also made several more phone calls. As before, all these attempts were without response. I was terrified the answer would be that Jacj had been posted as missing or dead, but even that reply never came. Hope remained alive, but the feeling of dread was larger.

Then the day arrived when the troopship carrying the 286th Battalion was expected. I travelled down to Glaund City, intending to be there when it berthed in Questiur.

31

When I stepped off the train I was already concerned about being late. We had been delayed at a small station halfway along, one the trains rarely called at, and I had seen several armed police officers boarding. They walked through the carriages, regarding everyone, but saying nothing. Finally, the train had moved on. Half an hour had gone by.

At the central station in Glaund City three male army officers were standing on the platform, precisely in front of the door I was about to step out of. They looked young to me, but by their insignia and medal sashes they were clearly high ranking. I glanced at them, then away. I moved rapidly past them.

'Sir, we believe you to be Msr Alesandro Sussken.'

Astonished, but also alarmed, I turned my head incautiously, clearly acknowledging I was who they thought I was. The one who had spoken to me remained where he was, facing me, but the other two stepped sharply forward, each of them at my side. They took my upper arms.

'You will come with us now, sir.'

They began marching me away.

'Are you arresting me?' I said as loudly as I could, a wild hope that someone around us would hear, perhaps help me.

'Not at all, sir. You are free to go about your business if you wish.'

They swept me through the ticket barrier, briefly held open by a station worker to allow us through. I was being supported so that I would not fall, but I could barely keep to my feet. If I stumbled they immediately slowed their pace, allowing me to recover. Some of the passers-by did stare at what was happening to me but they looked away again quickly. I was dragged swiftly across the concourse, swerving neatly through the crowds, then up the flight of steps to street level, a scene familiar to me from so many past visits to town. It was raining.

I was pushed hard but not roughly into the rear seat of a large, black-painted car. It had been waiting for us, the door already open and the engine running. Two of the officers sat one on each side of me, while the third sat in the front next to the driver. He immediately turned in his seat so that he was facing back towards me. None of them responded to my demands, but politely requested me to remain calm until we arrived at the place where they were taking me.

'Where is that?' I shouted.

No reply.

The car was a heavy, powerful machine and it was driven fast. The windows were darkened thick glass. From the thudding sound the doors made as they closed I guessed they were armoured, bulletproof. There were never many cars in the centre of Glaund City but the drivers of the ones that were there obviously saw us coming and moved swiftly to the side.

We did not travel far: a short distance down the street outside the station, a fast dash across the open ceremonial square called Republic Plaza, then a dive into the wide boulevard that led down towards the river. All this was familiar to me. I often walked along much of the same route, heading for the recording studio, whenever I arrived by train for session work.

The rain was sweeping heavily across Republic Plaza and spattered on the windshield as we accelerated along the boulevard. Then the car turned sharply off the road into a narrow access lane between two huge buildings and braked to a halt beside a side door. The rain suddenly intensified, hammering down on the metal roof and bodywork. I saw pellets of ice dancing on the hood and the narrow roadway.

The car door was opened by a man who moved swiftly out from inside the building. He was holding an immense black umbrella. First one officer scrambled out of the car, then I was pushed from behind by the other. For a few seconds I was outside in the freezing cold air, the darts of the ice storm rattling on the taut fabric of the umbrella. The sharp wind made ice water swirl along the sidewalk. Three steps through all this, then I was ushered quickly through the door.

We emerged into a large corridor, high and wide – windows to the lane outside ran along that wall, and a number of closed doors were opposite. I had barely time to look around. I glimpsed repair work going on – I saw some workers on stepladders, protective sheets draped over furniture, there was a smell of paint or plaster and the screech of power drills or sanding machines, or both. While I stood there for a few seconds, getting my bearings, while the three officers were still coming in from outside, brushing their uniform jackets with their hands where the intensive rain had struck them, a group of at least fifteen or twenty civilians appeared at the far end of the hallway. They were being conducted by two women wearing military uniforms, who led them in complete silence through one of the side doors.

I was propelled, less roughly, towards an elevator, which was standing with the doors wide open.

The doors closed against us and the elevator began to rise.

'Msr Sussken, would you care to tidy your appearance?'

'Before what?' I said disagreeably.

If my appearance needed tidying it was only because of the way I had been manhandled. My hair was untidy after the dash from the car, but I usually wore it informally so that did not matter to me.

'Before you attend your meeting, sir,' the officer said.

I started to protest. I knew of no meeting. I had clearly been arrested for some reason. You heard of such things happening: the armed police or soldiers who arrived at your address in the dead of night, the army trucks that came and went, the disappearance of a neighbour no one would discuss, the rumours of internment or punishment camps in the mountains, the harsh treatment, the terror of the unknown. When you knew what was happening to the people around you there was always the fear that one day it would be your own turn – but I led a life of such inconsequence, wrapped up in my own concerns, enthusiasms too, that I never took it too seriously. I had no business with politics and thought the reverse was true.

As I watched the elevator's floor indicator light climbing steadily up the array I suddenly thought: this must be something to do with Jacj!

I had spent a great deal of time recently trying to locate him, calling government departments, generally making a nuisance of myself, as one of the officials put it. I had broken a self-imposed rule, instinctively developed throughout my adult life: keep out of sight, don't become known for anything except what you do, and therefore what you have some control over.

'We think you should tidy your appearance, sir. There is a cloakroom available to you.'

'No!' I said. 'This is about Jacj, isn't it? Do you have news of him?'

'Jacj?' one of the men said.

'I think he means his brother Jacjer.'

'Yes!' I said.

'Oh no, Msr Sussken. This has nothing to do with your brother. Not at all.'

The indicator light flared briefly as it reached the top of the array. The elevator lurched and halted – the doors slid open. Directly opposite was an open door – I glimpsed a tiled floor under a glare of fluorescent light, a row of hand-basins, towels. I was not asked again about my appearance.

We turned to the right and walked briskly along a deeply carpeted corridor towards two large metal doors. We waited while one of the officers went through a code-and-accept ritual using a microphone built into the wall. After his identity had been acknowledged, he slipped a plastic card into a slot on the door, which opened it.

He was the only one of the three officers to follow me into the room beyond. The door closed swiftly behind us. We were in an unremarkable ante-room or waiting area: a few chairs, a table, a telephone, overhead lights. A house magazine published by one of the steel factoring companies rested on the table.

'Raise your arms, Msr Sussken,' said the officer.

I complied, feebly, reluctantly. He patted me down expertly and swiftly, then ran a hand-held detector device across my upper body. My music case was taken from me, briefly inspected, his hands fluttering around inside, sifting my papers, my journal, my pens, then he placed it on a shelf at one side.

Another door led out of this room and again the plastic card was used to open it. This time he went in ahead of me, stamped his feet, drew himself up smartly and made a military salute. I followed him in and heard a hubbub of conversation.

'This is Msr Alesandro Sussken, madam,' he said loudly.

The hubbub died. The officer made a second salute and exited, his feet stamping noiselessly on the thick carpet. He closed the door behind him with a sharp but precise motion.

I was in a huge, high-ceilinged room. The area where I had entered was unoccupied, but the far end, where there was a sort of low rostrum and a display of national flags, was crowded. My entry was, by the sudden silence it caused, obviously expected. Everyone present turned towards me. Many of them were holding wineglasses. All were dressed formally – I saw numerous military uniforms and most of the women not in uniform were wearing suits or long dresses. All the civilian men were wearing business suits, and several of them had the coloured sashes that indicated ambassadorial or diplomatic status.

I stood still, stunned by what I was seeing.

There was then a ripple of applause, silenced instantly when one of the women stepped forward towards me from the crowd. She was not especially large but the splendour of her military uniform made her distinct from everyone else. She had several rows of medal ribbons on her breast, a rope sash of office, brightly shining epaulettes and many other honours and insignias attached to her upper sleeves. A large golden medal of some kind hung at her throat.

She went to a lectern which stood in the centre of the room, directly opposite to where I had halted.

I recoiled inwardly. My heart started racing. I recognized her!

She was less tall than I had imagined from the television news, or from the wall posters. Her hair was shorter, and a nondescript grey. She was stouter. Her face was paler than I had thought from photographs. I felt an habitual fear of her, a deep and instinctive dislike. The press always called her madam.

She was an antagonist who stood against everything I held dear. She had power, she was dangerous, she regulated almost every aspect of everyday life. I hated her.

'Welcome, Monseignior Sussken!' she said, and her voice was amplified somehow so that it filled the cavernous room. The shock of seeing her made my memory temporarily fail. What was her name? Everyone called her madam. I tried never to speak of her. She was anathema to my life, my music. If I had an enemy in the world, this was she.

Generalissima Flauuran.

She was speaking, making an announcement, reading from a card which lay out of my sight on the surface of the lectern.

'Today it is our deepest pleasure to welcome Monseignior Alesandro Sussken, the greatest living composer in the nation of Glaund. His music is beloved by us all, and includes the following major orchestral works—'

She began to recite the names of most of my compositions,

with the place and date of their principal performance. I listened, I could not help but listen, stunned by what was happening, the attending crowd, the huge hall, the flags, the armed guards. Above all, stunned by hearing this woman mouthing the names of the pieces I had written. In this place it was like glimpsing loved ones held in a punishment camp. She mispronounced many of the titles, but did not stumble or hesitate. I realized that never in my life before had I ever heard the sound of her voice. She almost never spoke in public, avoiding it somehow, allowing other members of the ruling junta to speak for her. I was amazed to hear her accent: she spoke with the rough accent, the abrupt vowel sounds, of the mountain people in the far north of the country!

She concluded the list of my compositions.

'Monseignior Sussken,' she went on. 'As you no doubt know we shall be celebrating next year the tenth anniversary of the establishment of the Democratic Council of Leaders, we who have brought peace and prosperity to this great nation. There will be many festivities throughout the course of the year, both public and private, and these will be announced in due course. However, the culminating event will be a gala concert of contemporary music and it has been decided that you will be granted the honour of composing the climactic orchestral piece. Do you accept this honoured commission?'

Everyone in the room was looking towards me. Everyone, I could not help noticing, except this woman. She had not yet looked directly at me. What was happening here? The whole thing was madness. I had been dragged in from the street—

'Do you accept the honoured commission, Monseignior Sussken?'

What could I say? What choice did I have? I had never written celebratory music in my life. I had no idea how to do it. The thought terrified and appalled me.

'Msr Sussken, do you accept the honoured commission?'

'Yes,' I said.

A tumult of applause and cheering broke out from the crowd, soon silenced by the Generalissima raising a hand.

She was reading from the card again: 'We graciously concur

with your patriotic desire to celebrate our nation. What you will write is entirely within your wishes and ability. Amongst other intentions we have of you we expect you to demonstrate the full range of your creativity and imagination, totally free and under no sense of duress.'

She paused for a moment, presumably to allow this to be noted by everyone present. I was barely taking any of it in.

'However,' she went on, still reading in her weird regional accent. 'It is customary for a work of national importance to conform to certain expectations and in this case we do expect that your celebratory music will include the following elements. You are free to compose them however you will.'

She then recited the list of what the music was to contain. Her words went past me, irrelevant, meaningless, ridiculous. Was this really happening? I heard her say there would be a full symphonic orchestra. A minimum of four movements. At least three major instrumental soloists had to be featured. A mixed chorus of a minimum of three hundred voices. Four operatic soloists. There was to be a triumphal march at the beginning or end (my choice, of course). Serving soldiers would troop through the hall with a display of battle colours. It was to include a sequence of peasant celebration, with performers from the Glaund National Dance. Poetry was to be recited entr'acte – the words would be supplied by the current Laureate. When she said 'cannon effects in the climax' I almost laughed.

Was I losing my mind?

Finally, she said, 'And in recognition of the greatness with which you will fulfil this commission, your country offers you a single royalty. Kindly step forward, Monseignior Sussken.'

To the sound of more cheering and applause I went towards her. She handed me a large, stiff envelope. Her hand never touched mine. Her eyes did not meet mine. I took the envelope from her and went back to where I had been standing.

'Ladies and gentlemen,' she said, turning towards the crowd of dignitaries. 'I shall now have a brief private audience with our honoured guest. Thank you for witnessing this important moment in the cultural life of our country.'

The crowd started to move away. I stood still. Not at all sure what was expected of me and in a mental state of confusion and distress I watched what was happening. I could not believe what had taken place. That woman, this place, those words!

Everyone dispersed with remarkable alacrity – presumably they had been told in advance what to do when they were asked to leave. There were two large doors on each side of the rear wall, and they exited through them. Someone came forward and removed the lectern. The armed guards stood alertly at each side until the last of these guests had moved into the next room, then they followed them.

The Generalissima moved back and away from me, until she was standing in front of the raised platform. A single large desk stood on this.

While her back was briefly turned, I slipped a finger into the flap of the envelope to see what it contained. There was a thick wad of pages held in a card binder, and a single slip of paper. I peered closely at the slip.

It was a banker's draft made payable to my account number, and it had been signed by some kind of printing device. The amount was thirty thousand gulden.

It was a huge sum of money, conferring instant wealth. It was much more than I had ever earned in my life, to date, in total.

32

She stood with her hands held behind her back, squaring her shoulders. Her knees were slightly apart. What more did she want of me? The steel desk was behind her, an expanse of grey metal. It was bare of papers, books, any kind of computer equipment. A sheet of white paper lay exactly in the centre of the desktop. Other furniture stood around: I saw without paying too much attention some chairs, cabinets, smaller desks at each side, two huge windows where the rain was streaking diagonally, roofs dimly visible outside through the veil of falling rain, a grey carpet, light-grey paint on the walls, nothing unusual. Glaundian drab, but clean and recently placed there.

What was going to happen to me?

On the wall behind the desk: one large photograph, five smaller ones. The smaller photos were of groups of military men and women, standing in tiers like football teams. The large photograph was of the ruling military junta: five people in army uniforms, four men and this woman, the Generalissima, at the centre. All the men were wearing dark glasses. Two national flags were mounted above the main photograph, cruciform, dark grey and deep red.

What was this private audience to be about?

I was alone with her.

Just me and this woman. It was an effort to breathe.

'Msr Sussken, it is an honour to meet you in person. Your music is distinguished and beautiful. You are a credit to our country.'

I had no idea what to say.

'You may relax, Msr Sussken,' she said. 'May I offer you a drink?'

'I was brought here against my will,' I said.

'You must address me as madam.'

'Yes, madam.'

'You were free to go.'

I knew I had not been. If the ceremony was what it had seemed to be, why had they not issued a formal invitation? There was more to come. I said nothing, feeling my hand and lower arm starting to tremble.

She said, 'I have a few extra matters I must raise about the agreement you have made. There is a full contract in the envelope. You must read it and abide by it. Your signature is not necessary. The prime qualities it insists on are your manner and your means. The piece of music you are being commissioned to write must be wholeheartedly patriotic. You are expected to write it from the heart. We have no wish to hear –' and unexpectedly she pulled from her breast pocket a slip of paper, and read aloud from it '– we do not want irony, subversion, subtlety, cryptic statements, cross-references, allusions, knowing asides, quotations, hidden meanings. Is that clear?'

'Yes, of course, madam,' I said.

She put away the piece of paper, her cultural crib.

'The other matter concerns your wife. We know your present situation of separation from each other, but you are still in fact married to her.' (A mental image of Alynna suddenly formed: still young and delicate as she had been when we met, years ago, time lost, not gained.) 'Your wife is to appear beside you at every function. This is non-negotiable. We do not know how you will arrange your affairs but the appearance you and she give at all your public functions must be plausible and consistent.'

The Generalissima still had not looked directly at me. She was addressing a point on the grey carpet approximately two-thirds of the distance between us.

I waited. I could not bring myself to speak to this woman.

'Now, Msr Sussken. We know what you were planning to do today. You were intending to be at the harbourside when a troopship docked. We decided we should see you before you went to the harbour.'

I suddenly knew that my first thought had been correct. 'So this is this about my brother?'

'It concerns Captain Jacjer Sussken, yes. It also concerns your attempts to elicit information about him from officials. It concerns your unauthorized use of library archive equipment. We have information that you have taken a particular interest in a non-aligned territory called Dianme.'

An army captain? Jacj had become a captain? My harmless, lovely island, Dianme?

The Generalissima was dizzying me with hints at what they might know about me. And what they were suspicious about. And what measures they would take.

'I've done nothing wrong,' I said.

'Msr Sussken – this country is in a state of emergency. Address me as madam.'

'Yes, of course, madam,' I said, remembering how deeply I loathed her.

Only the week before this woman had authorized the execution of two dozen people the junta called subversives. She, Madam Generalissima Flauuran, had issued the orders. Although she would have been too young to have led the original military coup, she had emerged in recent years as the leader of the junta, a dominant and extreme personality, legendary for her ruthless control over the other generals, and her ways of ridding herself of them when they under-performed or had outlived their usefulness to her. All laws and directives were commanded from this building, or another like it somewhere else in the city. There was no civilian police force – only an armed militia, trained and regulated by the National Affairs department, answerable to the ruling military junta, answerable to this woman. Many of her enemies were in barracks or forts or hidden camps, imprisoned for life. I had nothing I wanted to say to this woman, the Generalissima, I wanted nothing to do with her.

I suddenly knew that with this enforced interview with Flauuran my life in Glaund was coming to an end. I was known, marked, identified and tagged. I was in danger. Anonymity, insignificance, were no longer mine.

Kill her! The thought came from an impulse, a shock. *Kill her now!* Never mind how, you are alone with her, there's no one watching, knock her down, stamp on her, kill her. Kick her in the gut, kick her face in, kick her to death. Make it swift before they stop you. Afterwards, they would ... but that's later, worry about that later. Kill her now! *Grab the chance!*

I reeled inwardly, appalled by what had coursed through my mind. I exhaled breath – I had been holding it in. Never before, never ever, had I felt the urge to kill someone. I honoured life, I treasured life. No enemy was ever so loathsome that I would kill.

'Your brother joined the 289th Battalion, we believe.'

But how would I do it? I mean, how do you actually kill someone? What is needed? I had never even struck anyone in my life. How would I kill this woman, how would I in fact do it? A fantasy of violent physical attack: a sudden assault, pushing her to the ground, holding her throat, kicking her.

Me? I couldn't do it. Not just *wouldn't* do it, I could not. I had no idea how. I would fumble, mess it up, fail even to hurt her, I would damage myself instead.

I tried to expel the fantasy of practical action. Greater than that was the abhorrence. But the fantasy lingered in me, like the rise of nausea.

'Msr Sussken. Your brother?'

'The 289th,' I managed to say. 'Yes, madam.'

'You look unwell.' A statement without concern.

I had no idea how I looked – internally I was in a kind of panic. I felt hot, shaky, on the point of falling over.

'May I have some water?' I said.

And with those words, it seemed on their instant, a door opened at the end of the room, behind the Generalissima. A man in civilian clothes walked in with a tray. It bore a carafe of water and a glass tumbler. He put down a cork mat on the surface of the desk, then placed the water and the glass on top. He paused for a moment to arrange them symmetrically opposite each other on the mat.

I had to step past the Generalissima to pour the water. The man was leaving with the tray, after a curt but civil bow to the woman. How did they know I was going to ask for water? As I picked up the carafe I looked up at the walls, the ceiling. I had not noticed them before, but tiny cameras were embedded above the photographs. Another was between the crossed flags. Two more were high in the walls, close against the ceiling.

The water was cold, refreshing. I did not drink much of it – I felt better as soon as I had swallowed the first mouthful.

'Thank you,' I said to the woman I was fantasizing about, kicks to the head, a stranglehold on her throat, death.

'Do you have any questions, Msr Sussken?'

I was facing her again. I left the carafe and the glass untidily on their mat.

'I am interested only in finding my brother,' I said, and I could hear my voice was revealingly pitched higher than normal. Already my throat and lips felt dry again. 'Is Jacj still alive, madam? Is he unhurt?'

'That is the case.'

'Then where is he?'

She said nothing.

It was so long since I had had any contact at all with Jacj – it was impossible to count the years because of what had happened to me. So much had changed since he was drafted, the family in which we grew up was destroyed. I had aged, he had aged. I could not imagine what so many years of army life would have done to his personality. All I felt by this time was his absence. I had known him only as my elder brother, a sensitive young man, a teenager. He was musically skilled if not prodigious, but a good violinist, a sometimes emotional musical performer, a passionate advocate for justice. He was a lover of books and film, never physically fit nor even competent at active things. Like mine, his childhood had been blighted by the air raids on our towns – he had been affected by them more than me because he suffered them longer.

I had never forgotten his apprehension and concern when against all our expectations he accepted the draft order and reported for training. My parents had pleaded with him to abscond. But Jacj had spoken instead about a perverse sense of duty, of having to serve, that to infiltrate these people was a way of informing himself and strengthening his resolve. He said he wanted to be within, inside their system.

It made no sense to me, but he tried to reassure me. He showed me the promises that were spelled out in the draft order. The enlistment would be short in duration, the military duties were arranged to minimize danger to the recruits, the major part of the fighting would be conducted by regular troops, there would be an honourable discharge at the end. Against everything that he had said and argued in the months before he was drafted, Jacj believed these promises.

The same promises now looked like glib lies. The short enlistment was obviously the first of all that followed – what about the other false promises, the ones less obvious?

I could not help glancing past the woman towards the discreetly mounted cameras. Every move I made was being observed, and no doubt every word was being recorded. I knew what would happen if I made any aggressive move towards the Generalissima.

I could hear no sounds from other rooms but the icy rain continued to rattle in hard flurries against the windows. I saw the slate-grey sky, the pall of dark clouds moving quickly from the direction of the sea.

Her hands were no longer behind her back. Now she was letting her arms hang straight at her sides. She still had not looked directly at me. She silenced me with her inscrutable cold manner. I could sense we were coming to the end of this interview. I noticed that a small red light, embedded somehow in her desk surface, had come on.

How would this meeting end? Was I still under arrest and to be kept in custody? Punished? Forced to join the army? Shot as a traitor? Anything seemed possible, because the régime she led was capable of anything. I had started trembling again, terrified of the unknown, but wishing once more I had the courage to make an attempt on her. That's what it was: a lack of guts. My lack. She rendered me useless. I had never before met anyone like her. The physical steadiness, the lack of gestures or eye contact, the deadly calm. The mountain country accent, modified by a military inflection. I still hated her, hated her more than before I met her. I had had no idea what she was like. I had not known that were I to meet her she would terrify me.

The stillness of her standing there, the manner of her waiting, the hidden cameras, the implied threat.

'You said I might leave, madam,' I said. 'May I do so now?'

'Are you still intending to visit the harbour?'

The actual answer was that I wanted to be anywhere that was not in this bare and terrifying room with its neutral, monochrome appearance, the cameras, the single red light, unblinking. The longer I was there the more the danger to me increased, even if it was only the psychic damage of realizing the depths of my hatred. She was not alone – she could not be alone. Aides and associates and armed guards would be poised invisibly around her, behind doors, a few paces away from where we stood.

'I don't know about the harbour,' I said, making an ineffectual effort to sound as if I had changed my mind. 'That is why I came to Glaund City today, but if you are saying I am forbidden to go there, then I will not.'

'You are free to leave, Msr Sussken. Remember you are a contract artist.'

She turned away from me, stepped back to the desk. She touched something beneath the rim of the desk top, and instantly the red light went out and three doors opened. Two were behind her, the other was the one by which I had been brought in. Four armed soldiers walked quickly in and stood in a rank behind her.

I turned. The senior officer who had escorted me had already entered behind me. He was standing to attention, saluting the Generalissima.

It was loathsome, alien, horrifying. I wanted to be out of there. I backed away from the woman, turning and heading for the door as quickly as I could, but I could feel my knees shaking. The knees would betray me – I did not want the weakness in me to be noticed. The lust to kill had still not entirely fled: even as I made my ignominious exit, it was in fact a retreat, a part of me was thinking that in spite of the numbers against me, in spite of their weapons, if only …

I reached the door feeling ashamed and frightened and relieved. The officer ushered me swiftly through and closed the door behind us both. He said nothing. My music case was still on the shelf where it had been placed. The officer passed it to me. The doors to the elevator were wide apart in the short corridor beyond. I went in by myself. Even as I took my two steps across the threshold of the compartment, the officer reached brusquely past me and jabbed the button. The doors closed swiftly as he jerked back his arm.

I was alone under an amber glow coming from a light dome in the ceiling of the compartment. As the elevator bore me downwards I turned to look at myself in one of the mirrors – I hardly recognized the person I saw. I looked shrunken, defeated, crushed down. I grimaced at myself, as we do when we are alone with a mirror, and the face that looked back at me seemed alien, older, pathetic.

The elevator stopped automatically and the doors opened to the wide hall I had been taken through before. The workmen were still on their stepladders, the busy movements continued of people crossing to and fro, a group of tourists was standing close to two large paintings of military personnel, a guide of some kind was pointing up at one of the figures, proudly describing insignia.

I hastened to the street, desperate to be out of there. Moments later I was back in the narrow lane where the official car had deposited me. The sleet, stinging as it fell against my head, leaching an acidic taste into my mouth, hammered unrelentingly down.

33

For about a minute I felt I had lost my bearings. I could not concentrate. I remembered the car crossing Republic Plaza, but where was that from where I was standing? I walked back down the way I thought the car had brought me, but the road that the lane opened into was a narrow service road. I headed back, the sharp wind blowing the rain directly against me. I felt it on my face, my eyes, my throat. My ears were unprotected and stinging. It was freezing cold, depressing and discouraging. I always hated this kind of weather – you never grew used to it, even in Glaund.

I found the boulevard. It was largely free of traffic, vaingloriously wide, with huge institutional buildings on each side, many soldiers standing guard by entrances and access points. I turned to the left, walked along as quickly as I could and the wind seemed perversely to re-angle itself against me. It made furrowed, spreading patterns on the inundated road surface. I kept my head down, hoisted up my jacket as far as I could to protect my neck and ears from the stabbing pellets of frozen rain.

Somehow I had walked in the wrong direction because I never found Republic Plaza, but I was relieved when I came into a familiar part of the city without really knowing how I had got there. I knew of a small café in a side street so I went straight to it and dived inside, shivering. My clothes were soaked. There were a few other customers already in the comfortingly stuffy and overheated room. I took a large cup of tea to the window where there was an electric heater. The glass was thickly covered in condensation. I found a seat and slowly recovered.

I was trying not to think about the Generalissima, but she was haunting my thoughts. Now I was away from the building I realized my obsession with a violent attack on her was inappropriate, to say the least. I was physically inept, out of condition, congenitally non-violent in every way. I hadn't the faintest idea even of how to thump someone's arm. An assault on her would have been a disaster for every reason.

Perhaps she would never know how the fear of her protected her. Then again, she probably did know, and that was how she operated, how she manipulated those around her.

I opened the envelope, which had become dampened by the weather. I took out the card binder. This contained, as the Generalissima had said, a contract of employment – one printed page after another of conditions, warranties, reprisals for breach, remedies of recovery.

Beneath it, something that was for me even worse: a prospectus for the sort of music they were trying to commission from me. I glanced at some of it, mentally shrinking away. It could only have been put together by a committee, and a committee of non-musicians at that. It was a kind of fantasy wish-list of every known musical trope, good or bad, fashionable or otherwise, serious or frivolous. If it wasn't so manifestly purposeful, so intentionally pompous, and so backed up by implicit threat, it would have been ridiculous.

Any attempt to fulfil even a part of this commission would destroy my reputation as a musician for good.

Also in the envelope there was an old photograph of myself, standing next to Alynna. We were holding hands, smiling at the camera. I well remembered the occasion, a friend's wedding, a happy day, innocent then of the future. How had these people found the photo?

Beneath it, a copy of the list which the Generalissima had read to me, her moral guidance, the avoidance of irony, crypticism, subtlety, and so on.

And the banker's draft.

I took it out, quickly confirmed that it said what I thought it had said, then slipped it back into the concealment of the envelope. It was not the sort of thing I wanted seen by anyone else in this humble café. Thirty thousand gulden was a veritable fortune, enough money, in all probability, to see me through the rest of my life. It was not something I could ignore. Equally, I could not accept it, because of the conditions surrounding it. It was a sickening amount, for the temptations it offered, for the implications.

It all amounted to the same thing: if I remained in Errest,

in Glaund, I was finished. I would be a chattel of the state, I would have lost all integrity as an artist and as a human being. I was marked. Everything about me was known. They even had suspicions about Dianme! I was in the grip of the people I loathed and feared more than anyone else in this world.

Sitting there, clothes slowly drying, my cup of tea gone cold, I knew that only one freedom was left to me. I had to run. I had to hide. I must find somewhere safe.

When I had finished my tea I wrapped myself up in my outer clothes as well as I could and went outside. The rain and sleet had been replaced by falling snow. Although it was colder, at least the snow did not soak me.

I went to a bank, presented the draft, and it was accepted without comment. I asked for the money to be paid into my existing account. It was a routine transaction – even the amount seemed not to impress the clerk who dealt with it. He told me that I could access the money within two working days. I went back outside, into the vile weather.

There was a metro station two hundred metres away and I hurried towards it. Inside the booking hall I stamped my feet and shook my arms, dislodging the flakes that had landed on me. A current of warmed air rose reassuringly from the platforms below, with the unmistakable smell of electric trains.

It was familiar and for me it was real. Had I imagined that interview with the woman who ran this country? It had all happened less than an hour before and already it felt like a horrible imagining. The terminal hall where I was standing was filling with people. Some like me were sheltering from the weather but others were passing through on their way to the train platforms below. After every flow of warming air from the tunnels, people ascended on the escalator from the trains and were forced to push their way through the crowd in the ticket hall.

From where I was standing I could still see over the heads of others out into the street – the wintry storm had intensified to fine, fast-blown blizzard. It was weather I well understood, as most likely did everyone else who was crammed into the booking hall with me: this kind of snowfall, dry and powdery and borne by air too cold to allow any thaw, could continue for days.

I wondered again if I should abandon my planned trip to the harbour – maybe by now the troopship would already have docked? I knew that waiting around on the bleakly unprotected quayside in this weather would be unpleasant. I also knew that winter storms like this one often disrupted the train service in my overground route home. I began thinking I should leave, try to get home before the weather closed in completely.

I rode down to platform level. If I turned to the right when I reached the landing at the bottom of the escalator any train from that platform would take me via two intermediate stations to the overground terminus. If I went the other way I could catch a train to the dockside metro station in Questiur, which was only a short distance from where the troopship was likely to dock.

I hesitated a little longer, then a train happened to come in on the left, so I walked through on impulse and boarded it.

34

Ten minutes later I was on the windswept wharf, the snow blustering insistently around me and starting to form drifts wherever something protruded above ground level. I knew that in under an hour the snow would be too deep for safe walking, and not long after that the overground trains would be subject to delays and cancellation.

With no sign of any ship, either tied up alongside or heading in from the bay, I walked as quickly as I could around to the next quay, keeping my face down to avoid the snow. As soon as I emerged from behind the stand of immense mobile cranes I saw a darkly painted vessel already tied up. No identifying name or mark was visible. Two covered companionways led down from the ship's side to the dock.

Dozens of young men were pouring off the ship, their boots making a clumping noise inside the hollow passage. They emerged in a single file into the whirling snow. A group of soldiers in full uniform were at the base of both of the companionways, quickly patting down the men as they stepped down on to the wharf.

Each one had to raise his arms then turn a full circle. After that he was made to pass through a tall metal detector gate. Once free of this the men lowered their heads and ran slithering across the slippery dock towards a windowless dockside building. None of them was wearing army uniforms or fatigues. Most of them were clad only in jackets or woollen sweaters, with ordinary civilian trousers or slacks, and none wore hats.

No one challenged me as I walked along the quay. I headed for the nearer of the two companionways, watching as the men continued to thud down the passage from within the ship.

When I was closer to them I could see that they were all much younger than I had thought at first – they were youths, teenagers, young men. If they had clearly not been part of the armed services on active service, or returning from it, I would describe most of them as boys.

Bowing my head against the wind I went to the group of soldiers waiting at the base of the companionway.

'Is this the 286th Battalion?' I shouted, over the noises of the ship, the docks, the wind, the tramping passage of young soldiers. Snowflakes flew into my mouth, and I spat them out and shook my head.

One of the soldiers heard me and half turned. His upper lip and eyebrows were crusted with blown snow. His face was grizzled, impassive against the cold and the job he was doing. He indicated the military flagpole propped up beside him: a colour drooped at the top, partly obscured by old grime and recent snow. On a yellow background, formerly bright, I could see the numbers '286' picked out in white stitching.

'Are these the troops?' I said, feeling stupid for having to ask the question. The young men were pushing past me, not looking up, trying to protect their eyes and heads from the swirling flurries of snow.

'You can't speak to them down here,' the soldier said. 'If you're a parent there are facilities for meeting your son in the reception hall. Discharged women from the 286th will arrive tomorrow.'

He indicated the grey concrete building at the rear of the quay. He turned away from me impatiently, barked an order at the next young man waiting in line, then roughly searched him.

35

I had to leave Glaund as soon as possible. The only place open to me, and indeed the only place I wanted to go to, perhaps forever, was the Dream Archipelago.

Although that night I returned home with relatively few travel problems, because of the snow it was impossible to leave my apartment for more than a week. I was still feeling paranoid after the meeting with the Generalissima, but I soothed my worried mind with music: I loved my piano, my violin felt like an extension of my soul, and for many years I had spent winter periods of isolation practising, learning new pieces, and, as often as I could, composing. Like most Glaundians I kept reserves of food in the flat during the winter months, and the place was always well heated.

I felt unsafe. I had banked many thousands of gulden given to me by the régime, and I was not intending to hand the money back or earn it in the way they intended. At first I was constantly afraid of being watched, of being followed, but the confining weather gave a sense of security, perhaps false, but anyway calming. No agents from the secret police came to my apartment in the middle of the night. Nothing sinister arrived in the mail. My phone and internet services seemed undisturbed. No one moved into any of the other apartments in my building. Time went by. The fearful feelings gradually faded. I was eventually able to sleep through every night. I felt life was becoming steady, comprehensible once more, but the quietness did not delude me.

My resolve to leave Glaund hardened. I began to plan how to shed myself of some of my belongings, how to prepare for a major change of life.

Once I had decided to flee, the money from the Generalissima was something I could not afford to lose. It took a long time but in the end I succeeded in transferring a large portion of it to an anonymous account in Muriseay. My friend Denn Myrtie, who knew nothing of how I came by such a fortune, helped arrange this for me.

I carried on with my other plans. I disposed of many possessions but decided in the end to keep the apartment in my name. I made arrangements with my bank that no matter what the bills would always be paid. I had learned a lesson, and I set aside the remainder of the junta's money for this long-term commitment.

I could barely see the offshore islands through the low gloom of the winter. I often sat at the window, staring across the sea, hoping for some sort of sign.

At last spring arrived. I was ready.

36

The warm weather came early to the island of Muriseay. I was there at last, my old life abandoned, my new one before me.

It was an escape, an ambition achieved, but I was not full of hope. I worried about everything and everyone I had left behind me. I missed my apartment and its view, even though I had exchanged the narrow vista of three islands for the full reality of the hundreds of thousands. Leaving behind the piano on which I had played and composed for so many years was painful, a real wrench. I was still missing Alynna, even though I knew I had lost her forever. Also, whatever my negative experiences and feelings about Glaund it was still my birthplace. It was politically stagnant, and I could see no end to that. The military coup had taken place around the time I was born, so I had never known any other kind of government or society in Glaund. Though it was repellent and repressive, the junta had at least brought a form of stability – the allegedly liberal republic that preceded it had been capitalistic, decadent and corrupt. That was what the history books said, reflecting the junta's own version of history. The reality and truth of the past were almost impossible to discover – whatever they might be, it made no difference on an emotional level. Glaund would always be my home. And the junta could not last forever.

But now I was a quarter way around the world, in endless warm weather, feeling balmy sea breezes, drowning in the scents of luxuriant flowers, being shaded by huge and mysterious trees, and learning the ways of a benign government that had devised a modern way of operating the ancient feudal laws of the islands.

I did not live easily in these easy circumstances. The political relationship between the islands and Glaund was ambiguous, to say the least. It was undisclosed, undiscussed, at least in Glaund – I was still too new to Muriseay to be able to read between the lines of what was in the local newspapers. Officially the islands still did not exist as far as Glaund's junta was concerned, even though I knew from my own experiences that certain cultural and a few sporting contacts were opening. The armed forces, whose ships constantly crossed the waters of the Midway Sea, were a real presence, and Muriseay itself was known as a place of R&R for the transiting troops.

For these reasons I did not feel secure at first. I had become a fugitive, and for a long time after arrival I half expected to be snatched by undercover officers from the north. Once I reached Muriseay I found a small and fairly decrepit pension in a backstreet of the city, and lived there as inconspicuously as possible. The first few days were the worst. I hardly left my room, but gradually I started to understand the easygoing nature of the place. Although I never entirely relaxed my guard, within a week I was beginning to think I might be safe from the Generalissima's version of justice.

As the days turned to weeks I did start to relax. I was charmed by the place. Who would not be, after enduring the gloom of my home country for so many years?

Muriseay's capital city was the largest conurbation in the Archipelago, home to more than two million people, and at times the centre of the town was a busy, crowded and noisy place. Muriseay was an island so large it exceeded the total land space of Glaund and Faiandland combined – which were themselves the major countries in the north – and one which although technological and industrial in outlook operated wide and deep environmental rules.

Much of the island was uninhabited because the huge central mountain range, and most of the extensive hill country surrounding it, had been designated as an area of ecological uniqueness. Temperate and subtropical forests covered most of the slopes. A vast coastal wetland lay on the eastern side. No roads or other tracks crossed the centre of the island, no building development was allowed anywhere in it or even near it, no mining or farming or logging or any kind of industrial activity went on. Even aircraft were banned from overflying the area. Only walkers could enter, and then were obliged to stay within designated zones. Muriseay was a wilderness, thought to be the last truly undamaged ecology of the world.

Most of the smaller towns and other settlements were built along the coastline, concentrated along the southern or western shores. As well as a network of railways, all the main ports were linked to each other by ferries. Muriseay was the acknowledged hub of the inter-island ferry system throughout the Archipelago – it was possible to book passage to a bewildering number of islands and island groups.

I was not yet ready to leave Muriseay so I tried to do some work while I acclimatized myself. It was difficult to stay focused on what increasingly I saw as austere musical theorizing, especially now that everywhere I went I could hear the gay popular romanticism of the island music. The people in the islands knew the classics too, the worldwide great masters, but the music they played and sang and listened to was quite the opposite of the work I had been writing for most of my life.

I realized it gave me a quiet insight into what And Ante had done with my music, transposing it into popular music, to rock, to a kind of jazz. I was beginning to understand, beginning to adapt and modify my views. I liked that feeling, even though this too tore me emotionally in half: the tension was deepening between my past and my likely future.

Meanwhile, I basked in the warm air, loved the feeling of daily sunshine, admired the casual good manners of the Muriseayan people, revered their happy homeland. The easy way of life on Muriseay soon won me over. I could happily have ended my journey there. I had the money to live wherever I wished, I could have found a suitable apartment on an attractive stretch of the coast, settled down to the rest of my life's work.

Muriseay was not where I wanted to be, though. I knew I would have to move on, but even on the relatively short journey from Glaund, my escape, I had been reminded of the enigmatic rules that affected travel through the islands.

37

The worst part of the escape from Glaund was the fear of being caught, because in practical terms it was fairly straightforward. Denn Mytrie told me that his own route into and out of Glaund was by way of an island called Ristor, situated off the coast of Glaund but at the furthest western extremity. This was a part of Glaund I did not know, a largely unpopulated area of lowland farming. It was at the opposite end of the country from the border with Faiandland, so the presence of security measures was less obvious than elsewhere. Although Denn himself had only ever travelled with official approval, he said that he knew there was informal trade between the people of Ristor and the mainland. Privately operated boats frequently made the crossing, strictly illegally but never interfered with by the Glaund authorities. Many luxury goods passed through Ristor on their way to unnamed customers in Glaund City.

When the time came I packed my bags, I walked to my local train station, I changed trains in Glaund City and within five hours I was at the other end of the country in a tiny port called Plegg. Money was no longer a problem for me, and the following night I paid for a covert passage across to Ristor. I endured three hours in an open boat, but I was taken to a small harbour on the southern coast of Ristor. The next day, one of the larger inter-island ferries made a brief stopover. I joined this, and after she docked in the main town of Ristor Parallel I went ashore with the other passengers.

I was one of the last to disembark so I had to wait in the drizzling rain outside the Ristor Shelterate building. Already it felt like a familiar process. I noticed that here, not far from the mainland, the same sort of young people I had seen on my earlier trip were hanging around in a group outside the entrance. There were five of them. Unlike the others I had seen in warmer zones, these were dressed in thick puffer jackets or bulky rainproof coats. They all wore caps or hoods. Two of them had the same knives I had seen before. They barely looked at us as we dragged our luggage slowly towards the Shelterate building.

Then one of the young women left the group and came directly to me. She was wearing a quilted jacket darkened by the rain. Beads of damp from the mist that covered the dock area had settled on the filthy cap that she wore crammed down on the top of her head. A knife was attached to her wrist by a silver chain.

'Are you coming to stay on Ristor?' she said without preamble.

'No – I'm in transit.' Denn had suggested an informal itinerary across to Muriseay, but I had not yet had a chance to buy the actual tickets.

'To Callock? Gannten?'

'Why do you ask?'

'I can help you,' she said. 'Callock? Then Muriseay?'

'Callock is next.'

'Then other islands, and Muriseay? Would you buy one of these? One hundred thaler.'

With a swift movement she pulled something from an inside pocket. As she moved her hand the knife attached to her wrist swung upwards. She produced a wooden stave.

'I don't need one of those,' I said. 'I have one already.'

'Let me see.'

'Why?'

'I can help you.'

I had brought the stave with me, but it was buried deep inside my holdall. I reached around inside for it, then handed it to her. She looked at it with interest.

'You never use this,' she said, holding it lightly in one hand and resting the fingers of her other hand on the wooden shaft. 'If you have come from the mainland, where do you find it?'

'I was here before – in the islands.'

'It is registered – but it has expired. Or nearly. I can extend the expiry for you. Thirty thaler. Fifty simoleon.'

'What do you mean, expiry?'

'Three days unused. Maybe four.'

'How can you tell?'

'Fifty simoleon.'

I reached across and took the stave from her. She released it easily.

'I'll wait until it has fully expired,' I said.

She lost interest in me then, turned away and wandered back to the others. I continued to move forward slowly towards the Shelterate building and soon I was allowed inside.

When my turn came to approach the desk I had my travel documents and stave at the ready. The official gave my documents the briefest of looks, but took my stave, turned to the scanning device which was mounted on the wall behind him and pushed it down into the aperture. As many times before the stave was drawn down mechanically a little further, an indicator light came on and went off, and the stave popped back up.

The official peered at it as he turned back towards me.

'Is it due to expire yet?' I said.

'No.' Then he said, 'Have a good journey, Msr Suskind.'

'It's Sussken.'

He had already lost interest in me. I scooped up my papers, grabbing them with the hand that was holding the stave, and I moved on through. I had no wish to stay in Ristor Parallel. I knew that the ship I had been on briefly was sailing to Callock next.

I found the shipping office in a street close to the harbour and discovered that although that particular ship would not call at Muriseay, I could travel on her to Callock, then take a succession of other ships to where I wanted to be.

I returned to the port in time to board the ship, and was given a pleasant cabin on an upper deck.

Ristor was part of the Dream Archipelago even though its proximity to Glaund lent it the appearance and grim climate of the mainland. For that reason I was glad to be ashore for not much longer than an hour. As the ship sailed, turning to the south, I knew I was transferring from being a traveller leaving the warring north, to a wanderer among the islands.

The transit experience in Ristor was repeated with minor variations at every island where I had to change ships: Callock, Gannten, Derril, Unner, Olldus, Leyah, Cheoner – the names and places slipped past, becoming interchangeable with each other in memory. Two or three of the islands I hardly saw at all: we docked at night, and I was aboard the next ship before daybreak. But everywhere the ships made landfall there was the same official delay, the same baffling but annoying bureaucracy.

My papers were generally passed over. My stave was used and examined everywhere and it remained unmarked.

Gradually the succession of ships bore me southwards into vivid sub-tropical seas. The temperature rose with the passing of every day, the sun glaring down from a sky that seemed to act like a concentrating dome of reflection. The waters were calm and metal-bright. Currents and tides stirred beneath the surface but each stretch of the journey was a stealthy, calming voyage through untroubled seas.

I protected myself from the steadily increasing hot weather by wearing a long linen robe and a broad-brimmed hat, both of which I bought from a stall on the deck of the ferry between Gannten and Derril. I covered my face and arms with barrier cream. After the first day away from home I stopped shaving and soon I grew used to the appearance of my new-growing beard.

Music returned to me. Every island had a different note. I leaned on the rail, crossing the sea, staring at land. The music sounded in my head and resounded in my body: the vessels' movements through the water, the slow rocking of the ships with their mechanical, unidentifiable sounds from deep within their hulls, the distant murmuring of the engines, and the steady vibration. Islands never failed me. Seabirds hovered and swooped in the wake of the ships and everywhere there were glimpses of fish and other swimming animals, surfacing intermittently, perhaps curiously, to see us churning past. Islands released their notes. With the sudden blasts of sirens and horns, the close encounters with other ships in the narrows between islands, I felt rhythms starting up, syncopations. When we passed between two islands I did not know on which side of the deck to be first.

Where once before I would have sought discordance, challenge and surprise in the music that I dreamed about, now I whistled tunes quietly to myself, tapped my foot as a rhythm came to me. I would stand close to the prow of every boat, responding to the slow rise and fall as we moved across the swell. Much of the time I had my eyes closed as I reacted to the sounds in my mind, or I stared away across the water to the nearest island, not focusing, just looking. Passengers on passing ships waved across intersecting wakes – soon I became one of them, joining in and waving back, loving this marine adventure, this journey into unknown zones, not only of the vast, island-crammed ocean, but also into the new musical impulses, lighter, happier, that were rising from my soul.

38

So a good end to the first part of the voyage. And so to Muriseay, and after waiting for him for many days because he was making a record at the far end of the island, Denn Mytrie.

The day before I was due to start the next part of my long journey, Denn took me for a drive in the hills that surrounded Muriseay City, finally arriving in a small village on the southern coast. We stopped for a long lunch: we ate on a shaded terrace overlooking the sea far below us, the white and terracotta houses ranged on the hills around the tiny cove. A score of small boats and yachts were tied up against the jetties.

I took it all in, pretending to take the view for granted, but in fact the simple beauty made me feel breathless. Denn and I sipped a chilled wine, picking slowly at the salad we had chosen for a first course. With the food half eaten I put down my fork, leaned forward so that my elbows rested on the wicker arms of the chair. I was staring down at the sea, breathing the clean air, the scent of the vine hanging from the trellis above, the flowers, the waft of strange food. Insects stridulated around us, unseen in the trees.

A huge dark ship was moving slowly across the view, heading in the direction of Muriseay City, a long way in the distance, beyond the hills.

Mytrie was not eating either. He saw what I was doing and leaned back in his own chair. For a long time we said nothing.

'Do you realize what that ship is?' he said.

'I think so. A troop carrier?'

'Yes. One of yours, I think.'

His words shocked me. I had said nothing to him about Jacj, and he meant nothing by it, but it was a sudden reminder of my old concerns.

'What's it doing here?'

'The harbour in Muriseay City is a treaty port. Most of the troopships halt for a few days.'

'Are you sure it's one of – are you sure it's from Glaund? How can you tell?' The ship was flying no flag that I could see, but it was too far away for me to be certain.

'There was another ship in the port last week. One from your enemies. Although this is neutral territory, the seigniory has made an arrangement with the army staff so that arrivals and departures are spaced apart. Didn't you see the news of what happened a few weeks ago?'

'No – of course not. I wasn't here. Anyway, I've left all that behind. The war was a nightmare.'

'This wasn't about the war,' Mytrie said. 'Although you might think it has followed you. There was a fight on the harbour front, outside one of the R&R clubs. It was a ship from Faiandland. Nothing serious, a drunken brawl – but a big one. A lot of the men were hurt, several of them were arrested.'

'I can't believe it happens here.' I indicated the peaceful view. 'What is there to fight over?'

Mytrie pointed deliberately at the troopship. 'This is a beautiful place, Sandro,' he said. 'But those ships are filled with boys coming back from the war. They've been cooped up on board for several weeks. They let off steam.'

'In this place?'

'Yes – in this place. There's an area close to the harbour – clubs, prostitutes, bars. The authorities try to clean it up from time to time, but not much changes. The same thing happens on other islands too, where there are places for the troops to go. It's a feature of everywhere they land.'

'Then couldn't it be stopped? Doesn't it invade the neutrality?'

'Would you know how to change things? They have a right to land here. The treaty ports go back centuries.'

Our second course was served then, and for a while Mytrie and I returned to silence while we ate. I was again thinking of Jacj, of course, who had once been on one of those ships, heading to or from the war. I had been trying to put Jacj somewhere in my mind where I did not have to think. Now there was the ship, that ship, the one I could still see, sailing slowly without a visible flag, to a berth in a harbour in a civilized city in a beautiful, undesecrated island, where there was an excess of pleasures provided for the young men crammed beneath the decks. I knew Jacj had travelled at least as far as an island called Winho, although I still had only the vaguest idea of where that might be. Jacj would therefore know everything about life on a troopship. Perhaps he was even on the ship I could see? I had despaired of ever seeing Jacj again – the interview with the woman general in Glaund had made me lose hope, and one of my most painful moments before I fled to these islands was the realization I would be abandoning Jacj to his fate. I had accepted that Jacj was dead, or missing, or lost in some other way. He would now be more than fifty years old – I could not imagine that. So much time had passed. I knew that the returning ships carried only the recent recruits, young soldiers, boys. It was unimaginable what might have happened to him, so I tried not to imagine any more.

'Tell me what you know about the ones who manage to escape from the ships,' I said eventually. Mytrie had left half his food uneaten.

'The deserters?'

'Yes.'

'Not a problem here.'

'But elsewhere?'

'Every island in the southern hemisphere, or any of the ones which have R&R facilities, receives its share of deserters. All wars leak young people who want no more of it. Some of them are here – the ships are allowed into the port, and once they're ashore some inevitably abscond.'

'But not a problem, you said.'

'This is a big country with a liberal government. We don't encourage it, but we are constitutionally against war.'

'I've heard about the havenic laws. I know you have them here.' I was thinking briefly of my own arrival in Muriseay, with a longer than usual examination of my papers by the official in the Shelterate building.

'Yes, but we are one of the main havenic islands. Many of the soldiers who escape from the ships try to hide, but on Muriseay it's not necessary. Most of the ordinary people who live here will give them a spare bed, or even a job. Eventually they assimilate. Few of them cause trouble here, and after a few years they usually apply for citizenship.'

I started telling him about Jacj, the loss of him, the background dread that I lived with every day. Denn listened sympathetically.

'In the Guildhall there is a register of people who have applied for citizenship,' he said. 'Anyone can consult it. Are you sure your brother's here on Muriseay?'

'No – he could be anywhere. I would have no idea how to start looking.'

'I suppose you have to start somewhere. This is as good a place as any. The records are probably complete. At least, there's a staff in the building who maintain the database. I don't know about other islands.'

Other islands. Sitting there in the warm sunshine, looking out across the sea, I was distracted by the sight of other islands. Of course there were other islands. Islands always filled the sea views. There were too many to count: five or six of them were in clear sight from where we were sitting, distinct and separate, with boats around them, signs of habitation, but each of them was surrounded by smaller islets and rocky outcrops, reefs, crags. I knew already that most of those would be counted as islands too. Some were inhabited, but surely not all of them? And named? Beyond them were more shapes, but it was unclear from my seat if what I could see was higher land on the islands, or if they were parts of other islands behind or further away.

Beyond even these was the distant view that I had often experienced while sailing on the ships, the sense of enclosure created by the wealth of islands.

Islands in large numbers are like cumulus clouds: they are separate from each other but the ones further away, towards the horizon, tend to create the impression of continual banks. It was unusual to see a view of the horizon as open sea. When the weather was clear, sailing across the Midway Sea sometimes felt as if the ship was crossing an immense lake, where the shores were far away but ever-present. These distant shores were an illusion – as the ships sailed onwards the land far ahead separated into individual islands, a continuum of the Archipelago, the feature of the ocean. It was exactly the same here, from this moderately elevated restaurant terrace, a sense that there was another country, perhaps a new continent, lying towards the horizon. The islands clustered.

It soon became apparent to me that Mytrie had little interest in the subject of deserters. He had his own preoccupations, and because they were similar to mine we soon drifted back to talking about them, comparing notes: he composed, played, reviewed for a newspaper and a couple of magazines, carried out session work, travelled around, tutored. The music we wrote could not be less alike, but our daily lives were more or less interchangeable.

He told me because he had been able to visit Glaund a couple of times he had more experience than most musicians of witnessing the effects of our war – I noticed he did not call it 'the' war, but the war I was in, the one my country was in, my war. Again, it was not prime among his interests. Some of the many still-unrepaired buildings and streets in Glaund City had made an impression on him. He told me he had later composed a galop extraordinaire in an attempt to illustrate the repair work that was going on in Glaund City. Like everyone else in the islands he followed the news when it was reported, which in Muriseay usually meant stories about the behaviour of the troops on R&R visits. Sometimes there was coverage of important victories or retreats in the southern continent. But it remained my war, our war, not his.

We drove back to the city. I was already thinking ahead to the next day, because I was intending to book a passage, but I was so attracted to the way of life on Muriseay that I was pondering a change of plan, a possible longer stay.

When we arrived back in Muriseay City we walked around on foot for a while, looking at the cathedral, a large park, a brief visit to an art gallery. He showed me where the Guildhall was located, but we did not go in. He did not take me to the port area. I am not an enthusiastic tourist, and we soon repaired to a large, noisy coffee bar in one of the main streets of the city.

At last I asked him what he knew of my former plagiarist,

And Ante. When I said the name Mytrie looked blank.

I said, 'You played a session on one of his recordings. Maybe two or three years ago?'

Mytrie shrugged his shoulders. 'Perhaps I did.'

'You don't remember?'

'Do you remember every session you've played in?'

'I suppose not. But I wondered if you recalled this man Ante. It would have been a small group. Ante would have played guitar – you were the pianist on every track.'

Mytrie looked unconvinced. But I had seen his name on the label – he had been more than an anonymous session player that time, more of a guest artist sitting in for the recording.

'Was it rock music?' he said.

'It was described as jazz, but I'm not familiar with that.'

'Not your kind of thing, then?'

'I'm not familiar with it, that's all.'

We talked about the record I had heard, and I began to wish I had brought it with me. In fact, it was one of the many things I had stored away in my loft at the apartment. I then mentioned that Ante came from the island of Temmil, and I asked Mytrie if he had travelled there for the recording, or if the session had taken place here, in Muriseay.

'It would be here. I have never recorded on any of the other islands. You say he's from Temmil?'

'That's where he lives. I don't know if he was born there.'

'And he's been re-recording some of your music?'

'Not recently – but he was for a long time. Several long-playing records.'

'The fact he's from Temmil is not a good sign.' Mytrie was looking sceptical. 'It's the sort of place many people want to live in and a sort of colony has grown up, half-talented artists, people with lofty ideas who make big claims for themselves, but who really aren't much good. They self-publish their poetry, put on exhibitions of each other's paintings. Many business people retire to Temmil. A lot of the biggest houses are owned by exiles from your country, or Faiandland. They have money, so they can afford to pay to have books published, records released, exhibitions put on. None of them actually produces good work, and they'll never amount to anything.'

I was remembering my short visit to Temmil and what an attractive, harmonious place it had felt like. It had stimulated me, made me wish to be there, to stay. I did not like what Mytrie was saying, or even why.

'When I was touring, we featured a soloist from Temmil, a young pianist called Cea Weller. Do you know her work?'

'Weller? Yes, of course.'

'So it can't be all bad there.'

'I'm only repeating what I've heard from people here in Muriseay. Friends, people I respect.'

'That sort of thing makes me nervous,' I said. 'It can't be true of everyone on Temmil.'

'I shouldn't have said anything, Sandro. You're right. I was only trying to reassure you about what this Ante person did to you. He was stealing from you. It's exactly the sort of second-rate behaviour that people here associate with Temmil. Someone like Ante comes along, takes a shortcut. He pinches what's yours, pretends it's his. He thinks no one will notice, and most people don't. You do, of course, but he thinks you won't find out, and doesn't care how you will react if you do. He's younger than you, so you say you start feeling forgiving about him, but that doesn't change what he did.'

'I have forgiven him – but I still want to meet him.'

'You're probably not the only one he plagiarizes, Sandro. But he's picked on you for a reason. Admiration, perhaps – have you considered that?'

'When I first found out about it I tried to think of everything. Mostly I wondered why it was me. It didn't feel like admiration to me.'

39

I spent much of the next day searching the microfilm archive in the cool and air-conditioned records section of the Guildhall. As Mytrie had said, there appeared to be a comprehensive record of every young soldier who had managed to get away from the armed forces and settle on Muriseay. I began with those records. The database was huge, at first forbiddingly so until I learned how to select. It was, for instance, divided into two main sections, one for the Faiandland Alliance, the other for Glaund and her allies – I saw no point in opening the Faiandland records.

I searched on names, of course, including 'Suskind', acknowledging the mistake people often made. Then I filtered birth dates, then dates of recruitment, then with a feeling of desperation I tried a picture search. There was a warning attached to the archive notes that many of the people who became fugitives supplied false names and dates to the authorities, even after they had been granted havenic asylum. I turned up no record for anyone who might by any stretch of hope be my brother.

After a break for lunch I started looking through more of the databases. There were similar records for other islands, but the notes gave a clear warning that these were known to be incomplete, could not be properly checked or updated, and should be used only for a coarse-grain search. I opened the archive for every island I had ever heard of, starting with Winho, the one island I was certain Jacj had been to. Next was Temmil, since I knew that was a place artists and musicians fled to. Then I ran through the database of every island I had already visited, however briefly, or knew I was likely to visit on my next travels – nothing. (I discovered that no records existed for the three islands which lay offshore from my home: Dianme, Chlam and Herrin. They were anyway so close to the mainland of Glaund that no one was likely to have sought refuge there.) Finally, I tried the databases of the islands whose names I had only vaguely heard about. There were thousands more. It was hopeless.

I abandoned the search, thanked the Guildhall staff who maintained the archive, then walked down to the harbour office to investigate what sailings might be available.

It turned out to be a day of immersion in a mass of data. After the Guildhall records I had hoped for a simple choice, but instead was presented with a dizzying array of travel options: packages, conducted tours, cultural visits, open-ended journeys, express routes, museums and sights, shipping lines, car rental options, as well as an apparently endless choice of accommodation standards, on board and in transit hotels, at an overwhelming range of prices.

The only destination I had in mind was Temmil, but before I landed there I wanted to make my way indirectly, explore more of the Archipelago. As it turned out, Temmil was one of the islands I could not find in the dozens of catalogues and brochures. The only thing I could establish about Temmil was that a couple of the people I spoke to in the harbour office thought it was in 'another part' of the Archipelago, or 'on the other side' of the world. As usual, it was impossible to find any reliable maps or charts of the islands. Even the few brochure maps I came across were vague and stylized, the alleged sea-routes shown in broad swoops of generalized lines. Few of the smaller islands were identified or located, and the drawings of the island sizes or shapes were approximate.

I went across the street to a tourist agency which had an office close to the harbour, told them what I wanted, and with remarkable efficiency I was offered a pan-Archipelago open ticket, a package tour, unrestricted as to routes, cabin and hotel accommodation that was claimed to be of higher-than-average standard while not being in the luxury bracket, no time limits on departures or arrivals, the freedom to change, cancel or extend routes as I pleased. It sounded so close to what I had been imagining that I agreed to it with feelings of relief and gratitude, passed over a substantial sum of money, and in return was handed a vast plastic wallet containing all the brochures, street maps and optional vouchers they assured me I would need.

A ship called the *Serquian* was due to depart on an easterly five-island cruise at mid-morning the next day, and I was guaranteed a single cabin, all meals and 'entertainments' on board included, plus the option to break my journey in any one of several tourist attractions en route.

I had travelled in the islands long enough to sense that there was something I was not being told, that there was going to be a snag of some kind, but the helpful young woman at the desk in the agency assured me this was one of their most popular packages, which combined comfort and security while travelling, as well as the freedom to explore many islands, and choose my next destinations freely and easily.

I returned to my hotel to pack.

40

I was awake early the next morning, ate a solid breakfast in the hotel restaurant, then hired a taxi and was driven down with all my baggage to the harbour. I was heavily laden. As well as two weighty suitcases containing all my clothes and the personal possessions I had thought to bring, I had my violin in its protective case and a holdall in which I carried everything I would need easy access to while travelling. This included my travel documents and maps, spectacles, a couple of books, pens, notebooks, a portable CD player, several discs, the stave, barrier cream for my face and arms ... much more. I could hoist the violin case across my back, freeing both arms, but the two suitcases and holdall were a problem to carry around in the heat.

When the taxi pulled up on the harbour approach I could see a large ship tied up at the quay, painted cleanly in pale blue and white. Her name, the *Serquian*, was visible on the prow. A long thin stream of pale smoke was rising from her single funnel and drifting away across the harbour.

I paid off the taxi driver then approached the Shelterate building, knowing that I would not be allowed to board until I had gone through their system one more time. I paid a few coins for a wheeled metal trolley from a rack set along the dockside, and loaded it with my luggage. Other intending passengers were also there.

As I stacked my luggage I was aware I was being watched – the group of casually dressed young people lounged around under their canopy, watching me, watching the other people as we made our slow way towards the building.

One of them, I noticed with surprise, was the young woman who had approached me when I landed on Ristor, who had tried to sell me a new stave. Gone were the thick clothes – in the heat of Muriseay she was wearing a pair of denim shorts and a white T-shirt. The knife dangled on a silver chain attached to her wrist. As soon as I saw her I gave a smile of recognition, but she looked away quickly.

The young man seated on the bench next to her must have seen this, because he stood up at once, as if to approach me. He was tall and painfully thin, with lank hair, dark over his eyes. He was wearing jeans and a dirty open-fronted shirt. With one of those knives dangling from his belt on a long silver chain.

I pushed my trolley in through the entrance. There were other passengers waiting for their papers to be checked, but with three officials on duty I did not have long to wait. I was soon called forward.

'Papers – where are you heading?'

The official this time was a woman. I pulled my plastic wallet out of my holdall, opened it and laid it on the counter in front of her. Lying on the top was the itinerary the travel agency had printed for me.

'I'm on an open tour ticket,' I said, trying to explain, not wanting to wait while she slowly read the whole thing. 'The first port of call is the island of Quy.'

'Let me have your stave, Msr Sussken.'

I handed it over. While she held it in her hand, running her fingers lightly across the wooden blade, she leaned forward to read my planned route. Then she lifted some of the pages, riffling through them .

'Visa?' she said. 'Let me see your visa.'

'I don't have one. I thought—'

'You can't go anywhere without a visa.'

'I'm travelling between islands,' I said. 'I'm not leaving the Archipelago.'

'You're departing from Muriseay. You need an exit visa.'

I felt a familiar dread in me: the almost inevitable feeling of insurmountable problems whenever I travelled. I imagined having to go back into the town somehow, walking or hiring another taxi, weighed down by my heavy luggage, finding whichever government office it was that issued visas, waiting around while someone completed the paperwork ... while my ship, my single cabin, my included 'entertainments', sailed away to Quy without me. Why hadn't the woman at the travel agency told me about this?

'This has nearly expired,' the official said, meaning the stave. 'Want me to check it for you?'

'I thought it was still good,' I said.

'Depends when it was last checked.'

She turned around, prodded the stave down into the scanner. The light glowed green, but this time when the stave popped back up she pressed it down a second time and punched something into a number pad. Another light glowed, this time a bright yellow. She came back to me.

'You had ninety days on the chip, but you've used almost all of them. Only two hours left. I can top it up for you.'

'Is there a charge?' I said, expecting there was.

'Not for that.'

How could I have used up ninety days? I assumed most of those were on the first tour? How many since I had left Questiur? I was trying to remember how long, trying to calculate, wondering if the lost, or gained, time counted. The woman official returned to the scanner, pressed more keys, then gave me back my stave.

'OK – that's fully recharged now. It's also blank at the moment. You shouldn't risk any more travel until the gradual has been marked.'

'What do you mean?'

'Talk to one of the adepts. There's a gradual increment showing and you'll need to adjust that. And don't forget to keep the stave topped up if you're moving around the islands without a visa.'

'Adepts?' I said.

'Outside.'

'So, do I need an exit—?'

'Next!' She had already closed my large plastic wallet and pushed it back to me. Another passenger was wheeling his baggage trolley across, holding up several sheets of printed papers.

I stumbled out into the glare of hot sunshine, trying to push my trolley and return the wallet to the holdall in one move. The exit led me directly towards the canopied area. The tall young man

I had noticed earlier was standing before me. He was holding out his hand. When I was close to him I realized that his youth was something of an illusion: close up he looked fairly fit, in a stringy way, but his face was wrinkled and cracked by years in the sun, and the mop of untidy dark hair only partly concealed an area of pattern baldness on the crown of his head. His eyes were glistening in the sunlight, straining against brightness.

'Alesandro Sussken,' he said, but his voice was deeply accented and it took me a moment or two to realize he had said my name. It sounded like *Zoozkint*. 'Let me have your stave.'

'Are you an ... adept?'

'Let me look at your stave. You should not travel any further without it.'

'I don't understand.'

'Ristor, Callock, Gannten, Derril, Unner, Olldus, Leyah, Cheoner. This is Muriseay, next will be Quy. I have followed your route. You must let me have your stave, Alesandro Sussken. Quy is to the east of here. Great danger awaits.'

'I'm booked on the *Serquian*.' I waved a hand in the direction of the large ship still waiting at the quay. 'What do you mean by danger?'

'Eastward travel always a hazard. Steep gradual.'

'I thought I was travelling to the south.'

'East and south.'

He still had his hand extended so at last I passed the stave to him. At that moment the ship's siren sounded a deep and extended blast, a signal I had grown used to on earlier voyages. It normally indicated that the ship would be sailing within the next quarter hour.

'That's my ship,' I said. 'I can't afford to miss it. I have this itinerary—'

'You can't afford to be on it, Msr Sussken. Let me take scrutiny.'

He began examining the stave – the familiar movement of lightly balancing the object between thumb and forefinger, the gentle touch of fingertips running along the wooden blade, while he closely regarded it. He took a long time, and I soon began to grow impatient. I could see other passengers in the distance, boarding the *Serquian*.

'You have been gambling with time, Msr Sussken. Are you aware of the steep tide between here and Ristor? I can trace you no further back than that. You have accumulated seventeen days. Detriment.'

'The woman in the Shelterate office said there was an increment.'

'Detriment. Seventeen days.'

'Do you mean I have lost seventeen days?'

'Gained.' He waved the stave in front of my face. 'You have travelled without score. Maybe that is how you choose? Detriment is risky.'

I said nothing, feeling a renewed sense of confusion, alarm and anxiety about being able to board my ship in time.

He held the stave in his left hand, then reached down and behind him and pulled up the knife that dangled from his waistband. He flipped off a leather cover that was protecting the blade and the sun briefly glinted from bright metal. He raised it and brought the blade to the side of the stave, squinting intently at what he was doing. Now that the knife was close to me I could see that it was not really a knife at all, but a bladed tool like a chisel, but with a vee-shaped pointed edge. The man turned the stave in his hand, and etched a tiny line in a short spiral close to the tip.

'Now – this is Ristor. One of my friends saw you there. You showed no interest. But on Ristor – this is what you should have. OK – that is about, I don't know, maybe twenty minutes.'

'Twenty minutes of what?' I said.

'Time corrected. Not much gradual tide between wherever on the mainland, and Ristor. Now – my friend Renettia. You saw her.'

I glanced behind him, thinking that the woman would still be there, but she had moved away.

'She was trying to sell me a stave.'

'You walked past her on Callock. No sale there. New gradual.'

Again he scraped lightly with the sharpened tip. This was a longer, looser spiral, further away from the end of the stave.

'So that corrects how much of the detriment?' I said, starting to glimpse what he might be doing.

'This is increment. Callock is south but to west of Ristor, so time lost, not gained as detriment. Very complicated. Now you are still behind, but not for so long.' He showed me how the spiral he had etched went in the opposite direction from the short one for Ristor. 'OK, so after Callock it was Gannten. Beautiful painters, I think. Dryd Bathurst, you know, famous artist? You are artistic man too. You did not stay, but passed through. It was night, you did not look. You were thinking of getting to your cabin, I am certain. You passed me as always, but I understand, I understand.'

'Gannten is to the east?'

'To the east. A great deal, but not far by ship.'

He etched another line along the stave's wooden blade. This was not a spiral but was straight, with intermittent gaps.

So it went, each of the islands I had visited or transited on my journey to Muriseay was marked with an etched line on the stave. He carved the marks with intricate care, checking his work by eye and with his fingertips, brushing away the tiny splinters of the wood carved out by the knife. Muriseay itself received a deeply gouged line. He wiped down the stave with a rag, which he pulled from his pocket.

'OK, now detriment is shown.'

I glanced past him towards where the ship was still against the quay. There was some activity around it and I noticed that the plume of smoke issuing from the funnel was much thicker. 'May I go now?'

'First you must record the detriment.'

This involved a thankfully brief return visit to the Shelterate counter. One of the officials took my stave, pressed it into the scanner, waited for the green light to shine and then handed it back to me. As I walked back outside I glanced at the wooden blade. The etched lines were still in place – I had half expected that the scan would remove them somehow.

The man was waiting for me outside.

'Now we remove the detriment,' he said.

'Haven't we already done that?' One of the gangplanks had been rolled back from the side of the ship, although I could see two crew members in white uniforms standing by the ship's hatch of the other one – passengers were still climbing slowly aboard.

'We have displayed the detriment, it has been recorded. Now we remove it.'

'I have to board,' I said. 'They will be closing in a few moments. I don't want to miss my ship.'

'You have already missed it, I tell you. Not as you think. As I think. It is not safe for you to travel with detriment.'

'I thought we had dealt with that.'

'No – we must remove it. Your ship will wait for you. No worry. Give me fifty thaler.'

I stared at him in amazement. 'You want money?'

'Of course. That is charge for removing the detriment.'

'Then I'll live with it.'

'So – you want to repeat what happened before? When you returned home with an unremoved detriment? One year eleven months?'

'You know about that?'

'It is on your stave. Fifty thaler.'

It was a large sum of money, almost as much as I was carrying in the Muriseayan currency. It was most of what was left after I had paid the travel agent.

'You say it will put everything right?'

'Not everything. What's done is done. But from the day when you arrived on Ristor – no more detriment.'

'Would you do it for thirty?'

'No discount. Fifty thaler is the price.'

He stood blandly before me, his eyes moist in the heat and sunlight. Why was he not wearing dark glasses, like some of the others there with him? Preparing for the voyage I had changed most of my cash into simoleons, as the travel agent had advised, but I had kept a small wad of thalers. In case of emergencies.

'Will you take simoleons?'

'Thaler.'

I handed the money over. I counted out the banknotes into his hand then he elaborately checked them, licking his thumb and forefinger. He folded and slipped the notes into the pocket of his filthy shirt. As if a signal had been sent by the closing of this transaction, the ship emitted two short blasts on its siren. I gripped the handle of my luggage trolley.

'Follow me. Leave the trolley. Carry all bags yourself, or risk losing them. And keep this in one of your hands all the time.'

He thrust the stave at me.

41

The man turned away from me and set off across the quay, away from the ship. He walked with his head down and his shoulders hunched. His gait was stiff. The etching tool swung at his side. I removed my luggage from the trolley, hefted my violin case across my back, then piled the holdall on my shoulders on top of it. It was uncomfortable, but it left both my hands free. I held one of the cases in one hand and used the other hand to carry the stave, clutched with the lighter of the two cases. By the time I had everything the man had reached the far side of the quay and was about to move out of sight around the corner of a building. I hurried after him with ungainly steps, the two cases banging against my knees. The sun's radiant glare was deadly on the unshaded parts of the concrete apron. Warm air drifted listlessly under the cranes and winches that littered the place. It smelled of hot oil, rusty metal, rotted food, the salty sea.

I followed him from the commercial section of the harbour and soon we came to a rundown area littered with grounded old boats long beyond seaworthiness, a tangled mess of torn fishing nets, many large pieces of rusty and unidentifiable equipment and a huge number of lobster pots shrouded in the remains of ancient seaweed. Here a small boat with an outboard motor was waiting at the bottom of some uneven stone steps leading down from the quay. The man had barely waited for me. As I was clambering awkwardly and unsafely down the disintegrating steps he was already pulling on the starter cord. I had to lean out from the lowest steps, swinging my stuff on to the boards. Trying not to lose my grip on the stave made everything twice as difficult. The boat was actually moving as I leapt aboard. I sat down heavily on one of the thwarts.

He speeded up and we steered out into the main area of the port: for the first time I gained some idea of the immensity of the facility. I could see ships, masts, cranes, chimneys, flyovers, warehouses stretching away from us into the distance. We headed past the harbour arm, the small jetty that enclosed the area we had been in. I was glad to be sitting down and not trying to manage my heavy bags but as soon as we were beyond the protection of the jetty the estuary was packed with ships, large and small, many of them under way. The water was rough here and the little boat threw spray high around us. The man steered the boat skilfully, eventually turning dramatically in front of the churning bow wave of a huge trawler. Now we were heading across the wide river mouth towards the further shore.

The water was just as choppy but I was glad of the cooling effect of the spray.

We closed with the opposite shore, which was undeveloped scrubland. The man turned off the outboard motor before we beached and the boat started drifting with the current. He stood up and stepped past me to stand in the prow, looking from side to side, shading his eyes against the sun. He appeared to be searching for somewhere on the shore, but when I asked him he snapped at me to be quiet. We drifted along, roughly parallel to the shore. This went on for several minutes. I had become resigned to the fact that I had missed my ship, so I sat quietly, waiting for something else to occur.

Finally, the man stepped back across the thwart where I was sitting and restarted the engine. He drove the boat ashore.

I managed to get my heavy luggage off without his help. He was already walking away from me. I knew then that I had had enough of this treatment. Annoyed, I dropped my bags on the ground and dashed after him.

'What's going on?' I shouted at him, tugging at his arm and swinging him around. 'Why are you doing this?'

He looked at me mildly. I saw there were traces of salt spray on his face and hair. His eyes were narrowed.

'Be quiet, Msr Sussken.'

'Why?'

'I am removing the detriment you have created.'

'Is this what I paid you for?'

'Fifty thaler.'

'This is hell. I can barely walk with all my baggage. I'm hot, tired, you've made me miss my sailing. Why are we out here?'

'The luggage you are carrying is yours. Maybe you travel lighter now? The gradual is being compensated. We have tides to cross, tides to cancel. Your ship will wait. You should have used the adepts before.'

'No one told me what to do.'

'Not my fault.'

'I don't see how this helps.'

'OK.'

'You said you could fix the problem.'

'Fix is what we do.' He glanced back towards where the boat had beached. My bags and violin case were in a heap on the ground next to where the prow had rammed into the sandy bank. I still held the stave in my hand. 'You are about to lose your stuff,' he continued. 'Your choice. Leave it if you never wish to see it again. Now I have to walk back to the bags with you. It is against the gradual we crossed. I charge extra for reversals. Normally.'

We went back towards the boat, the man a step or two ahead of me. He led me by an indirect route, crossing a sandy spur where prickly bushes snagged at my legs. I loaded myself up again, with bad grace. The cooling effect of the river air and the spray had already worn off and grit had penetrated my thin shoes. When I was holding everything the man set off once more.

I called after him, 'Won't you even tell me your name?'

'Why you need to know?'

'I don't know what to call you. How to address you.'

'I am adept. Keep up with me.'

Adept. I followed the adept up the long and sloping bank, having trouble getting a grip on the sandy soil. A long walk across untamed scrubland ensued, with the weight and unwieldiness of my luggage a constant and worsening problem. Low, tough plants spread stiff tendrils across the ground, making every step difficult. My whole body was aching and sweat was running down and across my face. It plastered my long robe against my back and legs. I tried several times to redistribute the load but all that I achieved was to transfer the heavier weight from one side to the other. The adept was always ahead of me but whenever I had to shift my load he did at least stand and wait. He never offered to assist.

Finally, after what felt like an hour of painful scrambling across the uneven ground we reached a darkly metalled road where traffic was moving by at speed. To my relief the adept waved down a car and after a long discussion in island patois the driver agreed to take us back into the harbour in Muriseay City, on the far side of the estuary. I saw a couple of banknotes passed across to him. They came from the adept's shirt pocket, the money I had paid him.

With my bags loaded in the trunk of the car I sat holding my stave as we rushed along. The fierce draught from the car's open windows was welcome, but the air was hot.

The car took us by an indirect route to the harbour – the adept dictated every turn and, once, a reversal. The driver finally took the car beneath the huge legs of the mobile cranes towards a wharf where a ship was berthed. She was painted cleanly in pale blue and white. She was the *Serquian*, still at the same berth. A long thin stream of pale smoke was issuing from her single funnel and drifting away across the harbour.

The adept and the driver climbed out, but I remained seated in the back. I was still clutching my stave. I was feeling despairing and exhausted. I watched as the two men spoke to each other outside the car but then without warning the adept walked away. I saw him take out the rest of the money I had given him – he fingered it, then transferred it to a pocket in the seat of his pants. After a few moments he had passed beyond the line of cranes and I could no longer see him.

The car driver opened the seat beside me, jerking his thumb to indicate I should leave. As I did so the *Serquian*'s siren blew a single long blast. I gathered up my stuff as quickly as possible, then went to thank the driver. He had been waiting only for me to take my property out of the car. He drove away without acknowledging me.

The trolley I was using before was still more or less where I had left it, so I loaded it up. The young people I now knew to be the other adepts were sitting casually on their bench beneath the canopy, watching me incuriously. The adept, my adept, was not there with them.

I was concerned only with getting on the ship before she sailed – I could see that other passengers were still boarding ahead of me.

I hurried into the Shelterate building but the long counters where baggage was opened and searched were not staffed. I made a noise with my bags, clunking them down on the counter. I had to continue waiting, anxiously glancing through the window towards the ship, but eventually an official appeared. It was the same woman I had spoken to before. She walked in casually, unsurprised to see me.

'Let me see your papers – where are you heading?'

I laid my itinerary open on the counter. 'I have a reservation on the *Serquian*,' I said, and passed over my stave. 'You'll find this is up to date now.'

'Did you say the *Serquian*? She sailed more than two hours ago.' She looked down at my itinerary where I had laid it, then turned to consult a printed timetable pinned to the wall behind the counter. 'If you are trying to get to Quy, the next service will leave here tomorrow morning. Around midday. Not from this part of the harbour, though. You will need a new ticket and your stave must be made ready.'

Again, briefly, I suffered the familiar panicky feeling of broken travel plans. But through the window beyond the woman I could see the pale blue and white hull of the *Serquian*. One of the gangplanks was still in place. The official looked through my documents with agonizing slowness but finally she impressed a rubber stamp on several of the pages and passed everything back to me.

'My stave?' I said. It had been lying on the counter next to her hand.

She picked it up without much interest, but turned it in her fingers, briefly sensing the etched lines. She turned to the scanning machine, thrust the stave inside, pressed a button and in a moment it popped back out again. For the first time during this unexplained procedure there was the sound of something being printed, then the scanner ejected a sheet of paper. The official took it without looking at it, and handed it to me with the stave.

'This is valid until you disembark at Quy,' she said. Then, inexplicably, she added, 'The *Serquian* will be sailing in ten minutes. It is at the quay next to this office.'

I quickly removed my luggage from the counter and parked the trolley in the allocated bay at the side. I staggered out clumsily into the hot sunshine. I was aboard the *Serquian* with several minutes to spare, long enough indeed for me to be settled in my own cabin, and standing contentedly in the shower cubicle under a cooling spray.

I heard and felt the engines powering up. The ship began to slide away from the quay.

42

I was so relieved to be out of the relentless heat of the Muriseayan dock area that I remained inside the luxury of my air-conditioned cabin. I had planned to be there for a few hours until the ship was well under way but in fact I stayed put in the cabin for the rest of the day. I knew the crossing to Quy would take more than three days, so I was in no hurry to explore the ship. The stresses of the day had taken away my appetite. I found chilled bottles of drinking water in the cabin, and a few complimentary pieces of fruit laid out for me to find, and they were all I needed.

After my shower I stayed naked, slowly unpacking and making sure that everything of mine had made it to the ship without loss or damage.

I checked my violin first, because although it was superbly well protected in its reinforced case it was the most valuable thing I owned. More than that it was the only instrument I had brought with me. The idea of having to travel day and night without being able to play was unthinkable. All was well but

I should have to tune it, of course. I had opened neither of my suitcases since checking out of the hotel in Muriseay City, and even after the rough treatment of the day everything was undisturbed inside. I removed a change of underclothes, another long robe, my toothbrush and other bathroom things.

I went to the mirror and checked to see how my new beard was coming along. I was pleased with what I saw. Even in spite of wearing my hat all day, my face had suffered sunburn while I was lugging my property around behind that annoying adept, but other than the slight redness I thought the flesh of my face looked better, firmer, more angled than it had for years. Although my arms and back were stiff I felt good – it seemed to me I was developing a little muscle tone.

I tuned my violin and began to practise, but I laid it aside after not very long, feeling disappointed. Maybe it was the acoustic of the small cabin, or the movement of the ship, or simply an after-effect of the tiring day, but nothing I tried sounded right. I was still disoriented by events. So many pieces of my life were in disarray, and as yet I had not really come to terms with any of them: my risky fleeing from the military junta with all that money, my worries about Jacj, my loss of Alynna, the Ante business, and now to make things even more complex, the adepts.

Not to be able to play well, even well enough for myself, was an unexpected blow in an evening, alone and cool and comfortable after a rough day.

It was a reminder of my earlier expectations about the stimulation of being in the islands. Standing on a boat deck and staring at scenery was not what I had had in mind, however tempting it was, however much I loved to look. I craved a little stability, the opportunity to hear myself play, to write some new music.

The next morning, after a long and deep sleep, undisturbed by the many sounds I now half expected on board a ship, I showered and dressed and walked the length of the main deck to the saloon. I was hungry at last. I wanted breakfast and coffee, then I planned a few hours alone on the promenade deck, succumbing again to the scenery. I remembered what I had resolved the night before, but I needed to sate my appetite for this beautiful and complex new world I had chosen.

Islands were all about me, irresistibly. Simply to turn towards one of them, any one of them, was to receive a stunning sense of that reality, that island. I crossed from one part of the deck to another, hands on the rail, leaning out over the white water thrown aside by the bow of the ship, seeking a new island, the next one, whichever it was. I soaked up mysterious feelings from each one, a thrilling inspiration. Tides flowed to and fro. Heat rose from the wooden planking of the decks, while a fresh breeze tended to moderate the ferocity of the sun, soothingly penetrating my thin clothing. Seabirds called around the stern of the ship. Passing ferries played their sirens. Light glinted from the waves. Around me, close and distant: cliffs and green hills and high mountains and shipping buoys and pretty shoreline villages. White surf broke over rocks and reefs. All seemed well.

43

On the third day out from Muriseay I left my cabin early in the morning. This was always the best time of day to be travelling at these latitudes. Within not many more minutes the sun would be blazing down, but for now it was still fairly low above the eastern horizon and a brisk crosswind was making the ship roll. The boat yawed and dipped as it cut through the white-crested waves. I was walking around the upper deck for a few moments before returning to my cabin. I wanted to make this a working trip and my head was spinning with ideas for a new composition. There were still several hours before disembarkation and I was planning to spend them usefully in my cabin.

I was pausing by the rail to think for a moment when a woman appeared beside me. I had not heard her approaching. She touched me lightly on my arm. She had a mane of strikingly grey hair billowing around her face.

'Msr Sussken?' she said. 'My name is Renettia. I assist you when the ship arrives in Quy.'

I recognized her then: she was the young woman who had

spoken to me at Ristor. I knew there would have to be another contact to make with an adept, but I had not expected to be approached while we were still en route.

'Renettia?'

'I will see you through the next stage of your journey. When we arrive in Quy, and afterwards, for your next departure. May I see your stave?'

'I don't have it with me – it's in my cabin.'

'You should always hold it.'

'Not now. It isn't convenient.'

'I need it. I also require payment. You are heading east. Please pay now.'

'Couldn't we talk about this some other time?' I said, starting to bridle. 'I have work I must do.'

'Forty thaler.'

'Please let us discuss money later.'

Renettia was standing directly in front of me, blocking my way. We were on the narrow part of the deck, between the high superstructure and the rail. The dazzling sea swept along below us. The ship rolled as another blustering crosswind hit us. I could have walked past her with a little effort, but she was determined to halt me. I heard other passengers approaching from behind, but whoever they were turned aside and went into one of the companionways inside.

'Forty thaler.'

'I only have simoleons. You'll have to be satisfied with those. What is the equivalent?'

'Thaler. Every ship has a currency bureau.'

I gave way. She followed me down to the purser's office at the aft of the ship. It had just opened. I waited in a short line behind other passengers, then expensively changed nearly all my simoleons into thalers. Suspecting I was going to need more of them I bought several extra thalers, drawing on the gulden in my mainland bank account. The disadvantageous exchange rate was irritating, although I could well afford it. Many years of past financial nervousness still made me reluctant to spend money.

I returned to my cabin, collected my stave, paid the woman. After she left I sat and tried to work, but I was annoyed with her and inspiration did not come easily.

I took a break near midday and went up to the boat deck. She found me there. She handed back my stave.

'Nothing to be done,' she said.

'Then why did you ask for money?'

'Nothing done now. We still to reach Quy. Pheelp has prepared you well.'

'Pheelp? Was that the guy in Muriseay? He wouldn't tell me his name.'

'Pheelp never says name to clients. He has removed your detriment. It was complicated.' She pointed to the filigree of etched lines that ran along the blade of my stave. 'Few of us could have achieved that so brilliantly.'

'I paid him well.'

'You travel east,' she said. She smiled briefly, put her hand above her eyes to shade them, took in the view, then walked away from me. For a moment I wondered if I was supposed to follow her, but she went along beside the rail without looking back, and entered the main part of the ship.

I do not know what happened to her after that. She would have been somewhere in the ship, because there were no other ports of call before Quy. When did she eat? There was only one small saloon for the passengers, most of whom I could already recognize by sight. She must have a cabin somewhere. I did not see her again until the end of the day, when the *Serquian* finally docked in Quy.

Quy turned out to be a steeply mountainous island with only one navigable harbour a short distance inland from the mouth of a narrow river. We arrived at the end of the afternoon, the shadows deepening. The ship crept slowly between high, wooded banks, unseen insects stridulating noisily in the sweltering air.

The adept woman, Renettia, appeared at my side but did not speak. The ship was being navigated carefully as we approached the narrow harbour. Renettia stood with her face raised towards the sky, closing her eyes against the brilliance of the lowering sun, her arms spread wide to support herself against the ship's rail. I said nothing, still wary of the weird behaviour of these adepts and feeling again a mild resentment about the way they intruded on me. I waited while the ship manoeuvred so that its stern was towards the quay. As the engines reversed with a violent white agitation of spume spreading back alongside the hull, the ship moved gradually astern to the berth. Finally the vessel came to a grinding halt and dockworkers on the shore secured it with hawsers slung across to the quay by the crew. Throughout this the woman barely moved and did not speak to me at all.

But then, suddenly, she did.

'You have been here before,' she said. 'To Quy.'

'I have not,' I said, certain of that at least.

'You forget. On your earlier voyage.'

'You know about that?'

'It is recorded.'

'We were nowhere near this island,' I said. I remembered nothing about Quy. Even seeing the spectacular scenery around the little port struck no reminders.

She frowned disagreeably and it crossed my mind to wonder if her adeptness for this work, the gaining of time, the removing of the detriment, whichever it might be, was as competent as that of Pheelp. She herself had praised Pheelp's skilled work. What made her think I had been to this island before?

'I need to examine your stave.'

'It's packed again, in my cabin,' I said. 'You have seen it already.'

'I'll wait here while you collect it.'

I was not planning to stay long on Quy, but I had an expensive overnight hotel room booked in the town. I was looking forward to exploring the place on my own, perhaps finding a local restaurant or bar. I liked the shipboard life but I did sleep better on land.

'Tomorrow,' I said. 'At the Shelterate building, before I set sail again.'

'No.'

Renettia insisted that she must urgently see the stave again, so with some bad grace I went below to collect it. When I was back on deck she looked closely at it, fingering the tiny lines carved into its smooth surface.

'Some islands have similar coordinates,' she said. 'This is perhaps why I thought you had been to Quy before. Manlayl is in gradual terms congruent with Quy. Manlayl is an island I know you have visited. Maybe I am wrong about Quy. Pheelp also made the same mistake. A problem for us.'

I had been to Manlayl – it was an early port of call during the first tour. But while I was below decks collecting the stave I had remembered that Quy was one of the islands I had given as a post restante address to Alynna. Whether or not I had any actual recollections of the place, I realized I must in fact have been here before, if only briefly.

'What do you mean by congruent?'

'The same size, the same shape.'

'That seems unlikely.'

'You have been everywhere in the Archipelago? Many islands are congruent. Is a big problem for us.'

'That could be solved if there were a few maps.'

'Not the same physically. Unlikely, yes!' She laughed, but I felt it was directed at my misunderstanding. 'Congruent is the size and shape of the gradual tide. Every island has gradual profile. Quy and Manlayl are congruent with more than two hundred other islands.'

'And you say Pheelp made the same mistake?'

'Yes.'

'So, he was not as skilled as you thought.'

'When we interpret the gradual tides that flow between the islands it is an art we perform, not a science we practise. We make honest mistakes. For us, a mistake is a learning skill. In this case it is easily corrected, made not to matter. It requires a short boat trip to one of the small islets. You and me.'

'I was planning a quiet evening in the town,' I said. 'A boat trip would take too long. I am only here on Quy for one night.'

She seemed unconcerned.

'What you do is what you do. You have paid me.' She passed the stave back to me. 'It is your decision.'

Her shrug was the sort that said the decision was mine, but also responsibility for the consequences of it.

'What does that mean?' I said.

'You have accrued another gradual detriment. It may only be removed while you are here.'

'How much is it? A loss of a few minutes?'

'A few hours. They seem nothing to you. Perhaps they are. Time does not matter as it elapses. But those few hours are permanent – we can remove them here. They create bias. They always increase future detriments, out of all proportion.'

'So you don't agree with my decision?' I said.

'It is no problem if you wish to carry a detriment forever. For me no problem.'

'Then we will do it your way.'

'I am pleased.'

When I disembarked half an hour later, struggling again with my luggage, there was no sign of Renettia. I followed the group of other passengers to the quay and to the Shelterate & Havenic building. We waited in the hot evening air as we moved slowly forward in turn to have our papers checked. The cicadas were gradually quieting as sunset proceeded. Darkness was falling quickly. I saw the familiar group of adepts sitting on the canopied bench beside the entrance to the building, waiting for business. They were all young, or young-looking, and all were lightly dressed. They were taking little notice of the passengers – in fact, most of them were sitting with their backs turned against us. Two of them had the triangular knife dangling by a silver chain from their belts. Another had the same instrument poking casually out of a back pocket. Renettia was not with them. I did not stare, did not want any of them to notice me or pick me out because they had caught me looking at them.

Pheelp was there. I could not see his face, but I was certain it was him. I recognized his narrow, rounded shoulders, the straggle of hair and the balding patches, the filthy shirt. I had seen him from the back for most of the time I was with him. As I moved slowly forward he contrived to keep his face turned away, almost as if avoiding me.

Did this mean he too had travelled on the *Serquian* from Muriseay?

Inside the Shelterate hall my papers were checked only briefly and when I produced my stave the official gestured it away. I noticed that none of the other passengers around me were carrying staves, so I returned mine to my holdall.

There was a luggage storage area in a room set aside from the main hall. Because I had transferred to my backpack the few things I would need for an overnight stay, I bought a key token and placed everything else inside one of the lockers.

Renettia was waiting for me outside the Shelterate hall.

'We sail to the little island now. I have arranged a boat.'

'I'd like to go to my hotel first, and check in.'

Again I saw the displeased look on her face. 'Give me your stave. We go now.'

'I want to register at the hotel, and make sure my room is as I reserved it. I won't be more than a few minutes.'

But seeing the expression on her face I slipped the stave out of my pack and passed it meekly to her.

'Hotel not option. Check your wristwatch now!'

She turned away from me and set off up the sloping ramp of the quayside. She was holding my stave aloft, like a trophy, or a beacon I should follow.

Feeling stubborn I stayed where I was, pretending to check my watch. After a few more steps she turned back. 'You following me. Bring all your luggage.'

'I've put it in the lock-up, and I'll pick it up before I sail tomorrow.'

'You never want to see it again?'

I argued feebly but there was no resisting her.

44

I retrieved my bags from the lock-up. Manhandling them as awkwardly and reluctantly as before, I followed her up the concrete slope, away from the harbour and through the cluttered wharves, and after them the narrow streets of the port area. At one point we walked past the hotel where I had reserved a room, but I was learning that while I was with an adept I went where I was told.

Renettia always walked a short distance in front of me, not appearing to calculate or measure in any way. She held her head forward so that she could stare at the ground. Sometimes she appeared to be counting the number of buildings we were passing. She changed her mind several times, returning the way we had just walked. Once, for a short distance, she walked backwards and insisted I should copy her. She always made me follow her moves exactly. She took hold of the wooden blade of the stave several times, fingered it sensitively, stared around, deciding where to walk next. I had no choice but to accept all this, wait for her, follow her. My arms and back were aching.

I was learning something from the adepts at last, though. I was going to have to free myself of some of my luggage. In one of my suitcases, for example, I was carrying the two formal suits I had brought with me to wear – a last-minute thought that at some point I might be called upon to perform or appear in public. I knew now I would never need them. There was no point my hauling them around while I was sailing from one subtropical island to the next. If for any reason I needed formal clothes in the future, I could replace them.

Once started on this line of thinking I remembered the two pairs of patent leather shoes, a seemingly endless pile of socks, dress shirts, neckties – and warm clothes, ridiculous in this world I was now in, but the habits of a lifetime in a cold climate are hard to drop. Then there were the books I had brought and which were buried somewhere in my bags. And there were the many records – for which I had no playing equipment.

I was beginning to wish I had left everything in the lockers in the Shelterate hall, from which by some unexplained means they would allegedly disappear.

The sun had set soon after Renettia led me away from the harbour. We walked down darkened streets, where overhead lamps were intermittent and not bright. Finally we came to the river again. Steps led down to where several small boats were tied up. There were enough lamps on the jetty for us to see, but the river itself was dark. I was nervous of all this but Renettia walked to the far end of a narrow wooden mooring. A motor boat was there.

Looking around at the darkness, I said, 'Couldn't we do this better tomorrow, in daylight?'

Again I received the quick look of shedding responsibility, but this time she said, 'No.'

She climbed aboard ahead of me. It was a familiar moment. Did every accrual of detriment have to be removed by uncharted trips in small boats? I followed her on to the boat and dumped my bags in the passenger well at the back. It was a slightly larger vessel than the one in which Pheelp had taken me around: the engine was inboard, and there was a tiny cabin in the bow.

Renettia gave me the stave to hold, injuncted me never to let go of it, then started the motor. Soon we were out on the dark river, the town on one side and a thickly forested hill on the other. The calm water looked black and our engine was the only sound. We passed other boats moored on the river but they were indistinct shapes. I was nervous of a collision and I stared ahead across the cabin housing, on the alert for other vessels moving about in the gloom. I could not understand how Renettia could steer so confidently.

After a few minutes we emerged into the sea. Almost as if the steep banks had in fact been shading us from the sky, there was a sense of twilight here. We could see ahead. The boat rose and dipped in the gentle swell.

We were steering in the general direction of a tall rocky outcrop far out to sea, presumably one of the islets Renettia had mentioned. I tried to relax, sitting upright on the hard bench around the well of the boat, but leaning out over the side, still watchful for other boats.

Renettia changed direction again, swinging the wheel, and I happened to glance towards her as she did so. She was standing. I saw a glow of brilliant golden light fall on her face and hair, her eyes shining. I stood up beside her to look at the source, and saw to my amazement that the sun, which had set at least half an hour earlier, was now low over the western horizon. It was a steady orange colour, the calm globe of sunset, but far too bright to be stared at. I shaded my eyes with my hand, trying to be certain of what I was seeing, that it was in fact the sun, not some other source of light.

Renettia looked across at me but she said nothing.

We continued to sail across the calm water. Gusts of warm air swept over us. Even the sun seemed to be radiating renewed heat. When I looked again the sun had risen higher still. At first I could think only that I had somehow missed the night, that I had lost consciousness and was now seeing the dawn of the next day. But the sun was looming in the west, the direction from which I had sailed only an hour or two earlier. Then the daylight had been starting to fade.

It was not a sunrise. I was seeing a sunset in reverse.

'Where you going after you leave Quy?' Renettia's abrupt question surprised me, shaking me out of my confusion about what was seeming to happen.

'Do you mean which island?'

'Next island, town ... it doesn't matter.'

'I think it's Tumo,' I said. 'Is that likely?'

'You tell me.'

'I meant – is that close to here?'

'Could be. Don't you know?'

'I'm travelling with an itinerary. It's printed out in a folder, somewhere in one of these bags. I'm going from one island to the next – most of them are just names to me.'

'Same for me.'

'I thought you knew where we are.'

'I'm a gradual adept, not a tour guide.'

'To be honest I'm not sure what the difference is.'

She swung the wheel suddenly causing the boat to tip and rock. Still worrying about her skill as a sailor I strained to see what it was she had been avoiding, and saw a patch of troubled water dead ahead of where we had been going. The erratic shapes and brittle edges of rocks broke the surface as the swell moved across them. When we were past the danger she turned the wheel again and resumed our former course. I noticed she briefly reached over to touch the wooden surface of the stave.

'So after Tumo, where?'

'I can't remember every detail, every island. I'd have to look in my itinerary.'

'Where is it?'

'In one of these bags. Do you need to see it?'

'No – where are you going, at the end, finally, ultimately?'

'Temmil. Do you know it?'

'Choker of Air – what they call the place. You been there already?'

'On my last trip,' I said. Of course I knew the patois name, but it was not something that had immediate associations for me.

'Then you know the place stinks. Volcano fumes.'

'I never noticed that,' I said.

'Lucky. Must have been asleep then.'

'The fumes are only around the crater. I was taken up there – a tourist excursion. It smells of sulphur dioxide, unsurprisingly. But you can't smell it in the town. In fact, what I remember best is the scent of flowers.'

She frowned disbelievingly and turned away from me, staring ahead across the waves.

She was making me think of the day of that trip to the summit of the Gronner, then later, looking back across at Temmil from across the strait, on the beach of Hakerline, the island adjacent to it. It was then that my determination to move to Temmil, perhaps forever, had formed. From Hakerline I had seen the plume of grey from the mountain: ash or smoke, whatever it was, but I had never been aware of the smell in the town, and the plume was not normally visible from there. I had been in Temmil Waterside for a few days.

I briefly remembered the night I had spent with the concert pianist, Cea Weller. A twinge of familiar guilt rang through me. Guilt then because of being unfaithful to Alynna, guilt now because the feeling had never left me, even though I had rarely thought about Cea in the years since the tour finished.

There was a long silence from Renettia as the sky brightened and the waves seemed higher, but then she spoke.

'Your itinerary. You know without adepts, you miss every ferry, lose all your property. Time betrays the eastward traveller.'

'I'm aware of that,' I said. 'The last time I was here I was travelling west.'

'It's on your stave. No difference, east, west. You can go south too. Tonight you'll be safe in your hotel, tomorrow the ship will be there to take you across to the next place.'

'Will you be on the ship?'

'Might.'

The air temperature was rising noticeably, from afternoon warmth to midday swelter. I glanced up at the sun again – now it was high in the sky. Filmy white clouds in the stratosphere were skimming past at great speed, semi-transparent, filtering the light. They looked like they had been filmed with a time-lapse camera. There was only a light breeze at sea level and in the open well of the boat, where there was no shade, the radiant heat from the sun was oppressive. The hat was protecting my face and neck, but where my arms were bare I could feel the sun burning down. I was shifting position as the boat moved about in the waves, trying to keep my exposed skin in the shade.

We were now close to the tall outcrop of rocks, steering a wide circle around them. I stared down at the water, knowing how relatively shallow the sea was around any of the islands and anxious about what might be perilously present beneath the surface, but the waves made it too difficult to see anything.

We completed a circuit of the rocks, then, instead of heading back, Renettia took us for a second loop around. After this, I noticed that the sun had passed back through its noontime zenith, and was appearing to head on down towards the east, from where it normally rose. Renettia's silence was constant. Whenever I glanced at her she was sitting in the stern of the open boat, holding the wheel, staring intently ahead at where we were sailing. She was alert and upright, watching what she was doing.

After the second circuit we made a third, this time unnervingly close to the broken rocky wall, but after that she steered a more direct course back towards the mouth of the river. Behind us, waves were breaking on the sharp rocks where they jutted out of the sea, the swell itself appearing more marked, speedier in rising and falling than the height of the waves suggested. I was glad that as soon as we were clear of the islet she opened the throttle of the engine and the boat moved more quickly.

The sun remained high above, the glaring dazzle of mid-morning. There was no shade, no escape from the heat. I was glad not only of my loose robe but also for the breeze that swept against me. Around my feet, on the floor of the boat's well, lay my heavy luggage, almost a recriminating reminder of the chore of carrying it as soon as we landed. I was beginning to hate my own property.

Renettia steered the motorboat into the main harbour, where the ferry had berthed earlier, but no large ships were tied up. Trying to orientate myself I wanted to locate the *Serquian* on which I had arrived, but there was no sign of her. Could she have sailed already? Renettia helped me with my luggage up to the concrete quay, then returned to the stern of the little boat. She said something inaudible, so I asked her to repeat it.

'I said goodbye.'

'No – it was something else.'

Frowning, she said, 'Your earlier visit to Quy. I should have realized. You were here before. Before is the same as now. Sorry.'

'But I did come through Quy before. I have remembered.'

'Then is twice the same as now.'

She still had my stave, so she hurried up the steps and passed it back to me. 'You must go through the Shelterate office and register.'

'I've already done that.'

'No – you do it for the first time.' She pointed insistently at the stave.

'Are we complete?'

'Complete? I don't understand.'

'With what you do for me.'

'There is no detriment, no gain. This is the same day, and you have slightly over five and a half hours returned to you.'

Nothing we said to each other was understandable. We stared at each other in the scorching heat, a kind of silent impasse having been achieved. I felt the sun's rays, an intolerable, inescapable constant. They beat down on my back, they reflected up from the whitened concrete surface of the jetty.

Renettia returned to the boat, whose engine was still idling. She paid no more attention to me, concentrating on swinging the boat around, steering beneath the ropes that angled down towards two other boats close by. I was irritated with her, annoyed by everything to do with these adepts. I waited until she was away, making sure that there was not going to be some other weird or inexplicable ritual to perform. When she was on the far side of the water I loaded myself up with my bags and began to walk slowly and painfully along the jetty.

45

I must have trudged more slowly than I thought, because when I reached the Shelterate building I noticed that Renettia was already there, sitting with the other adepts under the shading canopy. She did not acknowledge me as I passed, and anyway I had nothing more to say to her. I did notice, though, that in the short time since I had seen her, not only had she left the boat somewhere, but she had managed somehow to change her clothes. She had been wearing a grubby yellow shirt and white pants when she was with me, but now she had on a long, gauzy smock dress.

I went into the building. There were two officers sitting idly behind their counter, with no other travellers in sight. One of the men stood up, putting on his cap, and I handed over my stave together with my travel and identity documents. I said something about the fact I had already had my papers checked earlier, but he did not react. Examination of the stave took no time at all – he placed it inside the slot and a printed sheet was immediately produced. He handed this across to me without looking at it. However, my arrival when no ship was scheduled to dock for several hours aroused his interest.

He and the other officer began going through my luggage, looking for whatever it was that concerned them. Knowing I was almost certainly carrying nothing controversial I let them get on with it. I meanwhile had a close look at the stave and saw that Renettia had inscribed several new lines along the shaft. One ran the whole length and was cut deeply. Others circled the shaft near the handle, while an extremely light spiral was etched about halfway along: it was exact and deliberate, circling the shaft four times, and at each end fading away into faintness.

'What work do you do, Msr Sussken?' one of the officials said. He was holding up one of my pads of manuscript paper, notation written all over it.

'I'm a musician and composer.'

'Is this your writing?'

'Yes. I'm a composer. That is what I do. I write music.'

He peered at it more closely.

'Do you intend to work while you are on Quy?' he said.

'No – I'm passing through, staying one night. I am leaving in the morning.' I pointed to the itinerary, where the agency had clipped the ticket for the next part of the journey, to Tumo, dated the next day. It was clear.

'So you are not here to work? You need a permit if you plan any kind of work, paid or unpaid. Serious offence otherwise.'

'I suppose you could say I'm on vacation,' I said.

The officer paused in what he was doing.

'You suppose what?' he said, looking me in the eye for the first time since I had walked in. 'Are you or are you not on vacation? Are you intending to do any more of whatever this is?' He pointed to my manuscript paper.

'No,' I said at once. 'I'm touring the islands.' I realized I was being taught a lesson. I had never before heard this warning about a work permit – was there the same rule throughout the Archipelago, or was it just on Quy?

He demanded to see the stave again, which I handed over. I watched as he scrutinized it closely. Then he asked me to open my violin case. Apparently never having seen an instrument at close quarters before he made me take it out, show him how I held it to play, then demanded to hear some notes. I told them I played it for my own pleasure, and gave him the first four bars of the allegro maestoso from my Violin Concerto in D major. The violin needed retuning, but I don't think the man noticed.

After all this I went slowly across the harbour to the quay where the *Serquian* had berthed earlier, because when I and the woman at the tourist agency on Muriseay planned the long journey to Temmil we used the published schedule of shipping times as a way of deciding the route. She had said, casually, that the announcements of the ships' arrival and departure times provided the best framework for planning. I had already noticed that the ferries rarely left or arrived late, and then not by much.

I was therefore disconcerted to discover that the *Serquian* was not at the berth where I had expected her to be. If she had already sailed then I wanted to know at what time. She was not my next ship for Tumo, but on an island where the sun rose in reverse sunset she was, to say the least, a symbol of the known. But *Serquian* was not there.

I went to the harbour office where there was a display board of arrivals and departures. The *Serquian* was shown prominently – in fact, her arrival appeared to be the most important of the day. She was known to be on time but was not expected to arrive until late afternoon. About an hour before sunset.

The date was unchanged.

I decided I should not be in the harbour area when the ship did dock – I did not want to see the passengers disembarking. Five and a half hours returned to me, Renettia had said. I looked at my wristwatch, which was showing the same time as the clock on the wall of the harbour office. Who would I see stepping down to the quayside from the *Serquian*?

I struggled one last time with my bulky luggage, then went slowly and painfully up to the centre of the town, looking for the hotel where I had reserved a room.

46

Shedding personal property has always been something I find difficult. My family owned so few material possessions in the years when I was growing up that in these financially easier times I was still careful with money, tried to keep and use possessions for as long as possible. But I knew now that most of what I was carrying around with me had become unwanted deadweight, an unavoidable penance. I was cursed with carrying my baggage through time.

Once I decided to rid myself of as much as I could it felt like a new start, a purging of the old me. It did not take long to choose what to keep: changes of underwear, my manuscript paper, my violin, the book I was currently reading, a few other things. They all fitted into the smaller of my two cases with room to spare.

The morning after I arrived on Quy I checked out of the hotel, first making use of the huge recycling centre at the back of the building staffed by a local charity – I realized it was probably likely that many of the hotel guests decided to get rid of things, and often for the same reason as I did.

Clad in one of my lightweight robes and my broad-brimmed hat I returned to the harbour.

During the night, cool and comfortable in the hotel room, I had found at last the mental space to think about what I wanted to do. Life on a ship had many constraints and distractions, and the mystical adepts, and to lesser extent the obtuse officials, maddened and annoyed me. In the calm of the night I had had a chance to reflect.

I realized that I was beginning to feel a slave to my travel schedule. When I left home I was full of fears. I had no real motive for this long journey, other than to make myself safe from the Generalissima. Solving the mystery of my brother, perhaps, and finding a new life on an island I had visited only once, and in doing so indulging in a final uncertainty: to try to meet the man who plagiarized me. A kind of desperation had gripped me.

I was used to a regulated life. Like it or not I had the Glaundian way of thinking, acting, preparing. Life in Glaund was controlled, contained, observed. There had to be a reason for everything we did and that reason had to be acceptable to the monitoring officials. My work as a musician was as close as possible to a free Glaund life, but even then I had been bound by the same restrictions as everyone else. I carried government stamped identification everywhere – the stamp was renewed every three months, causing a time-consuming visit to a government office. I always carried a minimum amount of cash, as I was required to, as everyone was required to. If I stayed away from home more than three nights at a time I had to register with the police. There were certain days of the year when the whole country was under curfew and I could not be outside my home after nightfall. I had to be assigned to a church, even though I was not religious. Like every man or woman under the age of fifty I was in theory capable of being drafted into the armed forces at any time, or into one of several mandatory occupations. I was a registered user of the internet, but access to it was strictly controlled and there were severe search limits. All emails were automatically copied to the government department responsible for overseeing communications. Social media, briefly introduced, had been comprehensively and effectively banned ever since. Freedom of expression was not permitted – members of the Glaundian public were not allowed to know what each other thought.

These were just some of the limitations on daily liberties; but there was a host of extra minor regulations applied to Glaundian life. I had grown up with them, I had forged my career within them, I had grown used to them. And, I was discovering, I had made a habit of them.

When we travel we take our expectations with us, our prejudices, our sense of normality. We see what we see through eyes trained by home.

Now, though, I was regulating myself and it was because of conditions I had never really known before. I felt constrained by time – the self-determined need to catch certain boats, confirm pre-booked hotels. But I was in the Archipelago – nothing was urgent, there were no pressures of time. No authorities knew where I was or where I was going. Even the Shelterate officials, with their banal enquiries, always seemed surprised to see me.

I knew I could follow my existing schedule across the Archipelago to the end of my planned voyage, taking the ships and staying at the hotels booked in advance. But I had also learned that the calm and shallow seas of the Archipelago were criss-crossed by hundreds of different ferries, and that there was no reason why I should not strike out on my own, make spontaneous decisions about whether to travel or not travel, stay longer on some islands, skip others. Finding places to stay whenever I landed was even less of a problem: there were dozens of inns, guest houses and hotels in every port I had visited. I was beginning to feel like an experienced Archipelagian traveller.

It had taken until now for me to realize this, to gain some idea of the freedoms I was enjoying, or at least was potentially able to enjoy.

Even so, a realization that change is possible does not lead to immediate change. In Quy's harbour I cautiously established that the next ship where I had a cabin reserved was expected to arrive within the next two hours, and that she would be reprovisioned and refuelled, ready to sail late that evening. She was the *Scintilla Queen*, destined for the university island of Tumo, with eight ports of call en route. I confirmed my booking, telling myself that I would decide later if I would stay with the ship all the way to Tumo. I felt in conflict with myself, that I was denying a genuine change in me, but I had a luxury cabin reserved for me, and the old habit-follower in me did not want to lose it.

Then I changed my mind. When I boarded the *Scintilla Queen* it turned out to be the last time I followed my original itinerary. I never went as far as Tumo. I changed ships and my plans at a small island called Sanater. For two days I explored the Sanaterian hills, villages and cliffs, striding around unencumbered by everything except overnight essentials. I had left what remained of my luggage in storage in Sanater Base. When I decided to continue my voyage I abandoned my eastward quest and impulsively headed north, seeking cooler weather. That was hopeless because I was in the equatorial zone, but I did find an island that briefly felt a little fresher. This was on Ilkla, a place of high, windswept moors, but Ilkla turned out to be a bleak place of subsistence farming where almost the entire population seemed to speak a heavily glottal patois. It was picturesque in a bare sort of way but it was also unwelcoming. Nothing about it inspired me. If music there was somewhere beneath that scrawny grass and those rocky escarpments, it was a dull, distant beat of a drum. I moved from Ilkla to a larger island called Meequa, further south, still subject to the same winds but because of a warm ocean current it was as hot as the islands in the zone I was briefly trying to leave.

I had cancelled my planned itinerary by this time, sometimes having to pay penalties for changing my mind. I did not care: I wanted at last to be free, at least in the sense I understood it then. After the next fifty-six days and more than twenty ships later, all of which I boarded on impulse, I was feeling completely at home in my new mode of casual and unhurried travel from one island to the next. I changed ships and destinations at will. I chose short crossings and long voyages, but primarily the shorter ones – I was still attracted by the novelty of a succession of small places. Some of the places I visited did not even appear on the shipping schedules of the main ferry companies, and could be reached only by small boat. One ferry was pulled by underwater chains, across a fierce tidal channel.

All these sea journeys ravished my eyes, and once again I started responding to the rhythm of a seaboard life, to the stimulus of discovering one new place after another. Each island called to me – my mind was overflowing with music. I found the discomforts of an onboard life only relative, even on the smaller boats and the ones with few facilities. When I sailed overnight I made sure I would have a cabin to myself, and then slept soundly and ate well, and during the long hours of the afternoons, when the ships' engines settled into a routine throbbing from deep below, and most of the other passengers went below-decks to avoid the glaring sunshine, I would find a shaded place and work happily in my notebook. Ideas for new music were coming constantly to me, sometimes in such profusion that I worried that I could not get them down quickly enough before they were lost or supplanted by others.

But the mystery of the adepts remained. I never understood why or how, but they appeared to be following me.

So long as I was aboard a ship and travelling between islands I rarely saw any of them. I knew or suspected, though, that they must be with me, also sailing on the same ships I was aboard but concealed somewhere. There was no other explanation for the fact that whenever I arrived at a port of call they were already there, able to get ashore before me, waiting for me, lined up or in a group by the entrance to the Shelterate halls. I never understood how they did that.

I usually saw the same faces: Pheelp and Renettia were invariably there at the Shelterate entrance but so too were many others. Most of them I came to know, by sight if not by name, because at every island disembarkation one or another of them would step forward and present me with a solution to my endless problem with the gradual tides of time. Money was invariably involved. There was some kind of hierarchy among them, about which of them would take the job. I never worked out how these choices were made, and anyway it seemed to make no difference.

Because my voyages and crossings were mostly short the

adjustments of the detriments were often minor, although not much less expensive. Many of the detriments that emerged during this part of my journey were a matter of seconds, cancelled by a short walk along a quayside, or a drive in a car, or a climbing of steps into the main town. Once, after the chain ferry, the adjustment was achieved by a shaking of hands. It cost me ten thalers, even so.

Some of the adepts worked with me more than once: for instance, I had a second short encounter with Pheelp, who took me for a brief walk around a couple of large buildings on the island of Sentier, then brusquely abandoned me in the middle of a street. Afterwards my wristwatch was again showing the right time and I was forty thalers poorer.

Renettia also worked with me again – she took me on a longer detour, a dull car ride in residential streets at the back of a port, a long walk by the sea, time regained, wristwatch inexplicably corrected, money spent.

The wooden shaft of my stave was looking well used. Every adept made new marks. Most of these lines were short, or ran alongside existing scores. Many of them crossed and re-crossed earlier ones – in places there were so many lines they created a hachure effect. One part of the stave, close to the handle, was deeply marked to the point that the wood was scored almost halfway through. I still believed there must be something buried inside the visible wood, something metallic or perhaps silicon, with the capability of recording or noting whatever it was that happened when the Shelterate officials scanned it, or downloaded some sort of information about me into their device. But even in this relatively exposed part of the blade there was no hint that the stave was made of anything other than the wood I could see.

As well as the adepts known to me there were of course more I often saw but never worked with, and so had no knowledge of them at all, certainly not their names. There were others I saw only once – these I assumed must live on whichever island I happened to be passing through at that time, but there were more of them who followed me, or seemed to, wherever I went.

They were always there, hanging around with the others by the Shelterate office of the island where I had just landed, sometimes regarding me furtively from behind a hand, or a skein of long hair which had fallen across their eyes, or, more often, staring away from me as if I did not matter. They all carried knives.

Gradually, the number of adepts around me was increasing. At first there had only ever been half a dozen of them, then the number swelled to about ten, but after my fifth day of spontaneously chosen voyages there were at least twenty of these people waiting for me every time I disembarked. The number went on increasing the further I travelled.

And the central mystery about them remained unsolved. I never saw how they moved from one island to the next.

They did not appear to board with me. Although in some cases I was able to watch the boarding ramps after I was aboard the ships, I did not see them following me up the gangplank. They were invisible to me while the ship was under way except on rare occasions, when for some reason the adept needed to speak to me before we berthed. Then he or she would materialize quietly beside me for as long as it took, before retreating quickly to the decks below. Then when I arrived at the port, there they would be: the waiting group outside the Shelterate building, lurking in the canopy's shade or standing in the bright sunshine. Sometimes, if it was a night arrival, they would be clustered in the glow of the harbour's floodlamps, letting their knives dangle suggestively on chains.

It was obvious to me that there was no way they could reach the islands at the same time as me unless they were on the same boat, but I never knew where they were. Did they hide somewhere deep in the bowels of each ship? In a separate section of the vessel, reserved for them? It would have to be away from the passenger cabins, or the open decks. But if such a hiding place existed I never found it.

On the larger steamers there were multiple decks and cargo areas, and I could not search them all. Anyway, I had other things I wished to do with my time.

Some of the boats I sailed on were so small, so simple in design, that it seemed impossible that anyone could be on board without being immediately noticed. This profoundly puzzled me.

Less mysterious, but in its own way intriguing, was the

fact that the adepts rarely worked alike. I recalled Renettia's remark that what they did was an art, not a technique. Each had developed his or her own ways and the practical imperfections always interested me. There was clearly some kind of calculation involved in what they did: they balanced what they knew or felt about the gradual against what they perceived from me. The stave was crucial somehow: was it a record of what they had done, or some means of holding true whatever they had determined was the detriment? And how was that discerned, as a matter of interest?

Some of the adepts did their work by mental exercise: they stared into space, or looked down at the ground or the deck or wherever we were standing. Most of them looked out to sea but a few did so only quickly, while others deliberately scanned the islands that could be seen, or gazed towards the horizon for several minutes. One young woman took me to a beach, then stood immobile on the sloping sand – she warned me to stay well back from her and for about an hour she waited while the rising tide lapped around her legs. From time to time she turned a full circle where she stood. The waves were about to reach her waist when she appeared to break out of her trance, waded back to dry land, then told me to follow her along the beach. Throughout all this I stood in the unshaded glare of the sun.

One of the male adepts used a battery-powered electronic calculator. Another carried a little pad of paper on which he scribbled inscrutable sums. One counted on his fingers. Most of them had a pen and paper in addition to the etching knife, and they would take notes as we walked or drove along. Some of adepts ignored me as they led me through the areas of time's tidal gradients – others were talkative, almost informative.

The first contact with them was always the same. One adept would detach from the group, approach me and request a sum of money. Mostly this happened outside the Shelterate building, but occasionally it was while I was still on the ship – once I was approached in mid-voyage, a few other times just as the ship was about to dock. The matter of the detriment was never in doubt, because it was a given problem in every encounter. Sometimes it represented time gained, but in most cases it was a true detriment, time that had been lost.

I believed what they told me.

If I ever doubted, a glance at my wristwatch was evidence enough. Although, oddly, the time difference on my watch was never the same as the detriment, and after the process was complete, my watch had invariably returned to the correct local time.

Every ship on which I sailed had chronometers which reported *Mutlaq Vaqt, Kema Vaqt* – absolute time, ship time.

47

My zigzagging course across the Archipelago was taking me in an overall westerly direction. Ahead, somewhere ahead, lay the island of Temmil, my final destination. I had plenty of time to think, and as I sat day after day on the boat decks, in my cabin, in the bars and saloons, I tried to focus on what I was really intending by this journey. The Generalissima and her junta gave me a reason to flee but once I reached the islands the need for flight was less urgent.

Setting aside my quotidian needs to sleep and eat, my increasingly enjoyable habit of lounging around in the shady corners of the decks, and my obscure but also preoccupying need to gain or lose time detriments, it could be summed up in one word, or one name: Ante. At the root of it all, finding And Ante and confronting him was still a motive for taking this journey.

But the constant presence of the islands, as I sailed slowly past, changed priorities. Ante was of less and less interest to me. I had hated the idea that he was profiting somehow from stealing my work, but what had I lost by his actions? What had ever been at risk? My reputation as a musician, such as it had become, was specialist but secure. His crude copies of my work had no perceptible impact on my standing, nor even on my earnings.

The more I saw of these beautiful, sun-wrapped islands the less important became the concerns of my former life. I reminded myself that Ante's plagiarism had happened a long time ago, and perhaps was even the consequence of a coincidence, or an accident of some kind. Maybe I should be lenient, try to understand how it had happened, rather than confront him?

It was a peaceful feeling, a familiar instinct, in accord with what had become my normal outlook. I loved the easy allure of the islands, drifting from one of them to the next, and I relished my lazy new existence of lounging around, drinking and eating as much or as little as I wished. I could all too easily imagine seeing out the rest of my days on the warm beaches and in the fragrant forests of this tropical paradise.

After several weeks at sea I knew that I was drawing inexorably close to the group of islands known as the Rullers – this was where Temmil was located. I even saw the Ruller Group sketched in faintly on a chart in the saloon of one of the ships, so I knew it could not be far away. The islands lay in what was described by some of the other passengers as a picturesque jumble in the horse latitudes, not far north of the Equator. There were said to be eighty-three inhabited islands in the group, and according to a recent estimate there were five or six hundred more, small and presently uninhabited. Most of the islands were lush with forests and wildlife, with steep hills and shallow lagoons.

With the prospect of Temmil so close I decided to make my intermediate island stopovers less frequent, but there were several where I still had to change ships. One of them was a large island called Demmer. I was told the restaurants and hotels on Demmer were first-class, that Demmer Insula was an attractive and cultured town with much local musical activity and a world-class concert hall, and that the scenery inland was wild and beautiful. The passenger I was talking to, a man who came from the island, recommended that to fully appreciate the place I should plan to stay for at least two weeks. That was more than I wanted, but I thought I might stay and explore for two or three days. I was still travelling on impulse.

As the ship moved towards the harbour in Demmer Insula, I was approached by one of the adepts, a young woman whose name I had already learned from some of the others was Kan.

She said to me, 'Are you intending to land?'

'Yes, of course. The ship goes no further.'

'Are you sure you want to? You could stay aboard and return.'

'What are you telling me, Kan?'

'I am asking, not telling.'

I pulled the stave from my holdall. 'You'll want this,' I said. 'How much is the charge?'

'No charge on Demmer.'

'I need you to do whatever is necessary about the detriment.'

'No charge on Demmer.'

But she had taken the stave and was squinting along the blade, one eye close to the rounded end. The ship was going so slowly that its motion was almost imperceptible. I looked across at the town, prettily built in terraces around the bowl of hills stretching back from the coast. I sensed nothing unusual about it, nothing that alarmed me.

Kan slipped my stave into her belt and said, 'I will be outside Shelterate. We can adjust time gradient there.'

'Why don't you want to be paid for this?'

'No charge on Demmer.'

She slipped away. I made no move to follow her, or even to try to see where she went. I had tired of that futile pursuit many voyages ago.

The ship shuddered as we came alongside the quay and grated against it. Whistles blew, hawsers were thrown and secured, cargo cranes started making their roaring, whining noise. I went below-decks to retrieve the rest of my luggage. A familiar process lay ahead.

48

I stepped ashore and at once I realized something was wrong, something was different. I stood still, regarding the terraced town, the busy harbour, the cranes along the quay. Demmer Insula looked like a pleasant town, probably cultured and almost certainly with local music activity – I could not see anywhere that looked like a concert hall, though. It was late afternoon, the sun at its brightest and the air at its hottest, although the shadows were deep and starting to lengthen. There was an oppressive feeling in the atmosphere and when I looked back across the strait behind me I saw what must be the reason. A huge thundercloud was darkening the sky. It was so low that it appeared to be scraping the sea itself. A vast black anvil shape soared into the stratosphere, reaching out. Winches turned and the cranes were working but I realized that no insects were rasping, no seabirds hovered. A hot breeze lightly lifted the brim of my hat.

Thunder rumbled, a long low growling, still at a distance.

I walked across the quay, heading for the familiar sight of the Shelterate office, wanting to be done with the formalities so that I could find my hotel before the storm came ashore. The building was back from the main harbour, beyond a small warehouse. I climbed up a flight of stone steps to reach it.

Only Kan waited outside. She stood under the canopy, away from the sun, my stave in one hand and her knife hanging by its thread. But alone.

Where were the others?

She handed my stave back to me, but at a glance I could not tell if she had already etched a new line.

'No detriment,' she said. 'The gradual of Demmer is neutral.'

'Have you scored the stave?'

'The gradual is neutral. No need, no charge on Demmer.'

Thunder growled again – louder, closer, more of a thudding bang. The air was still, sweltering. I felt perspiration running down my neck, between my shoulders.

Kan was one of the youngest of the adepts and whenever I had seen her in the past she had seemed to hang back, allowing the others to deal with the time gradients. I glanced past her in the direction of the coming storm, but a harbour building blocked most of the view.

'Are you sure about the money?' I said.

'What worries you?'

'The detriment – if it is not removed it could start accumulating. And where are the others?'

She pouted her lips, made a dismissive sound.

'Take the stave in there,' she said, tipping her head back and towards the entrance to the Shelterate building behind her.

Another heavy roll of thunder. The sun was quickly occluded by the cloud. I wanted a better view of the sea, so I took a few steps to the side. When I looked down and across the harbour I saw that in the short time I had been talking to Kan the storm had moved much closer. I could see sheets of rain falling in the near distance, blocking most of the visible sea. A strong wind was arriving with the storm cloud. Waves were breaking hard against the harbour wall. Inside the harbour, men and women were working swiftly to secure the small boats and yachts in the private moorings to the side. In a few moments, the hot tranquillity of the town had been transformed by the shade of the thundercloud into a dark, shuttered place.

A pink-white sheet of lightning flashed four or five times. I did not see the fork, but I had never seen brighter lightning before. A second or two later the thunder sounded again, this time a terrifying crash followed by echoing rolls. Within a few moments the rain had reached us: it swept in, pouring down heavily. I looked towards the Shelterate building with its open door, a few metres away. I was tempted to dash across, but I was closer to the adepts' canopy, so I hurried beneath it, next to Kan.

Someone inside the Shelterate building slammed the door closed, and moments later the windows were pulled shut too.

The rain turned rapidly to hail: a terrible downfall of white marbles, crashing unrelentingly on the concrete apron. I wondered if the canopy would be strong enough to withstand the violent deluge, but Kan saw me glancing up and shouted something I could not hear, over the noise of the hailstones.

The hail was accumulating on the canopy, making it sag down towards us. Kan reached up and prodded the fabric, and a new cataract of ice balls rattled deafeningly on the ground around us. I ducked, stepped away, went too far and nearly backed into the hailstorm on the other side of the shelter. A cold and sharp wind blew around us, bulging the canopy roof and ejecting more of the captured ice balls.

Then the hail stopped as suddenly as it had begun. Thunder

was roaring almost incessantly, and the lightning was forking with terrible energy across the sky and down to parts of the town which were visible from where we huddled, but the hail stopped. An uneven sea of ice spread across the concrete. Overhead, the underside of the massive cloud was dark grey, streaked with red. It was flashing like an immense, faulty light bulb.

I felt warm air blowing up from the sea.

Kan said, 'Don't move! It is still dangerous.'

As she spoke, a second storm of hailstones began falling from the sky. If anything these stones were larger than in the first shower and were rattling down more intensely, but the fall was over more quickly, in less than a minute. The thunderstorm continued above us, around us, frighteningly close and deafening – some of the thunderclaps felt as if they were shaking the whole of my body.

The warm air brought again the familiar feeling of tropical humidity sweeping in behind the storm. It was not over yet, because a drenching fall of rain quickly followed the hail, a hard, insistent cloudburst. Almost at once so much water began to accumulate on the concreted area that the hailstones floated, drifting away as the rainwater flooded to one side.

To my surprise Kan stepped quickly out from the shelter of the canopy and walked into the heart of the cloudburst. The rain drenched her clothes and hair, but she stood still, her face tipped up to the sky, her eyes closed, her mouth open, letting the water pour all over her. She stood there as the storm began to abate, moving away noisily towards the interior of the island. The lightning and thunder continued and the rain flooded down, but it was obvious the worst of the storm was over.

The doors to the Shelterate building opened abruptly, and three officials emerged – two women and a man. They too walked into the open area outside the building into the full flood of the cascading rain. They stood close to Kan, circling themselves around, their faces and arms raised to the sky, soaking up the cleansing water.

Beyond the area where I was standing, in the street that ran down to the harbour, many more people emerged from their houses and stood, fully clothed, to embrace the downpour.

When the sun came out and the rain finally ceased, the return of the tropical heat was like the sudden opening of a furnace door. Great waves of warm air flowed up from the direction of the harbour.

Kan shook her head to make her wet hair fly out, then she swept it back with both hands. She eased the front of her shirt to separate it from where it was clinging to her body, and without even glancing in my direction walked away down the short flight of steps and along the quay. The officials returned to their building. The people in the street dispersed. Water flooded rapidly along street-side gutters, gurgling and bubbling as it coursed away.

I waited to see if Kan was going to return but finally I gathered up my things and opened the door to enter the Shelterate building. The officials were waiting for me behind their counter, their hair and clothes still soaked through. Water sloshed around our feet.

49

An hour later I emerged, shaken up by what had happened in the office, angered and humiliated by the officials who had insisted on searching every part of my luggage and person, but also, now that I had left and when I had calmed down a little, concerned at what underlying meaning the incident might have. I had grown to expect the Shelterate interview to be a slightly mystifying but banal encounter, soon over. Why was it different on Demmer? What had aroused their suspicions about me, and what were they looking for? They looked at first comical to me in their wet clothes, but there was nothing at all funny about the interrogation and intrusive search that followed.

With my property intact I walked through the evening heat in search of my hotel. It was close to sunset. The air was humid, steamy, but the ground everywhere had dried out within a few minutes of the passing of the storm. In most places it was if no rain had fallen: everywhere looked as parched as before. I was deliberately trying not to think about what had happened after I disembarked from the ship – the intrusive search by the officials was one thing, but what had Kan meant by saying the gradual was neutral in Demmer?

My wristwatch was showing the correct time, something I confirmed as soon as I arrived at the hotel and checked in. In my room I changed my clothes, then ate a light meal in the dining room and took an early night. I left the large window open, letting the breeze pass across my body as I tried to sleep. The room felt stuffy and airless, even so. I was restless all night long, hearing the sounds of the town around – some people were talking and laughing at a dinner table on a terrace somewhere outside, below my room, and they continued into the early hours of the morning. Even after they had left I was disturbed by the low roaring noise of the ventilator and somewhere outside my room the intermittent, jarring sound of the hotel elevator. People seemed to be riding up and down all night long.

I finally drifted into sleep but when I awoke it was already close to mid-morning.

I had booked to stay in the hotel in Demmer Insula for two more nights, but by this time I was so disliking the place, although for no good reason, that I decided to leave early. It turned out not to be possible: the hotel would only cancel the rest of my reservation if I paid a substantial penalty. Later I discovered at the port that there were anyway no more ships heading westwards until the one for which I already had a reservation.

I walked around the town, trying to understand why I disliked it so much. I came to the conclusion the tiredness was probably in me: I had been travelling too long, visited too many islands. Demmer was no more or less attractive than most of the islands I had passed through – I could see that objectively, but still I felt frustrated by being trapped there for two more days. I was set on reaching Temmil as soon as I could.

I decided it would make better use of the time if I set off to explore some of the interior. I found an island map in one of the shops on the seafront. It showed paths, villages, areas of woodland, viewpoints where scenery could be enjoyed, and so on. I set out immediately after I had eaten lunch, and in spite of the heat and the unrelenting glare of sunlight I enjoyed the day and slept well that night.

50

The next morning I set off early, striking out in the opposite direction, where the terrain was less hilly. I knew that several small villages lay along the coast. I passed through three of them, stopping in the third to have a drink and a meal in one of the inns. The air was still, with no sense that there might be another storm of the magnitude of the day before. The fields and hedgerows were vibrant with the sounds of birds and the rich scents of wild flowers drifted around me. Few cars or other vehicles passed me.

I soon reached the fourth village, intending at that time to have a brief look around, then turn back and return to Demmer Insula. I had walked a long way. But as I went down a curving lane towards where I could see the village houses ahead I came across a pole barrier set across the roadway. I hesitated, not sure what the barrier meant, nor how I was supposed to react. As it was a single pole it would have been a simple matter to scramble beneath it but something warned me not to try.

I stood there, thinking that I had walked far enough and I might as well turn back, when two young men in military fatigues emerged from trees by the side of the road. They came towards me. They were both carrying automatic rifles. Instinctively, I raised my hands.

'What do you want?' one of them said, tipping the barrel of his rifle in a threatening way.

'I'm on holiday – walking,' I said. The soldier looked like a teenager. His uniform fit badly and it seemed to me his hold on his weapon was unsteady. My heart was suddenly racing with fear of him, because of his immaturity, because he looked so nervous. How could anyone so young and slight be in control of such a deadly looking weapon?

'Where you going?'

'Down to the next village. I – don't know what the name of it is.'

'Then what do you want there?'

'Nothing. Just walking. I will go back now.'

But the other one had moved around to stand behind me. He looked even younger than the first.

They were both wearing a strange kind of cap, or helmet – it was difficult to see exactly what it was, but the size and shape of it was bizarre. It looked wrong, not only on these youths, but also in the gently green surroundings of this country lane. The caps were narrow and tall, made of, or covered in, some kind of intensely black matt material. The cap was four-sided, worn straight on the top of the head with one of the angles over the forehead. There were no marks or tags to identify which unit they were from, and the caps looked impractical for armed soldiers engaged in some kind of operation. The rest of their uniform was much as I thought military fatigues should be, but the strangeness of the tall caps they were wearing was unnerving. What was signified by them?

'Show your papers,' the first one said.

'I'm on vacation – I'm not carrying identity.'

'Then who are you and what do you want?'

'I have this,' I said, suddenly remembering the stave. I pulled it out from my holdall, and both soldiers momentarily tensed, as if I was producing a weapon. I also froze, mentally cursing myself for making an unexpected move in front of armed soldiers. But the moment passed – they obviously recognized what it was.

'Put that away. We're not bothered with it.'

Greatly relieved, I said, 'Can I go on, or should I walk back?'

The two young men glanced at each other. One of them nodded and then the other did too. The first one signalled with his rifle towards the village. The other walked around to the weighted end of the barrier and raised the pole. I went through quickly, stooping so that I went underneath even as the pole was still being lifted. I walked on without looking back.

Once I had gone through the sloping bend in the road I came into the main part of the village, where small houses were built along both sides of the lane. The place was deserted: there were no cars parked anywhere in sight, and no pedestrians were moving around. The only vehicle that was visible anywhere was a large truck with closed sides and a solidly constructed rear access. It was painted in dark camouflage colours.

None of the other villages I passed through had been empty, or had seemed so silently abandoned. It was as if I was alone. I thought at once of turning back, so uncomfortable was the vacant feeling of the pretty, prosperous-looking place, but the two young soldiers would still be manning their barrier back there along the road.

I slowed my pace, looking ahead and around me, wondering what was happening here, what I should do.

I walked slowly down the main street, hoping things would seem more normal further along. Perhaps there was some kind of village celebration somewhere on the road?

A sudden burst of loud bangs! I spun around in horror then crouched desperately in the shelter of a low brick wall that happened to be there. I had never heard the sound of close gunfire before, but that is what the noise sounded like. They were nothing like the detonation of bombs, which I had grown up with, but sharp, repeated, deadly. Was the gunman, whoever he was, firing at me? I was terrified of what I had walked into.

I pressed myself against the ground, feeling prominent and defenceless. What if I was on the wrong side of the wall? What if the gunman were to change position?

Nothing in my life had prepared me for this. Now voices were shouting: loud but indistinct, not fearful but ordering, commanding. I was certain they were yelling at me, but I kept still and silent. I began to realize I was not the target of the words being shouted, but I stayed put. Then another shot – I pressed myself harder against the surface of the road.

A minute went by in silence, then I heard a commotion. From the house close to where I was hiding came the sound of a door being booted open. Wood splintered, the door crashed against a porch pillar. I heard another voice crying out – this time it was with fear and hurt. Another shouting voice silenced it, or mostly.

I ventured a look, peering over the wall at the house. I saw a group of men struggling violently. Four of them were in army uniforms, but the fifth was clad only in a singlet and underpants. He was being dragged, forced along, fighting to get free, but the soldiers had him in a fierce hold, both arms pushed hard up against his back, his head held down with a soldier's clamping arm.

The fourth soldier took no part in the struggle but was shouting instructions to the others. He was carrying a machine pistol. The other three had automatic rifles but they were slung across their backs. Two of the soldiers were wearing the tall black caps I had seen earlier but the other two, struggling with the victim, had lost theirs.

The officer detached himself from the fight, strode quickly away and went to the truck parked in the street. He wrangled the rear door open: I glimpsed a filthy interior, a cage, boxes, ropes, other junk. A mechanical ramp lowered itself automatically from the rear, and it reached the ground just as the captive man was brought up to it. They kicked and pushed him up the ramp and he sprawled on the floor of the truck.

I looked away. I wanted to see nothing more of what they were going to do to him, but as the ramp closed again I could not help but hear the sound of a continuing struggle. I was appalled, feeling helpless, terrified.

Were they going to kill him? Now? Here?

And what if the soldiers saw me? I was not concealed by the wall – I simply squatted beside it. I believed that if I tried to run away they would attempt to stop me, perhaps by shooting, but they would find me anyway if I stayed where I was.

I stood up, my knees trembling as I put my weight on them. It reminded me of the fear the Generalissima had struck in me, the knowledge that all these years of close work with music was no preparation for the more sordid, threatening aspects of real life. I had sheltered myself all through my years, and I sheltered myself even now – my gentle voyages across the shallow seas between islands were no way to confront reality. I was engaged with the finer problems of gained or lost time – the man held inside the truck was immeasurably worse off than I would ever be. Even though I did not want to I could still hear the muffled sound of shouting voices coming from inside the truck's closed compartment.

The fourth soldier, the man I presumed to be the officer, moved away from the truck. He glanced in my direction – he must have seen me but gave no sign of it. He was sure of himself, certain of his power over me. He headed slowly back towards the house, staring from side to side as he strode in a measured way up the narrow path to the door that had been kicked out. I saw him bend down and he scooped up one of the caps that had been knocked off during the scrap. Then he found the second one.

At the door he checked inside the house by leaning in through the door: it was hanging open, its lock surrounded by broken wood. He turned around and with a swing of his hip he shoved the door back more or less into place. He returned towards the road.

He came towards me, his machine pistol held ready for use but aimed at the sky, not at me.

I raised my hands defensively, dreading the worst. He walked slowly, with precise steps, a military stride, the product of discipline and training. His face was masked with a thick green-coloured fabric and he was wearing close-fitting dark glasses. He wore the tall black cap on his head, square and upright. The two caps he had picked up were hooked over his belt. I could not see any of his face, or read his expression. I was shaking with fear.

He came to a halt two or three metres away from me, then brought down his weapon so that it was pointing straight at me. He did something to it and there was a terrible noise of metallic readiness as it was armed. It emitted a brief electronic signal.

'This is a closed military zone. Explain what you are doing here!'

'I—'

I found I could not draw enough breath to speak. I tried again, but this time the only sound I could make was a sobbing noise.

'I am authorized to eliminate witnesses. Explain!'

'Please!' I shuddered another breath into my lungs. 'Please!' I said again abjectly. 'I saw nothing.'

'You saw. Explain why you are here.'

'I'm on vacation – a short walking holiday. I came by accident. I had no idea this was a military zone. The men on the barrier let me through.'

'What's your name?'

'Sussken, Alesandro Sussken.'

'Say that again.'

'Alesandro Sussken.'

'Why do you use that name?'

'It's mine. I have had it all my life.'

'Sussken – that's a Glaundian name. Is Glaund where you are from?'

'Yes. I'm on holiday—'

'I heard that. Be silent, sir.'

There was some kind of electronic device strapped to his forearm. While he kept the weapon trained on me he changed his stance with the same military precision as before so that he could access it. With his gloved fingers he punched a panel, looking intently at the display, while managing to keep me in view.

His sudden use of the word 'sir' had startled me. It partly defused the threat I felt from him. It appeared to acknowledge, for instance, that I was a civilian, beyond his area of authority. Even so the pistol was still being held unwaveringly towards me. His stance was aggressive, ready for violent action, but his concentration on whatever he was looking for on his wrist device again tended to mitigate that. He continued pressing his fingers to the keypad, reading whatever response it was he was getting.

I noticed that an identifying number was sewn into the shoulder of his armoured jacket: *289*.

Under the bulky fatigues, the panels of body armour, behind the packs and accessories strapped to his belt and webbing, under the mask and the shades, he was a slight figure. There was something youthful about him, even boyish. His voice was that of a young man. He spoke with what I knew was a Glaundian accent.

I felt a surge of irrational certainty.

'Sussken,' I said. 'Is that the name you're searching for?'

'Be silent, sir.'

'A lot of people spell it Suskind,' I said.

'I know about that. I can spell it.'

'Sussken,' I said. 'Are you Jacj? Jacj Sussken?'

'Please be silent.' But he had looked up from the device. He stared at me along the barrel of the pistol. I was certain who it was, certain. 'The report I have read about you is that you, Alesandro Sussken, formerly of Errest in the Republic of Glaund, have absconded with thirty thousand gulden of public money. You are a fugitive, hunted by the police and the armed forces. I have downloaded a warrant for your arrest.'

'Jacj! It is you, isn't it?'

'Please be silent.'

51

He lowered the machine pistol slowly, but he held it ready and I noticed that he did not reverse whatever he had done to arm it.

'Jacj, I am your brother, Sandro!'

'I have no brother. I am not who you think.'

I wanted to rush to him and embrace him. 'Let me see your face!'

'My identity is of no importance. I am a serving officer. Keep your distance!'

'We thought you were lost, killed, injured. It's been so many years!'

'I am not who you think. I know no one called Sandro.'

'You were called Jacjer but everyone in the family called you Jacj. Surely you remember that? Please, let me see you.'

'You must address me as Captain, sir.'

'Captain Jacjer Sussken? Do you still play music, Jacj? You must have time off from your duties sometimes. Do you still have the violin you took with you when you were drafted?'

'I am not who you think. I have no violin.'

His voice remained controlled, steady, revealing nothing. But it was his voice, Jacj's adolescent voice, the familiar sound of my elder brother, heard all through childhood, my closest friend, the boy I looked up to, admired, tried to emulate. My partner in a hundred duets of piano and violin. The sensitive teenager, easily frightened, who abhorred violence and military might.

'You refused to avoid the draft notice, said you would try to subvert the military from within by being part of it.'

'That would be illegal. I am proud to serve my country. You are a criminal, a thief, a wanted man.'

I thought of the young man they had captured, pulled violently from the house half-dressed, defenceless against the combined strength of these troops. Was I about to follow him, thrust helplessly into the closed truck with the cage, the shackles?

With his free hand the captain reached up and removed his dark glasses. He slipped them into a pocket on his chest. Then he unhooked the piece of cloth that covered his nose and mouth, and at last his face was revealed to me.

He stared directly at me, expressionless, neutral, unshielded.

'Jacj, why won't you admit who you are? I have been searching for you for nearly forty years.' He showed no reaction. I said, 'May I look at you more closely?'

'Keep your distance.'

He did not try to prevent me from approaching, though. I took one cautious step, then another, then three or four more, until I was only an arm's length away from him. Still he stared blankly at me, not avoiding me, but not acknowledging me either. His eyes were pale blue, as Jacj's had been. Was that enough so that I could be certain? His nose, mouth, his whole countenance ... he could have been Jacj, he might not be. I looked and looked at his young face, still a teenager it seemed, not much older in appearance than he had been that day he walked down to the town centre and boarded the army bus. It was forty years since I had been with him, but he looked the same. I did think he looked the same. Maybe he was fuller-faced now, tougher, more determined? I was sure he looked the same. I was certain it was him. I thought it was him.

I could not be sure.

'Don't you recognize me?' I said quietly in the silent street, while the sun beat down on us both. 'Do you remember me, Jacj?'

'Please address me as Captain, sir.'

'Captain, I am your brother, your younger brother, the kid you played with while we were trying to shelter from the bombing. We used to sing together, and when the raids were over we would take out our instruments and play for a few minutes. We used to say it was our way of defeating the enemy. You must remember our parents – Mum and Dad? You've been gone so long … it's hard to tell you, but they have both died. They never gave up hope of you coming home again. They loved you, Jacj. We all loved you. They were waiting, we were all waiting, for your battalion to be shipped home. So many years have passed—'

His gaze remained level, steady, but I noticed that he was longer looking straight at me, but somewhere in the distance, somewhere behind me.

Then a cat emerged from one of the houses, moving gingerly around us, its body low. When it glanced up at us I saw it had large green eyes. It was long-haired, mostly white.

Jacj looked down at it.

I said, 'Djahann is dead, Jacj.'

If I had struck him physically he would not have reacted more. He stepped back, half-turned away from me, the hand holding the weapon sagged for the first time. He stared at the white cat as it scuttled away from us, dashed across the street, leapt into some bushes and disappeared.

'You promised to look after her,' Jacj said.

'I did – I thought you were coming home and I think she waited too. Djahann had a long life, a happy life. She often slept in your bedroom, on your bed. She seemed always to miss you. She became old and at the end she died peacefully. She was never in pain. I buried her in our garden and I marked her grave.'

He exhaled, and I heard an intermittence, a controlled sob.

But the weapon came up again, and he tensed his shoulders.

'If you leave now, sir,' he said. 'I need not arrest you.'

He swiftly clipped the fabric mask over his face again, but he did not replace his opaquely dark glasses. His breathing was still unsteady.

The other three soldiers had left the truck and were moving up the road towards us.

'The deserter has been secured, Captain,' one of them said. 'We have given him water, according to regulations.'

Jacj took the black caps he had been carrying in his belt, and handed them over. The two soldiers replaced them, straightening the stiff fabric, settling them exactly over their foreheads.

'Jacj – may I contact you again?' I said. 'Tell me how, tell me where you'll be.'

'If you leave now, sir,' he said. 'I need not arrest you.'

The machine pistol was pointing straight at my chest. With his other hand the Captain took the pair of dark glasses from his pocket and slipped them back on.

'I am not who you think,' he said. I backed away from him, frightened again of the deadly weapon. He went on, 'I have no brother. I carry no violin. I have a warrant for your arrest and if you resist me any longer I will be forced to restrain you physically. I am an escouade leader, I have an open brief to apprehend deserters and a statutory order that enables me to detain or eliminate witnesses. You are such a witness and a fugitive from our country, at risk of instant death, but if you leave now, sir, I will not arrest you.'

His enigmatic face, hidden, hiding. His light stature. The voice.

I turned away from him, then looked back. He remained poised, the weapon trained directly at my chest.

'Jacj?' I said.

'No. Leave now, Sandro!'

I stumbled away. I hurried back up the road. I did not look back. As I rounded the curve in the road, the two soldiers on the barrier saw me approaching and one of them raised the pole. I went quickly through, then once I was away from them, when the village was no longer in sight, I started to run. I ran in the merciless sunshine, through the hot still air of the country lane, dense with flowers, busy with birds, running until I had to stop at last to collect my breath. I leaned over, clasping my knees with my hands, staring down at the gravel.

52

Once again a litany of island names: Foort, the Ferredy Atoll, Mesterline, the Coast of Helvard's Passion, Lillen-cay, Salay, Fellenstell. They seemed to speed past, even though the ferries followed their usual circuitous routes, made their slow ports of call. I changed from ship to ship. I watched the varying chronometers on the walls of my cabins, absolute time, ship time. I met with the adepts, they adjusted my detriment. My stave became increasingly scored. I stayed in hotels, some humble, some grand, some awful. I burned on sunny decks, I sweated in unventilated cabins. I drank too much alcohol. I was lonely, emotionally drained, undecided about practical things, abandoned by music, beaten by life. I was not attending to what I saw, what I went past, what happened to me.

I was obsessed with thoughts of my lost brother.

How could I not be? Jacj was the last remaining member of my family. He was all I had of the past life, the growing up that had made me what I have become. When he joined the army his childhood ended, but so too did mine. Now, nearly half a century later, I was grown into a man, and Jacj – into a soldier, a boy soldier with a slight body and the voice of a teenager.

I travelled only to put distance behind me, to use up the distance that lay ahead. Distance was time: absolute time, my time, ship time. My brother and I were separated by distance, but also by the years lost and gained in repeated detriments, the temporal tides that eroded reality, the gradual encroachment of time. It was difficult to understand rationally – it was impossible to comprehend emotionally. The gradual was a kind of endless, inexplicable madness.

For the time it took to make most of these voyages I thought of no one else but Jacj. The tragedy of a life lost to the military. The tragedy of two brothers who could not recognize each other. The tragedy of lost music, because his music had gone from his life and mine was slipping away from me. The tragedy of his great youth, my advancing years.

I was sailing nearer to Temmil. Every ship I boarded, every timetable I consulted, had a port of call in Hakerline, the resort island adjacent to Temmil. I knew that I had only to remain on a ship, virtually any ship, and I would end up in that place with the view of the narrow strait and the dark volcano.

I broke my journey in the Salay Group – Salay consisted of five large islands set around a central lagoon, like the petals of some immense flower. Many of the passengers I was travelling with were heading for Salay. It was a popular tourist attraction, the place islanders liked to visit to take a vacation. I noticed then that the saloons of some of the ships had large paintings or photographs of Salayean views. I could see what an attractive place it was, how at some other time, in some other mood, it might have been the sort of place I would enjoy visiting. The time was wrong, though. I simply needed a break, a period of solitude, an opportunity to rethink, reconsider.

The ship called at all five of the Salayean islands, and I chose to disembark at the one called Salay Raba – the name meant it was the fourth of the five islands. It appeared to be the least commercially developed of the group. I rented an apartment in the main town, paying in advance for fifteen days. I settled down to rethink, reconsider, as I desperately needed to do.

I was calm and contemplative in my thoughts and actions for the first ten days or so, coming to understand, perhaps, a little of what Jacj had endured under the military régime, but then I realized that a couple had moved into the apartment directly below mine. It was only a few days after I had arrived. I knew nothing about them, although their names suddenly appeared on a tag in the hallway: Emwarl and Sophi. The names were familiar – they were often used in Glaund. This was confirmed when I overheard them speaking to each other in the hall. They were speaking Glaundian.

My first reaction was a friendly thought: that I should be interested to meet them and perhaps hear news from home. Almost at once, though, I was on my guard. Memories of the arrest warrant were still fresh. How much of a coincidence could it be that a couple should be placed here, on a remote island on the other side of the world from Glaund, in the apartment below mine?

I moved out of the apartment that night, dozed on a bench in the harbour office until dawn, then crossed to Salay Tielet, third island of the five. I checked into a small pension in a backstreet, and set about finding the next ship that would be sailing to Hakerline. I had to wait in a jittery mood for two more days, but in the end I caught a small ferry to the island of Fellenstel. The voyage took three days. In Fellenstel, without delay, without seeking the help of an adept, I took the first ship I could find that would call at Hakerline.

Absolute time, ship time, were hours apart. I had not attended to the gradual. I found it difficult to sleep on the narrow bunk in the cabin deep in the ship, and during the airless nights I would watch the twin dials of the chronometers, *Mutlaq Vaqt* and *Kema Vaqt*, as they steadily drifted further from synchronization.

53

Three days later, give or take whatever hours I had lost, or gained, I was standing at the rail of the ship as it closed on Hakerline Promise, the name of the main port. I saw a murmuration of brightly coloured water-birds bursting up from the lagoon in the late afternoon sunlight, and watched while the dense swarm took shape and reshape as the birds swooped across the sea away from the harbour wall. Pleasure boats speeded around my arriving ferry, some of them blowing their horns in welcome. I looked across the wide lagoon towards the forest which touched on the edge of town, the trees growing down to the edge of the water, many of them leaning precariously over the waves.

I did not want to leave the ship – I felt safe on the ship, anonymous, unknown to those who might still be seeking me.

I had spent so long travelling and sailing that it had become almost second nature to me. I knew, though, I was at the end of that: all that remained was a short trip across the narrows to Temmil. Afterwards I would settle.

An adept came up behind me and I was pleased to discover it was Kan. I had not seen her since sheltering from the storm with her in Demmer Insula. Until this moment I had not been aware she was on the ship – indeed, I had not seen any of the adepts aboard, although as soon as I saw Kan again I realized she and the rest of them must have been somewhere there with me. I was convinced she was one of the youngest of the adepts: they all looked youthful, but Kan had a kind of innocent glow that I liked. I was pleased to see her, and I turned towards her with a smile of greeting.

'I want sixty Hakerline talents,' she said without preamble, moving to my side. 'Please pay in cash before the ship docks.'

I was startled by her abrupt manner but in truth I had become used to the adepts' brusque way of opening the transaction.

'I was hoping to see you again, after we left Demmer,' I said.

'Sixty talents. There is not much time before we dock.'

I produced my stave. 'Don't you wish to read this?'

'Not now.'

'So you just want the money?' She nodded. 'I would need to change notes in the office,' I said. 'Couldn't I pay you later, Kan? Or I have plenty of simoleons.'

'I will wait for you here. I need talents. Who told you my name? You are not supposed to know!'

'I knew it before – when we were in Demmer Insula. Someone must have told me – I think it was you. Maybe one of the other adepts.'

'Which others? I am alone.'

'The group you work with.'

'I am alone,' she said again. 'I have not been to Demmer. No adept goes there. The gradual is neutral on Demmer.'

She was giving me a sharp, suspicious look, then she glanced away, apparently annoyed with me.

I did not press the point.

So, once again, I had to spend time below decks, lining up with a few other passengers to change money in the purser's bureau, while the bustle and noise of the ship's arrival went on around us. I would have much preferred to be out on the deck, enjoying the sunlight and watching as the resort of Hakerline Promise came into view. Although I mostly enjoyed the pleasures of solitude I was often lonely while a long voyage went on. I had found Kan attractive company when we together, all too briefly, that time on Demmer.

Or perhaps we had not been. Whatever was true was whatever she told me, not what I remembered. It was sometimes a shock to remind myself of the madness of the gradual.

I just wanted to disembark, find somewhere to stay, then in

the morning take the first ferry I could to Temmil.

By the time I completed the transaction and climbed back to the boat deck to find Kan the ship had stopped moving. I thought at first we must have docked but then I saw that the vessel had hove to some distance away from the narrow entrance to the harbour. I could see members of the crew in the bow of the ship, doing something with the winch mounted there. As I looked for Kan I noticed that while I was below-decks the ship had manoeuvred around towards the harbour entrance. The island of Temmil was in view. The tall cone of the mountain Gronner was glowing with reflected sunlight, made a deep orange by the quality of the afternoon light, or because of whatever plants might be growing on the slopes.

I found Kan and handed her the cash, which she counted twice, pedantically, before she accepted it. She slipped it into a small leather purse, which she wore on a cord around her neck.

'Now your stave.'

'You didn't want it before.'

'Now.'

I had in fact been waiting for her to ask for it, so I had it ready. She held it in one hand so that it was upright, then ran the fingertips of her other hand lightly down the wooden blade. Her eyes were half closed.

When she looked at me again her demeanour had changed. She smiled, handed the stave towards to me with a playful pass, pretending to tug it back so that I could not reach it. She kept hold if it, fingers of both hands lightly gripping it.

'Now I understand what you say about Demmer. You must have been there.'

'You can tell that from the stave? Don't you remember the storm while we were there?'

'Demmer is never recorded,' she said. 'I do not go there. But you were in Foort, so it is likely. And you came to Hakerline before?'

'Is all this on the stave?'

I was uncertain of her mood. She had transformed in an instant from someone making a cool business deal to informal, almost teasing friendliness. It was so sudden I could not believe it was genuine.

'No – not everything is shown. But the Shelterate records are here. You were touring with an orchestra—'

'That was during my first visit to the islands.'

'Big detriment lost. How did you manage when you were home? Was difficult? But you are a piano player and violinist. A composer too! Why did you not say? You went to many islands, big success. Then Temmil. Big success. Then here to Hakerline.'

'We returned home after we left Hakerline.'

'You were concerned about what you might find when you were home. I see now. Yes. You were worried about a relative. An older brother?'

'Does it say what his name is?'

'Jacjer Sussken. Is that right?'

'What else is recorded there?' I said, reaching out to take it from her. This time she let it go.

I looked closely at it but the dozens of etched lines made no sense to me. Much of my life was recorded somehow there, or at least the actions and movements I had made. The loss or gain of gradual time, the entries and exits to islands. Little pieces of information I must have let slip, or deliberately imparted.

'Does it tell you what I went through when I reached home?' I said. 'What I found, what I had to discover?'

'There is nothing. You have heavy detriment now.'

'How much?'

She held out her arm, where there was a tiny wristwatch. I looked down at it.

'It is a heavy detriment,' she said again. 'You were in Salay, moved between the five islands, did not find me.'

'I never saw you,' I said. Then I pointed at her wrist, and showed her my own watch. 'There isn't much difference in time.'

She laughed. 'You want to leave it like this? You think it is not much?'

'A few minutes.'

'You are nearly twelve hours ahead of me. That what you want?'

Absolute time, ship time – I had seen the chronometers drifting in the gradual.

'So what should I do?'

'First we wait for the ship to dock.'

She stood close beside me at the rail, leaning forward with her weight on her elbows. I could feel the warmth of her arm – she was standing much closer to me than perhaps a mere working acquaintance might stand. I liked the sensation of her near presence, but wondered what she meant by it, if anything. Her manner was casual. A gulf of difference lay between us – age, background, culture, her adeptship. The ferry was manoeuvring slowly in the approaches to the harbour but there were so many small boats milling around us that we were barely moving. The ship's siren sounded several times, a warning to the boats to make way for us. Nothing much was affected by the noise and the colourful chaos around the harbour continued.

Looking across the water at what I could see of the town I watched the crowds moving about on the streets, the gaily coloured bunting strung from trees and high posts, the profusion of bright electric signs. When I had stayed on Hakerline before we had been in a large hotel on the edge of town, used its private beach and only ventured into Hakerline Promise after dark to visit restaurants and bars. I recalled an infectiously happy place, full of loud music, noise and crowds. Even as we moved into the harbour, amplified music came thundering to us across the water.

'You like that sort of music?' I said to her.

I felt her shifting position. Although she remained beside me, leaning forward with her arms across the rail, she was suddenly on her guard.

'Some,' she said.

'You like some of it?' I said. 'Or you like it somewhat?'

'No difference.'

'Have you ever heard of a young musician called And Ante? He lives on Temmil, Choker of Air.'

'Are you travelling to Choker of Air?' she said.

'Yes.'

'Leaving soon? Or staying in Hakerline Promise?'

'I haven't decided. There is someone I want to meet on Temmil. That man – Ante. But I need to think about it.'

'If you stay in Hakerline a few minutes, OK. But here an

overnight stay, or part of one day, and you will need me. The time gradual is steep, and erratic. I would have to follow you constantly.'

'What exactly do you mean?'

'You could not walk down the street without a detriment. You cannot even cross a room in this town without losing or gaining a few seconds. Even to move while you are asleep is dangerous.'

'You need to be with me constantly.'

'Not at night.'

She started telling me a story. At first I expected the short sentences she normally came out with, but for once she was loquacious: this was something she wanted to tell me about. It concerned her parents. They had met as young adults, she said, while they were on holiday, part of a group travelling around this area of the Archipelago, sailing from island to island in a fleet of small boats and staying at hostels or inexpensive hotels. There had been couriers, organizers, who were with them all the way. Kan said that when islanders travelled about the Archipelago, or they went on an organized tour, they did not need the constant attention of adepts. By law, each booking agency, each tour operator, had to be licensed to an adeptive agency. At the end of each journey, or at the conclusion of a tour, the detriments were corrected collectively.

'Everyone you can see,' Kan said, pointing across to the crowded street alongside the harbour, where the crowds ambled by. 'All these people are travelling with that sort of licence. They each have a profile, defined on the licence: which island group they were born in, on which island, the time of day, blood group – everything like that. Before computers it was difficult to calculate groups. They made many mistakes. That was when the staves started to be used. But these days it is centralized. When you buy a ticket, or book a tour, you fill in a form or use a website. The tour operator does the rest.'

'You were telling me how this affected your parents?'

'They met each other during their holiday, fell in love and wanted to be together. The tour operator refused to amend their licences, or more likely didn't know how to. They had to travel on different coaches, or follow separate routes. They had to keep taking different ferries planned in advance for them. When the tour arrived here on Hakerline they ran away from it and went off on their own. I think they found a hotel somewhere. Then at the end, when they went to catch up with the ship, the one booked for the return journey, they discovered they had lost seventy-eight days. The rest of the tour had departed weeks earlier. They were stranded without much money, unable to make contact with home. It was romantic, but it made their lives chaotic. In the end it was sorted out by adepts, but by then they had decided to stay here, on Hakerline. They found somewhere to live, married, found jobs, had me, had my two brothers. They still live here, in the Promise.'

'Do you live with them?'

'Not now.'

'So – why couldn't I be given a licence too?'

'You were born in the north. The stave says Glaund.'

'Yes.'

'All mainlanders are outside the system. You have to use the stave because even though you're a mainlander you're still vulnerable to the gradual. Hakerline is a problem for everyone. This is a gradual vortex within another vortex.'

The ship had passed the harbour arm and was slowly manoeuvring towards the long wall, the engines turning slowly. The familiar, insistent sound of cicadas rasped, but they were for once almost drowned by the ambient noise from the loudspeakers mounted on the town buildings. Without the breeze created by the ship's motion the air felt sticky and hot. Rich scents drifted from the shore: too strong for flowers, but varied, alluring, illicit, foreshadowing night-time adventures.

Kan straightened. The ship was being secured to the quay.

'The ship is at the dock,' she said. 'Give me your stave and wait here. Do not try to leave the ship.'

She took the stave from me then slipped it into the large bag she was carrying. Without another word she left me. She passed quickly through into the superstructure of the ship.

54

When I walked back through the ship I saw that most of the other passengers were crowding by the gangways. As soon as the gangplanks were in place they began disembarking, jostling each other in their haste to be off the ship after the three-day voyage. I saw them streaming across towards the Shelterate building, prominently placed on the quay here as everywhere else. I could see the familiar striped awning, with the ambiguous figures of the adepts sitting or standing beneath, affecting not to look closely as the passengers walked past with their wheeled suitcases and backpacks. Every now and again one of the adepts would walk out from under the canopy, apparently at hazard, to speak to a selected passenger.

Money changed hands.

I did not see Kan leave the ship.

I stared across at the town. I had memories of Hakerline Promise, but on the first trip I had only ever visited the town at night. I remembered drinking too much, eating food I found too spicy. It was the end of a long tour. In reality I knew nothing about the place.

A wide road ran beside the harbour in front of a long parade of buildings and this was where most of the crowd was. Everyone I could see was dressed in holiday clothes. Cars and motorbikes weaved slowly through the throng, with a noise of revving engines and rude blasts of horns. Music blared out from several places: a cacophony of sounds and rhythms, in brutal competition with each other. Everyone seemed to be shouting at once. Many of the cafés and restaurants had tables and chairs placed outside on terraces and these were crammed with customers. Neon lights shone from every vertical surface: places to dance, to drink, to eat, to meet people, to watch live performances. When night came those signs would light up the town.

Kan returned unexpectedly, coming up beside me as I stood at the side of the ship. I had not seen her crossing the harbour area although I had a clear view of it and I was watching for her. Once again she stood disconcertingly close beside me. She handed back my stave.

'We thought you were in transit through Hakerline,' she said. 'You wish to stay, so tonight you will remain on board this ship. It is the only place that's safe for you.'

'Safe? Wouldn't a hotel be as safe?'

'No.'

'I'm tired of being on boats. I want a normal bed in a room that doesn't rock from side to side. I want to take a long shower, eat in a proper restaurant.'

'No choice. The gradient is extreme here. If you went ashore we would lose you.'

'We?'

'I have talked with the others. There is one called Renettia. You know her?'

'I do.'

'Renettia is my supervisor, my mentor. She trained me. I always go to her for advice. She agrees with me about this – you must stay aboard the ship tonight. Tomorrow will be better.'

I stared back at her, feeling rebellious. So many times I had accepted these directions from the adepts. So many times I believed what they said would happen, or what would not happen.

'What if I just do what I think is right?' I said.

'Can't stop you. Stay on the boat, though. You can't leave the harbour without Shelterate clearance. They will want your licence. You don't have one. They will insist. You will offer your stave. They will take your stave away. Hakerline is different from other islands. No one lands without licence.'

'You sound certain.'

'I was born here. I know. No one goes ashore without licence. This is a resort island. This is how it works. No licence, no entry. They would put you back on the ship anyway. Or intern you.'

'But I came here before. On my first tour.'

'Then you were licensed.'

'I couldn't have been,' I said, thinking of everything that followed the tour, when I was back in Glaund. But I knew I was losing this argument. A resigned feeling was growing in me.

'Renettia will try to get you a pass from the Shelterate office, but that can't be done now. Tomorrow. So you stay aboard here one more night. We've arranged that. The cabin is available until tomorrow midday. The ship sails then. Be ready before that.'

55

It was still only afternoon. The temperature was high, the humidity awful, the noises from the town intrusive. I felt trapped and abandoned by Kan, left on the ship to fend for myself. I felt I might be at risk: maybe the crew had not been told about me, and a routine search of the ship would discover me. Would they think I was a stowaway? I glanced up at the windows of the bridge, but they were half silvered, like those of many of the ships I had been on. It was impossible to tell if any of the officers were there. And because I was no longer on the move, the thought would not go away that some authority figure with a warrant for my arrest might come on board to find me.

I picked up my belongings, which I had brought to the deck ready for my departure, then carried them down to the ship's passenger decks, looking for the cabin I had been using. Now that the ship's engines were not running there was no air conditioning, but for the time being it was cooler and the air was more breathable inside than in the open. The narrow companionways were lit only by emergency bulbs, but in my cabin the electrical power sockets and the lights were still working. The water that came out of both taps was lukewarm.

I sat on my bunk, which I had left unmade, and considered what I should do. I was full of inertia: my mind felt blank, my spirits were low.

I explored what I could of the rest of the ship. The passenger areas – cabins, companionways, the stairs, the exits to the boat decks, one of the gangplanks – were all open to me. I realized I could look around for a bigger or better cabin, but after I had looked at a few others I realized my existing cabin was no better or worse than any other. I stayed put.

I did wonder if this was a chance to see if could discover

where it was in the ship that the adepts travelled but I soon found that most other areas had been locked.

The ship had a restaurant on board but it closed when the ship docked. I was already hungry. I could not get through until the morning on an empty stomach, so flagrantly breaching Kan's instructions I went briefly ashore to a kiosk at the end of the quay. I had spotted this earlier from the ship. I bought some bread rolls, processed meat, cheese, fresh fruit, a can of beer and a couple of bottles of mineral water.

As I walked back to the ship I was met by one of the ship's officers. He confirmed what Kan had told me: the captain had received orders from the company office that I would be permitted to stay on board overnight. The ship would be locked down for the night, he went on, with only a skeleton crew: two men, whom I probably would not see.

I passed the long slow evening alone. After eating some of the food and drinking the beer my mood lifted and I took out my violin. I practised on it for more than three hours, absorbing the music into my system like a recharge of energy. For the last hour I walked slowly along the companionways like a wandering minstrel, listening to the way the sound changed in the narrow, irregular spaces.

I finished playing in one of the large saloons. The huge and empty room, with its multitude of bright surfaces and many fabrics on the walls and floor, had a resonant acoustic. It was an area of the ship soundproofed from outside, so the endless racket from the town was not a problem. I played until my arms and shoulders were aching, then returned to my cabin, restored in spirit.

Later I took a shower, standing in the half-hearted and tepid dribble. The water ran out just as I had finished rinsing my hair and beard. Towelling myself I did something for which I had rarely had time or interest while I was travelling and stood before the full-length mirror attached to the wall of the shower cubicle.

I first glanced quickly at the reflection of myself, then with a feeling of surprise I looked again, then I looked more closely, and finally I stared in astonishment.

I had of course been looking at my reflection several times a day, but only superficial moments when brushing my teeth, combing my hair, and so on. I was used to seeing myself. I had felt for some years I was not ageing well – my skin had a sallow appearance, the flesh of my cheeks was starting to sag, deep creases had appeared around my eyes and mouth, there were wrinkles on my forehead, my neck, and worst of all a dewlap was starting to dangle around my throat. My new beard helped disguise it, but only partly.

I was more than fifty years old, well into middle age. There was no escape from the reality that all the blessings of youth had fled. My physical appearance was frankly unappealing and I knew it was because I took hardly any physical exercise, or when I did so it was the wrong sort and was over too quickly, that when I worked I was usually seated, that I was careless with the kinds of food I ate, but mostly it was because I was no longer young and took poor physical care of myself.

That night, alone on the ship, alone in my cabin, with time on my hands and little else to think about, I looked at myself as if at a stranger. I was amazed by what I saw.

It was my eyes I noticed first. I was used to what I saw in the mirror: the invariable surrounding of dried or darkened skin, the puffy eyelids with scattered lashes, a distinct yellow tinge in the sclera, with several visible papillae. My eyes always made me look tired, strained, as if I had been reading too much and too long, staying awake instead of sleeping, a revelation of a generally unhealthy lifestyle. But now I saw that my eyes had cleared! The whites were almost untrammelled, with no trace of that unpleasant liverish tinge. The irises were the calm pale blue I had cherished when I was a young man. The eyelids looked taut. The darkness and looseness around the eyes had disappeared.

I started examining myself with a feeling of increasing surprise and a growing sense of mystery. My face was more or less unlined, except for tiny creases where I smiled. My cheeks were smooth and firm. I pulled at the area below my chin, lifting the tufts of my beard and trying to see my throat and neck clearly. There was nothing loose there, no sagging, no sign of even an incipient dewlap.

I found a hand mirror and held it behind my head while I looked in the main mirror. My hair was dark again, dark all over without a single streak of grey. There were none of those faded areas which had been spreading inexorably, and which, if I thought of them at all, I had deluded myself that perhaps they made me look mature, distinguished. And my hair was growing thickly again. I now had the same full head of hair that had been mine throughout my twenties and most of my thirties. The thin patch that I knew about but tried to pretend away, the increasing spread of baldness on the crown of my head, had entirely disappeared. I touched my scalp with a press of my fingers, feeling the healthy growth.

My stomach was flat, my legs and arms were firmly muscled. My shoulders looked broader. The mat of untidy grey hair across my chest, straggling up around my throat, had all but vanished: I now had a faint sheen of dark chest hair. My buttocks were firm. My back was straight. When I expanded my chest the motion felt strong, pleasing. I reached down, touched my toes. I could not remember the last time I had been able to do that. Overall I was leaner without being thinner. I was in terrific shape.

In some way I could not understand, something like two decades had been stripped from me. My body was once again that of a young man. I was still at least fifty-four years old, I thought and felt the same, the substance of all my memories and my experiences in life remained with me. I was unchanged. But I was also renewed.

I had been vaguely aware that something was changing. I had been feeling a gain in strength, in stamina, I had been sleeping better. And I had seen some of the physical changes in the mirror. But small daily changes are imperceptible, and it was only during this solitary night in the ship that I fully noticed what had happened.

Time fled from me – I suffered gradual detriment. Youth attached to me – I gained gradual increment. Balance remained.

Absolute time, ship time: the difference became personal time lost.

Absolute age, travel through the gradual: the difference led to personal rejuvenation gained.

I slipped on some clothes then ran the length of the companionway, breathing the warm stale air but invigorated by the feeling of agility, strength, stamina that coursed through me. Afterwards my increased heart rate returned to normal almost immediately.

How had this happened? The constant fresh air cleansed by the sea winds? The endless bounty of sunshine? Even, perhaps, the frequent stresses and strains of marching around island shores, burdened with my possessions, following the opaque and sometimes inconsistent instructions of the adepts? Certain parts of my body had felt the effects and after-effects of those incidents. But, no. That could not be the only reason. Other people exercised far more often and consistently than me and they did not see the years slipping away from their appearance.

Once before, when I returned home after the first tour, I had been faced with a radical turn of events I could not comprehend. In the end, that baffling loss of time, or gain, had an explanation of sorts. I never fully grasped it, but for all that it was an explanation. Now I had suddenly lost years of my physical life, decades of my physical life, but in an altogether different way.

Could this be another manifestation of the gradients of time, the gradual?

When I was back in my cabin the feeling of being trapped bore down on me again. I took to the bunk. The small room was still too warm for comfort but I kept the cabin door wedged open. I lay awake.

After an hour of this I managed to force the porthole open, sealed with rust or paint, but which gave way after a struggle. This allowed a refreshing breeze but also admitted the noises from the town. I sat up, leaned with my back against the cabin wall and the open porthole beside my head, listening to the racket from the shore: the shouting voices, occasional screams or loud laughter, music belting out from five or six separate loudspeakers, engines revving and roaring. At times I heard the penetrating electronic sirens of emergency vehicles, their warning lights flashing, as they pushed slowly through the crowded area, nudging the pedestrians aside.

The night wore on. I remained unable to sleep. Eventually most of the motorbikes and sports cars were driven away, the rowdy shouts died down, no more ambulances appeared. Only the music remained, maddening me, because it was always difficult for me to hear music and make it unimportant. Any kind of music made me listen to it.

When I first had the porthole open I found it more or less impossible to separate the music from the rest of the commotion in the noise-filled streets, but in the early hours the lack of other sounds meant I could discern the tunes, the harmonies. What they were playing was what I thought of as the lowest denominator of popular music: repetitive chords and simple tunes, heavy bass lines, a thudding, unchanging drumbeat, the words chanted or shouted. It was for me a form of private torture. It drilled into my mind, blanked my thoughts, gave me back nothing I could like. It made me fail to understand why others might like it.

Then suddenly I was fully alert. They were playing something based on the main theme from *Tidal Symbols*!

Who was it? A live group? A heavily amplified recording? I turned, pressed my face to the porthole gap, then my ear, to try to hear better, but the small circular window was designed only to open to a crack. There it was again! The main theme, the chordal progression, the brief elaboration, the shift of key. The music was mine because it came from my soul, my life, my emotions, because it was the first work of mine to be recorded, because it came from a remembered part of my life, because I loved it. It was a part of myself.

Whoever was playing it, whoever was on the record, had turned it into something bland and loud and rhythmic, had made it cheap and repetitive, made it obvious and moronic, but it was still mine.

The army had made my brother into a soulless soldier, but he was still mine.

From my narrow view through the porthole I tried to see what I could of what was going on out there. Most of the buildings were at last darkened for the night, but a short parade of bars, cafés and clubs at street level were still lit with flashing neon signs. One of them had a picture window, brightly illuminated from within. I could see hardly any details but I could make out the blurrily silhouetted heads and shoulders of the people by the window, moving up and down, dancing to the repetitive, obvious, brainless version of my music.

In the end I barely slept even after the music finally went quiet. I may have dozed for an hour or two, but it was with that unsatisfying feeling of semi-sleep, restless and aware, constantly shifting position. The sky was lightening in the east. Large cleaning vehicles moved slowly through the streets and the harbour zones. Some of the operatives yelled to each other and bins crashed and rattled as they were emptied into the hopper. Grinding motors roared from within the trucks as the trash was crushed and compacted.

56

I moved outside to the promenade deck before Kan returned to the ship. From the deck I had a good view of the harbour as well as most of the other decks. The ship was slowly returning to life as members of the crew filed back on board then went below to start up the pumps and generators. I saw two uniformed officials going to the Shelterate building and unlocking it. The striped awning was permanently in place but there were no adepts anywhere around.

I was glad to breathe the fresh air and stretch my legs – I was still quietly celebrating the ease with which I could use my body. There was none of the stiffness I had felt in the past during the first hour or so after waking every morning. I realized it must have been the norm for some time but this morning was the first in which I really appreciated it.

The town seemed quiet and clean, not at all as it had been during those long hours of bright lights and hideous loudness. The night-time revellers were presumably sleeping off their excesses. All the bars and nightclubs along the front were closed and shuttered. A water truck whooshed down the road beside the harbour, spraying over the few small pieces of rubbish that remained on the road after the night's celebrations. Some traders appeared with wheeled stalls and set up their displays of fruit, flowers and wines. I saw a team of cleaners walking aboard the ship, hauling trolleys of fresh towels and bedclothes. Supplies of food and drink were being delivered to the ship from the shore by catering companies, carried aboard by young staff. Other goods were loaded into the two large holds by the crane that stood above the harbour.

I noticed that a group of passengers were waiting around outside the Shelterate building, but no ships had docked recently and the boat I was on was the only one in the harbour. The adepts' area was still unoccupied.

The temperature was starting to rise with the sun.

I finally saw Kan and the other adept, Renettia, walking along the quayside. I went down through the ship to meet them at the companionway, but inexplicably I must have missed them somehow. I found them waiting for me back on the promenade deck where I had been standing. My bags were beside them. I was ready to leave but Renettia raised her hands to halt me.

'Msr Sussken, you must remain on the ship. We have to discuss your options.'

'My options? I've been waiting all night. I want to go ashore.'

'Not yet.'

'Kan told me there was a problem with the Shelterate rules, but that you would resolve it.'

'Yes, but options are to be discussed.' I glanced at Kan for confirmation but she was staring away from me, across the outer harbour wall. 'This is Kan's home island. The gradual effects are so complex here that you need a native of the island to help you. If you are to leave and cross to Choker of Air, there will be problems for you when you arrive unless you are prepared properly.'

'This means you want more money?' I said.

'If you leave Hakerline, Kan's adept abilities will be diminished. You will need both of us to accompany you.'

'So how much more?'

'Understand – the gradual here on Hakerline is strong, has a complex field pattern. Kan is trained to deal with that. But if you cross to Temmil, Choker of Air, you enter a new gravitational agenda. Gradient on Temmil is unidirectional. You know what that means?'

'I just want to be there,' I said.

'The two islands have an intense temporal stress between

them, but they counter-balance, one against the other. Each compensates for the other.'

'Where do my options come into this?'

'You told Kan you are planning to meet someone on Choker of Air.'

'It can wait,' I said. 'Mostly I want to get off this ship.'

'You were on Temmil once before?'

'I was.'

'And you crossed from here to Temmil?'

'The other way around. I came to Hakerline from Temmil. You know why – the tour organizers made the travel arrangements. None of us knew anything about gradients and gravity.'

'You know now the consequence.'

'Are you asking for more money?' I said.

'One hundred Hakerline talents.'

That surprised me, but I said, 'I've already paid Kan sixty. I'll give you fifty.'

'We don't bargain.'

'What do I get for the extra? I've spent nearly all the cash I'm carrying.'

'There is a bank here in Hakerline Promise. We take you there.'

'You said there were options. What if I don't pay?'

'That is an option.' The two women were both standing so that they were facing me. Kan was right at my side. If the intention was to make me feel I had been cornered, it worked. 'Is that what you wish?' Renettia said.

'But what would happen?'

'Kan will accompany you so long as you remain in Hakerline. You paid for that. If you wish to leave the island, she will be with you part way. If you travel to Choker of Air, you have options. I will accompany you, or you travel alone.'

'Those are options?'

'For you. We do what you need us to do.'

Around us, the ship was being readied for its next voyage. The main engines had started and were throbbing gently in the depths of the vessel. The passengers who had been waiting at the Shelterate office were walking across the quay to board. A drift of pale brown smoke idled out of the squat funnel towards the stern of the ship. Several of the crew moved to and fro on the deck, one of them speaking into a portable radio. An officer, smartly clad in tropical white, came down to the main deck and inspected something in a lidded compartment two of the young sailors had been working on.

'All right,' I said, resigned as so many times before to the fact that I never had any options at all when dealing with the adepts. 'We'll go to the bank.'

Kan spoke for the first time that morning. 'I need to check your stave again, Msr Sussken.'

She took it from me, and once again she touched the surface lightly with her fingers. Renettia was watching her closely.

We disembarked. I carried my belongings easily, recognizing and fully savouring the physical vigour that had been gifted to me. We went straight to the Shelterate office. Outside the main entrance Kan gave me back my stave.

'All you do – hand this over. Say nothing.'

For some reason neither of them would enter the building with me. I went in alone and did exactly as Kan instructed. My stave was pushed down into the scanner – after a pause it popped out again and the official handed it back to me. No paper note was printed out this time.

The two women adepts were waiting for me by the exit. We walked up through the rest of the harbour area and into the town itself. Up close, in the bright daylight, the buildings which the night before had been so crammed with celebrating holidaymakers now looked shabby and unrepaired. There was a bank two streets away. I went through the time-consuming and tiresome procedure of identifying myself, then waiting while identity and credit checks were made through the banking system. I had done this before on other islands – I always had a background nagging fear that I was about to be informed that the Glaund military junta had traced my account and frozen it. However, after a long delay all was well and I collected a substantial sum in cash: talents for use here on Hakerline, but also thalers and simoleons for the future.

I paid Renettia what she had requested.

57

Half an hour after leaving the ship all three of us were in a car, speeding away from the town and along the coast, Renettia at the wheel. Kan was in the front passenger seat. I sat alone behind them, my possessions stacked beside me.

I had had nothing to eat or drink since leaving the ship's cabin, but the women gave no sign that we were about to stop for a meal. There were bottles of mineral water in the car, from which we all drank as the morning temperature rose steeply. The hills around Hakerline Promise were thickly forested, so for much of the way there were only fleeting views of the scenery or the sea. Occasionally I was able to glimpse in the distance the familiar shape of the volcanic cone of the Gronner when it came into view above the trees. Renettia brought the car to a halt at intervals while she and Kan consulted each other, speaking quickly and quietly in island demotic.

They were intent on what they were doing. Kan was using a calculating device which I had never seen before – it was somewhat like an abacus, but the beads were strung along wire guides held in a frame, made in the shape of a five-petalled flower. She fingered the beads deftly, spinning the wire frame around the central support, checking and confirming Renettia's decisions. Once, she read out a sequence of numbers as we drove along. In one tree-shaded valley she called out for the car to be stopped – Renettia braked sharply and pulled the car over to the side of the road in a cloud of dust. After Kan had recalculated, Renettia reversed a short distance, then waited again while Kan shuffled beads to and fro. We resumed. At another place we turned off the road to follow an unmade track through the forest, before swinging across to an even smaller track to the side and eventually returning to the road we had left. Or it might have been one that was like it.

We came to a village, the road winding down from the hills into a crescent-shaped bay, where a stretch of white sand lay in contrast to the calm and translucent aquamarine of the enclosed lagoon. A reef lay about five hundred metres from the shore: the open sea beyond was a deeper blue. Dozens of small boats and yachts were sailing on the still waters of the lagoon. There were many people on the beach, but it was not crowded. Renettia drove the car along the road that skirted the beach, into the village itself. She parked in a central square.

We climbed out into the blazing sunshine. Renettia said she and Kan had to make some enquiries and told me to wait by the car. I had already entered the state of mind familiar to me whenever I was being escorted by an adept. I became passive, accepting, not enquiring, letting myself be moved around and told what to do.

So I stood meekly beside the car while the two women walked away across the sun-baked paving stones. They went together into an alley leading off the square, disappearing into the deep shadows.

When they were out of sight I glanced around at what I could see of the village. The square itself was almost deserted of people. Two elderly men sat side by side on a bench under the largest tree. They both had walking sticks propped up between their knees. Several other cars were parked on the far side. The surrounding buildings were tall, old-looking, with a kind of well used grandeur. The windows blankly reflected the radiant sky. There was a café with tables on the outside terrace, protected from the sun by overhead screens, but no one was sitting there. The interior was too dark, relative to the brilliant outside glare, for me to see if anyone was inside.

I was of course wearing my light clothing and protective hat but the sunlight was intense and heat was pumping up around me from the ground. My sandals hardly protected me from the heat of the paving stones. There was no wind even though the square opened out towards the sea. It was so humid I was finding it difficult to breathe.

I moved away to stand in a narrow strip of shade against the wall of one of the buildings. I drank some cold water from a fountain set in the wall, feeling the delicious chill as it went down. I splashed water over my face and hair, letting some of it run down over my shoulders and chest.

When I looked back across the square I discovered that the car we had been in was no longer in sight.

Everything else appeared much the same – except that under the tree, where the two old men had been sitting, a drastic change had taken place. One of the men had toppled forward on to the ground and was lying awkwardly face down, his walking stick lying at an angle across his legs. The other man was standing beside the prone body, leaning heavily on his own stick, looking around the square desperately, seeking help.

I was tempted to hurry across the square to do what I could, but something about the suddenness of the situation, together with Renettia's injunction not to move away from the car, warned me not to.

The car, though, had disappeared. My first thought, as passive as always when adepts were around, was that Renettia and Kan must have returned while I was drinking at the fountain and had driven away without me. Nothing surprised me any more. My possessions were still inside the car, and those included my violin, which normally I would hardly let out of my sight, but I felt unconcerned. There were always reasons for what they did – their reasons, not mine. But as I walked back across the sun-bleached paving the car returned into sight. It was still exactly where Renettia had parked it. Both women were standing beside it, staring around the square, clearly looking for me.

I looked around too: both of the elderly men were again seated side by side on the bench beneath the tree.

Kan saw me.

'You should not leave the car when we are driving you,' she said, explaining nothing.

'I needed something to drink,' I said ineffectually.

'We have found a restaurant,' Renettia said, pointing towards the alley where they had walked. 'More than water there. Bring your luggage.'

I collected my stuff and followed them to the place they had found. We took a table under a huge canvas shade, where an electric fan blew a cooling draught across us.

58

After a good meal, a most welcome and delicious meal, for which I paid, we did not return to the car but instead walked on further down the alley to the edge of the lagoon. Here a short curving jetty had been built. I was enjoying the sensation of having drunk a little too much wine, adding to my general passivity about their instructions.

Moored to the jetty was a small yacht, a simple sailboat. Another boat trip – it passed through my mind to wonder: why all that again? But I was feeling cooperative so I swung my bags into the well at the rear and sat down where they told me, to one side.

They went about the preparations to cast off, but it seemed to me they did not know much more about sailing than I did. They had trouble loosening some of the knots – Kan succeeded in tightening one and tangling the rope. I helped her untie it. There was no engine. Neither of them said anything as they struggled with the ropes but at last they managed to get the sails raised. Fortunately the wind was light, so as the little boat moved away from the jetty and headed into the lagoon it did so slowly and in a steady direction. Kan took the tiller and seemed confident while Renettia kept her hand on the mainsail's boom, and worked the ropes as necessary. I could not help feeling relieved that a small dinghy was being towed behind us.

The sea remained calm, even when we went through a channel in the reef and entered the gentle swell of the open sea. Here the breeze was stronger. The boat sailed more quickly and I relished the wind and the occasional splashing of spray. Ahead, not too far ahead, I could see the dark green bulk of Temmil. All I felt was a sense of relief that this long journey would soon be over. I was content. The food and wine felt good inside me. I began to relax.

I dropped an arm over the side of the boat, trailing my fingers in the cool water, listening to the sound of the boat breaking through the waves. The water swirled past, a trail of thin foam and small bubbles created by the boat's passage. The water was so clear I could see beams of sunlight shafting down, but the water was too deep for me to see as far as the bottom. I wondered what was below: a sea floor I could barely imagine, sand and rocks perhaps, fish of course and other forms of marine life, live coral growing, even wrecks or lost treasures. The sea was still a novelty to me, a romantic mystery. I listened to the intermittent, arhythmic gusts of the wind, the ropes straining under the pressure, the sails flapping and beating, the mast creaking. Constant sounds of water. Seagulls followed low above the water. Harmonies formed inevitably in my mind and I tapped my fingers against the wooden side of the boat.

Musing enjoyably in this way, I was no longer taking an interest in what the two women were doing, except that after I had been drifting contentedly in this lazy, acquiescent state for about twenty minutes, eyes half closed, I sensed a different kind of movement. The boat rocked with their footsteps.

Without turning my head to see what they were doing I assumed they were sailing the yacht, stepping past me to reach the sails, the ropes. Then a shadow fell across me, and I looked up. The sun dazzled me.

Kan was beside me, standing over me. She was holding her flower-shaped abacus.

'We are leaving now,' she said. 'Good day.'

I struggled to sit upright. 'What did you say?'

We were still out at sea. I knew that the tract of land we were moving towards was Temmil but when I looked back I could see that the hilly coastline of Hakerline was roughly the same distance behind us.

'This is gradual balance. Time standstill.' She thrust her wrist at me, showing me the face of her watch, but because of the dazzling sunlight and the rocking of the boat I could not see it clearly. I looked at my own watch – I assumed the time it was showing was the same, that usually being the point of checking our wristwatches.

Renettia was securing the tiller with a length of rope and as Kan stood beside me she was holding on to the boom of the mainsail.

'You can't abandon me,' I said.

'No further. If we stay with you all we have done is undone.'

'What have you done?' I had kicked myself out of the passive mood – now I was feeling defensive, unhappy, threatened.

'We have brought you to Temmil,' Kan said. 'We have finished.'

I leaned over to look at Renettia. She was standing at the stern of the sailboat, pulling on the painter, drawing the dinghy towards us.

'I'm nowhere near Temmil!' I said, raising my voice. 'I paid you a lot of money to take me to that island.'

'You paid us standard fee,' Renettia said. 'Your fee is for correction of gradual time detriment, not for travel. You are safe to continue. We have provided you a boat. '

'Safe? What do you mean by safe?'

I was standing now and in my sudden onrush of anxiety I was making the sailboat wobble alarmingly. Renettia had brought the dinghy alongside and was transferring the few things she and Kan had brought with them.

'The boat won't sink,' Renettia said. 'That's safe. I have set the rudder, but you must control it. Wind won't change. Press rudder against it. Tide is flowing in the direction you want. Here is your stave. Take care of it, in case you return home.'

'You're not serious!' I said, now really frightened – alone on the sea in a boat I had no idea how to sail.

Renettia stepped across to the dinghy, lifted up the oars and settled them in the rowlocks.

'Kan – couldn't you at least come with me the rest of the way?' I said. 'Just as far as the harbour?'

'Sorry, Msr Sussken. No problem. Believe me.'

She stepped into the well of the sailing boat, climbed up to the rail then leapt gingerly across the narrow gap to the dinghy. She was holding her abacus in her hand, steadying herself with one arm as she landed in the dinghy. Renettia released the rope she was holding and the dinghy immediately began to drift away.

I shouted to them, appealing to them not to do this. The dinghy had already half turned. Kan was sitting on the thwart immediately behind the other woman. She took up the spare oars. They began rowing, leaning over their oars, straining their arms and backs as they pulled away. Their inexperience with rowing was obvious – the oars frequently splashed and they barely moved forward. Although because their boat had turned away they were facing me, neither of them would look in my direction. They were heading in the approximate direction of Hakerline, but the tide was against them and their progress was slow. Most of the increasing distance between us was caused by my sailboat drifting on the same tide, towards Temmil.

I was genuinely terrified of the predicament they had put me in. The immensity of the sea, its vast depth, the unlimited range of hazards it was likely to contain – all these frightened me. I sat down clumsily beside the tiller. The bulk of the yacht's hull was before me – I could not easily see ahead. I stood up again, then leaned from side to side as far as I dared, glimpsing the coast of Temmil. The mainsail swung towards me with a change in the wind and I sat down again.

I took up position beside the rudder and loosened the tie. I calmed myself with six deep breaths, a practice I had taken up in the days when I was performing or conducting and had to walk out to the platform in front of an audience. It was a technique that always helped me make sense of potentially complex situations.

Now, six breaths later – the sea was calm, the wind was light, there were no other ships close by, several hours of daylight were ahead. No storm or violent gale seemed likely. I knew that the yacht was a simple design, that the sails were already hoisted and that Kan and Renettia had managed to bring it this far without much practice beforehand.

A long gust of wind came at me and the boat reacted. It turned away from the island, leaning alarmingly to one side. I pushed the rudder against the direction of the wind. The boat responded at once, twisting back, bucking against the waves it met. It was still leaning over because of the wind but I had been aware of that while Renettia and Kan were sailing so I knew it was normal. The larger of the two sails filled with the wind, bulging out, and I could feel a continuous pressure from the rudder.

I glanced back. The dinghy was still in sight, almost within shouting distance. The two women were rowing hard.

I began to feel more confident. The weather was unlikely to change, the rigging of the sails was something I could not alter, but it seemed all right, or probably all right, and my destination was obviously not too far away.

I remained tense and alert, though. I was constantly aware of possible dangers, but as I sailed inexorably closer to the island I could see houses and other buildings along the shore. I also saw the long, low arm of a harbour wall stretching out into the sea.

My entry to the harbour turned out to be surprisingly straightforward, although not incident free. Once I had managed to turn the boat towards the harbour entrance I tried to see ahead to some sort of safe landing area, or somewhere not already crowded with other boats. I managed to pass the harbour wall with only one slight scrape and with part of the mainsail torn when it snagged on some kind of metal fitting that jutted from the end of the wall. After that the boat simply headed towards a part of the jetty where dozens of other boats were already tied up. It slid heavily against them. Someone on the quay noticed what was happening and he and two other men managed to grab the rail with a boat hook. They dragged me without further damage to a spare mooring.

Embarrassed and flustered, but immensely relieved, I climbed ashore. As I stood on the concrete wharf, gladdened beyond words that I was on solid ground again, I knew my legs and arms were trembling and that sweat was pouring down my face, neck and chest.

59

I already knew that it was impossible to go ashore without having to submit to formalities in the Shelterate building. There was no hope of a quiet or unobserved arrival in Temmil Waterside – my erratic approach had been monitored almost from the moment the two adept women abandoned me. I learned that had I drifted into real danger the harbour guards would have launched a high-speed rescue boat. For a short while I was notorious and of course the Shelterate officials were interested in me.

First I had to visit the harbourmaster's office because I had not booked a mooring and my arrival was unscheduled. A mooring fee inevitably had to be found. After that I carried my luggage across to the Shelterate office. Because I was not a transit passenger I had to enter the island formally. The officials confirmed what I already knew: that I had landed in Temmil Waterside, capital of the island of the same name. A seignioral seal was affixed to my visa. They then searched my baggage and the familiar conversation ensued when they opened the case and found my violin. I offered them my stave – this time a paper slip was printed by the scanner and handed to me. The amber light shone from the machine, and without asking me the officer added another three hundred and sixty days to the stave's memory.

At the end I was made to sign a form of indemnity, declaring that I was immune from gradual anomaly. By this time I was so tired of the endless obsession with the vortex phenomenon that I signed without reading anything beyond the first couple of lines. A copy of my declaration was then stapled to the back of my visa and I was charged another ten simoleons.

I walked out into the street.

I did not feel like celebrating. I did not even feel a sense of completion now the long journey had ended. I simply felt tired.

I walked into the town, barely looking about me. The place seemed quiet – that was not how I remembered it from before. I headed for the hotel where the orchestra had stayed. It was a large manorial building in its own parkland but when I located it at the top of the town the main gates were closed and chained. A sign warned me that twenty-four-hour security surveillance was in place. I could see that the windows of the main block were shuttered. I walked back down towards the quayside, went to the first hotel I saw. I was checking in with the receptionist when the manager emerged quickly from his office and announced in an annoyed voice that the hotel was full. I knew from the way he regarded me that I appeared too scruffy for his high-class establishment. I was weary, much in need of a bath and a change of clothes. I gave up without an argument and continued the search, eventually finding a small, over-priced pension near the harbour.

By this time I was too tired to care about the expense.

I checked in and paid for five nights in advance. I did not even notice the name of the place. I went to my room and was soon asleep.

60

The succession of long sea journeys had worn me out but after three days of lazing around in the town I was physically restored. I had caught up with sleep. I had adjusted to being on solid ground once more and I did not miss the shipboard life at all, so much a part of normal daily experience. All my clothes had been laundered by the hotel staff and I had bought some extra new ones. I was eating regularly and well, I had my thickly growing hair cut, I secured my finances by moving all my funds to a non-seignioral Waterside bank, and I had explored the town and much of the surrounding countryside.

The first feelings of restlessness brought on by the impermanence of staying in a hotel were starting to matter, though, and Temmil Waterside itself began to reveal its limitations.

Much had changed since my earlier visit. It was not just the loss of that large hotel where the tour party had stayed, but the hall where we had performed the great concluding concerts had also closed. It too was shuttered and locked, with security guards on patrol. I was escorted none too politely from the site. On the way out I noticed a large board had been erected by a property company, announcing that the area had been acquired for redevelopment. A gated community of sixty-five retirement homes for select buyers was being planned. I was shocked by this but saddened too: the existence of a well equipped concert hall always acts as a focus for musical activity, drawing in young players and performers.

Remembering what I had seen of Waterside's café culture I went in search of the bars and restaurants I had briefly visited, where live music was played. In one place on the waterfront a string quartet had played most evenings of the week, and other bars in the same area featured guitarists, pianists or singers. As

I walked around in the daytime it was difficult to see which of the places now would have facilities for music, but it was worse at night. Almost everywhere was closed after dark. Many of the smaller places I had seen on my first visit appeared to have been converted into fast food outlets.

Because of the volcano dominating the island, Temmil had richly fertile soil and wildflowers grew in profusion. Wine was grown on the lower slopes of the Gronner, and the plains in the north of the island produced many different fruits and vegetables. I learned these facts from a seignioral pamphlet about the island.

I was interested in the Gronner from the start, never having lived anywhere near an active volcano before. Waterside itself was on a distant, lower slope of the Gronner, but because the volcano was surrounded by several smaller hills there were only a few positions in the town from which it was possible to see the cone or whatever outflow there was. On the hotel's television I discovered a local station which routinely carried data and pictures from the scientific stations set up to monitor the activity. Every night there was a news update about the state of the volcano: around the time I arrived it was said to be active but stable, with what the authorities described as Reduced Amber: in other words, not much probability of an eruption producing lava or ash. After I had been on the island about seven days this state was upgraded to Average Amber, but the likelihood remained low. There were occasional minor tremors in the ground but some of the local people I spoke to said these were normal. The worst known eruption had occurred more than a hundred years earlier. No one at all was concerned about the mountain and soon I too felt the same way.

I realized that whatever I had thought of Temmil on my first visit, much had changed since. There were few signs of anything I would recognize as cultural activity. There was only one bookshop, for instance, and their stock was to me unadventurous and dull. There were two galleries near the waterfront, but although they both claimed to support local artists the kind of work they had on show, predominantly views of the harbour, cliffs and the Gronner, was the kind of conventional landscape painting found in most tourist resorts. There was no theatre, the concert hall had closed, the only cinema was a small one that showed commercial films. There was a modern leisure centre on the edge of town and this had a swimming pool, a gym and craft shops.

It was not long before I was questioning my decision to be there. Everything about Temmil except the scenery had changed, and beautiful scenery was the norm all over the Archipelago.

I had to decide what to do – the choices were simple. I thought hard about the journey home. Temmil was a disappointment and without it my long travels lost all meaning. It was depressing to think about giving up and going home, and the thought of all those ships I would need to sail on was a daunting one. There was also the likelihood that if I tried to go back into Glaund itself I would be arrested. It did not feel like a real choice, so maybe I should move on further and try to find another island? Then, six days after my arrival in Temmil Waterside, I noticed an advertisement for a villa that was available to rent. The printed photograph made it look attractive so I went to view it, even though I had already started browsing through the shipping brochures.

The house was on a hillside close to the town and with a view across part of it. It was halfway up the hill, at the end of a narrow track leading between two flowery banks. The house had two main rooms and a large single bedroom, with a balcony running around three of the four sides. It provided shade, but also, from one side of the house, there was a view of the sea.

There was a piano in one of the rooms, a good quality baby grand. This clinched it. I could hardly believe my luck, because I knew I would not stay sane without a piano in my life. I could play my violin well enough, but I could never compose on it. As soon as I saw the piano I decided I would take the house, no matter what else might be wrong or unsuitable about it. The agent showing me around pretended to ignore the instrument but I could not stop staring at it. Finally the agent said the piano had been requested by a previous tenant and that naturally it would be removed before I took possession. I would hear of no such thing – my decision about what to do had suddenly been made. I paid the agent twelve weeks' rent in advance and moved into the villa four days later.

I was happy in the house from the outset. An expanse of the sea was visible from where I sat at the keyboard, with Hakerline across the narrow strait and four other islands spreading out towards the horizon. Many small crags, rocks and reefs broke through the shallow waters close to the shore. The Gronner was not in sight from the house because of the hills. Dense woodland grew on the slopes behind the villa.

At the beginning of my first full day in the house I walked down to the town and purchased many sheets of manuscript paper. Imaginative excitement was at last coursing through me.

I quickly settled down into the way of life I knew best, what I could only describe as compositional bliss. The endless voyages across the Archipelago had left their imagic impressions, and I could sense the music of the islands swirling inside me. I started with a simple piece, almost an exercise after so long away from a piano: I wrote a sonata for the piano, a melodic and conventional piece, a private route towards a rediscovery of my art. I gave it no title – just the Sixth Piano Sonata, for that is what it was.

Something had changed in me, though. While I was still in Glaund I had been inspired by the islands in a general way: their actual existence, their presence offshore from the mainland, the unspecified promise they seemed to hold. It had all been how I felt, rather than what I knew. Now I related to the islands in a direct and personal way, knowing them as well as having feelings. Each one had communicated something to me, something personal and unique. My sonata, with its unrevealing title, was in fact about the island of Quy. For some reason, images of my time on Quy flooded through my imagination as I composed.

After that I began some melodic sketches for what I thought would probably grow into a larger orchestral work, but I became restless with it. Again, images of individual islands were dominant.

As I turned from one piece to another it was as if, internally, my consciousness also moved. I was on, or in, or somehow submerged by, the island of Callock. Then I turned to Leyah and was across warm seas and through new currents into a weird islander sensibility I barely understood. I moved on to Unna, tiny Unna, which I had only glimpsed from afar, late one night on a deck beneath the stars, yet something from that lay within me, bright, a derived dazzle of arpeggios.

But I did not want to commit to only one piece at a time, especially not a large work which would take some time to complete. I was still not in contact with any classical musicians on the island and I would need at least a small ensemble to work with so that I could try out my ideas. I stopped composing and the mad consciousness of the islands left me.

I turned to another idea I had been nurturing while I crossed the seas from island to island. I had become fascinated by the idea of time slippage, the experience of gradual time. How might that be translated into music?

It made me think of an unsuccessful early suite, which I had called *Dream Island*, written in the difficult period after I returned from the tour. I had long thought of that as a failed piece, an experiment with counterpoint and randomness. I had known all along that it would be difficult for the performers to play and probably baffling for an audience to hear. I wondered now if the same idea of betrayal by time, of the undetectable detriment, might be better achieved if I worked it into a more conventional format.

I wrote at the piano keyboard, page after page of draft, some of it satisfactory, some of it less so. It was the transition that I found difficult: I had clear musical images in my mind, but working them into the actual score often defied me.

At night I dreamed of the islands I had seen and visited, the slow progression of one after another as the ferries ploughed their routes across the calm straits between them, places varied and mysterious, land close at hand but often unattainable, each small island with its invisible, indiscernible power of time distortion. I began to realize that I best understood the effect of the gradual if I interpreted it in musical terms. The Archipelago was in my dreams, and every morning I would rise from my bed and go straight to the piano, trying to capture, define, describe, use the fleeting impressions, the unreliable memories of the music of dreams.

61

One evening, after a long day at the piano keyboard, I walked down into Waterside. I had been living and writing alone too long and needed the company of other people. I went after sunset, relishing the quiet as the cicadas stilled at last. A warm wind blew from the sea.

I went first to the harbour, where I watched the departure of the regular motorboat that acted as a ferry between Temmil and Hakerline Promise. The lights in the harbour were dimmed after the boat left, so I walked into the town. The streets were mostly quiet, although a few of the restaurants were open. I had eaten already.

I wandered further away from the centre and eventually came to an area I had seen during daytime, where there were several large warehouses or stores. I noticed a lighted doorway leading off from one of the narrow streets. I heard music drifting up from below. There was a man standing by the door but he ignored me as I walked past and went down a narrow wooden staircase into the darkness of the building's cellar. The low ceiling created a claustrophobic environment, but the air was clear and breathable. Tables were scattered about, where customers were sitting with drinks. The place was not full.

A woman was seated at a piano, leaning forward across the keyboard, her back towards the crowd. She swayed gently from side to side as she played, responding to the rhythm. She was playing jazz, a slow piano blues. The only other musician on the platform with her was a double bassist, standing beside the piano, his eyes closed as he played.

I took a seat at a table and ordered a large glass of beer.

The place was so dark I could barely make out who else was there – the only lit area was the tiny platform and a patch of dance floor in front of it. I watched the pianist, admiring the lightness of her touch, the way she appeared to feel the music more than play it. I had never had much time for jazz, but I was quickly won over to the sort of music she was playing, and the skill with which she performed.

After about thirty minutes she came to the end of her set. While she remained at the piano she pushed the stool back and turned to speak to her bassist. She was holding a long glass of light beer, which she sipped several times.

Staring at her, I suddenly realized I knew who she was. The lighting remained diffuse, the sort of stage light that illuminates without making detail clear. I could hardly see her face, but her manner, her bearing, was completely familiar to me.

I left my table and walked across to the raised stage. She turned towards me with a ready smile as I approached – the bassist laid his instrument on the floor, and walked down from the stage, heading for the bar.

I said, 'You're Cea, aren't you? Cea Weller?'

'Yes, I am.'

I had the light behind me, so I could see that she was trying to peer at me to see my face. 'I am Sandro,' I said. 'Alesandro Sussken. Do you remember me? You performed my—'

'Sandro!'

She stood up quickly, smiling with recognition and presented her face to me. We kissed briefly, coolly, on each cheek. Then she sat down again.

'I've moved to Temmil,' I said, still standing, my body throwing a shadow across her. She did not seem surprised to see me.

'Yes, I heard you were coming here. My father told me.'

'Your father?'

'You met him that evening at the concert.'

I thought back – I had been introduced to many people that evening. Nothing about him registered now. Why he should know my movements I had no idea.

'Yes – that's right.' I said. 'But he wasn't my main interest that evening.'

'I thought you'd forgotten about me, Sandro.'

'We agreed, didn't we?'

Just one night. I had been due to sail across to Hakerline the next day, while she was in the process of preparing for a series of recitals on another island. Demmer? I could not stay on Temmil, she could not leave with me, I was full of remorse because I was married, we had to part and knew we would and then we did so.

She stretched out and briefly took my hand. 'I know what happened, Sandro. I've no regrets.' When she let go of my hand I crouched down on my haunches so that I was no longer standing over her. 'We obviously have some catching up to do,' she said. 'So where are you staying?'

'I've rented a house on the edge of town. Just for a while.'

'If you're renting that sounds like a more than temporary stay.'

'I'm not sure what I want to do. For now I will stay put but I might even settle down here. I like being here on Temmil and I like the house. There's a baby grand in there.'

She looked impressed by this news. The bass player was heading slowly back towards the platform. At that moment he had paused to talk to a couple of people at one of the tables.

Cea said, 'I will be playing for another half-hour. Are you going to stay on and listen to the rest?'

'Of course I am.'

'Let's have a drink or two afterwards to celebrate.' The bassist had stepped up to join us on the platform. Cea looked towards him and said, 'Teo – this is Sandro Sussken. An old friend of mine.'

'Pleased to meet you, Sandro,' he said pleasantly. When we shook hands I felt the hardened fingertips of someone who regularly played a string instrument. The fingers of my left hand were similarly callused from the violin. They had been like that all my life.

I walked back to my table and sat down. After a few moments Cea made an announcement into her microphone but because of the muffled acoustics I could not hear exactly what she said. I thought I heard her say my name. In a moment she and Teo began playing again.

The piece started with a slow introduction, Teo leading with a series of long bass runs, while Cea played quietly sustained chords, but then she took over the main theme.

I was suddenly fully alert. I recognized the music – it was an improvised, extended, subtly restructured version of the cadenza from the second movement of my piano concerto, the one Cea had performed at our final concert. As I realized what she was doing I saw her shifting on her stool before the piano, turning and looking back towards me across the wide cellar space. She was smiling.

Shortly before she completed the second half of her set I ordered a bottle of wine and two glasses, and had them brought to my table.

62

Someone put on records after Cea had finished her set and a few people began dancing in the space in front of the platform. We wanted to talk so we had to raise our voices to hear each other. Our heads were close together.

I told Cea the story of what had happened to me since the last time I saw her. She had known at the time that I was married, but said she was shocked to hear that the marriage had ended so suddenly and irretrievably. When I explained about the time detriment, it was a subject obviously familiar to her, but she nevertheless sympathized. I described in some detail my long journey across the Archipelago, the dealings with the adepts, and much else.

'You didn't give them money, did you?'

'I had to.'

'No you didn't. It's a racket – a way of taking money from tourists.'

'They wouldn't help me unless I paid them.'

'That's what they tell you. But the detriment can be corrected in other ways. No one who lives in the islands would ever go near the adepts. They're a bunch of crooks. There's an inexpensive insurance policy you could have taken out. You claim exemption at the Shelterate offices. You should talk to my father when you meet him. He travels around the islands a great deal.'

I was remembering the annoyance of dealing with the adepts, the apparently endless walking or driving about as a way of correcting lost or gained time, while I hobbled along with my luggage. I said nothing. I did not like the idea of having been rooked by those people, but I didn't want to go into the subject with Cea just then.

She was drinking quickly and soon we ordered a second bottle. She told me what had happened to her since we parted. The most serious change was the closing of the concert hall. Audience numbers declined sharply after our tour and several sponsors had withdrawn funds. The social nature of Temmil was changing, Cea said. More and more people were coming to the island to retire. Many of them were business people with a lot of cash to spend. There was some kind of scheme the seigniory had set up to attract wealthy people to Temmil, few of whom had any interest at all in the arts.

The sense of excitement about having an orchestra on Temmil, of greeting visiting artists, of setting up workshops for young musicians – all this had begun to fade away. Her own career as a concert soloist had come to an end, partly because of the loss of the hall but also because she had become the unwitting carer for her elderly mother. She said she was more or less trapped at home on Temmil, until what she called the inevitable happened. Her mother was in her early eighties. Cea said she adored her, of course, but—

'I loved what you were playing tonight,' I said. 'How does that sit alongside your classical training?'

'Music is music,' she said, which was of course something I entirely agreed with. 'When you hear the great jazz musicians you realize how skilful they are. My father played jazz – I grew up listening to him and playing the records he had. He took me to some of his gigs. I enjoyed his music but it was always the great classical composers I felt most drawn to. When I realized my career as a concert pianist was most likely over, playing in clubs like this was the only work open to me in town. It was really difficult for me and not simply because of money – I had never played jazz before and I had to learn the hard way. Back then there were more bars where they wanted live music so I was able to pick things up as I went along. That wouldn't be possible now – these days there's just this place still open. And one other, but that only opens at weekends.'

A new record came on, a slow number with romantic lyrics.

Several couples stood up and began to dance. Cea pushed back her chair.

'This is the one they always play before closing,' she said. 'Come on – let's celebrate. I'm happy to see you, Sandro.'

We went to the dance floor and she pulled me close against her. I realized she was slightly drunk, but then so too was I. We began moving around the dance floor, hardly in step, holding on and leaning against each other. The side of her face was against mine. I breathed her scents.

When we finally left the club she declared she wanted to see my house and try out the baby grand. She said she had recently retrained as a piano tuner – playing in clubs didn't pay enough, so she needed a secondary career. Tuning was interesting and lucrative. She promised to put everything right for me. I said I would like that. We laughed at what we saw as a double meaning. We were soon alone in the darkened street, unsteady on our feet. We walked slowly and deliberately up the gentle hills towards the edge of town. It was another hot night but there was a breeze from the sea and the stars were out. We held each other, arms and hands touching, and sides pressing. I was full of excitement – it had been a long time.

When we arrived at the house she forgot all about the baby grand. We went straight to bed.

63

I awoke in the night, unused to feeling the body heat of someone else sleeping against me. The windows were wide open and there was a draught from outside, but it was still a warm night. I shifted position, trying not to disturb her. Cea obviously sensed me moving, turned towards me, her hand resting on my chest. She settled down again. Her breathing was steady.

I was fully awake, though, and I lay on my back in the dark, as contented as I had ever been. This at last seemed to represent the real reason for my quest back to Temmil. I had not personified it directly to Cea but now that we were together again I realized that I had been burying, suppressing, a long-held wish to be with her again.

I suddenly saw in a different light all that guilt I felt after our one night together at the end of the tour. True, I had walked away from her and left her, but she had done much the same to me. That night we had been attracted to each other by the glittering excitement of the moment, the orchestra and the music, the heady roar of applause, the drinks party and excited conversations afterwards. We both knew this. Neither of us pretended anything else, consented to it, made no secret of what would happen soon after.

And soon after, it did happen. I travelled away the next day, Cea returned to her life here on Temmil.

I had regrets, I had a feeling of guilt, but these feelings were swamped by everything that happened on my return to Glaund. When next I had the mental space to remember the time with Cea, all that remained was the guilt.

As I was lying there beside her, with her unclothed body sprawling on the bed, dimly lit by the night glow from the window, I wondered if what I had been really going through was not guilt but a feeling of longing, of missing her, of wanting to be with her again. Now here I was.

I was happy that night in the warm dark, feeling the movement of her breath across my face and neck, sensing the strands of her hair lying against my shoulder, knowing that when I woke up in the daylight she would still be there.

I drifted back to sleep – then, suddenly, with no sense of subjective time passing, the sun was up, I was half-awake and Cea was still there beside me. She had turned over so that her back was towards me. For a few moments the euphoria I had felt during the night returned to me, but then, unexpectedly, my mood shifted.

In the bright daylight I looked around at the room we were in, the room with the bed. That is all it was. There was nothing personal or individual about it. Just the bed and a small table, my clothes dropped on the floor. Cea's were scattered elsewhere, probably on the floor by the other side of the bed. I had put no pictures on the walls, there were no books, the blinds, still wide open, were the ones that had been there when I moved in. It was not a room I could call my own.

Temmil itself was a disappointment. It was no longer the place I thought I had found, the place I wanted to be. A creeping conventionalism was taking the place over: restaurants with unimaginative menus, bars without live music, places that closed early every evening, gated communities, single-storey houses built on the slopes of the hills. The roads were being widened, streetlights were going up. I felt out of place, wanted something from the island that no longer existed. It was a paradise being concreted over for the sake of new and safe suburbs.

But I had been here only a short time. Perhaps I should stay for a while, learn the place, not rush to opinions about it?

I was fretting as these thoughts went through my mind. Beside me, I could sense Cea was waking up too.

I needed the stimulus of other people working in the same way as me. I was feeling my music slipping away. In the past I had thrived on the muscular difficulties of modernist music, the challenge, the satisfaction of being awkward and novel. Now I felt myself writing tunes, enjoying natural harmonies. Would this streak of easy familiarity also work itself out if I embedded myself more firmly in island life?

How deep should I go? How long should I stay?

Cea turned over to embrace me, laid her head on my chest.

'I have to go home now, Sandro,' she said quietly.

'At least stay and drink some coffee with me.'

She raised her head, looked at me.

'My mother can't get out of bed on her own. I have to be there for her. I should go now.'

'Will you come back?'

She was already sitting up, looking around for her discarded clothes.

'Maybe this evening. I have to be with her today – we planned to go shopping. She needs all sorts of things.'

She pulled on some of her clothes then used her mobile phone to call a taxi. She hurried to the bathroom before the car arrived, so I dressed too. There were so many things I wanted to say to Cea – I had imagined a relaxed morning with her while our mild hangovers slowly disappeared. Then some time together – perhaps a swim, a walk, a tour around the town? I wanted to talk with her about music, how she had come to adapt that cadenza of mine, where she and I would head next, what our future might be. All we had together was an instant of past, and an even shorter present. Could two people's future be built on such a flimsy basis?

I was no longer sure what I wanted: of me, of her, of this island. Most of all I did not want her leaving me like this. So soon, after last night.

I went down the lane with her and we waited until the taxi arrived. Then she was driven away, a dust cloud thrown up by the car's tyres from the unmade surface and drifting briefly. I walked back to the house. The day, hardly begun, had already lost its point.

I took a shower, put on some fresh clothes. I made myself breakfast and a large flask of coffee. In my music room – like my bedroom, it contained hardly anything personal, the usual mess of papers spread randomly on the floor – I sat at the piano while I sipped my first cup of coffee but my mind was empty. Nothing stirred inside me. I practised for a while, but I could still hear in memory Cea's fluid playing at the bar and all the pieces I usually went to for relaxation now sounded spiky, academic, cold.

I poured myself a second cup of coffee, returned to the piano, sat and stared at the keyboard. I had placed the coffee precariously on the floor beside my feet because there was nowhere else to put it. I could not risk standing it anywhere on or near the piano in case of accidental spills. I was thinking about Cea, the pleasures of the surprise meeting with her, what we had done, the promise of more. I was daydreaming about her, completely unprepared for what then happened.

Like a roaring in my mind I heard a great swelling of music – an imagining of complex orchestral music, intriguing, unique, complete. Above all, complete. A whole work.

It was over in less than a minute but in that time, in some kind of imaginative shorthand it is impossible to understand or describe, I heard the whole of what would probably be an extended orchestral suite of at least twenty or thirty minutes' duration. My normal method of composition was a slow and sometimes painful process of seeking notes on the piano, making marks on the manuscript, following an unending series of changes of mind, abandoning and restoring certain phrases – but this piece had come to me entire.

I knew it as well as something I had played all my life. I started playing the piano, hesitantly at first, but with an increasing sureness. The music was mine, coming from within.

I turned around, reached down to the floor for paper and pen, tried to scribble notes, but I knew immediately that my old way was no longer the right way. I rushed from the room, found my digital recorder, checked the battery, stood it beside me at the piano – then I started playing again. The sureness remained.

I played the piece through to the end. It was as if my mind and hands and heart were being guided by a spirit force, almost an example of automatic playing. I came at last to the finale, which was as whole in my imagination as the rest of the piece.

When it was over, shaking with excitement and relief, and still not at all sure what had happened to me or how, I sat slumped on the piano stool. I was glad no one was there with me – it was a moment of necessary solitude, beyond anything in my experience, beyond expression.

I checked the recorder: everything was safely stored in the memory.

I stared down at my cup of coffee, which, neglected while the spirit of the music absorbed me, had gone cold. I saw concentric rings fluttering across the surface, peaking briefly in the centre. I was thrilled by the music – was I trembling enough to transfer my excitement through the stool to the floor, and thence into the coffee? The rings shivered again to the centre, then again.

This time I felt it myself – the floor was shaking.

I heard a loud, frightening noise: a groaning, rasping sound, unlike anything I had experienced before. When I stood up it was as if vertigo had struck me. I staggered in terror across the room, recovered, felt myself toppling again. I reached out towards the piano, the most solid thing around me. The house was shaking – dust and pieces of plaster showered down from above. I lurched against the piano, trying to get my balance, because I knew I had to leave the house as soon as I could.

Then it stilled. The tremor passed. Silence fell once more.

The dust cloud started to drift and settle. The light fixture, hanging in the centre of the ceiling, continued to swing to and fro but that too was steadying. My heart was racing – brief and minor though it was, the earthquake had been terrifying.

I went out on to the balcony. Most of my view was across the open hillside or the sea, so there was not much difference to normality, but I saw that several people were standing out in the road that led down to the town. What I could see of the town from this position looked normal.

A siren started howling somewhere in the centre of Waterside, the eerie signal distorted by the distance.

64

Back in the house I switched on the television. I tuned to the scientific station, the one that monitored the volcano, and was immediately rewarded with an intense amount of information and commentary. Everyone who spoke or was interviewed was excited.

The likelihood of an eruption was now set at red – Imminent – and as if this was not warning enough the graphic in the corner of the television picture was flashing on and off urgently. Listening to the comments I learned that the alarm level had been steadily increasing during the night, a sense of emergency gripping the people who ran the project. There were several gradations of amber: Negligible, Minor, Small, Reduced, Average, and so on. Through the night it had climbed through Increased Amber, Large Amber, Dangerous Red. It had been upgraded to Imminent about an hour earlier. Tremors were being reported from several different parts of the mountain's environment, but for the moment emissions from the crater of the volcano were still at a normal level. The scientific stations had been evacuated and the seignorial policier forces were on standby for civilian evacuation, should that be necessary.

I found this exciting and alarming, but also thrilling. I called

Cea's mobile phone to see if she knew any more, but the call went to her voicemail. The recording mentioned a landline number, so I called that too. Again there was no answer.

I went back to watching television.

The full eruption began about half an hour later. All three of the remotely controlled cameras monitoring the crater and the largest of the fumeroles lost their pictures more or less at once – a spokesperson said they had been built to withstand huge physical pressures, so the cameras were still thought to be working, but there was suddenly so much steam and smoke that nothing could be seen.

I went out to my balcony and stood on the part of it from which I knew I could look in the direction of the Gronner's cone. I saw a vast, bulging plume of dark grey smoke or ash, rising in the distance above the trees that stood in the way. The plume was already high in the upper atmosphere. The wind was taking it towards the north-east, away from Temmil Waterside.

Later, it was announced on television that three active lava streams had appeared and were moving rapidly down the mountain. Two of them were already disgorging into the sea, while the third was moving across a thinly populated area to the north. Everyone on the island was informed that no emergency evacuation was necessary at present, but that people living in the vicinity of the Gronner should make themselves ready to be moved out at short notice.

Wondering if that meant me or Cea, I tried calling her again, without success.

There was something else, too. I was burning with the need to see her again, because I wanted to tell her about the astonishing music that had come flashing to me just before the eruption. I had never known music to present itself to me in that way: the completeness of it was uncanny. But beyond even that, in the excitement of the earth tremor, and the news of the eruption, I had almost overlooked the fact that the same thing had happened again.

As I had been standing on the balcony after the tremor, in the last few moments before the volcano burst forth, I had heard and felt in my imagination a beautiful romantic song, the complete music and the words as well: it was a ballad about a young man who discovers a wounded seabird on an isolated beach, repairs its wing somehow and despatches it to his loved one with a message of undying devotion. It was amazing, inexplicable.

Whence had such a song arisen? Unlike the time when I discerned the miraculous orchestral work, so much was happening then, just as the eruption was about to start, that I had been unable to play or record the song. I was already beginning to lose it. The details of it were fading. I could remember the sentiments and much of the story, but not the actual words – similarly, I could still sense the melody, but the phrasing and the arrangement of the voice were already leaving me.

The third time I tried to phone Cea I heard an electronic howl of broken communication. From the television I later learned that much of the island's digital network was temporarily out of action: masts had been destroyed and there was immense electrical disruption from the eruption. Some areas were already unable to receive television signals, and several telephone landlines had been cut.

However, the larger news, about the eruption itself, was optimistic. The pressure of the discharge was lessening and volcanologists were predicting that within a day or two the mountain would be starting to stabilize. Two settlements on the north side of the volcano had been evacuated but there were no reports yet of any serious casualties.

So the day went by. It was a memorable time for most people on the island, no less for me, although perhaps for slightly different reasons. Minor earth tremors continued at unpredictable moments throughout the day but the danger from the volcanic outflow diminished. I returned to the piano, listened to the recording I had made and began the slow, painstaking work of transcribing.

I had never known work like it – I had to invent the method as I went along. I had created the work myself, spontaneously, completely, but now I was having to re-create it in reverse, following the recording, which was itself taken from a sort of recording of my own creation.

I could not get in touch with Cea. The phones remained

unusable. I was missing her, but I was also starting to worry about her. I knew she had been planning to take her mother out – had they been caught somehow by the eruption? She had said she would try to see me in the evening but nothing had been arranged. I had no idea where she lived although I assumed it was somewhere in Waterside. The only way I knew how to contact her was by phone.

Long after dark I walked down into Waterside through the quietude of the warm night, to see if by chance Cea might be playing at the bar again. I was anyway curious to see how the town seemed after the disruption of the day but to me it looked fairly normal. There were no evident signs of damaged buildings and no new fissures in the ground. The town was quieter than usual though, and when I found the bar I discovered it was closed.

I went down to the harbour. The dark shape of Hakerline loomed across the narrow strait, with a blaze of intense light coming out of Hakerline Promise. It was so vivid I felt I could almost hear the raucous sounds of the night-time revels. I stared for a while, then I turned around and looked inland. From here it was normally possible to see the peak of the Gronner, but in the darkness that was of course difficult. I could see an intermittent flashing of yellow or orange glare, close to the crater.

Later, I walked back to my house.

65

Two days passed. Silence from Cea, a gradual diminution of activity from the volcano. The telephones were said to be returning to normal, but for some reason I could still not get through to Cea. I continued to try at two- or three-hourly intervals.

On the second morning, after a change of wind direction, spill from the outflow passed over the Waterside, dimming the sun and leaving a shroud of fine grey dust everywhere. This was a minor inconvenience compared with what some of the people who lived on the other side were putting up with. We heard about roads and rail lines blocked, farmlands submerged by fallen ash, one river diverted by a lava flow and many houses destroyed.

Motorized cleaners, operated by the seignioral authorities, moved along the streets of Waterside, sweeping up much of the spill.

I suppressed the feeling of frustration about losing contact with Cea, and concentrated on my work. I was deeply engaged with the challenge of first transcribing, then scoring and arranging, the music that had come to me shortly before the earth tremors. It was one of the most fruitful efforts of composition I had ever taken on but through it all I felt awkward questions nagging at me.

How did this experience come to me? Why had nothing like it ever happened before? I marvelled again and again at the completeness of the piece: had I been working on it in my unconscious for weeks? Was it based on other works I'd written earlier? (I thought and thought about this, without result.) Worse, could it possibly be based on some other piece of music I had heard, or overheard, then by some trick of the mind had claimed for myself?

I ransacked my mind and memory for any clues but always came to the same conclusion: by some miracle this music had passed into my consciousness, not only complete but completely original.

By the end of the third day of work I had achieved most of the reconstruction, and to be honest I was well pleased with the result. It was identifiably a composition that had all the hallmarks of my other work, but it was throughout an adventurous and unusual piece of writing. It had moments of pure excellence. The opening had shocks and surprises; the second passage of the suite was lyrical and sentimental; the third passage was an awakening; the climax was a restitution of order.

Cea called me on the morning of the fourth day. I was so pleased and relieved to hear from her that at first I hardly said anything. She told me she and her mother had been shopping in Waterside when the first tremor struck but that they had returned to their car and she had driven them back to their house. They had stayed there throughout the eruption. We talked about our separate experiences, which actually amounted to much the same: keeping up with events by watching television, eating, sleeping and waiting for phone connections to be restored. Cea said her mother been brave through the entire experience.

I did not mention, while we were still on the phone, that I had composed and scored an entire orchestral suite. I wanted to tell her in person, perhaps play her some of it on the piano.

'My father has turned up,' Cea said. 'He came in on the ferry last night from Hakerline. He's planning to stay here for a while.'

'Am I going to see you soon?' I said. 'There's something I want to show you. I've been writing. How about this evening?'

'We could meet during the day, if you wish. My father says he'd like to meet you.'

'I was thinking – just you and me. Alone.'

'Yes, but we could do that later this evening. Why not come over now? My father's here.'

I took a deep breath. 'Cea – I want to see you. Why should I meet your father?'

'Because he admires you. Because he knows what you mean to me.'

'Maybe tomorrow?'

But she was determined I should meet him immediately. She gave me the address of her house, told me how to find it, offered to drive over and pick me up. I said I would walk, even though by this time the sun was high and the dry ground was baking. The shrill sounds of insects filled the hot air.

The house was not far from the centre of Waterside in an area of old and grand houses, many of which were being converted to apartments. Cea came to the door to greet me and we embraced quickly but affectionately. She led me through a short darkened passageway beyond which was a paved courtyard, the inner walls of the house rising up around it. There was a pool with a source of water trickling down from above and several bushes were planted in huge ceramic pots. Two electric fans circulated air but the walls were so high that the sun did not strike straight down.

It was there I met Cea's parents, who were waiting for me to arrive. Her mother, whose name was Ellois, was much as I expected from Cea's description. She was elderly, shrunken and unable to walk. She would not shake hands with me and Cea explained that she was afflicted with arthritis. The wheelchair in which she sat had a parasol shade above it and she was wearing dark glasses. Throughout my time in the house she was to speak barely more than a few words to me.

But Cea's father was there too and he was not at all what I expected. His name was Ormand.

66

If before this meeting I had a mental image of Cea's father it was a vague one. Cea said I had met him at the concert on Temmil, which I did not doubt, but at best I recalled speaking to many strangers in a blur of excitement and pleasure, so many friendly people of all ages, male and female, wanting to congratulate me or speak well to me of the orchestra's performance. I assumed that her father, Ormand Weller, would have been one of the older ones. When I met Ellois – as Cea had described her, being in her eighties and suffering from problems of disability – I instantly assumed that Cea's father would be in the same general age bracket.

When I turned around to meet the other person there I saw a tall young man, straight-backed, slim, face unlined, and with a head of long dark hair. In the instant before Cea said anything I made the snap assumption that he was someone else: a neighbour, a friend, perhaps a brother of Cea's?

'Sandro, I would like you to meet my father,' Cea said. 'This is Ormand Weller – Alesandro Sussken.'

I was shaking hands with him politely before I could react.

Confusion and questions were coursing through me! I tried not to show the reaction on my face, but—

How could this young man be Cea's father?

How could this young man be the marriage partner of the sickly, elderly lady in the wheelchair?

Could this young man not be the partner of the woman, but a father to Cea by another relationship?

(Above all, negating the other questions): how could this young man be Cea's father when he seemed approximately the same age as her, and by all appearances a few years younger?

He was staring directly, frankly, unwaveringly into my eyes as we shook hands. The greeting and the close regard went on longer than I wanted – I wished he would release my hand, step back from me, allow me a space of some kind in which I could understand who this was and what he represented in Cea's life.

I said quietly and ineffectually, 'Your name is Ormand?'

'Yes. Ormand Weller.'

'I'm so pleased to meet you,' I added politely, as the handshake went on and on. Inside I was thinking: who the hell is this?

'We must speak together, Sandro. I hope you will not mind.'

At last he let go of my hand and turned away to where a small table stood, laden with various drinks and glasses. He opened a bottle of beer for me, taken from a chill-box standing there. Condensation immediately formed on the cold glass. I looked around for Cea but she had moved across to her mother and was leaning down beside her. The two women were speaking quietly together.

'I happened to be away from Temmil when the Gronner erupted,' he said. 'I was playing a gig in a nightclub in Hakerline Promise. I came back as soon as I could. They cancelled the ferries for a day or two, but I was finally able to catch the boat last night. You benefited from the eruption?'

I said in surprise, 'Benefited?'

'Did it speak to you?'

'I don't know what you mean,' I said.

'I think you do.' He took my arm, then led me away to a sort of alcove behind the flow of water into the pool. The water sounded louder there. I gained the impression he did not want to be overheard. 'All islands speak,' he said. 'Some of them speak louder than others. Cea does not know this. Nor does her mother. But I believe you understand that.'

We were both now standing in direct sunlight, which because of a sloped roof at the top of one wall was admitted for the time being into that corner.

'I have been sensing something,' I said cautiously. I did not want to tell him about the whole suite that I had gained just before the first tremors. 'You are Cea's father?' I said. 'That's right, isn't it?'

'Of course. Why should she and I pretend otherwise? And you are Cea's lover, I believe.'

I did not know how to reply to that. Much was still uncertain.

'You are younger than I would have thought,' I said directly. 'If I might say so.'

'You might. And I would have thought the same of you.' He drank from his beer bottle and gave a short, humourless laugh. 'Appearances can be deceptive.'

I quietly indicated Ellois and Cea, who were still together. Cea was sitting beside her mother's wheelchair on a small wooden chair. They were not looking towards us. Cea had her head turned away, nodding as her mother said something to her.

'You are Ellois's partner?'

'She is my wife. We have been married for many years. And before you ask the next question – yes, Cea is our daughter.'

'I don't understand.'

'I think you do. I am the same age as Ellois – in fact I am a year younger than her, but that's not what you are asking me, is it, Sandro? I hope you don't mind me calling you by your first name – for many years I have been a great admirer of your music, and I defer to you. For a long time I thought of you only as Sussken. The traditional compliment of one artist to another, using only the surname. But, Msr Sussken, now we have met—'

'What is it you are saying?'

'We have travelled in the islands, you and I. Not together, of course – we both know that. But we have followed the same routes. East or west. Across the straits, following the currents, responding to the allure of the islands. Time has a gradual effect. The direction makes no difference in the end. Look at the both of us!' He was standing in front of me, staring directly at me. He opened his hands towards me. 'You are in fine physical shape, for a man of your age.'

'And so are you.'

'We have both travelled through the islands. Look at me.'

We were standing only a short distance away from each other.

Suddenly, I could see past the superficial evidence of youth. His skin was clear, his eyes were bright, his hair was full. He looked fit. He looked agile, strong. He looked like a healthy man in his early or middle thirties. So did I – every day I relished the return of the youthfulness gifted to me by the gradual.

But beyond the suppleness of Ormand's body, the physical energy, I could now detect something in his expression, his demeanour. There was a sense of weariness, of experience of the world, of a history of achievement and disappointment and hopes and happiness and despair. He had the look of someone who had travelled a great distance, lived long beyond the normal span.

'Drink your beer, Sandro,' he said and tipped his own bottle against his lips, swallowing twice or three times. He wiped the back of his hand across his mouth. I had felt the neck of the bottle warming in my hand so I drank some of the beer while it was still cold. In the corner where we were standing the volcanic ash had accumulated – blown there, perhaps, or swept deliberately to clear the larger area. It was all over my sandals, clinging to my bare lower legs. I tried brushing some of it away, but it made no difference. 'What happens to you and me when we cross the gradual tides does not happen to everyone,' Weller continued. 'My wife, my daughter, all my friends, my neighbours, the people who pass me by in the streets, the musicians with whom I play, the audiences who come to watch us – they also travel, they too move from east or west, they too sail across the straits that lie between islands, but they do not, cannot, respond when the islands speak.'

'Speak?'

'The islands speak. We both know that, Sandro. We are adept.'

'Why do you use that word?'

'What other word would you use?'

'I don't know. I met some adepts while I was travelling. I wasn't sure who or what—'

'You would have met them, I know. There are many of them, hanging about in our seaports. Cea thinks they are all thieves, but I am more sympathetic. They assume they are the same as us but we are different from them. What I mean by that is that we have the same skills, the same sensitivities as them, but you and I are musicians and they are not. Musicians are not more greatly adept, but music gives us a focus for what we perceive of the islands, what we hear when the islands speak. Some of the adepts I know have a commitment to the arts of other fields, some of them are philosophers, writers, painters, innovators, entrepreneurs, doctors. They hear the voices of the islands too. But you will not meet adepts of that sort hanging around outside the Shelterate office on a small island. Those people you have met, and will probably meet again, are adepts who have become skilled in the gradual slippage of time. Time graduality does not interest me, and I assume you feel the same. They draw from the islands the strength to resist the gradual and with that they make a living from the tourists who pay them. But their adeptness is superficial, variable. Tell me now, more interesting to us both – have you heard the music of the islands?'

'I heard music a few moments before the first tremor in the ground, when the volcano blew.'

'A long piece?'

'A whole orchestral piece,' I said. 'I had never known anything like it. It was scored, arranged. It came to me as inspiration.'

'Yes – inspiration!' he said.

'Then there was another when the volcano erupted but there was so much going on around the house that it faded, and I could not recollect it afterwards.'

'You were never before inspired by the islands?'

'Well – yes.'

A hundred times, in fact, from a hundred islands in the stream. I knew all their names, knew their harmonies. But suddenly I remembered the day when I was seven years old, in my parents' junk-filled loft beneath the roof, pressing my hands against the steep window. Looking out to sea for the first time, looking out at three island shapes in the sea beyond my town, dark, mysterious, full of promise. Something had resonated then. That first time. Music had flowed on that day, music had been heard. I could do nothing about it at that age, but my talent was prodigious.

'I too have heard music all my life,' said Ormand Weller,

Cea's impossibly young father. 'Some of it was what I now know to be yours. I heard tides and winds and the sounds of seabirds, the blast of wind on a moor, the suck of a retreating tide. It was beautiful, moving, mysterious, deeply true. I was young, I thought the music was mine. Inspirational, as you say. Later I discovered it was Sussken's, not mine. Yours, Sandro. The music that speaks to us from the islands is not unique, as we believe or as some of us prefer to believe. It is in fact communal, consensus, shared, part of the gradual. It is present in the fields of time that lie around every island. It is the great hall of music, the fundament, the sky, the world. Some of the other adepts describe a vortex, a gradient, a distortion of time, but to me the gradual is a heart, a living soul, a continuum of musical response, sung to us, played to us, spoken to us by one island, by the next island, by all islands. We alone understand it.'

'You say you know the music was mine?'

'Yours as much as it was mine. It's a commonality, Sandro. I found out about your work, what you had made of the islands. I was confounded by what I had done. As soon as I understood what the gradual was capable of, I never used it for inspiration again.'

'I know you,' I said. 'I know your work. I know what you have done. I have bought copies of your records.'

He nodded his acceptance of that.

'You are And Ante!'

'I am. I was. I am no longer. I am also sorry for what I did.'

He raised the beer bottle to his lips once more but this time I noticed that his hand was shaking. His eyes were moist and for the first time he looked away from me, evasively.

Cea said, 'I am going to take my mother for a short walk.'

She had already turned the wheelchair around and was pushing it towards the passageway. I wanted to go with her. I did not want to be left here alone with her father.

'You have to embrace the gradual, Sandro,' he said as Cea went away. 'It comes to you, but you have to surrender to it. It is not an option for you. Or for me. It is not a creative force as we think, but a reflection of our own imaginings. All your life you have felt that response, the surge from the islands. That's right, isn't it?'

I stood there in the courtyard with Weller, still not truly understanding, still remembering the music I had heard in my mind, still not able to acknowledge the truth of it. Dust and fallen ash we had stirred up with our agitated movements were drifting about in the sunlight, fine debris from the volcano. I could smell it in the air I was breathing, feel it stinging my eyes.

But I knew the music would come again.

Ormand Weller, And Weller, And Ante, went across to his guitar case. He took out his instrument, slipped the strap across his shoulder, then he sat down on the low wall around the pool and he started to play.

It was the same music that had come inspirationally to me from the earth tremor.

67

I left Weller in the courtyard. He remained seated on the wall of the pool, one leg crossed over the other, the guitar resting on his lap. His head was bent low as he played. The tips of his callused fingers made the strings squawk as he moved his left hand across the frets.

The sun was at its highest, the heat a kind of unmoving mass in the street between the tall houses. I walked along, feeling as if I was forcing my way in the heat, heading back the way I had come, hoping to see Cea again. Ash flurried around my legs as I walked.

It was briefly possible to glimpse the Gronner from this part of the town and I could see that although the outflow had decreased the eruption was still going on. The wind was spreading the ash cloud – some of it was moving above the town. The rotten-egg smell of sulphur dioxide was stronger than before.

If the island was speaking to me then, I could not hear it.

The way back towards my house led past the harbour, but because of the smell, the unhealthy feeling of ash and dust and expelled gases, I turned off down a narrow side street, which I thought would give me a shortcut to the sea and the chance of a fresh breeze.

As I reached the coast road, with the harbour in sight, I met Cea. She was walking alone, holding a cloth across her mouth and nose. There was no sign of her mother or the wheelchair. When she noticed me she reacted at once, looking quickly to one side, as if seeking an escape route. Or that is how it seemed to me.

'You were deep in conversation with my father,' she said, when we came up to each other. 'I didn't want to interrupt.'

'We finished. Where is Ellois?'

'I took her to the ... the residence.'

'I thought you said— She doesn't live with you, then?'

'Not all the time. Are you returning to your house?'

'For the moment.'

'I hardly saw you, Sandro.'

'You wanted me to meet your father,' I said. 'And you said we would get together again this evening. Shall we?'

We had moved to the side, into the shadow of one of the warehouses on the edge of the harbour area. When we were out of the direct sun it was a little more comfortable, but the hot air and the ever-clinging dust were just as unpleasant. Cea was keeping her distance from me, still holding the cloth across her mouth.

'Let me phone you later,' she said. She edged around me, stepping out briefly into the sun's glare, then pressed herself back into the shade. She was looking along the street, towards where she lived. She wanted to get away from me.

'Cea?'

'Yes.'

'What's happened? Why are you like this?'

'I heard what my father was saying to you.' She moved out from the shade and began walking back towards the house. I followed her. 'I realized what you are,' she said. 'I've always sensed it in you but today I realized what it really meant. You're the same as him. I can't deal with another like him. He knew all about you before you came to Temmil, but then he would. He has the adept abilities. Look at him, Sandro! He's in his eighties and he acts like a young man! He has spent most of his life as a young man. How can I ever understand that? My father! And now you.'

'I'm much older than you, in my fifties,' I said. 'You know that. I have never tried to deceive you.'

'It's not that.'

'Then what?'

'You are adept, like him. I can't – I want to leave this island, I want to get away, leave my parents, go back to the life I had before I met you—'

'Why should I prevent you from doing that?'

I tried to take her arm but she pulled it sharply away from me, changed direction, dodged into an alley running between the backs of two rows of houses. I turned to follow her, but she was walking more quickly. Her head was bent forward, the cloth was pressed over her nose and mouth. Of course I could have caught up with her, but her meaning was clear. I watched her hurrying away from me, into the deeper shadows of the narrow lane, past more houses, never looking back. Then she turned, climbed some steps that led up from the roadway. I lost sight of her.

I stood for a while where she had left me, wondering if she would come back, and also wondering if I wanted her to. Some quirk of the street layout made the sound of the volcano louder here, its intermittent rumbling channelled by the narrow roadways. I had not really paused to listen to it until now, because from the start it had been a deep sound, more a feeling in the gut than a sound, happening below the threshold of audibility. But as its own internal built-up pressure was eased its voice was less threatening, as if its throat was being cleared. I could not see the volcano from this part of the streets although the thin haze of its outflow was drifting across the sun.

I walked into the centre of Waterside, hoping to find a taxi to carry me home, but it was the early afternoon when everything closed down and the shops were shut. I saw several unattended taxis lined up in the town rank.

Half an hour later I was back at the villa. As soon as I was inside I stripped off all my clothes and went gladly into the shower cubicle. The dust and ash washed away, making a thin gritty smear across the white plastic base as they poured into the drain hole.

The shower spray made a light staccato sound as it bounced off my head and shoulders, a rhythm, a simple melody. Was it speaking to me?

I towelled my hair then went out to sit naked on my balcony, letting the sun dry me. I did not stay there long – I could feel the thin grit still drifting around me.

68

As once before I knew I should depart from Temmil as soon as possible. It was not the place I had imagined it to be, it was not a place I wished to stay. I had begun to dislike it. And the past – I had not come to Temmil to find Cea again, but that is what had happened and it could not be denied. I had also discovered that a fragment of the past does not fill the present, nor provide a future.

I slept uneasily that night, and alone. Cea made no contact and I did not expect her to. Her silence provided me with possible answers to questions I had glimpsed but in my half-awake state could barely form: will she?, do I?, can we?, should I?, what is it? ... and so on, the inevitable circling enigmas of insomnia. None could be answered, except by the breach she had made, by our absence from each other. If I did not see her, answers were unnecessary.

I was awake several times in the night, thinking about her, finding it hard to breathe in the tropical climate: the smell of gases, the feeling of dirt and dust everywhere, the ever-present heat and humidity. A thunderstorm rolled in, drenched the hillside with a cloudburst, soon rolled away. It was nothing like the storm I had experienced on Demmer but for fifteen minutes my room was intermittently lit up by the flashing lightning. Through the wide open windows I felt the thrill of being close to heavy rain without being caught in it. The thunder was loud and close but that was all. I did not sense any threat from it. For a few minutes after the storm moved away the air felt cooler, but that did not last.

The volcano grumbled all night long. It sounded less menacing than before but it was something I had grown accustomed to during the last few days. Was it speaking to me at this moment, as Ormand Weller had described? I drifted back to sleep before I could gain a clear reply. It was a night of questions without answers.

In the morning I sat at my table, ate some breakfast and drank two cups of coffee. The outflow from the volcano had shifted again with the wind, so now the sun was undimmed. The fierce rain in the night had washed away much of the dust and ash around my house.

I had to leave Temmil. The resolution I made the evening before returned. I felt it as surely as anything I had ever known. There was nothing to keep me here any longer. The town bored me, I knew no one except Cea, and perhaps her father, and it was not the place where I had thought I wanted to spend the rest of my life.

But I felt beset by practicalities, large and small.

The house: rent paid ahead, agreements signed for land taxes, the supply of electricity, water and so on. Unfinished work: I wanted to write and compose and now I had found a house that I felt comfortable in and where there was a splendid piano. I knew that if I set off on my travels once more it would mean another postponement of work. I could not compose while on ships. My illicit money: held for now in a Temmil bank and I wasn't sure how safe it would be to try to withdraw it from the account. Property: I had started accumulating books and magazines, and records, sheet music, manuscript paper, new clothes, pairs of sandals. I now owned four broad-brimmed hats made of different materials. The prospect of carrying all that stuff around with me, taking it on the ships into those cramped cabins, made me tired to think about it. And the ships themselves, with those cabins, the occasional need to share with a stranger, the constant engine noise and vibration, the smell of fuel oil, the long halts in ports. Much of the romance of a life on the sea had fled, or proved illusory.

I was all too aware of the inconvenience of shipboard life, the discomforts, the feeling of being trapped by it.

And I could not, should not, forget the fact of the arrest warrant. I felt reasonably safe from the long reach of the military junta so long as I remained on Temmil, but I worried that the moment I started making myself known to authorities by passing through official border controls I would be identified and arrested. I did not dare to imagine the retribution the Generalissima and her cronies would exact on me.

Above all I felt a dread of having to engage again with the gradual and the time detriment it created. Every port of call that I made on my travels would involve having to deal with the adepts, never resolving the mysteries of the stave, never finding a solution to the tiresome carrying of my baggage through hot streets and on small boats. Nothing would be explained and I would suffer a constant drain on my money.

All practicalities, some of them dreary. Music for me was the voice of the human spirit. It existed only in the space between the instruments that produced it and the ear that appreciated it. It was the movement and pressure of molecules of air, dispersed and replaced instantly and unceasingly. It lived nowhere in reality: gramophone records, digital discs, were merely copies of the original. The only real record that existed of music was the original score, the black pen marks on the staves, but they were cryptic, had no sound, were written in code – they had no meaning without the human spirit that could break the code, interpret the symbols. And music survived not only the lives of those who played it, but the life of the man or woman who composed it.

Yet for all this recondite idealism I was tied to the real world by its realities. I wished profoundly I could walk away from them.

I went down to the harbour in Waterside, thinking I would make some enquiries about travelling without the need for the stave, free of the adepts. Cea had mentioned the existence of an insurance policy that I had not heard of before, and the adept Kan had told me about a licensing arrangement provided by tour operators. Both of these seemed promising alternatives.

Regardless of the possible financial cost I felt either of them might be a better method, less involving, less annoying.

My hopes were disappointed. The tour operators would only provide the licence when a firm and pre-paid booking was made several months in advance and after the route had been set out in detail and agreed. Only standardized routes could be used – any diversion from these had to be surveyed in advance and an extra fee paid. The licence would in any event never be applied to a route that ended up in Glaund. The insurance policy was available solely to people who had been born in the Archipelago and had been permanently resident in the islands for at least the last ten years.

New practicalities, new oppressors of the spirit.

While I was in the harbour area I walked across to the Shelterate building, with a half-formed idea of perhaps speaking to some of the adepts who were normally waiting around for business. I was surprised to discover there was no one there. The bench and canopy where the adepts normally waited were empty. The Shelterate building itself was closed and locked. The harbour office told me no inter-island ships were expected that day.

I accepted that as an explanation yet as I walked back I noticed the familiar sight of the regular ferry that plied between Temmil and Hakerline. This was a large open motor boat, piloted by a single crewman – passengers sat on the thwarts around the inside rim of the hull, or stood in the main well. It was heading into Waterside's harbour at that moment. Did the ferry not count as an inter-island ship?

I waited around to see what happened.

It pulled up alongside the sloping jetty, the motor idling. Passengers disembarked, others boarded for the return trip to Hakerline. The arriving passengers walked across the harbour, past the closed Shelterate building and strolled into town or went to the line of waiting taxis.

That evening I walked down to the club where Cea played, but after I had paid the entrance fee and was inside the dance area I discovered that another small group was playing. Among them was the bassist, Teo, who had accompanied Cea, so in the interval I approached him.

'I was hoping that Cea would be playing tonight,' I said to him. 'Will she be here later?'

'Who did you say?'

'Cea – Cea Weller. You were playing with her a few nights ago.'

'Weller – is she a pianist? Guitarist?'

'A pianist,' I said.

'I'll ask one of the others.' Teo lit a cigarette then turned his back on me and went to where the other musicians were standing at the bar. I waited around for a few minutes but it was clear my message about Cea was not being relayed.

I walked home, following the road out of town along the coast. Because of the lie of the land along here it was possible to see the Gronner from a short section of the road. As I was approaching the side lane that led up eventually to my house, I heard a deep rumbling noise from the direction of the mountain and saw a brilliant yellow-white spill of flame bulging up from the summit. It was followed by a second eruption, even bigger, but not a third. I could see a torrent of lava, molten rocks, spurting up into the sky – from this safe distance the explosions looked like a wild fireworks display. The noise of the eruptions, delayed for a few seconds, reached me. They were powerful enough to feel like a pressure wave.

I hurried home, switched on the television and soon the science and news channels were describing what was happening. The lava flows had suddenly intensified – a new one had appeared on the town side but it had poured into a transverse valley and was not likely to threaten the main part of the town. I left the television playing but went through to the other room. I sat by my piano, hands on the keys.

I was in darkness. Behind me, visible through the open windows, was a view of the calm sea, untroubled beneath the night sky. If I looked back over my shoulder I could see a few navigation lights and the dark, vague shapes of the islands that were out there in the near distance.

I could not hear the eruption itself although I was as aware as always of a deep, throbbing bass note, the sound of the pressure of the magma releasing into the world. Even in the darkness

I was keeping my eyes closed. I was concentrating on what I understood to be the spirit of the music, the heart of the island, the explosion into the world.

I was where I wanted to be: islanded. This island, any island. My dissatisfaction with Temmil was based on the surface, so not relevant to the spirit – the true island lay beneath. My hands felt alert, the fingertips were tingling. My heart was beating a little faster. I was excited but calm. I was waiting. I remembered how Cea had taken the cadenza of my piano concerto, had clearly listened to it intently and deeply several times, learnt it as a classical pianist would, but then later through improvisation, the freeing of the spirit, she had disentangled the heart of the music from the notes I had written. What she then played was both instantly recognizable as my music yet was produced completely afresh, as new, as if it came from the soul, the spirit.

I found the basso profundo note of the eruption: a deep F sharp, wavering, half a tone up, down, back again. I sustained it, played it again and again. One note, unheard by any but me.

The volcano continued.

Later I improvised, sensing the relief of magmatic pressure as the eruption continued, clearing out the hidden passages of the mountain's core: a less deep note, less certain, more likely to burst, relax, find a different tempo. Music from the spirit of the island's heart.

As dawn came I was still awake, still at the keyboard, exhaustion holding me to account. My left hand ached, my head felt heavy, my eyes had been closed for much of the time. I sensed the growing lightness of daybreak from the window, but by then I had found the sound, the beating heart of the island. As Weller had said, the island spoke. I alone heard, I alone listened through the night. I alone responded.

69

I dressed. I put on my loose robe, my hat with the widest brim. I found my most comfortable sandals. I might need a little money so I took two small denomination notes, each of thalers, simoleons and talents. A handful of coins. I had been keeping a note of household bills in a pocket memo pad so I took that too, first tearing off the pages where I had written down what I spent on groceries, postage stamps, and so on. All the remaining pages were blank. I found a pencil, sharpened it.

I tidied my house then locked it up. I fed my arms through the straps of the case, and hoisted my violin on my back.

These were the only practical matters that interested me.

I walked down the lane, along the road, down the sweeping curve of hill that led to the town. The sun was up, but still low. White gauzy clouds high in the east filtered the rays. It was the coolest part of Temmil's day.

Overhead, the sky was clear. No outflow of ashes or smoke or steam or dust.

The road ran beside the sea for a short distance so I walked down to the beach. Temmil's lagoons were gentle in their action on the shores, so there was only shingle here. I crunched down to the waterline and squatted on my haunches to watch. Small waves broke. I stared across at the reef – a brown jaggedness was containing the lagoon. I had always intended to swim out to the reef one day but had never done so. I had seen photographs in the shops by the harbour, some of them taken underwater in brilliant colours. There was much of Temmil I still did not properly know.

When I reached the harbour the whole place was still. Small boats were at their moorings, others were drawn up on the shingle where part of the beach continued. The tide was low. No ship waited at the quay. The harbour office was closed without lights showing. The Shelterate building was the same.

I felt a breeze coming in from the sea, with a hint of the day's heat to come. It blew in from elsewhere, carried marine freshness, the scents of distance.

I walked around to the wharf side of the Shelterate building, where the adepts' canopy was strung above the metal bench on which they waited for custom. No one was there.

I went to the bench, sat down, stared at the cracked concrete floor, the remaining ashes and dust from the eruption, a few pebbles from the beach. A metal sign clanked lightly against a wall as the breeze moved it to and fro.

Renettia appeared. She was unsurprised to see me.

'Are you going to use a name?' she said, without preamble.

'I am Sandro. Is that good enough?'

'You should have a name to use. What's in there?' She was indicating the case on my back.

'That's my violin.'

'Then that is the name you should use. Never tell it to anyone you help. They will know who you are, because they will see that on your back.' She produced one of the hand tools that I had thought were knives and offered it to me. 'Do you have one of these?'

It appeared to be new. The handle was made of varnished wood and the blade, forged steel, was contained in a stiff little leather protector. A silver chain dangled from the handle. I popped open the leather cover, looked closely at the precisely milled point, sharp as a needle, cold as a chisel. I held the tool by the handle, felt its balance, the cleanness of a good knife, a craft tool.

'May I have this one?' I said.

'It's yours.'

'How much?'

She looked uninterested. 'No charge. Do you know how to use it?'

'I know how it is used,' I said.

'Not the same. Can you use it?'

'Show me.'

She sat down on the bench beside me, while I used the strap to attach the chain to my wrist. I was going to take out my own stave, which I had stored inside the violin case, but Renettia had brought another stave with her, new and untouched. She passed it to me, allowed me to feel it, hold it, run my fingertips along its smooth length. I felt the familiar sensation of awareness, of readiness.

'This is a stave for practice,' she said. 'Never, ever, give it to a traveller. Keep it or throw it away when you are ready, but it is for learning with.'

'No charge?' I said.

'No charge.'

She showed me how to hold the stave in one hand, the tool in the other. I would find the relevant area by touch. I tried it.

Halfway along the shaft of the stave I sensed something akin to a pinpoint of heat. It touched me with a spot of energy, without burning. I moved my finger over it several times to be certain of where it was. Then I moved the point of the tool to the place and held it there.

Renettia said, 'It detects a detriment. Move the blade forward, towards the tip.'

I did so and in the same instant, without my volition, I felt the handle turning within the grip of my hand. As I slid the point of the blade forward, an exact, precise spiral was etched around the stave. It stopped without my intervention.

'There is an increment too,' said Renettia. 'See if you can find it.'

I concentrated on what she was showing me. I became absorbed. I was mystified by what was happening but elated too. After a few attempts I could readily discern the difference between a detriment and an increment. The nature of the island was another challenge: a broader area of sensitivity, easier to miss or misinterpret. Renettia showed me how to slide my thumb along the main rod of the stave, feeling for the island.

'You will know it,' she said.

But it was difficult and my thumb went to and fro. I was seeking an area of heat, or vibration, or that more general sense of awareness, but nothing was there that I could sense. Then Renettia showed me – there was a tiny patch of roughness which I had thought was a flaw in the way the stave was smoothed. I held my thumb against it. The bass note I had sustained through the night was immediately clear to me. To my spirit.

'It's Temmil,' I said. 'I know it.'

'There's another one – find it.'

The second one was easier to locate because now I knew what I was looking for. This time the minute area of roughness was close to the tip of the stave.

'Name it,' Renettia said.

I struggled for a moment with an unfamiliar name, knowing nothing about it.

'Yenna?' I said. 'Also called in island patois Overhang. A treaty, a convention, the Yenna Convention?'

'Yenna. Can you tell what it is?'

All I could detect was a single note, a plaintive sound, but when I tried to describe it to Renettia it meant nothing to her. 'Can we go there?' I said.

'Go next.'

'Where is Yenna?'

'No idea. Mark it.'

I etched a new line.

The matter of the gradual was also not easy to grasp. Renettia said I would have to work out my own way of interpreting what the stave told me and then calculate the necessary correction of the gradient. She showed me some examples, which I drew with the sharp little blade. The stave was quickly gaining a wide hachure of criss-crossing etched lines. It was beautiful and enigmatic. I kept holding it up to admire it.

'When you need me I will come with you to help calculate,' Renettia said. 'It is an obscure matter, impossible to explain, but you will soon understand it in your own way. I cannot teach gradual calculation to you – I can only show how you learn it.'

The sun was soon high and the familiar swelter of the day was rising around us. I was completely wrapped up in what Renettia was showing me, focusing so closely that I was only half aware of all the growing business and activity of the harbour as the day started, the noises and the movement of people and boats. I was leaning forward with the weight of my violin pressing on my back.

When I did look around me, finally, I discovered that Renettia and I were no longer alone beneath the canopy – half a dozen more young people had arrived from somewhere and were sitting, standing or sprawling around in the shade. None of them acknowledged me. One of them was Pheelp and he ignored me as he always did.

Renettia said, 'A ship is about to dock.'

I turned my head and saw the long dark shape of a passenger ship closing in on the harbour wall. Black smoke was pouring from her funnel and a blast from her siren resounded across the harbour.

Renettia said, 'Don't look. Learn this now, Violin. Never look at the ship.'

'What? You told me to.'

'I informed you. Not point it out. Show no interest. And put away the stave. You must be ready – it might be you.'

I turned away, slipping the stave beneath my robe. Along with the other adepts I sat in an affect of uninterest, looking at the sky, staring at the ground, keeping my eyes away from anywhere near the direction of the dock. Time passed.

It was not long before a stream of passengers moved away from the ship and headed for the Shelterate building. We did not stare at them and none of them noticed us.

Later, when the ferry from Hakerline came in, a middle aged woman made contact with one of the male adepts who was waiting under the canopy.

I heard him say her name, then, 'Ten thaler.' The woman paid up immediately and handed over her stave. After he had etched a minute scratch on the wooden rod they walked together to the road that ran alongside the harbour. He waited while she spoke to one of the taxi drivers. After they had driven away he walked back to rejoin us.

I was getting hungry. I said to Renettia, 'Do we eat?'

'Of course we eat. We are people, Violin.'

We went to one of the harbourside cafés. I spent the rest of the day practising with the stave, but mostly just waiting.

70

On only the second day I was sitting with the other adepts when a cruise liner arrived at the port. I waited with the others to see how many people disembarked and from the stream of people who appeared, pushing luggage trolleys or tugging their own wheeled cases, it seemed likely it was going to be a great number. While I stared at the ground Renettia said to me quietly, 'Cruise passengers usually on organized tours without staves. Wait to see what happens.'

The crowd pushed on past us to the Shelterate building, where most of them had to cluster in the yard while the crush inside was eased. Many of them, in particular a large group of men wearing brightly coloured sporting shirts, were grumbling about the heat. From the amount of noise they were making most of them seemed drunk. We sat and sprawled beneath our canopy, making no move. One by one the mostly disgruntled passengers were emerging from the Shelterate building. They walked off towards the town, heading in many cases for the taxi rank.

Then suddenly I knew I was required. I did not understand how. I stood up, and walked towards a young man who had emerged from the Shelterate building.

'Taner Couter?' I said. He looked at me in surprise, noticing the top of the violin case strapped to my back. 'Let me see your stave,' I said.

'How do you know my name?' he said.

I took the stave from him and felt gently along the wooden shaft. There were already many curled lines and spirals etched along most of it. I discovered a small detriment immediately.

'You have come from Nestor,' I said. 'In transit to Ferredy Atoll?'

'Yes.'

I was aware that Renettia had also left the shade of the canopy and was standing behind me. I felt reassured by her doing that. I took out the etching tool and quickly drew a short line, a straight one, not far from the handle.

'Forty simoleons,' I said.

71

After Taner Couter had departed on his way to Ferredy, Renettia and I went to Yenna. This was outside the Ruller Group, in a remote part of the Dream Archipelago. Renettia had never been there before. We saw at once that the arrangements for the adepts were not good – there was no shading canopy, for one thing, and we had to stand exposed to the sun. No other adepts were there. Renettia said little to me – this was her way, as it was the taciturn way of most of the adepts.

As soon as we arrived, Renettia asked me for the stave she had given me for practice.

I gave it to her, but to my surprise she broke it over her knee – it snapped at the point where the blade met the handle.

'You no longer need it,' she said.

She dropped it in a bin. I wanted to have a look at it, see what if anything was inside it, but she warned me not to.

We adjusted our own staves. Renettia said this was always essential on arrival at a new island.

Other adepts began arriving and Renettia and I went to find some food. While we were eating she congratulated me on how I had removed Taner Courter's detriment.

'The first one is never easy, Violin, but you made it seem natural,' she said.

'How was that calculation done?' I said, remembering a long walk through streets behind the harbour, while Msr Couter followed with his luggage.

'It was your calculation, not mine,' she said.

'But—'

Silence.

Why had we come to Yenna? She did not say. Why was it called Overhang by the local people? She did not know, or she did not say.

When we walked across to the yard behind the Shelterate building I was surprised to see Kan was one of the adepts who was there. I tried to speak to her, but she turned her back on me.

The port in Yenna was a largely industrial one, so the arrival of passenger ships seemed to me unlikely. However, within an hour or so of our taking up position a small ferry did arrive and about twenty or thirty passengers came ashore.

One of the male adepts, someone I had not seen before, said, 'Hey, Violin. It's you again.' Some of the others laughed.

I went forward.

'Mave Louster?' I said to a young woman, who was burdened with a baby in arms and a small child in a push chair.

'You want my stave?' She appeared grateful I was there.

'Twenty thaler,' I said, holding the stave between my finger-tips. She had come from Mee, the island next to Yenna, a short trip, an increment of less than fourteen minutes. Renettia nodded her approval at my work.

After that we went to Cheoner, where the port was called Cheoner Maxim. I remembered having passed through this island while I was travelling. We adjusted our staves immediately we arrived but I waited in vain with the other adepts for two days. On the third morning a newly disembarked married couple selected me. I heard two of the other adepts commenting on my violin case.

The situation this time was unusual. The man had apparently lost his stave while on the ship and needed a replacement. I was not sure what to do about this but Renettia was standing by and she said that had to be dealt with before anything else. She sold him a new one.

One hundred simoleons.

She pocketed the money then passed the man's new stave to me. I identified the island location, then established the detriment, which was a fairly large one of just over seven days. My etched lines on the pristine blade were a matter of pride for me. Renettia and I set about the calculation that would correct the gradient.

Forty more simoleons – this was paid to me.

To enact the calculation we required a car, which Renettia obtained easily – she later told me that on Cheoner all the adepts used the same car. Some islands were more difficult and if they were needed cars had to be borrowed, or some other method had to be devised. I wondered about that.

Renettia drove us through an industrial complex, turning left and right, apparently without planning. I sat in the front passenger seat beside her while the couple were behind us. I was struggling with the calculation, trying to make sense of the gradual data that I was finding on the stave. I had no idea what I was doing. I had removed the violin case from my back to give myself more space, but it was in the foot well in front of me and my legs were cramped and uncomfortable. I had written down a string of values on my memo pad, all taken from the stave, as

275

Renettia had taught me earlier, but I was not sure what the next step would be.

Seeing my expression Renettia stopped the car and took the pad from me. We were in bright sunshine.

'What do I do with the numbers?' I said. 'What do they mean?'

She looked closely. The couple behind us were silent. Without the car's movement the temperature inside the passenger compartment was rising rapidly. Renettia frowned, checked the stave, looked again at what I had written down. Then she passed the pad back to me.

'OK,' she said.

'What does that mean?'

'It's OK. You finished.'

'But – what have I finished?'

'The calculation is correct.' She restarted the engine and began turning the car around so that we could drive back to the harbour. 'You have worked it out. Well done, Violin.'

'I'm not sure how,' I said quietly, not wanting to seem too inexperienced in front of the man and woman.

'It matters only that you have done it. You might never know how.'

Back at the harbour in Cheoner Maxim we watched as the couple went through the Shelterate process, then they walked out with their luggage to board the ship to their next destination. They had said to me it was an island called Slow Tide, but I had never heard of that. The stave had indicated the island of Nelquay.

'The same. They meant Nelquay,' Renettia said. 'You will have to be there for them, because the gradual between here and Nelquay is steep and irregular. Do you want me to stay with you? I think in fact you could work on your own now. It's your choice.'

'For now,' I said. 'Yes – please stay with me a little longer. I am nervous of doing something wrong.'

'We all are,' Renettia said. We were in the canopied shelter. My violin case was on my shoulders. The other adepts were sprawled in their self-consciously relaxed positions, but I had already noticed how a feeling of tension arose amongst all of them whenever a ship was due to arrive, or was preparing to depart. Their casual attitude was an affectation, a presentation of assumed confidence for their encounters with travellers. 'Adept work is an art,' she added. 'I told you this when we were in Quy. It's not a science. You know that now.'

'Yes,' I said.

We watched the ship moving away from the wharf, reversing and turning around in the cramped inner harbour, then setting out towards the south. A long cloud of smoke trailed from its double funnels. It was already late in the evening and we watched the ship until the darkness closed in.

'So we go to Nelquay?' I said.

'Their ship won't arrive in Nelquay for three days. First we eat.'

72

Immediately we arrived in the town of Nelquay Stream we adjusted our staves. It was a cold place, far in the north, close to the shores of Faiandland. Renettia and I were both dressed unsuitably for the island. We agreed that as soon as I had dealt with the gradual needs of the couple from Cheoner Maxim we would move south again. Some other adept could take over, if the couple continued their journey.

The harbour at Nelquay Stream was not much more than a huge building site: a tourist complex was being constructed on a spit of land beside the main quay, a planned hotel, marina, casino. We looked at the contractor's board at the gates of the development and saw that the project was unlikely to be completed for another two years. At the present time it was a wilderness of building materials, trucks, temporary buildings. The persistent wind blew clouds of construction dust across the harbour.

Other adepts were waiting by the Shelterate building – most of them were familiar figures, but unlike us they had managed to find warmer clothes. I saw Kan again – she was wrapped up in an old greatcoat with a scarf wrapped around her lower face. She had mittens on her hands. Once again she ignored me when I tried to greet her.

Not long after, when their ship from Cheoner arrived and had docked, the couple selected me once more. Their staves confirmed that they had come direct from Cheoner, without breaking their journey anywhere and were intending to sail to Muriseay. I observed that the long voyage from Cheoner had involved a dogleg around the Reever Fast Shoals and this had created a detriment of more than five hours.

Renettia checked what I had done.

Thirty-five simoleons each.

'We have to cross the harbour,' I said, thinking ahead. 'We must take them away from the town, then find the coast road.'

'I'll get a boat,' Renettia said.

I sent them through the Shelterate building. We then sailed across the bitterly cold waters of the inner harbour, the four of us, crammed together in a tiny boat with an outboard motor. The couple's luggage was piled high in the bow. When we landed on the far side we led them past the construction site where work was going on, then across a long stretch of broken ground, enclosed by a high fence, that looked as if it too was intended for future development. As we climbed higher the cold became more intense. My loose-fitting robe was completely unsuitable for this, as were Renettia's light clothes. However, the couple we were saving from the detriment were no better off, struggling with their heavy bags.

I paused to calculate the gradual, then we returned the couple to the harbour by the swiftest possible route. They were not satisfied with what we had done and the man complained bitterly that we had overcharged. They headed for their next ship, which was already waiting at the quay, destined for Muriseay.

Renettia said, 'I think somewhere warmer next.'

'Muriseay?'

'Perhaps not.'

Later, after the ship had slipped away from Nelquay Stream, Renettia and I found a small restaurant and while we were eating Renettia suggested our next destination should be Paneron. She mentioned that it was close to Winho, information that made me say that I would prefer that instead. This was the only island I knew my brother had been to, so long ago, so many years before.

'Not Winho,' Renettia said. 'Paneron. You'll like Paneron, Violin.'

73

Paneron was a lushly beautiful island, with high wooded hills and dozens of tiny islets scattered around in the area offshore. It was in a part of the Dream Archipelago known as the Swirl, close to the equator in the southern hemisphere. It was hot. We were suitably dressed once more.

As soon as we arrived in the harbour at Paneron Main, Renettia and I adjusted our staves.

Because Main was a popular tourist resort the Shelterate building was larger than any I had previously seen and three long canopied areas had been set up for the adepts in the adjoining compound. Ships came and went all the time and the port was always crowded. I had never seen so many adepts at work, so much money changing hands. I saw all the familiar faces and perhaps forty or fifty others.

We adepts worked with passengers for the next five days. Because Paneron was a popular island and the Swirl had so many more islands in relatively close proximity most of the people we worked for had accumulated only small increments or detriments. Our average fee was ten thalers or fifteen simoleons, although when two privately owned luxury cruisers docked one day we found that we could charge more than a hundred thalers a time. That became a busy and lucrative day.

Because there was so much traffic, and because the shipping routes were short and well established, the adepts had many regular procedures for adjusting the gradual effects. Most of these involved a short walk in a shady woodland area next to the harbour – several well worn paths ran through the trees. The calculation of the gradual was easy and routine.

On the fifth day, Renettia said to me, 'Go, Violin.'

'Go?'

'You are fully adept. You will work better alone. There is

nothing more I can guide you with.'

I had begun to like Renettia after so much time with her, for all her brusque manner. I still knew little about her but I had learned that she came originally from the island of Semell, which was in Archipelagian terms not too far from the Ruller Group. She was once married but her husband had died many years earlier. She had five children, sixteen grandchildren and three great-grandchildren. All but the three youngest were now adults. She would not tell me her age. From occasional remarks about experiences in the past I worked out that she must be at least eighty years old, possibly more. Aside from her distinctive grey hair, her physical appearance was that of a healthy young woman in her late twenties or early thirties.

'Will I see you again?' I said.

'Adepts are everywhere, Violin. Where will you go first?'

'I haven't decided yet,' I said, but that was not true.

We agreed I would set off alone, but not until the next day. Renettia revealed that some of the other adepts had worked out who I was and through her had made a request of me. When I found out what it was I accepted. It pleased and excited me.

The evenings in Paneron were quiet in the harbour because no ships arrived after dark and it was normally deserted, but that evening a crowd of the adepts gathered under their striped canopies.

Playing my violin I walked slowly along the narrow spaces between the three groups of adepts, to and fro, back and forth. I was under the stars. I gave them a few short pieces from the standard repertoire, some of which I had not played for years. Then I played the whole of the allegro maestoso from my violin concerto, a short virtuoso piece that I knew was liked by many people. I finished with the reels and jigs I had learned and played with my brother Jacj, in the social club in Errest. While I fiddled with a rhythmic energy I had not known since I was a teenager some of the adepts came out from under their canopies and began to dance. Someone turned on a floodlight mounted on the side of the Shelterate building – it threw a single beam into the compound. A few more of the adepts emerged shyly into the light and shuffled alone, some others held each other self-consciously, these old-young people jigging in the warm night, clumsy on their feet, laughing at their own mistakes, adept only at time and the gradual.

I played them every dance tune I knew, then played them all again. The insects in the dark surrounding trees were silent, lights from the town shone in the distance, the sea lapped gently against the harbour walls.

In the morning I went to Dianme, the island that had charged my dreams all my life.

74

Dianme at last! It was the culmination of a lifetime of hopes.

But the harbour in Dianme's only town, Deep, was on the north side, facing the mainland of Glaund. I was cold and I could smell the polluted air flowing down across the bay. I had arrived in the night. I adjusted my stave.

This change of subjective time – a cancellation of the most recent increment of seventeen hours – moved me back not only to daylight but to a slightly warmer day, with a wind from the south keeping the stench of Glaund temporarily away. It also made my transit to Dianme, in effect, instantaneous.

I had become an adept of time. I travelled free of time. I arrived at the same subjective moment as I left, Paneron to Dianme in an instant, wiping out several weeks of my subjective time.

I went from beautiful Paneron, with its rich clientele, luxury hotels and expensive restaurants to lowly Dianme, blighted by its proximity to Glaund, by its northern position, by its climate.

The journey took me several weeks in subjective time. I knew from the start that there were barely any facilities for passenger ships on Dianme. It was going to be a long and complex trip. Few travellers wished to be on Dianme, or to travel there, or for that matter leave there. The reality of this I had learned during my long voyage northwards, island after island, forced to follow an erratic, diverting course, seeking a combination of routes that would take me eventually to Dianme. In the hotter latitudes no one had even heard of Dianme, so my first task was to travel sufficiently far into the temperate zones that the name was at least discoverable. Then, with my ultimate destination identified, even to recalcitrant shipping lines, I had to develop a strategy of how to get there. Dianme was not a regular port of call for any of the main shipping lines, or indeed of the smaller ones. More devious routes were necessary, unexpected crossings had to be made. I reached my destination finally on a mail boat, one which sailed once a month from an island called Stemp to the three-island group that lay off the coast of Glaund.

I arrived on Dianme in the night.

I adjusted my stave. The long intervening journey disappeared. I was back at the same moment I had left Paneron. I was an adept of time. Provided I could stand the delays and inconvenience and slow journeys of subjective time, the stave allowed me to go anywhere I pleased in a split second.

I was looking good. I felt fit. I was young-old, renewed daily by my adeptness.

Now the reality of Dianme, which was a disappointment, a disillusionment.

The harbour of Dianme Deep was really not much more than a jetty and a harbour wall. Most of the boats were for fishing. No Shelterate office existed. There was a canning and freezing factory next to the port. The town itself was little more than a village. There were no restaurants but there was an inn where I was able to buy a meal. After that I found a place where protective clothes for manual workers were sold, many of them second-hand: thick working trousers, a woollen sweater, a rainproof hat. I put these on over my other clothes, feeling stiff and awkward but warm at last. I had to loosen the straps of my violin case to get it on over my bulkily padded shoulders. I went inland after that, hoping to learn history, hoping for views, scenery, some insight into how the legend of the benign wind-bringing goddess might have arisen.

I found subsistence farms, many hectares of marsh, and on the western side a few beaches. In a warmer climate, similar to those I had seen in the south, such beaches might have drawn the crowds for lazy vacations and other pleasures. On Dianme the beaches were cold, windswept, bleak, and as the day went on and there was a shift in the wind direction, the beaches suffered under the outflow of Glaund's polluted air.

The place was bereft of music. No sounds or impressions rose around me, I sensed nothing. The island was bare in every way. The island did not speak.

This was the worst discovery of all. My Dianme was not what I thought she was.

I made sure that I was back in Deep's port in order to the catch the same mail boat on which I had arrived, as I did not want to remain any longer on Dianme.

I was saddened, I felt obscurely betrayed.

But then I went home.

75

I arrived in Questiur as snow was falling. I adjusted my stave as soon as I was on the concrete apron and away from the ship. For a moment I thought the stave was no longer working, that because I was on the mainland the effect of the gradual was no longer present, because after the adjustment the snow was still falling.

It was another day, another snowstorm. I had arrived in a blizzard of fine, hard snow – after I had adjusted it became fine hard snow free of the effect of wind, falling vertically. The sky was a little lighter, suggesting a break in the snow might come. I had moved back to the day I wished.

This arrival in Questiur was not a matter of chance. I had planned the day because I knew what was going to happen on this day.

All journeys in subjective time were complicated, involving delays, diversions, changes of mind, many transfers in ports and between ships. This journey had been like all the others, but there had been an extra complication. It was not my first return to Questiur, to Glaund City. There was an earlier one, or perhaps it would be better described as a later one. I had increment, future time, I could make use of.

I was becoming adept at adeptness and I landed twice in Questiur.

The first time was at the end of the relatively short voyage from Dianme, in which I deliberately ran up much of the extra increment of time. As soon as I had left the ship I made no adjustment to my stave but went directly to the archive of the newspaper library in Glaund City.

Familiar with the conventions of the search engine I looked for and found the information I wanted, then I returned to the harbour. During my brief visit I noticed nothing unusual in the familiar city, although the newspaper library had been more crowded than I expected. The city itself was battened down for winter in a way I remembered well, the doors and windows closed against the weather, the people hurrying about their lives with their heads down. Until I went to the islands this was the place I knew best in the world. I had not come to explore or rediscover Glaund City, to notice it, to remark on it. I was collecting information that was to me personal and vital.

Back on the harbourside in Questiur I adjusted my stave. All subjective time disappeared and I returned to what I thought of as the present.

I then boarded another ship. On this I travelled away from Glaund, first to the south and west, using up subjective time. Then I returned north and east, using up more subjective time, adjusting my stave, watching and comparing the chronometers, *Mutlaq Vaqt, Kema Vaqt* – absolute time, ship time.

When the last of my ships approached the grimly snowed-in harbour at Questiur I knew not only the absolute time, but also the absolute day. Among many other islands I had visited Petty Serque, Nelquay, Ristor – a circular tour of northern islands in the wintry seas. Subjectively, the hours had dragged by. All I had was my violin.

The last of my several ships docked in Questiur. I landed. I walked across the concrete apron in the teeth of the blizzard. I adjusted my stave. The blizzard turned to a snowfall, with a promise of a break.

I had arrived on the day when I knew exactly what was going to happen.

76

I walked away from the civilian area of the harbour, to make it happen.

I had to keep my head bowed because of the falling snow but I kept looking up and around me to make sure I was going in the right direction. The docks in Questiur had not changed much since the last time I was here – I passed the entrance to the metro station. Lights were showing from the ticket office within.

I continued on, turned a sharp corner around a blocking warehouse wall, and finally I was rewarded with what I had come to find. A dark ship, black-painted but rusty, was moving towards the quay. Long securing ropes were already attached and winches were slowly tugging the ship to a secure mooring at the shore. The ship carried no identifying marks.

I kept to a rear wall of the dock, not wanting to draw attention to myself, but I had not gone far when I realized that not everything was as I expected. There were no troops waiting, as I had thought there would be, and the identifying battalion colours were not displayed. Suddenly, I was unsure.

I stayed where I was because although I had prepared carefully I could not be certain of my gradual calculations, on this one occasion when they mattered crucially to me.

The manoeuvring of the ship came to an end and for a few minutes nothing more appeared to be happening. I waited, feeling the wintry cold creeping around me. I had spent so long in the balmy heat of the Archipelago that I no longer had any tolerance of the cold. Before I set out on this I had made sure my clothes were weatherproof but even so I could feel the thickly falling snow building up on my shoulders and head. From time to time I shook myself like an old dog, and stamped my feet. My breath clouded around my head.

Two mobile cranes moved forward, bringing portable gangplanks towards the side of the ship's hull. There was another delay while they were lined up and attached and the hatches on the ship were opened.

Finally, people began marching quickly down the covered

ways from the interior of the ship, making the wooden structures shake and wave about. They tumbled out on to the concrete quay and once they were under the full impact of the falling snow they ran across towards the buildings.

They were all young men. None of them wore uniforms and nearly all were weighed down by their large packs of belongings. I went forward, tried to intercept some of them, but the weather was so cold and unpleasant that they pushed past me in their rush.

Finally, I managed to catch the arm of one young man and he swung around to face me. He was just a boy, hardly more than a teenager. He looked resentful that I had halted him. Everyone else was hurrying past.

'Is this the 289th Battalion?' I shouted at him.

'Of course it is!'

Then he too pulled away from me and rushed on towards the dockside building.

I moved across so that I was halfway between the two companionways. I stood unprotected in the falling snow, anxiously swivelling my head from side to side, trying to spot Jacj, who must be somewhere in this crowd.

A man with a violin strapped against his back suddenly emerged from the gangplank on my right.

He was not a large man and was shouldered aside in the rush. He staggered on the compacted snow, where so many footsteps had already been stamped, and slithered forward, leaning down with an outstretched hand to prevent himself from falling. As he did so the violin case slid forward across the back of his head. I hurried across to him, put a hand beneath his elbow, pulled him upright. At first he tugged his arm away fiercely, glancing angrily at me.

'Jacj! It's me – Sandro!'

He looked back at me in surprise and then he clearly saw who I was. He grabbed me, hugged me. I put my arms around him, pulling him against me. I felt him trying to get his hands past my violin case, just as I was trying to get mine past his. We were like two bears, two bulked up wrestlers, grappling for an effective hold.

The snow came down on us but we stayed there. The other

men continued to flood past but Jacj and I stayed holding on to each other until all the others had gone.

77

The snow was at last starting to slacken as Jacj and I walked back the way I had come. I led him towards the entrance to the metro station. Unlike those in the main part of Glaund City this one was crude and functional, with an automated ticket dispenser set behind a thick glass window and a gate which acted as a ticket barrier. The railway tracks were not deep below ground this far out from the city centre.

The ticket hall was empty as we hurried in – the snow outside was settling thickly. We brushed the loose snow off, rubbed arms and shoulders to try to instil some warmth. We kept looking towards each other curiously, recognizing, noticing the changes in our appearance that must have taken place. When he briefly removed his cap I could see how he had changed. He looked just as I remembered him, but his face was fuller, more mature. His hair was short in the military way. He was still not a big man but he looked stronger, healthier. More than forty years had passed. He looked as if he was still in his early twenties.

I could not help wondering what he was thinking about my appearance. I did not ask.

'How did you know I was to be released today?' Jacj said.

'I looked it up,' I said with a feeling that I had to avoid telling him the whole story for now. 'Troop returns are announced in the newspapers.'

'I thought they were going to cancel our demob at the last minute,' he said. 'Something weird was going on – I still don't know what it was.'

'What happened?'

He told me that for the last few days on the troopship they had been warned by officers that on arrival in Questiur the troops would be mustered in full uniform and they would march from the harbour through the streets, carrying their weapons, brandishing the colours, displaying their campaign medals. There would be cheering crowds to line the way. The rally would finish in Republic Plaza in the centre of Glaund City. They were going to be formally inspected by senior members of the ruling junta.

'Like everyone else on the ship,' Jacj said, 'I have spent the last two days making sure my kit was in good order, my boots were polished, my rifle was cleaned. But this morning, first thing, the parade was suddenly cancelled. We were ordered to dress in our civilian clothes before disembarking, leave our kit and weapons on board and as soon as the ship docked we could make our own way home. An hour after we heard the order another ship came alongside, all the officers and NCOs transferred to it and we were left to our own devices. Apart from the crew of the ship there was no one left on board but squaddies.'

'Have you any idea what made that happen?' I said.

'No – have you? Was there anything in the news?'

Of course I had no idea. I had been in Questiur for but an instant. Subjective time had vanished – I had been sailing a round trip, Petty Serque, Nelquay, Ristor. I could feel my stave where I normally carried it half concealed, tucked against my hip in a deep pocket, and clipped to my belt.

'Any chance we could get some food, Sandro? They gave us nothing to eat this morning.'

'I know a place in the centre of the city,' I said.

My brother. My elder brother. Forty years had passed and Jacj looked as if he had aged by only four or five.

We bought two tickets from the machine and rode the metro into Glaund City. Because of our violin cases neither of us could sit comfortably on the hard little passenger seats, so we stood in the area by the doors, holding on to the overhead straps, close to each other. We kept glancing at each other, revealing our cautious brotherly regard, our curiosity, a growing awareness of the gradual changes brought by time, and the mysteries of ageing.

78

As we crossed Republic Plaza it stopped snowing altogether, and by the time we reached the café where I had often eaten during my trips to Glaund City the sun was shining weakly through a thin veil of cloud. It remained bitterly cold. The café was nearly full but Jacj and I found a small table in a corner by the counter. Everyone already in the café was making a lot of noise, talking excitedly amongst themselves and moving about to talk to people on other tables.

Jacj and I ordered what we both thought of as comfort food, the sort of thing we had enjoyed when we were kids: mostly fried, greasy, tasty, full of fat and carbohydrates, delicious.

I asked Jacj how long he had been away.

'The full draft term: complete waste of time.'

'Do you want to talk about what you've been going through?'

'Going through?'

'Were you in much danger?'

'Only of dying of boredom. I've lost four and a half years of life, for absolutely nothing.' He shook his head, put in a mouthful of food, and while he chewed he looked around the packed tables of the unpretentious little restaurant. 'Is it always as busy as this?' he said. 'What about you? You look as if you've been in the sun.'

'I've been away too. I've only just come back.'

'Are you going to talk about it?'

'Not really.'

He shrugged, went on eating. We had never had much to say to each other. All through boyhood we did different things in different ways, our only point of real and regular contact being the music we played together. We had been reunited less than an hour and we were taking each other for granted.

All that worry about him, the fear he might have deserted, might have gone missing, might have been killed in action. Here he was. Brothers can be awkward with each other.

'Have you kept up the playing?' I asked him.

'Not as much as I would have liked. Soon after we were in a

camp down south they took the violin away. We were going on exercises. That's what I've been doing for more than four years, incidentally. Exercises, training, recognizing aircraft, marching about. No combat, no enemy. As far as I'm concerned the war is not happening.' Another piece of overcooked sausage meat went in. 'It hasn't been so bad for the last year or so. I was given the violin back so I was able to practise. What about you?'

'I've kept it up. I'm a composer now.'

'I thought you might be. You were always interested in that.'

'I'll play you some of my records later,' I said.

At that moment there was a sudden interruption. The main door of the café burst open and a group of young people came rushing in, all laughing. A flow of icy cold air swept in with them. The noise level in the room exploded. They shouted across the room to the people at one of the tables. '*Hurry up!* – *Starting soon!*' Other people in the room with us shouted back. I could not catch what they said but they all appeared to know each other. Someone pushed back a chair and stood up. Some of the men whistled loudly. Three young women let out high-pitched yells. One of them had a compressed-air siren and released a long squawk, which was so loud it made my head ring. Soon almost everyone but us was standing up. The door remained open. I could see that in the street outside a huge crowd was pouring down towards Republic Plaza. More noise and confusion out there in the cold. Amplified music was playing. I saw a big truck go slowly down in the direction of the square, and it was festooned with coloured banners and streamers. Someone was standing precariously at the back, leaning against the side, shouting through a bullhorn. People started leaving the café, throwing down money for what they had been eating.

The four young people who were on the table next to ours also began to leave, scraping back their chairs, grabbing their coats, talking across the room to others.

I leaned across to them.

'What's going on?' I said.

The woman who had been sitting close to me answered. 'Haven't you heard?' she said loudly, over the din.

'Heard what?'

'Where have you been – on another planet?'

'Yes – sort of. What's happening?'

'She's dead! She's gone! It's all over!'

I immediately sensed who she meant but I said, 'Who's dead?'

With her fists raised triumphantly, the woman said, 'Madam! Someone got to her!'

'When was this?'

'Last night! There's been a coup! The bitch is dead! The junta has collapsed and there's going to be an election.'

Jacj and I finished up and paid for our food but by the time we left the café we were the only ones left. We followed the crowd down to Republic Plaza, which was already packed with people. The mood was infectiously happy. A band had been set up close to the monumental entrance to the Glaund People's Museum and they were playing heavy rock, which I had rarely heard in Glaund. Many people were dancing to it, leaping around, waving their arms, trying to stay upright on the slippery ground. It remained bitterly cold, but the sun was still thinly shining.

Jacj and I stood at the edge of the huge ceremonial concourse, watching the celebrations. More and more people were flooding in from all sides. Cheering kept breaking out. Lights were being set up. Television vans had appeared.

Jacj said, 'Did you know this was going to happen?'

'No,' I said. I pointed towards the roofs of the buildings surrounding the plaza, most of which were government offices or departments. On every building the dour flag of the Glaund Republic was flying at half mast. 'This is the day,' I said, 'when I knew exactly what was going to happen. But I didn't know about this.'

We watched the crowd for a while longer but we were not really a part of it. We walked away into a quieter part of the town, went to the railway terminus.

79

The train to Errest was almost empty. Jacj and I stacked our violins and our other bags in the luggage area and sat down close together. By the time the train began moving the day was coming to an end under a mass of dark cloud. It looked to me as if more snow was about to fall. In Glaund at this time of year it usually was.

The train was warm and it travelled along speedily.

Jacj said, 'Where are we going?'

'Home,' I said. 'Where else?'

'You mean—' He sounded thoughtful, and there was a long silence. Then he added, 'Where do you mean?'

'Home. Where we lived.'

'And Mum and Dad?'

'I don't know,' I said. 'Do you know exactly how long you've been in the army?'

'The period of service was four and a half years. A bit more than that because they don't count the induction period. But I was demobbed exactly when I was expecting it.'

Four and a half years? What was happening four and a half years after Jacj went away? And everything that happened after four and a half years – ahead of us, events still to come?

I said, 'I think Mum and Dad will be expecting you.'

'Is there anything you're not telling me? It sounds as if there is.'

'No – but I've been away too. I haven't seen them for a long time.'

'What about Djahann? Is she still there at home?'

'I don't know,' I said again. 'She was when I left. But there's a lot I don't know. Almost everything, in fact.'

'How long have you had that beard? It makes you look older. Last time I saw you, you were just a kid.'

'You too,' I said. 'You've put on weight.'

'You've lost some. You were getting a bit plump when I joined the army, you know that?'

Then we said no more and the train journey continued.

We stopped at one place, then another. It was a line I knew

well after so many journeys to and fro in the past. Many of the stations were more brightly lit than I remembered, and the houses, the ones we could glimpse through the train window, seemed to be showing more lights. Could it really be true that the junta had fallen, that an election was being promised? The snow was falling again and whenever the train slowed I could glimpse through the window the fat flakes drifting down. It was as yet a gentle fall, not a blizzard, not a powdery assault that would leave a frozen layer that stayed around for weeks. There was nothing a new government could do about the weather in Glaund, but there were other things they could put right. I sat back, leaning against the headrest, eyes half-closed, wondering about that future and thinking about the islands out there in the night, in the wintry sea. Was snow falling on Dianme too? It was a moment of unreality, believing in what I had seen. Once I had not known the Dream Archipelago even existed and now once again it felt to me as if it had become unreal, distant, concealed. I reached down to touch the stave, which still rested inside the deep pocket at my side. My fingers touched the smooth wooden blade. I felt no responding sensation of awareness from it.

Tomorrow, I thought, tomorrow I shall walk down to the beach in Errest and look across at Dianme, restore my faith in what had once been an island of promise and loveliness, forget about the dream place I saw.

The train arrived in Errest. I needed to work. I had an idea for a new composition, inspirational, arising not from what Ormand Weller had called the consensus, the gradual and the imperceptible advance of time, but from my own reality, the life I knew. As Jacj and I stepped down to the platform I thought that at last it was the right time to compose what I had promised I would. The new Glaund would need a triumphal march – I would be happy to include cannon effects, folk dancing entr'acte and even a couple of sea shanties.

ABOUT THE AUTHOR

CHRISTOPHER PRIEST IS A CONTEMPORARY NOVELIST and a leading figure in modern SF and fantasy. He was born in Cheshire, England. He began writing soon after leaving school and has been a full-time freelance writer since 1968. He was selected for the original Best Of Young British Novelists in 1983. He has published thirteen novels, four short story collections and a number of other books, including critical works, biographies, novelizations and children's non-fiction. His novel *The Separation* won both the Arthur C. Clarke Award and the BSFA Award. In 1996 Priest won the James Tait Black Memorial Prize for his novel *The Prestige*, which was made into a film in 2006. Directed by Christopher Nolan, it went to No.1 US box office in its first week and received two Academy Award nominations. He has been nominated four times for the Hugo Award, and has won several awards abroad, including the Kurd Lasswitz Award (Germany), the Eurocon Award (Yugoslavia), the Ditmar Award (Australia), and Le Grand Prix de L'Imaginaire (France). In 2001 he was awarded the Prix Utopia (France) for lifetime achievement.

THE ADJACENT
CHRISTOPHER PRIEST

The eagerly anticipated new novel from "one of the master illusionists of our time." (*Wired*)

In the near future, Tibor Tarent, a freelance photographer, is recalled from Anatolia to Britain when his wife, an aid worker, is killed—annihilated by a terrifying weapon that reduces its target to a triangular patch of scorched earth.

A century earlier, Tommy Trent, a stage magician, is sent to the Western Front on a secret mission to render British reconnaissance aircraft invisible to the enemy.

Present day. A theoretical physicist develops a new method of diverting matter, a discovery with devastating consequences that will resonate through time.

"Utterly absorbing." *Library Journal*

"A wonderful piece of fiction, an intricate puzzle." *Publishers Weekly*

"A marvel of craft and feeling." *Locus*

THE ISLANDERS
CHRISTOPHER PRIEST

The Dream Archipelago is an endless sprawl of islands spanning a vast ocean between two warring continents. Some of the islands are deserts, swept barren by hot winds, while some are icy wastelands. Some have been sculpted into vast works of art and others are home to terrifying creatures. Many have multiple names, several have none and some may not even exist at all.

There are no reliable maps of the Dream Archipelago, but visitors are invited to travel with a mysterious gazetteer written by the islanders themselves—artists, authors and scientists; lovers, rivals and murderers—which documents their intertwining lives in a place where dreams are reality and nothing is certain.

"A glowing mosaic of a novel."
Sunday Times

"One of the most complex, challenging and satisfying fictions from one of our finest novelists."
The Telegraph

For more fantastic fiction, author events, exclusive
excerpts, competitions, limited editions and more

VISIT OUR WEBSITE
titanbooks.com

LIKE US ON FACEBOOK
facebook.com/titanbooks

FOLLOW US ON TWITTER
@TitanBooks

EMAIL US
readerfeedback@titanemail.com